The Missing Letters Of Mrs Bright

BOOKS BY BETH MILLER

The Two Hearts of Eliza Bloom
The Good Neighbour
When We Were Sisters

The Missing Letters Of Mrs Bright

BETH MILLER

Bookouture

Published by Bookouture in 2020

An imprint of Storyfire Ltd.
Carmelite House
50 Victoria Embankment
London EC4Y 0DZ

www.bookouture.com

ISBN: 978-1-78681-742-6
eBook ISBN: 978-1-78681-741-9

For John, who is nothing like Richard.

Chapter 1

Kay

The shop labels were still on the rucksack. I cut them off with my nail scissors, then threw in some clothes: comfortable jeans, black top, blue sweatshirt, a fistful of pants, a sensible bra and a not-sensible bra. I tipped in several pairs of shoes, my sponge bag, a fancy lipstick I'd never worn because it was expensive, the book I was reading, my passport, and the Swiss army knife my father gave me on my fifteenth birthday.

Then, as if I was playing someone on a sappy TV drama, I twisted off my wedding ring. That makes it sound easier than it was. That thing was a nightmare to get off. I did remove it occasionally. When I made bread, for instance, because I hated the feeling of sticky dough caught under it. But I probably hadn't taken it off for a year. I don't make bread very often. When it finally came off there were red ridges on my finger. I slipped the ring into my jeans pocket, put the rucksack on my back – God, it was heavy – and went downstairs.

Richard was sitting at the kitchen table, reading a thick book about the Second World War.

'It's going to be great,' he told anyone who'd listen, eighteen months ago, when he finally recruited someone to run his fourth shop. 'I'm going to read all the books I didn't have time for before.' As far as I could see, he'd been reading this same what-if-the-Nazis-hadn't-lost potboiler ever since.

'Kettle's still hot,' he said, not looking up.

I automatically went over to the counter then realised I didn't want tea. I didn't want anything in that room at all.

'I've got to go,' I said, and I guess my voice was different from normal because he did look at me then, and raised his eyebrows at my rucksack.

'To the shop?' he asked. We both automatically glanced at the clock; it was eleven, the time I'd usually head out on Mondays and Wednesdays. Those were my leisurely days, when Anthony opened up at Quiller Queen and I didn't have to be in first thing. But I didn't usually take a massive backpack with me. I wondered if Rich remembered that he'd given it to me as an anniversary present four years ago; a symbol that now both children were grown and independent, we'd finally do some of the travelling I'd been begging him to do forever.

'Are you going somewhere after work?' he said. 'I'm so sorry, I've forgotten what you're doing today.'

'I'm the one who should be saying sorry, Richard,' I said.

'Why?' he said, completely in the dark.

'Because…' I said, then stopped. He looked at me expectantly. I wanted to tell him, 'I'm leaving,' but it sounded so dramatic, so silly. Instead, I said, 'I'm, er, I'm going away.'

Richard's face lightened. 'Oh, to Rose's?'

'Maybe. I'm not sure.'

'What do you mean? Where else would you go?'

'Well, Sydney, first. Then Venice, perhaps. Or Prague. Then who knows? Lisbon, or Russia.'

'Um…' I could see he thought I was joking but couldn't work out why it was funny. It did sound like a joke, because I'd never been further afield than Winchester without him. Jovially, he said, 'Shall I make you a packed lunch?'

'Richard, I'm sorry.' I took the wedding ring out of my pocket, and held it out to him. 'I'm really sorry.'

He stared at my hand, then his eyes rose slowly upwards until they met mine.

'Kay, what's going on?'

'I'm going away.' I still couldn't say, *I'm leaving you.*

'But what does that mean?'

I shook my head. 'I'm… I'm going away from you.'

'Oh, Christ. Oh no.' He pushed his book aside. 'Have I done something?'

He stretched out his hand to me, but instead of taking it, I dropped the ring into it. He turned it over in his palm, as if he'd never seen it before.

'Is this really happening?' he said.

'Yes,' I said. It's such a little word, and it usually means something positive. But not always.

Richard looked from the ring to me, and then he just crumpled. His shoulders sagged, and the hollows under his eyes looked darker against his shocked white face.

'Please don't, Kay.'

I knew I should go straight away, but I also wanted to explain. Even though I knew he would never understand.

'It's just, there are so many things I want to do.' *Lame, Kay, lame.*

'Please sit down, Kayla. Take off your bag. Only for a minute.'

He hadn't used that nickname in years. But I shook my head. If I sat down, I would lose momentum, find reasons to postpone, go tomorrow, or next week, or never.

'All right,' he said, 'then I'll stand.'

We faced each other across the table. He was still easy on the eye, his salt-and-pepper hair lending him gravitas. His blue eyes, the exact same colour as Stella's, were clear and bright, though uncharacteristically watery right now. Sure, he'd changed since I first knew him as a spindly twenty-something, but who amongst us hadn't? For a man in his late fifties he was in pretty good shape. Broad-shouldered, six inches taller than me. *Age shall not wither him*, I thought pointlessly.

'So,' he said quietly, 'there are things you want to do.'

'Yes.'

'And they aren't things you can do while being married to me? Or even with me?'

I told myself not to get cross. I did that one-nostril-at-a-time breathing they were always going on about in yoga classes. It meant blocking my right nostril with my forefinger, but I'm pretty sure it just looked like I was thinking extra deeply.

I said, 'Well, they're not things I can do *with* you, that's for sure.'

'Oh, I see. I get it.' His voice got louder. 'It's someone else, isn't it? You've met someone else.'

I closed the left nostril with my thumb. Breathe *in* two, three, four. 'No, I haven't.'

'I'm such an idiot. You've been so distant lately, I assumed it was something to do with the menopause.'

'I haven't started the menopause, Richard.'

'Who is he, then? Do I know him? Christ!' He banged his hand on the table. 'It's that guy, isn't it, that guy you were in love with, the one you left for me? David. The one who wouldn't...'

'No!'

Our secret shimmered there for a moment, heady with a tiny puff of oxygen after years of starvation.

'Don't, please, Richard. I haven't seen David since then. I swear. I am not having an affair with him, or with anyone.'

Richard stared at me. Then he said, 'Do you want to know why Edward…' and stopped.

'Why Edward what?'

'Nothing.'

'Go on, what you were going to say?'

He shook his head, and returned to his previous thread. 'You must be having an affair, because otherwise this doesn't make any sense.' His voice cracked on the last word.

Gently, I said, 'It makes sense to me. There are things I want to do before I'm too old, and they aren't things you want to do.'

'Try me!'

'I have tried you.' I couldn't even remember all the things that I hadn't done, because he'd not wanted to. 'I've tried for years to do things with you.'

Out loud, it sounded pathetic. I could hear my mother-in-law's voice – *so he's a workaholic, well, there are worse things in this world!* I knew I had to walk out of that door, get into my car, but I felt incredibly tired at the thought of it.

Richard knew me so well, he could see that I was faltering. He began to smile.

'Kayla, sweetheart. Listen.' How well I knew that smile, the confident expression of someone used to always getting their own way. 'How's this for an idea? You go off for a while. A few weeks, a couple of months even, and see how you feel. No need to do anything drastic, we don't need to worry the kids or Mum. Why don't you go and find yourself, or whatever it is that you want to do, and I'll be here, waiting for you. Mmm? Kayla? Why don't you take off that heavy bag? We'll sit down and talk.'

I knew what he was saying was perfectly reasonable and sensible. In fact, it only had one flaw, which was that if I did that, if I took a Richard-sanctioned sabbatical, I wouldn't be able to walk into the future without a safety net. And I needed to do that the way a thirsty person needs water. I'd had a safety net my whole life; first with my parents, then for almost thirty years with Richard. Safe, knowable, no surprises. I wanted to try whatever life I had left without that net. Close my eyes and take a leap of faith.

How easy it would be to shrug off this bag – it seriously weighed a ton – and slide down into a chair. Talk, let him solve my problems, let him tell me how things would be.

But no. Not this time.

'I'm fine standing, thank you,' I said, and took a step back, one step closer to the door.

'Look.' He held out his arms. 'Maybe I've been a bit unadventurous. I'm sorry. We've been so busy with the kids…'

'Who are both grown up now.'

'Stella's only just left!'

'She's been gone six months,' I said.

'And with the shops.'

'But you're supposed to be taking more of a backseat now, Richard.'

'Yes, but you're not. You like running the shop.'

'Do I?'

'Don't you?'

'It was your dream, Richard, not mine. You did brilliantly. Built up one shop into a chain, four shops now, making enough money that you've officially stepped down. I thought we might finally do some things together, but you've kept on working.' As I said it, I knew it didn't matter what he replied, because actually, us doing things together was only one part of it.

'Well, thank you for being honest.' I could hear the old certainty creeping back into his voice. 'It's a wake-up call. Have your break, then let's go travelling. Let's do things. I'll book somewhere lovely for supper tonight.'

'It shouldn't take me saying that I'm leaving to get you to want to do things with me, Richard.' There, I'd said it. *I'm leaving.* 'And anyway, it's more than that.' I took a breath. 'I don't want to be married anymore.'

'Ohhh, fuck.' He sat down, abruptly, as if I'd punched him in the gut, and stared at me, like he didn't know who I was. An eternity passed in silence, him sitting, me standing, looking at each other. Then he said, 'What about the shop?'

It was a sign of how shocked he was, that it had taken him so long to get to the most important thing of all: the staffing rota.

'Anthony can manage on his own today,' I said. 'But he has Tuesdays off, so you'll need to get cover tomorrow.'

'Jesus.' Rich covered his eyes with his hand. Me saying he'd need cover was clearly the thing that convinced him I was serious. In the twenty-five years that I'd run his flagship shop for him, I'd almost never requested it. I took two more steps towards the door.

'What will you do for money?'

'I'll be all right. I'm sorry,' I said for the hundredth time.

He looked up. 'Don't go, then. If you're sorry.'

Me standing there was only prolonging the agony for both of us. I gripped the straps on my bag, and said, 'I'll see you.' Then I turned, and walked out into the hall.

'Christ! Kay!' I heard his chair scraping back and falling onto the wooden floor as he ran after me.

I opened our yellow front door and he sprinted towards me, as if he was going to push it shut, so I quickly stepped outside onto the path.

'Don't go,' he said. 'Please.'

I'd like to say that I coolly walked away, without saying anything more. But for some reason, I turned and said, 'Goodbye. Thank you very much for the marriage.' *Thanks for having me. I had a lovely tea.* Christ!

He looked as surprised as I felt, so maybe it was a fortuitous, if embarrassing, leave-taking, because it didn't give him anywhere to go. I suppose he could have said, 'You're welcome,' but he didn't. He stood and watched as I put the rucksack into the car boot, climbed into the driver's seat and pulled away from our house. I could feel his eyes burning into me even after I'd driven into the next street.

I wish I could have kept my confidence going for a little longer, but my hands started shaking so much I could barely hold the wheel steady. A few streets further on I pulled over, almost outside Stella's old primary school. Too far for Richard to come running after me, not that he was likely to.

Now what?

I stabbed uselessly at my phone. I couldn't remember my password, and my fingers were too sweaty for the thumbprint recognition to work. Finally the password came back to me – Edward's birthdate – and after a couple of tries, I broke into my phone. But once in, I wasn't sure what to do. I typed 'hotels' into Safari, but didn't know where I wanted to be. This was London – there were more Premier Inns than you could shake a stick at. Should I get one nearby, so Richard and I could meet to talk? Or somewhere further afield, so that we couldn't? What was the correct running-away procedure? I googled 'how to leave your husband', though it seemed a little late for that. Anyway, the advice was mostly financial, and scarily assumed that I might need a woman's refuge. I could hear my breaths loud in my ears, little strangled gasps. I tried to slow my breathing down, do the alternating nostril thing, but I couldn't seem to get control over it.

I needed someone to tell me what to do next. I rang Rose, the obvious person, but it went to voicemail, and I remembered she was away for a long weekend in Lille, not back till tomorrow. She was no doubt swanning round whatever the fancy sights of Lille were. I had no idea. I wasn't even a hundred per cent sure where Lille was. France, probably. Or Belgium? I also didn't know who she was with. Her kids? One of her Winchester friends?

My finger hovered over Stella's number, but would she appreciate me asking if I could nip up to Essex to see her, stay for a few days? *Just us girls, have fun, do some shopping, oh by the way I've left your father...* maybe not.

I was such a damn idiot not to plan this. I should have waited till Rose was around, or at the very least booked a hotel. But then, if I'd waited, planned it, would I have had the guts to do it? It was only this morning that the thought had pushed me out of the door, even though it was a thought that had been knocking around for a long while. A thought I'd always banished to the back of my head before it became too deafening. A thought of walking out on my life, closing the yellow front door behind me. I'd never breathed a word of this thought to anyone, barely even acknowledged it myself, and had assumed it would eventually go away. Something was different this morning, though, and the thought of leaving had turned itself, with little warning, into action.

It was so weird that Richard had mentioned David. We never spoke of him, and I myself hadn't thought about him for years. Not much, anyway. But a few weeks ago, looking for Bear's letters, I'd come across some of my old photos, and there was David in arty black and white, as beautiful as I remembered him.

I scrolled through my contacts, trying to breathe like a normal person, and thank God, saw Imogen's name. I don't know why I hadn't thought of her already. I pressed her number with such force, the phone asked if I wanted to delete it.

'Oh, Kay, chérie, how lovely to hear from you.'

'Imo, dear,' I said, as always, though I didn't usually punctuate each word with little gasp-gasp-gasps. 'I don't suppose lovely Bryn Glas is free?'

'Yes, do go up,' she said. 'Give it an airing.'

Thank God. 'I'm not sure how long I'm staying...'

'Long as you like, Kay. Have you got that horrid cold that's going round? Ignore any estate-agent bumpf that comes through the door. Some of my irritating relatives are trying to convince me to sell up, but I'm ignoring them. Over my dead body.'

I thanked her and hung up, praying that she would continue in rude health for many years. I programmed the satnav, noting with detached interest that my hands were slightly less shaky, and the gasping was a bit quieter, and set the car in a westerly direction. I was going where I should have gone in the first place.

I remembered David, three decades earlier, saying, 'Whenever there's the possibility of travelling, one should always go west.' He immediately undermined the solemnity of the pronouncement by breaking into the chorus of 'Go West' by Village People, but the sentiment was right. I needed to go west.

Letter written on 15 May 2018

Dearest Bear,

Well, this is getting to be a habit: the third time I've written to
you without one of your letters to reply to. Three missing letters
in thirty-five years doesn't sound a lot, except they've all been
in the last six months. Before that, I could have set my watch
by our letters. One month, you write. The next month, I write.
That's how it's always been, hasn't it? I hope everything's OK.
I'm hoping it's just a weird snafu with the postal service. But
I'm feeling worried about you.

   I'm writing from Bryn Glas cottage. I got here yesterday. I
know I've mentioned the cottage in letters before. As I've got
none of your news to reply to, I'll tell you about the cottage, as
it's such a special place to me. A refuge, particularly this time.

   I came here most recently with Rose, last year, for my fiftieth.
But I've been coming on and off for more than twenty years,
ever since Alice looked at my frazzled face – the kids were little
then, and hard work – and told Richard, 'Your wife needs to
get away. I know the perfect place.' I think I might have written
to you about it back then.

   That first visit, courtesy of Alice, was a wonderful break
from my busy, chaotic life. I left behind in her care two noisy

children, a largely absent husband, and an albatross of a job. When I retrieved the key from the outside safe-box – the first time I had seen one of those – and unlocked the heavy, old wooden door, it was like stepping into a fairy circle that we used to conjure up at school with chalk. Do you remember us doing that, Bear? A magical place that conferred special powers to anyone who stepped inside. The cottage felt like that to me, and still does. I am more myself here, more content.

It belongs to Imogen, a friend of Alice's from her cooking-for-minor-royalty days. Bryn Glas – meaning 'green hill' – has been in Imogen's family forever. Perhaps 150 or 200 years ago her ancestors even lived here. Imogen isn't royal, before you start to picture a grand mansion known as a cottage ironically. She was one of the upper-crust women Alice knew who worked as ladies-in-waiting ('In waiting for rich husbands,' Alice liked to quip).

When I first came here it was used as a rural bolthole for Imogen's friends and acquaintances, but as the years went on it was used by a dwindling number of people, and now I think, perhaps only me. Imogen never stays at the cottage herself, she hates to leave London, but she still pays for it to be cleaned every fortnight, and for a gardener once a month. After my first visit, I didn't need to go via Alice, but could call Imogen directly.

'Imo, dear,' I'd say, copying the way she and Alice speak to each other, though I've never met her in person. 'I don't suppose lovely Bryn Glas is free?'

I say that every time, even though it's always available. She calls me 'chérie'. 'Of course, chérie, go and give the old place a bit of love,' she says. She used to charge a peppercorn rent for it, but even that's faded over the years. The cheques I send her are rarely cashed. She seems happy simply if someone is using it.

When the kids were little they loved it here as much as I did. I'd drive the three of us, captain of the ship, listening to the radio on low while they slept in the back, four or five hours through the early morning, only waking when I pulled up outside the cottage and turned off the car engine.

In my memory the sun is always shining, illuminating floating columns of fairy dust, and casting a glow on Edward's golden hair. He almost tumbles out of the car in his eagerness to get to the wooden swing-seat at the front of the cottage. Stella gazes at me with huge blue eyes. 'My favourite place,' she says.

I get out, stretch my cramped-up back, let the sunshine warm me, feel the stillness of the mountains surrounding us. I open the heavy doors and breathe in the cottage scent, and for a moment, with the children playing nearby, I attain perfect peace.

Only for a moment, mind you. After that there would be unpacking and bed-making, while the kids ran around, and doubtless later there would be arguments over whose turn it was on the swing-seat. And for me it would be the hard work of managing yet another family holiday solo, because even if Richard did manage to join us for a couple of days, he wouldn't be involved in any of the planning or organising. The first few times I felt a little lonely being here without him, but to be honest, if he did come, something of the peace of the place would be lost.

As the children got older, they got less keen on 'the cottage in the middle of nowhere'. When they didn't want to come, I came here with Rose. The cottage was always available, has always been there for me, solid, its flint walls warm to my touch. And now here I am again.

So, I looked at your last letter, from October. I've read it through six times looking for clues as to why you might have stopped writing. But I can't find anything. Your job is fine, and Charlie is fine, you'd been to see him play the bassoon in a concert, the clever boy.

I've been reminiscing about the past. 'Oh no!' I hear you cry. 'That's a mistake!' But since Mum, I've been thinking a lot about when we were younger, and wondering if the decisions I made then were the right ones. I've even been thinking a little about He Whose Name I Shall Never Utter Again. Now that's a blast from the past, right? You're the only person in the world who might guess how painful it is to think back on it. But for the first time in years I've been reflecting on the anguish I went through then, the impossible decisions, the pact with Richard. Our Catholic upbringing has a lot to answer for, amirite?

Still to this day, only you, me, Richard and HWNISNUA know the truth. But is that the right thing? Should I tell other people, important people, before it's too late?

I'm still thinking about it.

However, there are things I am doing before it's too late. You'll be amazed when I tell you. I've done something drastic, something massive, and I feel jittery and strange and, frankly, a little close to hysterics. I can't believe I'm not pouring it all out to you, my most loyal confidante. But it feels weird to do that without knowing for sure that you're still at the other end of this letter. It'll have to wait till you write me back. Or when

I come and see you – I know I've been saying I'm coming over for years, but this time, I really am. I've already got my visa.

Till next time.

Miss you.

Always, Kay

Chapter 2

Stella

I was surprised to hear my phone ringing, because I'd thought it was completely flat. Gabby and I had been working hard all day at the market, and though the lunchtime rush was over, Gabby was hopeful of a few more punters. I fished the phone out of my pocket, and nearly dropped it when I saw it was Dad. He never phoned.

'Hello, Dad? Is everything OK?'

There was a silence. I was about to speak when I realised I could hear something – a very weird noise. Was Dad *crying*?

'Dad! What's wrong?' No answer. 'Listen, my battery's almost run out—'

'Stella?' he said. He *was* crying. 'I really need to—'

My phone cut out, and I stared at it in disbelief. It was doing that maddening thing where the little circle in the middle goes round and round, before it turns itself off.

'Shit, shit, shit.' I felt cold all over. 'Gabby, please can I use your phone?'

'Well, not really,' Gabby said, stirring one of the pots of food on the stall. 'I'm using it.' She gestured to her phone, which was plugged into the card reader.

'There's no one here.'

'But what if someone comes and wants to pay with a card, while you're using my phone?'

I stared at her. Our banner – 'Yummi Scrummi Authentic Sri Lankan Street Food' – flapped in the breeze above her head.

'I'm sorry,' she said, not sounding it. 'If you can wait half an hour we'll pack up and you can borrow it then.'

I took off my apron. 'I'll find a phone box.'

'So nineties,' Gabby said. She turned her attention to a woman who was walking past the stall. 'Hello, madam, can I interest you in some delicious fresh…'

'No thank you,' the woman said, walking faster.

I hurried off down the precinct, past the other stalls: Jamaican food, Indian food, noodles, Japanese. *Phone box, phone box.* Did the town actually have one? Did anywhere? I couldn't think when I'd last seen one. I certainly hadn't used one since I was a child. I walked quickly through the market and into the main shopping street. Maybe Mum was ill. Or, oh God, perhaps she was dead. Car accident, brain haemorrhage, a hold-up at the shop. I found that I was crying, and tried to get a grip. What would Bettina say? *You're catastrophising, Stella, imagining the worst. The worst rarely happens. Deep breath, now.*

Bettina was right. Mum was never ill. Nothing ever happened to her; she was reliable, safe. It was more likely something to do with Edward, or his kids. Jesus. Or maybe Dad had discovered that he himself was ill: prostate cancer, or bowel, could be anything.

Thank God, there was a phone box outside the library. I ignored the horrendous smell inside the cabinet and dialled my parents' number. But every time I pushed money in, it came out again. One pound coin rebounded out so violently that it fell on the floor, and seeing the pool of unspecified liquid it landed in, I decided to leave it there.

Trying not to give in to sobs, I ran into the library.

'The phone box isn't working,' I barked at the dark-haired guy behind the desk, as though it were his fault. He seemed willing to accept full responsibility for it, in any case.

'I know, it hasn't worked for ages, I keep telling them. Borrowers can use our payphone over there.' He pointed to the far side of the room. Despite my panic I couldn't help noticing that he was rather young and hot for a librarian.

'I'm not really a borrower,' I said, thinking foolishly of the tiny people in the children's book, *The Borrowers*.

'That's OK,' he said. 'It takes pound coins and fifty pences. Do you have enough money?'

The overly solicitous way he said it made me realise that he thought I was a homeless person. OK, so I'd slept in my make-up and got up way too early to bother doing anything about it, and I was wearing a cardie and baggy jeans. But surely it wasn't that bad... I became aware of an old smelly man waiting next to me, his tweed trousers tied round the waist with washing line, holding a large-print copy of *Fifty Shades of Grey*. I was only marginally better-dressed than him.

'Yes, thank you, I have money,' I said and walked over to the phone in what I hoped was a dignified manner. I pushed in a pound coin and dialled the landline – we'd all given up long ago trying to get Dad to use a mobile phone – but he didn't pick up. Instead I heard my mother's ancient and formal answerphone message: 'This is the telephone of Richard, Kay, Edward and Stella. We cannot come to the phone right now, but we will call you back.' A pause, then 'How do you turn it off, Richard?'

My static, unchanging parents. It was ten years since Edward had gone to university in Scotland. He'd stayed there, got married and started a family, yet his name was still on their message. Mind you, my name still being on the message made sense, embarrassingly; it wasn't that long since I'd finally managed to move out.

Dad's voice came in, cutting off the machine. 'Oh, thank goodness, Stella.'

'What's happened, Daddy? Tell me quickly.'

'It's your mother. She's left.'

'Left?' I felt my heart sink into my feet. 'Left for where?'

'*Left.*' He started crying properly. 'Gone. Gone and left me.'

I staggered back to the stall. I wished I knew Gabby well enough to fling myself into her arms. But I didn't. We'd hit the ground running when we started working and living together; we hadn't been friends for much more than six months. One thing I did know about her, because she'd told me often enough, was that she wasn't a fan of drama. So, as we packed up, I told her as calmly and rationally as I could about the awful phone call.

'I think my parents have split up.' My eyes welled with tears again, just saying those words.

'You think? Or definite?'

'I don't know. Apparently Mum's walked out, and Dad doesn't know where she's gone.'

'Then they have split up.'

'It could be a temporary thing.'

'Yeah, probably not.' Gabby untied one side of the banner.

'My parents have been married forever,' I said. 'Almost thirty years.'

Gabby whistled. 'Bloody hell, she's done her time. Guess she had enough.'

'That makes no sense, though. They were great together.'

'Really?'

'Yes!' I said. 'God, I feel so weird. My parents have always just been, well, my parents, you know?'

'Mine split when I was six, so I don't really remember them being together,' Gabby said. 'I suppose if they've always been all right, you take that for granted.'

'I didn't know I was taking it for granted! I thought things would just carry on as they were.'

Gabby shook her head. 'That's pretty much the dictionary definition of taking something for granted.'

I couldn't think of a reply to that, and we carried the stuff to her van in silence. Once we were on the way back to our place, she let me borrow her phone to call Theo. Luckily I knew his number by heart, but of course, his name came up anyway when I put in the last digit. Theo and Gabby had known each other for years; he was the one who'd introduced us to each other.

He picked up straight away and said, 'Gabs! So good to hear from you,' rather more enthusiastically than one would want one's boyfriend to address another woman. I tried to ignore any worry about this because my anxiety bucket was already full, and said, 'Theo, it's me.'

'Hey, babe! What's up?'

I told him, and started crying again, and he was lovely and kind, saying all the right things. I told him I'd be going to my dad's as soon as possible and he offered to come right over, as he was working at home.

At the house, Gabby and I lugged in all the gear, my mind full of logistics and fears. I was startled when she broke into my thoughts.

'Stell, listen, I'm sorry, I know you've had a shock. It's a shitty thing to happen. But I heard you tell Theo that you're going to your dad's.

What about the stall? We've got loads of events coming up. How are you going to work?'

'I don't know.' I bit my lip to stop myself from blubbing again. 'I don't know how I'm going to do anything. But I can't *not* go home.'

There was a pause, then Gabby nodded. 'OK. I'll think of something.'

I went to my room, plugged in my phone and started packing a bag. As soon as I got a tiny bit of charge I called Mum's mobile but she didn't pick up. I left her a voicemail, and messaged Edward and Rose, Mum's best friend. I could hear Gabby talking downstairs in the kitchen, presumably telling Piet what had happened, because a few minutes later there was a quiet knock on my door and he came in, stooping under the doorframe. Theo always called Piet 'the Flying Dutchman', because he was so tall – six foot six – that his head was way up in the sky. It was a handy feature in a housemate because he could clean cobwebs off ceilings, but you didn't want to be sat behind him at a gig. Oh, and also he was Dutch. He handed me a mug of coffee and offered me one of his comforting hugs, which I gladly accepted. Piet made up for Gabby in the humane-housemate stakes.

'I am so sorry to hear of your bad news, Stella.'

'Thank you,' I said, muffled against his chest – actually I was closer to his waist. 'I've got to go and look after my dad.'

He let me go, and sat on the bed. 'This happened to my parents also.'

I carried on putting random stuff into my bag. I didn't know what to bring, because I didn't know how long I'd be away. 'When you were little?'

'No, not at all,' Piet said, crossing his long legs. 'It was only two years previously.'

'Oh! When you were already grown-up,' I said. 'Like me.'

'It is becoming more common, I believe, amongst older couples,' Piet said. He continued in his usual calm tone, 'My father had an affair with the aunt of my mother.'

'My God, your mother's aunt?'

'She is ten years younger than my mother. My family is a little complex. But so are all families.'

'That's the thing, Piet. I didn't think mine was.' I wiped my leaky eyes and tipped some bits of make-up into the pencil case that served as my sponge bag.

'I am much older than you, Stella,' Piet said – he was only six years older, actually, 'and I have found that everyone has the complicated story, if you dig low down enough.'

'Not my mum, though!' I said. 'This is totally out of the blue. I'm worried she's had a funny turn. She's always been completely, well…'

'Predictable?'

'I was going to say stable. Sensible.'

'A woman in her prime,' Piet said, 'has many layers.'

'Is that a quote?'

'Yes, it is a quote from me, Piet Jansen.'

There was a knock at the front door. 'Piet, that's probably Theo, could you let him in?'

'Certainly,' Piet said. He unfolded himself from the bed and patted my shoulder. 'Try not to worry, Stella, I'm sure your mother will be all right.' He ducked under the doorframe and disappeared. Theo came running up the stairs, and seconds later I was in his arms.

'Ah, babe, don't cry,' he whispered, but I couldn't seem to stop. I sobbingly poured out all my anxieties about my dad, my fear that Mum had lost the plot, and my worries about my work with Gabby. Theo knew only too well how shatteringly relieved I'd been to get the chance to go into business with her, and thus drag myself out from the well-meaning but suffocating atmosphere of my parents' house. Even if I'd only been able to get my independence with financial support from them and Gran, it was my new hard-fought for life and I didn't want to jeopardise it.

'Look, Stell, I think I have a solution.'

'To what?' For one wild minute I thought Theo had a plan to convince my mum to return home.

'I'll take your place till you get back. Gabby suggested it.'

'Huh? When did you speak to her?'

'She called when I was on my way here.'

I pulled out of his arms. 'But you don't have catering experience.'

'I worked in a bar, remember?'

Theo and I had met in a bar, in fact, in our second year at university, when we'd both been working there to earn extra money. But now he was a junior designer at a graphic design place in London. All he knew about Sri Lankan food was from eating Yummi Scrummi leftovers.

'Come downstairs,' he said, 'we'll talk it through with Gabby.'

'Gabs, you mean?'

'Ha ha,' he said, utterly unabashed.

I knew I should be grateful that there was a solution to my taking time off work, at least, but I felt a bit weird. I avoided looking at Gabby when we went into the kitchen. Instead I went and filled the kettle, to top up Piet's lukewarm coffee. There was a mirror over the sink that Gabby had put up – she liked to be able to check her face in every room – and I caught a glimpse of myself. I hurriedly looked away, but not before I saw exactly how successful my sleeping-in-my-make-up-then-crying-every-ten-minutes regime was. I should probably switch to waterproof mascara until this thing with my parents, whatever it was, had passed.

I nodded at Gabby. 'Thanks for coming up with a solution.'

'I'm sorry I didn't ask you first,' Gabby said, and she did sound genuine. 'It's just, we've got so many markets on this week. And the weekend after next is our first party.'

'I'll be back long before then.'

'What if you're not, Stell? I can't do the whole thing on my own. Theo is a godsend.'

'But he doesn't really cook.'

'You love my Thai green curry,' Theo said, grinning.

'Well, yes, but that's just following a recipe.'

'So's our food,' Gabby said. I could see she'd already decided this was a brilliant idea. 'It's on a bigger scale, is all. And Theo has great people skills.'

The scream of the kettle boiling on the stove made me jump.

'How have you got time, though, Theo?' I said. 'You've got your own work, after all.'

'They love me, Stell, and you know how flexible they are.' Theo came and put his arm round me. 'Long as I get the work done, they don't mind.'

'I thought you'd be pleased we've sorted it,' Gabby said.

'I am! It's a great idea,' I said, trying my best to feel it. 'Thanks, both of you, I really appreciate it. I won't be away long.'

'It's fine, take as long as you need. It's a family crisis,' Theo said.

'Yeah,' Gabby said as I went out, under her breath but loud enough for me to hear, 'but, you know, no one's died.'

*

I finished packing, and Theo dropped me at the station.

'Good luck, babe,' he said. 'I know this is going to be a tough one for you.'

'You don't want to come with me, I suppose?' I wrestled my bag out of the back seat.

'I can, if you like, but that means I can't stand in for you at work…'

'No, OK. That's all right, thanks,' I gabbled, and got out of the car.

'Text me when you get there, OK?' he said, and his eyes were full of concern, which made me feel a little better. I nodded, and went to catch the train.

Chapter 3

Kay

My favourite place to sit in Bryn Glas was in the bedroom, on the grey Lloyd Loom chair. It was placed directly under a roof window, and I barely needed to tilt my head to see a beautiful expanse of sky. This morning it was bright blue, streaked with white. As I sat, my writing pad on my lap, a flock of birds appeared, swirling from one side of the window to the other in fluttery formation. When they disappeared from view I continued to watch the window as though it was a TV screen, and they came weaving back again, following some mysterious and ancient pattern.

Usually, sitting in this chair, gazing up at the sky, brought me deep peace. But not today. Not with the burning pyre of my marriage 300 miles away. I tried to trick my brain into thinking that I was here on holiday, but my mind wasn't as dumb as all that, and instead I thought way too hard about why I was really here, and let out an involuntary little wail.

Thank heavens Rose was on her way, my fourth emergency service. Being alone was emphatically not what I needed right now. She'd promised to hop off the Eurostar this morning, and get straight on a train for Wales.

I finished writing my letter to Bear, which was rather more stream-of-consciousness than my usual letters, then prised myself out of the grey chair, and went downstairs to unpack properly. After arriving yesterday evening, I was too exhausted to do anything more than make the bed and get into it, where I slept solidly for more than ten hours. Frankly, it seemed miraculous that I had got here in one piece; there were large parts of the drive I couldn't remember.

I walked over the cool kitchen flagstones, and ran the tap to make sure the water was running clear. One year it had run brown, to the children's horrified fascination. I unlocked the back door, and stood on the threshold for a moment, looking up at the beautiful, forbidding mountains, the morning sun climbing up behind them. Then I stepped into the overgrown garden, large enough for children to play satisfying games; for a moment I thought I heard Edward and Stella laughing out there. Possibly because I was genuinely starting to go mad. *Hurry up, Rose!* I walked round to the side of the yard to check the level in the oil tank, as I did every time I stayed here, because otherwise there would be no hot water. Then I looked in the doorway of the old barn, which had been slowly decaying as long as I'd been coming here. Light fell in strips from the missing roof slats, but it was still an amazing space. Several times I'd suggested to Imogen that she could do something with it, and she always politely agreed, but nothing ever happened.

Back in the cottage I checked on my food supplies. The nearest shop was a six-mile drive, but I'd bought bread and milk on the way here, and there was a decent store cupboard, which still had some tins and packets from the last time I stayed. I felt a strange sense of pride in my homemaking as I worked out what needed throwing out and replacing, a sense completely absent from similar activities in my kitchen at home.

My phone sat accusingly on the table. After speaking to Rose, I'd put it onto silent, because I couldn't face anyone but her. I glanced at it now, noting with fascinated horror how many missed calls and texts there were from everyone in my life. It made me feel very tired looking at it, despite my epic sleep, and without planning to, I went upstairs and got back into bed, intending just to rest. When I was woken by a knock on the door, I saw to my astonishment that I'd been asleep for three hours. I clattered down the stairs, almost tripping in my haste.

'Rose!' My voice was a little creaky after a day's disuse.

'Kay!' Rose said, and we flung our arms round each other. 'Thank God you're alive!'

I relaxed against her soft body, inhaling her familiar perfume. 'How was the journey, Rose? Have you spoken to anyone? Does everyone think I've gone mad?'

'Long; yes, everyone; and yes they do. Darling, do you really want to do dispatches on the doorstep? That train had won the world's most disgusting toilet award, and I'm busting.'

I stepped back and watched her jog urgently upstairs. Lovely Rose. We'd been friends since school, through college, through jobs and marriages and children and house moves and heavens knew what else. I went into the kitchen and put on the kettle.

She came back down and leaned against the counter, casting a critical eye over my tea-making.

'Revolting fiend,' she said, as she always did.

I grinned at her. 'My way's right and you know it,' I said, as I always did. I make tea in mugs and I put the milk in first and I'm not going to apologise for it.

I gave the teabags a final squash and we took our mugs into the living room and sat opposite each other.

'So?' she said.

'So?' I said.

'Kay, chick, how are you?'

'I'm fine.' She looked worried, so I added, 'Well, I'm all right. Fine is pushing it.'

'You don't look fine. You look wild-eyed.'

'Do I? I know this is weird.'

'Just a bit! What happened?'

What *had* happened? I scarcely knew myself. 'Well,' I said, 'I guess I've left Richard.' Out loud, it sounded implausible, almost silly.

'I know *that*. Your whole family's told me.' Rose smiled. 'Have you *really* left? As in, goodbye, here's your wedding ring back?' She looked at my unadorned left hand, cradled round my mug. 'Oh, *shit*.'

'I know, right?' I nodded. '*Heavy*.' I said 'heavy' like a hippy lad Rose and I had both had a crush on in 1983. I couldn't remember his name, but ever since, whenever something was a bit intense, Rose or I would say, 'heavy' in the way that cute boy had done. I got to kiss him first, but Rose went out with him for a couple of dates. She would remember his name. I was about to ask her, when I realised she was looking at me oddly.

'You are in a complete daze,' she said. 'Did something awful happen at home? It seems so completely out of the blue.'

'Nothing happened, honestly.' I put on a reassuring smile. I was glad that I remembered how to smile. You stretched out your lips and let your teeth show. Hopefully it looked more authentic than the odd grimace it felt on the inside. 'Actually, I have been thinking about this for a while.'

'You never said.' Rose looked surprised.

'I know. Sorry. I didn't really even tell myself I was thinking it.'

'How long have you felt this way?' Rose said, counsellor-style.

'Oh, a while. A few years, maybe.'

Perhaps twenty years.

'Oh, darling!' Rose came over, sat on the arm of my chair and hugged me. 'I had no idea things were so bad. I'm sorry.'

'It's quite shocking, isn't it? I've shocked myself.' I giggled, and the giggles segued into odd little sobs that I didn't seem to have control over. Rose held me until I got a grip, and then she looked at me so kindly I had to look away, for fear of crying again.

'Jee-sus, darling, this is absolutely massive.'

I nodded. I didn't trust my voice to acknowledge just how massive.

'You're the most married person I know!' She went back to her chair, still with the worried expression on her face.

'Is that how you see me?' I said shakily.

'Jeez, Kay! It's a huge thing to do. Are you scared?'

'Terrified.' A tear slithered down my cheek and I brushed it away.

'Of course you are. It's incredibly brave.' Rose sipped her drink. 'Ugh, your tea! It's lucky I love you.'

'How's my family doing?'

'Edward's calm.'

'Nothing ruffles that boy.'

'*Weirdly* calm, Kay. More flat than calm, really. When did you last see him?'

'Oh, not for a while, he's so busy with work, and the twins...' I tailed off, because I realised that Edward hadn't been down to see us for more than a year, other than for Mum's funeral. He'd missed Christmas, and two Easters.

Rose went on. 'Stella's being stiff-upper-lip but I can sense the panic.'

'God, poor Stella. And' – I steeled myself – 'have you spoken to Richard?'

'Several times. He insisted I was harbouring you in Winchester and said he was coming right over. Took me a while to convince him I was in France and knew nothing of your great escape.'

'Hell, I'm sorry, Rose.' Stupidly, it hadn't occurred to me that Rose would be the buffer between me and my family.

'It's what I'm here for, my love. Could have done without Alice, mind you.'

'Good God. How did she get in on it?'

'"My dear Rose, we are all going quaite insane here!"' Rose did a fair impression of Alice's 1950s' BBC voice. '"My Richard seems to have carelessly mislaid his wife, so it's all hends on deck to retrieve her. *Thenk* you!"'

'She didn't really say Richard had *mislaid* me, did she?'

'I'm paraphrasing. Anyway, I told everyone I'd spoken to you, and you were fine, and would be in touch soon.'

'Thank you.'

'I don't mind telling you, I was petrified, Kay Bright! Or are we going back to Kay Hurst now? I said all confidently to Stella that we should give you some space, but secretly I thought, what if I've called it wrong and I get here to find you hanging from a beam?'

'Wow, Rose, that's *heavy*.'

'*Heavy*.'

'What was the name of that boy who used to say that?'

'Ollie.'

I knew she'd remember. 'So, you were pretty relieved to see me, then?'

'You could say that. In fact, I need to text Graham, tell him he can stand the coroners down.'

'Who's Graham?'

'I'll tell you later.' Rose looked at her mug. 'Oh dear, my vile tea's gone cold, what a shame. I've brought French wine. I know it's a bit early, but…'

'It's almost four. Wine would be great.' I jumped up and fetched two glasses, stowing away the mysterious Graham for later.

Rose poured the wine and we chinked glasses, then to my surprise, I started crying again.

'Oh, Kay!' Rose reached for my hand. 'Don't tell me the wine hasn't travelled well? It was gorgeous in Lille.'

That made me cry-laugh, and I started spluttering. Rose gently took the glass out of my hand and I hid my face behind a cushion until I'd calmed down.

'You've done a massive thing, soft lad,' Rose said. 'Bound to feel a bit odd.'

I nodded, not trusting myself to speak because there were lots of tears still there, threatening to come out. Her using that daft affectionate name from our Liverpool youth, 'soft lad', didn't help.

'So, what now?' Rose gave me back my glass.

I sat up. 'I guess… it's hard to explain. I just have this feeling – I've had it for a while – that there are things I want to do. Things that I *must* do.'

'Like what?'

'It was all much clearer in my head before I left home. I do know that I want to go to Australia. I'm worried about Bear, she hasn't written for a few months.'

'That's not like her, she's always been regular as clockwork, hasn't she?'

'There are a few other things floating round. Climb Snowdon, for instance. I say every time I come here that I'll do it, but haven't yet. Go to Venice.'

Rose nodded. 'But, Kay, you can go to Venice and Australia and still be married.'

'Well, it would be tricky. Australia, for instance: I'd have to brace myself for endless complaining about how long I'd be away, the impact it would have on the shop. And then Rich would likely be upset because he hates to fly, so me wanting to go to Australia would be perceived as an attack on him. No matter how much I assured him that I was happy to go alone.'

'Marriage is very complicated, isn't it?'

'And then Venice, I've always wanted to go there. He'd feel obliged to come with me because it's a place for lovers. But he wouldn't fly, as already mentioned, or get the train, even though it would be fun, because that would be too long away from the shops. So, there would be a whole load of angst around that.'

'Surely he would climb Snowdon with you, Kay?'

'He'd plan it for weeks. He'd tell me my boots were wrong and insist I get new ones. He'd research the best pair for days.' Now I'd got started, it seemed difficult to stop. 'He'd buy me walking poles. It would be an expedition. And by the time we got it together, it would be too late for this year and we'd have to start again next year. I just fancy popping up there in my flip-flops.'

'Your knee is jiggling up and down like a buzz saw,' Rose said. 'I must say Rich isn't coming out of this particularly well.'

I put a restraining hand on my knee. 'Look, he has many positive attributes, I'm just not focusing on those right now. The thing is…' I took a breath. 'If I did those interesting things when I was still married, then after doing them I'd have to go back home and still be married.' I got up, unable to sit still, and started pacing the tiny living room. 'I've never really experienced not being married. Richard and I got together so young. Younger than Stella is now. I'm completely different from the girl I was then. If it was the Middle Ages Richard and I would be long-dead, and our marriage would only have lasted for ten or fifteen years. Now we're all living forever, and our marriages are going on longer than they were meant to.' I discovered I was shouting, and put my hand over my mouth.

'But none of this matters, chick,' Rose said quietly, as if to compensate for my volume. 'The only thing that counts is, are you unhappy with Richard?'

No one had ever asked me that before. I sat down abruptly, trying to stop the damn tears spilling out. 'Yes.' The gasping breaths came back. 'I – *gasp* – am – *gasp* – unhappy.'

'I'd no idea things were so rough between you,' Rose said. 'Clearly, leaving is the right thing to do. You don't need a to-do list as a cover story. If you're unhappy, you can leave your marriage. You don't have to climb Snowdon to justify it.'

'Thank you.' I put my head in my hands. 'Christ! What have I done? I have literally no idea what I'm going to do.' I jumped up. I didn't seem to have control over my actions. 'What! Am! I! Going! To! Fucking! Well! Do!'

'Right, miss.' Rose stood up. 'You're spiralling. Anxiety, hysteria, loud swearing. I recognise the signs. I was the same when Tim left. You need to do something to completely shift your focus. Get out of your head.'

'Drugs?' I said hopefully.

'I only have ibuprofen gel with me. Go and put on a jacket.'

'Why?'

'We'll go for a little walk.'

'Rose, you have literally just got off a train from France! Do you not want a nice sit-down?'

'Get your jacket! Stop shilly-shallying!'

And in the absence of a better plan, or indeed, any plan, I did as I was told.

'I'd forgotten how beautiful this place is,' Rose said, as we stepped outside into the late afternoon sunshine. 'What was that walk we did last time I was here? It ended at a convenient pub.'

'Oh, that's a very short walk,' I said, relieved. 'We cut across two fields and we're there.' I pushed open the gate at the edge of the garden, and we set off across a somewhat neglected meadow that was being decimated still further by sheep. They scattered as we passed, in their usual terrified fashion. At least I wasn't as timid as a sheep, I thought, randomly. The wine had gone to my head. I ought to eat something.

'So chick,' Rose said, 'what's happening with the shop?'

'I've decided it's not my problem.' How long had I secretly wanted to say that? It felt alarmingly good, as well as plain alarming, to be able to say it.

Rose gasped and put her hand on my forehead. 'Nope, no fever. Bloody hell, Kay, I have never heard you say that before.'

'You're more shocked by that than by me leaving my marriage? I think I've been worrying about the shop for too long.'

'Darn tooting! Well, look. I know it's not your problem, darling, and I applaud that. But I promised Edward I would mention one teensy thing. Have you, by any chance, heard from Anthony?'

'My sales assistant?' Oh hell, I was so thoughtless. It hadn't occurred to me till now that, of course, Anthony would be horribly upset I'd left without telling him. We'd worked together for years. I looked at my phone. 'Damn, there are some missed calls from him. I'll ring him soon as we get back.'

'Er, before you ring,' Rose said, looking embarrassed. 'I'm sorry to be the bearer of this news, but, er…'

I stopped walking. 'Oh God, what, Rose? Tell me!'

'Richard sacked him yesterday.'

I gaped at her. 'He what?! Why?'

'He thought you and Anthony were having an affair.'

'Are you joking, Rose?'

'Wish I was. Anthony's threatening industrial tribunals and lawsuits.'

'Good God!'

'Isn't Anthony gay?' Rose said.

'Yes! He has a boyfriend! We're not having an affair!' I spluttered. 'Bloody hell, what's Richard thinking of?'

'He's in a state, darling. Lashing out, trying to make sense of things. The kids think it would help smooth things out if you spoke to Anthony.'

'Of course.' I glanced at my phone. 'No bloody signal!'

'Try him after the pub. A couple of hours won't make much difference.'

We set off again, climbing over a stile into the next field.

'Who's running the shop, then?' I said. 'Is Richard trying to do it? Has it' – I could scarcely say the words – 'been closed?' It was unbelievably ridiculous of Richard to get rid of my assistant at the exact moment he most needed his help! Anthony knew Quiller Queen inside out.

'Stella's taken it on.'

'Oh no! I so didn't want her to get dragged in.'

The novelty of playing shop had worn off for both Stella and Edward when they were very little. The shops were Richard's life, and it was a matter of personal pride to him that a customer could deal with an emergency paperclip shortage or pressing need for Post-it notes as easily on New Year's Eve as on a random Thursday morning. Consequently, the shops were open ten hours a day, every day, except Sundays and Christmas Day, and our family holidays were always brief and meticulously planned, with folders full of instructions for temporary staff, and Richard very stressed and often backing out of the trip at the last minute. 'Shop' to the kids meant parental absences, and a grumpy, tired father.

'She's managing fine, for now,' Rose said, 'but I agree, it would be good to get Anthony back in there if at all possible.'

'I'll see if I can persuade him,' I said.

'Sorry to give you this to worry about,' Rose said. 'But you do seem a little calmer.'

'You were right about getting out. My head feels clearer.'

'Good, because tomorrow we're going to do a massive head-clearing excursion.'

'Oh dear, are we?' I unlatched the gate at the end of the field, remembering how Edward, aged about eleven, had tried to vault it and landed on his chin, requiring a visit to the hospital in Bangor.

'Yep. Tomorrow we tackle Snowdon.'

'You're kidding, right?' I stopped dead.

'I'm very not kidding. Is the pub this way?'

'Yes,' I said, distractedly, following her along the lane. 'But, we haven't prepared! Or got a map! Or anything.'

'What's your name, Richard? Look, I've been up a couple of mountains with, er, Graham.'

'Ding ding!' I hit an imaginary bell. 'Time out! Second mention of Graham!'

'Fine. Tell you what. I'll reveal all about him when we're up the mountain tomorrow. Is that motivation enough? Fresh air and a physical challenge, that's what you need.'

'I can't. I've never been up anything higher than Hampstead Heath.'

'This is what you want, right? Adventure and wild times.' Rose looked at me thoughtfully. 'Or at least, it's what you need.'

In the pub we ordered more wine, and two rounds of lasagne and chips, and talked about inconsequential things, the way people who've been friends for a long time do. Rose always knew when to change the subject, and I was grateful to not have to talk about Richard for a bit. I tried to trick her into telling me about Graham, but she wasn't falling for it.

'Tomorrow,' she said, 'when we're up that big ol' hill.'

We walked back to Bryn Glas, both a little tipsy, and after she'd gone up to bed I gritted my teeth and dialled Anthony's number. It was clearly a week for doing scary things.

'What?' he said.

'Ant, it's me, Kay.'

'I know.'

'I'm in North Wales.'

'Well, whoop-di-whoop, I'm at the bottom of the deep blue sea.'

Oh dear. 'I'm so sorry about Richard going mad. Don't worry, we can sort this out. What exactly did he say?'

'I left you enough messages telling you, Kay. What the hell is going on with you?' Anthony's voice sounded shaky. 'I thought everything was fine. I thought you loved working with me.'

'I did.'

'Then it's, oh Kay's buggered off and by the way you're having an affair with her, so you're sacked.'

'God, I can't imagine how—'

'Too right you can't imagine! I've been a loyal employee for twelve years.' There was a charged pause. 'I went in this afternoon and told Stella I'm taking legal advice.'

Poor Stella. How would I ever make up for this? 'I don't blame you,' I said. 'I'd do the same. It's an appalling thing to do to you, our best-ever assistant manager.'

There was a silence. Had I overdone the flattery? I went on. 'And even though Richard is clearly in mental turmoil, it is still absolutely inexcusable. If I was you, I'd take us to the cleaners.' I'd been a parent long enough to earn a PhD in reverse psychology.

'Oh, Kay. I don't want to take you to the cleaners. You know how I love that shop. But Richard can't fling false accusations around like that.'

'Too right he can't!' Forgive me, Richard, for the lie I was about to tell. 'In fact, he told me that if you would be willing to forgive and forget, he'd make you shop manager.' I knew how much Anthony would love to be in charge.

'I thought you had left him,' Anthony said suspiciously.

'Yes, I, er, heard that from Stella.' Oh God, it was a tangled weave.

'Manager, really?'

Bingo.

'On the same pay as me,' I said. 'More holidays, better pension, your own assistant.' Richard would kill me. But Anthony was more than capable. 'Make all the decisions about layout and stock…'

'I'll do it.' Anthony whooped, then said, 'I'll miss you, though, Kay.'

Not as much as you'll like being manager, Ant. 'I'll miss you too.'

'I'd better apologise to Stella. I was a teensy bit rude earlier. I told her where Richard could put a glue stick.'

I stifled a laugh. 'She'll understand. When do you want to start?'

'How about after a fortnight's paid leave?' he said, so quickly I realised he'd been prepared for this offer, the swine. Maybe he too had a PhD in something sneaky.

Sorry again, Richard. But for Stella and Edward's sakes, and for the sake of the business, I agreed. I'd be happy never to see Quiller Queen again, but it was where I'd spent most of my working life. It would be good to leave it in Anthony's safe hands.

He asked a couple of cursory questions about how I was, and my plans, but he was clearly desperate to get off the phone, presumably to tell his partner the good news. After we hung up I sent Edward and Stella an email explaining what I'd promised. Then I went to bed. I knew I'd never sleep, not after my huge nap. But somehow, seemingly moments later, it was morning, and the light was flooding into the room, and I was mildly hungover. I could hear Rose singing in the bathroom. The song was, 'Climb Every Mountain'.

Oh God.

Chapter 4

Kay

A quick breakfast, a lecture from Rose about wearing layers, and a short drive later, we were standing in the foothills of the tallest mountain I had ever seen up close. I was in utter shock, but Rose nonchalantly opened up a map.

'Don't people use phone apps these days?' I said, hiding how impressed I was that she seemed to know how to use it.

'Old school, darling,' she said, lining up a compass.

'Do you always carry a compass, Rose?'

'Yeah, I'm Dora the Explorer. No, it was in the drawer with the map, back at your cottage.'

The wind whipped round my ears worryingly, and I felt ill-equipped in a cheap waterproof, M&S leggings and old trainers. Mind you, Rose wasn't much better dressed in ancient yoga clothes and walking boots caked with dried mud.

We walked for about fifteen minutes, and I started to feel less manic. Hey, we were doing it: something I'd wanted to do for years. It felt good.

'This isn't so hard after all,' I said.

'It may get a little harder,' Rose said in a parental voice.

'It's not even very steep.'

'It's not even very steep, *yet*.' She glanced at me. 'How's your head? Do you feel a little less clogged up?'

'You know, I do. Hungover, but less clogged.' I smiled at her, and it felt like my first real smile since I'd left home. 'You should be a therapist, Rose.'

'Too right. Pull your socks up! Go climb a mountain!'

'It's great out here.' I breathed in a lungful of mountain air, and noticed with pleasure that the breath filled my lungs properly. No more gasping. 'Normally at this time I'd be opening up the shop and counting the hours till 6 p.m.'

'So, Kay,' Rose said, putting the map into a nerdy pouch hanging round her neck. 'Are you up for a brief interrogation?'

'Go on, then,' I said. 'I guess I can't just leave my husband of a hundred years and not expect a few questions.'

'Is there someone else?'

'Apart from Anthony, you mean?' I laughed. 'No. Definitely not.'

'And Richard's not having an affair?'

'Not as far as I know.'

We reached a small kissing gate, after which the path got noticeably steeper. I slowed down and, to my relief, so did Rose. I'd been worried she would go marching off and expect me to keep up.

'So, was it violence?' She gazed at me with her steady Rose eyes. 'Was he hitting you?'

'Good gracious, of course not!'

'Heavens, I'm glad to hear that! Were you hitting him?'

'I certainly wanted to sometimes. But no.'

'Was he doing that new thing? That gaslighting business, what's it called? It was on *The Archers*.'

'Coercive control? No, he wasn't, and before you ask, neither was I.'

'So, darling, we've established you were unhappy, but what was going on? Was it "irreconcilable differences", which is what that shit Tim said were our reasons, apparently, for divorcing?'

'Not really. I know it's difficult to understand…'

It was hard not having a single proper reason to leave Richard. None of the little reasons on its own was enough for someone to consider leaving a marriage. None of them on its own looked like anything at all. It was the cumulative effect that did for you. I toyed briefly with inventing a vice for Rich – he gambles! He drinks! He's a philanderer! – but my oldest friend deserved a truthful answer. Though how could I explain it to her, if I could barely explain it to myself?

'You've been married forever,' she said, saving me from having to try and unpack it.

'Twenty-nine years.'

'Twenty-nine years! I came to your silver anniversary party. I made a speech!'

'It was a beautiful speech.'

'I was a bit squiffy. I cried all through Richard's speech.'

Twenty-nine years of little things was what got you in the end. I don't mean twenty-nine years of Richard doing things wrong. Not at all. He was a great husband in so many ways. Kind, generous, funny, very hard-working. A good father. He'd make someone else a lovely husband now, if I hadn't used up all his husbanding.

'We need a water stop,' Rose said. She braced her feet against two ridges on the path and we took out our bottles.

'So, Rose. I'm up this crazy mountain…'

'We're not all that *up* yet.'

'And you promised you'd tell me about Graham.'

Rose mumbled something.

'What was that, chick? Sounded like "boyfriend".' I glugged down some water, surprised by how thirsty I was.

'The kids made me a dating profile.'

'Wow, go you!'

Rose made a face. 'It was so embarrassing. I had three horrific dates before Graham. I will take the details of those to my grave. But he's really nice.'

'How long have you been seeing him?'

'A few months. Four or five.'

'Gosh, why didn't I know about this?'

'Ah, Kay, when the boys forced me onto the website last year, it was not long after your mum… I didn't think it appropriate to talk about my dating travails when you had all that going on.'

Richard, of course, hadn't been much help during Mum's last illness. But Rose had been an absolute angel. For weeks before Mum died, I rang her nearly every day to offload.

'Come on then, tell me about Our Graham.'

'He's sixty-two—'

'Ooh! An older man.'

'At fifty-one we are hardly spring chickies ourselves. He's divorced. Two grown-up sons, like me, and a two-year-old granddaughter. He teaches English at a posh private school in Winchester. Very fit. Plays cricket. Goes up mountains.'

'And you like him?'

'I really do.'

'That is *wonderful*, Rose.'

'I'm sorry to bring tidings of my romantic door opening as yours seems to be closing.'

'Good Lord, Rose, no one deserves to be with someone nice as much as you.' Since Rose and Tim split up ten years ago, she'd devoted her time to her boys, and her part-time job and voluntary work. Tim had remarried quickly and started a new family in his mid-forties with the clichéd younger woman. 'He looks absurdly knackered, thanks,' was Rose's habitual response to being asked how Tim was doing.

'An English teacher too,' I said. 'A perfect match for your fine bookish ways.'

'Ah, he's the outdoors type, more Wordsworth than Proust. Thanks to him I have a rough grasp on the whole getting up a mountain thing. Talking of which, onwards.'

We started walking again. Climbing, really, as each step was a little higher than the one before. Minutes later, it became abruptly steeper and about ten times more challenging than the previous terrain, and I knew I would have to go slowly to avoid dying. An expression of Stella's crossed my mind – *Is this the hill you want to die on?* No, Stell, it's not. I had a sudden pang to see her pretty face.

'So,' Rose said, puffing slightly, 'another indelicate question: what will you do for money?'

'I've been putting some aside.'

'A few stashed tenners isn't going to go far.'

'Richard was always pretty generous with my wages, and every month I put away £150 in a savings account. I've never touched it.'

'Well, that's smart. That's what... nearly two grand a year. How long have you been doing that?'

'Twenty-five years.'

'Hell's bells! That's a lot of money.' Rose shot me a sideways glance. 'Have you been saving for an escape fund this whole time?'

'Of course not. I don't know what I was saving for. But anyway, even that wouldn't be enough for long on my own, I know that. I'm not an idiot. Then Mum's money came through a couple of weeks ago.'

'Ahhh, that answers my next question.'

'Which is?'

'Why now?'

'And also Mum didn't approve of divorce. I'd have hated to tell her.'

'No, she clung on to those ol' Catholic tenets for a long time, may she rest in peace. Longer than my mum, that's for sure. She took me out to dinner to celebrate when my divorce finally came through.'

'Plus, Stella's moved out.'

'Finally.'

'I know. God, poor thing, there were times I thought she'd never go!'

'How's she doing in Essex?'

'Great, I think. Nice house-share, good mates, working hard.'

'She's a good kid. Have you called her yet?'

I shook my head. 'Can't face it.'

'You must. She's really worrying about you.'

The path became even steeper, and we fell silent, save for the unattractive huffing of my breathing. All I could think about was sitting down, unhospitable a seating area as it was, but then, thank goodness, we reached a flat bit. I slithered down onto my butt, trying to calm my racing heart.

Rose rummaged round in her rucksack and pulled out a pack of trail-mix. She tipped some into my hand. It was the nicest thing I had ever eaten. I looked at her with big hungry eyes and she handed me the packet.

'So, Snowdon and Venice, and all that,' Rose said. 'Is this a random selection of activities you've plucked off midlife-crisis dot com?'

'No.'

'Or a bucket list?'

'I'm not planning on dying any time soon. Possibly if this mountain gets any steeper. No, it's just… I was looking through some old stuff from Mum's house, and found a list I made when I was a kid: "Things to do by the time I'm thirty". And I'd done almost nothing on it.'

'You need to make a new list, is all.' Rose nodded. 'Come on, we'll get cold sitting still.'

'It's not a bucket list,' I said, as we resumed walking, 'but I suppose there was something about losing Mum. Well. We don't have an infinite amount of time, do we?'

Rose laughed. 'Did you only just realise that?'

'No, but it used to be kind of an abstract notion. Then suddenly it was a real and constant threat. I'd be at Waitrose, for instance—'

'I too always have my most metaphysical revelations at Waitrose. Aldi just doesn't cut it.'

'Shut up. And I'd be wheeling my trolley round thinking, how many more times will I do this?'

'You could get online delivery, you know.'

'And it wasn't, how many more times will I do this, as in, what a bore. It was, this is a reasonably pleasurable part of my week, and how many more times will I get to do it?'

'No wonder you wanted to leave home, if the supermarket shop was a highlight.'

'I've learned to take enjoyment from the banal moments of my uneventful life. Please can we stop for a minute?' Despite the coolness of the day, I was pouring sweat.

We rested briefly, our hands braced on our knees. I glanced behind us, and realised that we still had so much further to go than the amount we had already come. We stepped off the path to allow a family of four to pass us. They all said hello, even the little kid at the back who couldn't have been more than seven. Compared to us, they were going at jogging speed.

'If you're feeling tired, take off a layer,' Rose said.

'Is that Mountain Man lore?'

'Yep. Or maybe you're having a hot flush.'

'I'm nowhere near hot flushes yet. Still getting my periods on the regular.'

'Poor you.'

'Being in one's fifties is very different, don't you think, from when our mothers were that age?'

'Totally. My mum seemed like an old lady,' Rose said.

'I remember. She wore a shawl.'

'That bloody shawl! All she needed was a rocking chair and a cat. Yet she wasn't much older than I am now.'

We started off again, a slow uphill crawl. The family were already specks in the distance.

'When Mum was very ill,' I said, 'a couple of weeks before she died, she said she regretted not taking one more walk along Parade Gardens.'

'Ah, I haven't thought about the Parade for years!'

'You haven't been back to Hoylake for a long time, have you?'

Rose shuddered. 'No, thank you.'

'She'd take me along the Parade when I was a kid, but she rarely went there afterwards. You don't, do you? You don't go for walks in the same way as when the kids were little. Well *you* do, with your new Wordsworth boyfriend who wants to take you up the Khyber Pass.'

'Pretty sharp banter for someone puffing like a rhino.'

'Anyway, Mum said, "I always thought there would be more time."' And I realised I was carrying on like that too. I was aware that I wasn't exactly happy, but I always assumed there would be time to do something about it. And then I thought, what if there isn't more time? You never know, do you? You never know if there's a bus hurtling round the corner with your name on it, or a heart attack, or something.'

'Jeez!' Rose said. 'This is heavy.'

'*Heavy*,' I said, like Ollie.

Rose was silent for a while. Then she said, 'It's about feeling that you need to spend your time in a different way from now on.'

'Exactly! An excellent summary of all my waffle.'

'So there really wasn't one particular thing Richard did to tip you over the edge?'

'No, honestly, there's nothing that I could put in an "unreasonable behaviour" petition. There wasn't any one thing. It was just a marriage-full of little things.'

We stopped again. The going was tough and we were, when all was said and done, not in the prime of fitness. Rose unscrewed the top of her water bottle and looked at me thoughtfully. 'Go on.'

'How do you know there's more?'

'I can see from your face.'

'You are so smart, Rose.' I tried to gulp down a lump that had found its way to my throat. 'Well, I guess... I was lonely.'

We started walking again.

'Loneliness is a bugger,' Rose said.

'Eventually, it makes you fall out of love with someone.' I drank some water, but it didn't dislodge the lump.

'Ah, Kay. I'm sorry. So when are you off to Sydney?'

'I don't know.'

'Good heavens, why not? You're worried about Bear, your new mantra is that there might not be more time, so what are you doing sitting here?'

'I'm not sitting! I'm toiling up Wales' answer to bloody Everest!' I was starting to feel out of breath again. 'And I already have my visa. I applied weeks ago.'

'Ha! You *have* been secretly planning this for a while.'

'Secret from myself, too, in that case. I only applied because I thought I might go to Australia this year.'

'It's natural to be scared about going off to the other side of the world,' Rose said.

I didn't reply, because at this point we had to do some single-file scrambling up a verge. Rose went first, and I struggled up behind, clutching pointlessly at tufts of grass. At the top, the path widened out again, but I was so breathless I sat on the ground. Rose joined me, and we gazed at the view: misty rocks and peaks as far as the eye could see. The world seemed dauntingly huge, all at once.

Man up, Kay, I told myself. It was a phrase I'd got from Anthony, whenever he had to do something that scared him. Which was quite often – he was an anxious guy. 'Man up, Anthony!' he'd mutter to himself. It didn't seem to help me this time, though.

'Oh, Rose.' I felt the tears come into my eyes again. 'I *am* scared. I wish you were coming with me.'

'I think you have to do this on your own, chick. I've been to see Bear a few times, but you never have. Not since that trip when we were eighteen. But I'll help you plan it, when we get back.'

We stood, and looked up at the mountain ahead of us. We were now at a point where we could no longer walk side-by-side. The next section would be more like rock climbing.

'*If* we get back,' I said.

We gave each other a Scouts' salute, and then Rose stepped forward.

The rest of the climb was the hardest thing I'd ever done. In some places, I had to stretch my leg so high with each step that I grazed my chin with my bended knee. Muscles twanged that I hadn't heard from in years. At one point, the mist came down and we climbed blind, with no sense of how high up we were.

It was often physically impossible to talk to each other, and my inner conversation went into crazy overdrive. I berated myself for leaving Richard, then berated myself for not leaving years ago. I worried about the shop, and about Stella being pulled back home so soon after she'd finally managed to leave. I worried about going to Australia, whether it was a stupid idea, and I worried about whether Bear was OK. Occasionally I wondered if the easiest thing would be to lie down and die quietly at the side of the path.

It took five hours to reach the top, and though we had been passed by dozens of climbers, including young children who sprang from rock to rock like mountain goats, I was taken aback to find hundreds of people in the mountain-top café. When Rose informed me that the majority had come up by train, I was too knackered to be outraged. We got tea and went outside. The fog had lifted, and we sat near the stone cairn marking the summit, surrounded on all sides by valleys and shimmering lakes, and by the rising jagged peaks of smaller mountains, grassy and sunlit. We were right at the top of the world, the clouds almost close enough to touch.

'This was voted the prettiest view in the whole of the UK,' Rose said, handing me a sandwich. She swept her arm across the landscape. 'Is it what you thought it would be like?'

'It's even better than I imagined,' I said. All the years I'd been coming to Bryn Glas, I'd been aware of Snowdon, so near, yet somehow the time had never been right to tackle it. Now the challenge was over, and I had a warm cup of tea in my hands, I felt something I hadn't felt for a long time: a sense of achievement. 'Thanks for making me do this, Rose. You were right. I needed to come out of my head for a bit.'

I put my arm round her shoulder.

I was physically tired but emotionally I was buzzing. 'So. Train back?'

She stroked my hair. 'Hell, no. Downhill's miles easier!'

Three hours later, as we limped back into Llanberis, I'd have punched her on the nose, if I wasn't too exhausted.

We fell into the car with screams of relief.

'Fuuuuucccckkk,' Rose said. 'I forgot something important!'

'Oh God, what?'

'I forgot we were in our fifties.'

This struck us as extremely funny, and we giggled tiredly all the way back to Bryn Glas. When we were through the door, Rose simply said, 'Good night,' and went straight up to bed. It was not yet nine in the evening. I followed her upstairs on my hands and knees, and crawled into bed without taking off any clothes. And that, dear fifty-something worried husband-leaver, is one way to get yourself a decent night's sleep.

Letter written on 21 January 2018

Dearest Bear,

Well, this is new: no letter from you last month. I hope everything's OK. It feels so weird to be writing without yours in front of me. I had another look at your last, but everything sounded fine. Charlie was happy, getting on with his studies and all his after-school activities, hats off to you. When Stella was a teenager I couldn't get her to do anything. She'd lie on her bed for hours on end, listening to music, or on the sofa watching telly. It was a miracle to me that she went off to university. When she came back, I wasn't surprised.

This last year, with her filling in hundreds of job applications, she was getting so miserable, losing all her confidence. I was thrilled when her boyfriend Theo set her up with someone he knows, Gabrielle, who's got a thriving business and needed a partner. I think I told you this in my last letter. So, Stella's moved out at last. It's hard for kids now, they've all got degrees so how do they stand out? I never got mine, of course. I was going to say that despite that, I did OK, but actually, I didn't really, did I, Bear? All those years when I might have been doing something interesting, I've been stuck behind the counter of the bloody shop. Ah well. You make your bed, you lie in it, as my dear old mum would say. Hell, I miss her so much.

And look here, Honey Bear, I miss you too! I'm hoping this blip is the Royal Mail's fault and that next month your letter will drop onto my mat, as always. Do you know how my heart lifts at the sight of it? The blue envelope, your slanting handwriting. I didn't even think how much I'd miss it till it didn't arrive. Sorry, I sound like I'm guilt-tripping, Bear, and I don't mean to. I just miss hearing you.

Till next time.

Miss you.

Always, Kay

Chapter 5

Stella

I got to Mum and Dad's at a little after five. Or just Dad's now, I supposed. I let myself in with my key, but he wasn't in. Oh God, surely he hadn't gone to…? I called a cab and raced over to Quiller Queen, Mum's shop. It was almost closing time, but there was an unusually long queue at the counter. A couple of girls at the back peeled off as I went past, and I heard one tell the other that they could 'get it in Smiths'. Thankfully they were too far away for Dad to hear. Where the hell was Anthony? Today of all days he should be here. Dad was stabbing wildly at the till, looking grey and tired, his hair un-brushed. As I reached the counter, he said to a customer, 'I'm going to have to take a card payment, this piece of crap is broken.'

'Hey, Dad,' I said.

'Stella!' He threw his arms round me in front of everyone, something he'd never done in the shop before. *Unprofessional*, he'd have called it. Mindful of the impatient customers, I extricated myself and took over. Dad stood limply at my side, smiling vaguely. Once I'd processed the queue and the shop was empty, I turned to him.

'Dad, let's close up. It's not long till six, anyway.'

'Am I being useless?'

'No, no. I think you're a little tired, maybe. You're in shock.'

'Your mother thinks I'm useless.'

'She's never said that, Daddy.' The babyish name seemed to come out at emotional moments.

'She might as well have done. She must have thought me pretty useless to throw me over for that mincing ninny, Anthony.'

'Pardon?' I looked at Dad closely. 'What's happened with Anthony? Where is he?'

'Rotting in hell, I hope.' Dad slapped his hand down on the counter.

'Daddy, what have you done?' Oh my God, had Dad... killed Anthony? My mind ran on feverishly. It was such a weird day, I honestly felt like anything could have happened.

'Only what any sensible man would have done in the same situation.' Dad locked the till.

'What would any sensible man do?'

'Sack him, of course.'

Phew. Though, hang on, what?

'I sent him packing. That conniving little bastard, taking my wages every month and secretly, behind my back, well it doesn't bear thinking about.'

'Mum's been having an affair with... Anthony?!'

Dad nodded gravely.

I couldn't compute this new twist. We went outside and locked up, then had a brief tussle at Dad's car, with him insisting he was fine to drive, then abruptly giving in. I got into the driver's seat and started the engine.

'Dad, did Mum tell you about this affair?'

'Of course not! She wouldn't have the balls.'

'So did *Anthony* say...?'

'A scoundrel like that *certainly* doesn't have the balls to admit it! I always assumed he batted for the other team. Shows how wrong you can be about people. *All* people.' He let out a strange half-laugh-half-sob, and closed his eyes.

'What did he say, when you confronted him?'

'Oh, he denied it, of course. Little runt seemed to think he could carry on working for me!'

'But…' I could see from Dad's face it was pointless to argue. He looked like a crazy man. I was sure Anthony was gay. Still, on this topsy-turvy day, who knew? Maybe he had somehow fallen for Mum's older-lady charms. Stranger things had happened, probably, though I couldn't think what they were right now.

I put the car into gear, eased into the road, and said, 'Let's go home, I'll make you something lovely for tea, and you can have a nice rest.' I realised I was soothing Dad, speaking as though he was going senile. Was he? Was that why Mum had bailed out? *Thanks a bunch, Mum.*

Back at the house, Dad went for a bath, something he'd always done after a day in the shop. The normality of that was encouraging. I began to put a curry together from ingredients Mum had left in the fridge. She had clearly stocked it up before she left this morning, as everything was fresh. This thought caught in my throat. How long had she been planning to leave? What preparations had she put in place? I looked at my phone. Nothing from Mum, but a few texts from Edward. As always, he was infuriatingly laid-back.

Wow, that's a helluva facer. Thanks for stepping in. I've spoken to Gran and she'll be there tomorrow.

No mention, I noticed, of him coming here. *Don't over-exert yourself, Eduardo.* I couldn't understand why he'd become so detached from us lately. He hadn't always been. Even when the twins were tiny babies, he and Georgia had come down from Glasgow to see us all the time. Things had changed, though, in the last few months, or maybe longer than that. A year, perhaps? He'd come for Granny Hurst's funeral, of course, but he went back the same day. I couldn't put my finger on when, but he'd definitely withdrawn from us. I mentioned it to Mum once, but she said it was probably because they had their hands full now the twins were toddlers.

I messaged him the latest revelation about Anthony – let's see how detached Edward managed to be with that one! – then sent Mum another text, my twelfth of the day.

Mum, so worried about you. Please call.

I prepared rice and vegetables to go with the curry. Cooking, as always, calmed me and helped clear my head. When everything was ready, it occurred to me that Dad had been in the bath for over an hour. I ran up and knocked on the bathroom door, but there was no answer. I could hear the radio blasting away. Would I prefer to have to go in there when Dad was naked, or for him to accidentally drown? It was a close-run thing.

'Dad? I'm coming in.'

I pushed at the door, but it didn't yield. Oh God, he'd locked it, and now he was in there, floating lifeless, or bleeding to death from self-inflicted razor wounds. I beat the door with my fists, but there was no response. *That's it,* I thought, *there's nothing else for it, I'm going to have to call the police.* I stood for a moment, my hand pressed to my chest, trying to calm my banging heart, then as I turned to go and get my phone, Dad opened the bathroom door. He had a towel wrapped round his waist and no visible damage to any major arteries.

'What's the matter?' he yelled over the radio.

'You've been ages,' I said, feeling foolish and a bit cross, 'and supper's ready.'

As I watched Dad push his food around, I realised I should have done a proper traditional meal, a pie or steak of the kind Gran would make him. Mum was the one who was adventurous with food, who tried all my experimental cooking.

Me and Dad ate/pushed food in silence. It seemed impossible to start any kind of conversation, from the small (what did he think of the curry?) to the big (would he reinstate Anthony if I could prove there was definitely nothing going on?) to the massive (how was he feeling about his failed marriage?). After a few minutes, Dad took his bowl to the sink and left it on the side, the food barely touched.

'I'm sorry,' he said – his first words since Bathroom-gate. 'I'm not hungry.'

'Shall I fetch you some chips?'

'Ooh yes please, love.'

I quickly finished my own food and walked up the road to the chip shop. It was only when I pushed open the door that I remembered that my old school friend Nita worked here.

'Well, hello, stranger,' Nita said. She was wearing a stripy apron, her long dark hair tied back neatly. 'What you doing back here? Visiting your mum?'

'Er, something like that… how are things here?'

'Oh, you know, the excitement never starts. Fish and chips, is it?' She started expertly turning chips in the hot fat.

'Yes please, one portion.'

'So how's your business going, Stell? Vietnamese food, wasn't it?'

'Sri Lankan. Yes, it's doing really well.'

'Lucky you. You escaped. I'm trapped here forever. Can't afford to get my own place.'

'I know, it's really tough. I'm only just scraping by, and I've got the tiniest room in a house share. And it's in the worst part of Romford.'

Nita raised a sceptical eyebrow. She knew how ecstatic I'd been to get out of my parents' house. As she shovelled chips into a bag, I thought, there but for the grace of God. Swap stationery for batter, and that could so easily have been me, stuck in one of Dad's shops.

'Salt and vinegar?'

'Yes please.'

'Well, if you ever have a vacancy in the business, or the house, think of me, won't you? My cabin fever is at critical. If I never see another blimming chip it'll be too soon. Say hi to your mum and dad for me.'

'Will do.' I wished I could tell her what had happened, but I was worried about Dad being on his own in the house. 'See you soon.'

After Dad scarfed down the fish and chips from the wrapper – Mum would never have stood for that – he said he was going to have a rest.

'Dad? Can I, I mean we ought to, shall we… I mean, should we talk?'

He looked straight at me, and I saw that he was starting to look old. His face seemed more lined than just a few months ago, and his hair was more grey than brown.

'Not now, thank you,' he said, and went out.

During that difficult time after university, there were days when getting up was a challenge, knowing that all I had to look forward to was filling in yet more hopeless job applications. Mum would sometimes say, 'Sweetheart, there's going to be a limit to what you can achieve today.' I whispered it out loud now, like a mantra: *there is going to be a limit to what I can achieve today.*

I cleared up, then went to find Dad. He was in the living room, asleep in an armchair. I draped a blanket round him, then went upstairs and got into my old bed – Mum always kept it made up with clean sheets – and texted Theo. I tried to stay awake long enough for his reply but couldn't keep my eyes open.

Chapter 6

Stella

I was woken by a noise I couldn't immediately identify. My phone was still clutched in my hand, and it was nearly eight o'clock. I'd slept for eleven hours straight. I realised the noise was Dad yelling, and I jumped out of bed and into the room formerly known as Mum and Dad's room.

He was lying on his side on the floor next to the bed, wearing nothing but pants, looking utterly confused. 'I banged my head!'

'Jesus, Daddy, what happened?' I tried to pull him up, averting my eyes from his belly rolls, but he was too heavy to move.

'I'm not sure.' He struggled into a kneeling position. 'I was sitting on the edge of the bed, putting on my trousers, when I, I don't know, I must have tipped over. I hit my head on the floor. It really hurts, actually.' He rubbed his forehead.

'Can you get back into bed, Dad?'

'We have to open your mother's shop.' He tried to stand up, then stumbled and sat back on the floor.

'You're going nowhere.'

'I'm not, am I?' he said, trying to smile. 'I don't think I had a very good sleep, I was in the living room for some reason.'

Heaving with all my weight, I helped him get up into a crouch so he could climb back into bed. He crawled under the covers, still protesting. 'You can't manage the shop on your own.'

I picked up his crumpled trousers from the floor – he must have been lying on them – and laid them over the back of the chair. 'It will be fine,' I said. 'Try and get some rest. Gran's on her way, so she'll look after you. There's no need to worry about anything.' My strong dad was falling to pieces.

'Thank you, Stella. You're an angel.' He closed his eyes, and I started towards the door, then his eyes snapped open. 'If the Sheaffer rep comes in, tell her—'

'To leave you the catalogue.'

'Yes. Thank you.'

My first day solo in the shop was anything but calm. Anthony came in and threatened to take us to court, but not before telling me exactly where Dad could put a glue stick, then Edward was infuriating when I called to tell him what had happened, suggesting I drop my life and work in the shop full-time. And to top it off, we had a run on gel pens so I had to deal with an irate mother complaining I'd ruined her daughter's birthday when there were none left. Things took a much-needed turn for the better when I got back to Dad's and discovered Gran in the kitchen, rolling out pastry.

'Dear heart!' she said. 'What a marvellous trooper you've been!' She glided round the table and planted a delicate, barely-there kiss on my cheek. She wasn't one of life's huggers, which was a shame as I could have done with one.

'Thanks for coming so quickly, Gran.'

'Not at all, Stella dear.' She went back to her pastry. 'How is your father?'

'Haven't you seen him yet?'

'Barely. He let me in, then went off to bed. That was three hours ago.'

I flopped into a chair, suddenly overcome by it all. Gran took one look at me and got the brandy out from the cupboard next to the sink.

'Stella, how are you really?'

I took a tiny sip of brandy – I hated the taste, but it was Gran's go-to in a crisis – and gave a brief precis of the rollercoaster couple of days: Dad's phone call, Anthony threatening lawsuits, Edward being weird, and Theo far away. Gran gave me her best: a pat on the shoulder and a top-up of brandy. I couldn't help thinking how Mum would have gathered me into a tight, comforting embrace and held me for as long as I needed.

I told her about Dad falling down/fainting this morning, and she nodded sympathetically. 'My poor little boy. I always knew Kay would break his heart one day.'

'To be fair, Gran, it did take quite a long time.'

'Thirty years might seem long to you, sweet child, but to me it's the blink of an eye.'

I was under no illusion about the prickly relationship between Mum and Gran. I'd noticed from a fairly young age that their conversational barbs were more edgy than affectionate. I'd asked Mum about it once, and she said, 'Oh, Alice wouldn't have thought anyone was good enough for Richard. She'd have been the same with Jackie Kennedy or Grace Kelly.' I hadn't heard of these women at the time, so for quite a while I assumed they were Dad's ex-girlfriends.

Probably their mutual abrasiveness was due to class differences. My grandmother was from a well-to-do Hampshire family and, of course, as she loved to remind us, used to work for (minor) royalty. Though Mum always described this as being 'in service', which made Gran furious. She sent Dad to private school and was thoroughly disappointed when he didn't get in to Oxbridge. Mum, on the other hand, grew up on an estate near Liverpool, and still had a soft Scouse accent that set Gran's teeth on edge. I couldn't help noticing that the accent came out more strongly when Gran was around.

'What are you making?' I asked her, changing the subject.

'Your father's favourite – steak pie.' She draped the pastry neatly over a dish full of meat. 'Ideally one would leave the pastry in the fridge for two days, but I'm going to simply shove it in the oven and beg for forgiveness.'

She brushed the pie with egg yolk, put it in the oven, and sat opposite me. 'Do you understand what's happened, dear? Richard's telephone message was so garbled I could barely follow it, and Edward was scarcely any more enlightening. Your mother can't really have been having some *folie a deux* with little Anthony, can she?'

'I don't think so, Gran, it's just a weird idea that Daddy's got somehow.'

'Well, that's *something*. But I truly don't know what's got into Kay. She must see that one can't simply walk out on one's life in this way. One has responsibilities, after all. Husband, children, work. I did wonder…' and she leaned forward and whispered, 'if she'd lost her marbles.'

'Gran! You can't say that.'

'Can't say it about your mother, or about anyone?'

'Anyone! It's not the right way to say… look, never mind about that. Are you saying you think Mum's got a mental-health issue?'

Gran rolled her eyes. 'If that's what we have to call it nowadays, then yes, that's what I think.'

Dad walked in then, luckily, as I didn't really want to hear Gran's diagnosis. We both jumped up. I put the kettle on, while Gran whipped out a plate of biscuits she must have made before I arrived. It was great that Dad was up, but even his own mother would have said that he looked awful.

And yes, here was his own mother: 'Richard dear, you look *awful*.'

Dad nodded. 'Thanks, Mum.' He slumped into a chair, and stared vacantly into space.

He was unshaven, and his hair lay flat and unwashed against his head like a limp dishcloth. The dark circles under his eyes were closer to panda than human.

'Are you still tired, Daddy?' I asked.

'Down to my toes. Bone tired,' he said, and then to my horror he started to cry. Though I had heard him cry once before, on the phone yesterday, I'd never seen it. It instantly went straight to number one of the top ten things I wished I'd never seen.

'She's not coming back, is she?' Dad wailed.

Gran and I both ran over and held him – well, I did and Gran patted him gently – while he sobbed his heart out. Could he be right? Was Mum really not coming back? The echoing silence of her disappearance was scary and final. There was no such echoing silence from Gran, though. She forgot momentarily, perhaps, that I was closely related to Mum, and called her a few things I was surprised to hear. But the dissing seemed to soothe Dad a little.

'I thought she'd have come back by now. I really did,' Dad sobbed. I handed him my glass of brandy, and he chugged it down as if it was water.

'Well, she easily might yet,' Gran said, then added, contradictorily, 'but good riddance, say I!'

'I miss her!' Dad said, leaning his head against my shoulder.

'Me too!' Gran said. *Make your mind up, woman.*

After a few minutes, Dad pulled out of my arms. 'I have to check in with the shops!'

Of course – Dad's daily ritual, never yet missed – was to email the managers at the other shops. What they thought of it, I wasn't sure. He started to get up, but Gran fixed him with her special stare.

'You're in no state, Richard,' she said. 'Stella can do it.'

'Sure. Just whip off a few emails, is it?'

'Aileen needs a phone call rather than an email,' Dad said. Aileen was the manager at Pencil Us In, Dad's second-biggest shop.

'You phone Aileen every day?'

He looked at me, baffled. 'Of course.'

By the time I'd checked in with the other managers, and handled Aileen's concerned/nosey questions about my parents, supper was ready. I shovelled in a load of Gran's comfort carbs and fell heavily into bed. I was almost asleep when Edward rang.

'Have you seen the email from Mum?' he said.

'No. I got a text from Rose saying they were both at the cottage in Wales.'

'She's sorted the Anthony problem.'

'Oh, hurrah!' I sat up. 'Did she sound OK?'

'It was a pretty weird message, to be honest. She said she was going up a mountain tomorrow, and went on about glue sticks. She possibly has totally lost her mind, but I can't process that right now. Anyway, she's arranged for Anthony to come back as manager. That's the good news.'

'Uh oh.'

'The bad news is, he's taking a fortnight's holiday.'

'What are you saying, Edward?'

'Can you just stay until he's back? Pretty please, Stell?'

'A *fortnight*? Surely you could come—'

'I'm sorry, but I can't drop everything. And I'm afraid you can. I've got responsibilities, and you're lucky you don't have any yet. That's simply the way it is.'

'I don't believe this!' I was too furious to cry. 'How can you be so cold? You haven't been here for months, and now we've got the worst crisis ever and you're all, oh dear I'm a bit too busy to see my father who's been walked out on.'

'I've spoken to him plenty. And you and Gran are there.'

'Yes! Some of us don't have the luxury of being able to opt out,' I yelled. 'I want to go back to my home and my job and my boyfriend.'

'But someone needs to look after Dad for a bit. And Mum's shop.' Edward put on his conciliatory voice. 'You're a superhero, Stell. You're my hero.'

Oh my God, he was every bit as maddening as when we were children. 'Don't fucking do that, Eduardo.' I turned off my phone. Bloody Edward. And bloody Mum! Just when I thought I'd finally managed to get my life together, and she went and kicked it out from under me.

Chapter 7

Stella

The next few days passed uneventfully, if such a confusing, upsetting, annoying situation could be described as uneventful. I worked in the shop, and worried about Dad's mental state, and watched Gran reorganise Mum's kitchen. The relish with which she tackled this made me wonder how long she'd been dying to get her hands on it, but on the plus side, everything was tidy, and there were delicious home-cooked meals every day. Plus a packed lunch for me to take to the shop so there was, 'No need for you to force down sandwiches made by people on dubious employment schemes, dear.'

Dad was distant, prone to tears, there-but-not-there. He greeted the news that Anthony, Mum's alleged lover, had been promoted to manager, with a strange lack of surprise. 'I suppose I'd better apologise to him?' he said.

'Yes!' Gran and I chorused, equally relieved that on this, at least, he seemed to have his senses back.

'I'll write him a letter,' Dad said, 'and take him champagne on his first day back.'

But other than asking for a brief shop report at the end of each day, he didn't speak much, and spent a lot of time sleeping, or hiding away in his bedroom.

The agency girl Edward had hired, Callie, was efficient at serving customers. But everything else was down to me, and it was so tiring. I tried hard each night, in weary, before-bed phone calls to Theo, to think of a more interesting topic than the shop. But it was all I had to talk about. He seemed very far away and was exhausted too, juggling his own work and the catering with Gabby. He didn't have time to visit, and I was too knackered to go and see him. Even when I went to sleep there was no respite, because I had panic-dreams about not having ordered enough stock. Had Mum felt this way too? In just a few days, I felt hemmed in by the shop. What had it been like to do this for twenty-five years?

On my fourth day at Quiller Queen, I sold our most expensive pen, a solid gold Cross, to a customer Gran would describe as a 'refined Arab gentleman'. It was thrilling to dig out Dad's instructions for opening the safe where the most expensive pens were kept, which led me to a piece of paper with the latest combination in Mum's handwriting. It was hard not to feel a little pang at this evidence of my parents' teamwork. I took the box out to the shop with care, and clipped the pen to a chain on the counter, put there specifically for this purpose since an incident years ago when a man tried to steal a Mont Blanc. This was one of Dad's favourite stories. 'He looked so respectable!' he would marvel. 'And I stupidly put the pen into his thieving hands!' It all ended in great excitement, with some of the regular customers tackling the villain to the floor and sitting on his back till the police came.

The customer examined the beautifully engraved nib. 'There is nothing like gold, is there?' he said, turning it so that the light glinted off it.

He didn't blink when I told him the price, though Callie gasped. When he'd paid and gone, she and I high-fived each other. My first thought was that I couldn't wait to tell Mum, she would be so proud.

Then I thought, probably she wouldn't care. At that moment I felt sadder than I'd done since this whole thing kicked off.

At closing time I texted Theo, telling him I missed him, and asked if he could possibly come and see me this evening, no matter how late. After I pressed send, three little moving dots appeared, meaning he was typing. I watched the dots for a minute, but nothing came through.

I locked the shop and drove back to Dad's. Gran gave me my regular glass of brandy, and I showed her my phone, the little dots still moving back and forth enticingly. 'He's sending a very long message, so that's good, right?'

'Mmm,' Gran said, looking at me thoughtfully. 'It's about time we released you from incarceration, isn't it?'

I looked at my phone. Theo's dots had disappeared, and there was no message. As I stared at it, the phone buzzed in my hand, but it was Rose calling, not Theo.

'Hey, kiddo,' she said. 'I'm phoning on behalf of your crazy mother, who is too shy to call you.'

'Oh, Rose.' I sniffed.

'Hey, hey. She would love to see you. She really misses you. Any chance you can come up for a couple of days?'

'I can't,' I said, though I did really want to see Mum. 'There's the shop…'

'Chip off the old block, aren't you?' Rose said. 'How many times have I heard that sentence from your mother!'

'May I interject?' Gran said, right next to my non-phone ear.

I heard Rose laugh in my other ear. 'I can hear your redoubtable grandmother.'

'Teach me to run the shop tomorrow, then go see your mother,' Gran said. In a quieter voice, she added, 'And talk some sense into her!'

'Really, Gran?' I stared at her in surprise. 'But you don't, I mean you haven't...' What I wanted to say was, 'You've always been very snooty about the shops.' But I couldn't think of a polite form of words. Luckily, she assumed I was hesitating for other reasons.

'I'm a very fast learner, I'll have you know.' She sniffed.

'Well, thank you.' I smiled gratefully at Gran. This was no time to start inspecting gift horses. 'I'll come Sunday,' I told Rose, and she whooped.

'Can't wait to tell Kay!'

When I hung up, Gran said, 'Still no missive from Theo, then?'

I shook my head.

She went on, 'Why don't you phone him?'

'I don't know. It feels a bit weird...' but to avoid Gran giving one of her 'suffragettes died so that you could ring the man rather than sit by the phone' speeches, I pressed 'call'. Gran discreetly slipped out of the room, and I counted the rings till Theo picked up. It seemed it would go to voicemail, then he answered.

'Stella?' He sounded his usual self, if rather far away. I felt my shoulders begin to come down from their previous all-time high position somewhere above my ears.

'Theo! Did you get my text? Can you come down tonight?'

'I can't, sorry, babe. It's all go here. You too, I bet. You've been too busy to even think of me, am I right?' He laughed, which seemed inappropriate as I wasn't exactly here on a fun holiday.

'No, I really miss you and think about you a lot.' I held my breath, my fingers tightening around the phone. The silence went on and on.

Finally, he said, 'Ah, that's so nice.'

'What was all that texting earlier? It looked like something huge was coming in, but then it disappeared.'

'Oh, I was trying to explain why I couldn't come, but I thought it would be easier to speak, it was a bit complicated. Listen, Stell, it's another early start tomorrow, crack of dawn at Chelmsford farmers' market, so by the time I got to you tonight I'd pretty much have to head back. Stell? I'm sorry, I don't think I'm safe to drive. I'm so knackered.'

'That's fine.' I forced a smile into my voice. 'Well, see ya.'

I clicked off the phone before he had a chance to say anything more. We'd never been brilliant at long-distance communication, and I knew we probably wouldn't reconnect until we were face to face. I'd go there after seeing Mum.

The next day I taught Gran how to run the shop. She was a surprisingly quick and enthusiastic learner.

'Adored it,' Gran told Dad that evening, as we sat down to another of her hearty dinners. 'Should have seen me, Richard. Sleeves rolled up, hair in a scarf. Figuratively, my dear, not literally.'

'Well, Mum, I'm impressed.' Dad looked a bit stunned at Gran's late-life flowering as a shop girl. After a few moments, he cleared his throat and said to me, 'So you're going to see your mother tomorrow.'

'Yes, Daddy. Thanks for lending me the car. I'll see Mum, go to my house for a couple of days, then bring it back.'

He nodded, then reached out and put his hand on mine.

'You'll tell Kay the shop's doing well, won't you?' he said. 'I'm sure she's been missing it.'

'Of course,' I said, avoiding Gran's eye. I wondered if she, like me, was picturing Mum sitting in Bryn Glas by the fire, setting her business cards alight and cackling with laughter.

'Will you take her a letter?' he said.

'Er, sure.'

He fished into his pocket and handed me a crumpled envelope. 'It's what I wish I'd said to her,' Dad said, 'when she went.' With his straggly beard, stale smell and air of bewilderment, Dad still had something about him of the tramp I'd seen in the library. He wiped his eyes and stood up. 'I'm going to bed.'

'I'll be off in the morning before you get up, Dad,' I said. I remembered from going there as a child what a long way Bryn Glas was. He pulled me into a hug, and though it was not as soft nor fragrant as the one I was looking forward to from Mum, it was still very comforting.

'Drive carefully, Sparkle.' He went out, and we heard him climb laboriously upstairs. Sparkle was Mum's nickname for me.

'Now Stella,' Gran said, breaking into my thoughts, 'you're not to go swanning round the country clutching love letters, pretending you're in *The Go-Between*. Your mother is no Julie Christie.'

'Huh?'

'I'm merely saying, dear, it's not wise to get his hopes up, is it?' Gran frowned at me, as if the love-letter carrier-pigeon scheme was my idea. 'Not that I don't want your mother back as much as the next person.'

I wondered who the next person was – someone who hated my mother, presumably.

'I'll give her the letter, Gran, if it's the right thing to do.'

Gran gave me an old-fashioned look. Well, even more old-fashioned than usual.

'Evasive,' she said frostily, 'like your mother.'

*

Despite this exchange, Gran was still up early to make me breakfast and see me off. It took hours to get there, but the sight of Bryn Glas gave me reminiscence-ache in my stomach. We'd had so many lovely holidays here when I was little. I got out of the car and stretched my stiff limbs, putting off the moment, aware that while I was desperate to see Mum, I was also rather dreading it.

Face your fear head on, Bettina said. *You can do this.*

I can do this, I told myself, and I stepped forward and banged on the door.

Chapter 8

Kay

When there was a knock on the door, I looked out of the window and saw Richard's car parked next to mine. Well, I very nearly had a heart attack. That certainly clarified how little I wanted to see him. My rational mind knew that Stella must have borrowed his car, but I nonetheless ran out of my room in a panic, and crashed into Rose on the landing.

'What if Richard's come too?' I said, doing mock-but-sort-of-real shivering.

'Hell's bells!' Rose said. 'Do we have a gun?'

Despite myself, I started laughing. 'No, but there's a poker downstairs.'

I flung the door open and Stella fell into my arms. There was, thank God, no sign of Richard. My girl clung onto me like a lead weight, and I stood in the doorway holding her, her warm damp cheek against mine, her arms tight round my back.

I whispered, 'It's so lovely to see you, Sparkle.'

At last, she pulled away, and I ushered her into the living room.

'Thanks for replying to my messages,' she said as she sat down. Her heavy sarcasm reminded me with a pang of her teenage self.

'I'm sorry, love. I've been struggling to know what to say. How was the journey?'

'Long.'

'That was my assessment too,' Rose said, coming in with three steaming mugs. She put them on the coffee table and hugged Stella tight. 'Hello, love.'

'Hello, Rose. Thank *you* for keeping me posted.' Stella picked up one of the mugs, and said, 'Can I go and have a wash? I've been in that stuffy car for hours.'

'Of course, sweetheart, there's plenty of...' she went out, and I finished pointlessly, '... hot water.'

Rose and I raised our eyebrows at each other. 'It'll take her a little while,' she said. 'Be patient. You've turned her life upside down.'

'I've turned *my* life upside down, Rose.'

'Stella and Edward are technically grown-ups, but when it comes to one's parents, we're always little children. By leaving, you've effectively said to them, "You know all those years you thought me and your dad were happy and in love? Well, surprise! It was all a lie!"'

'It wasn't *all* a lie, Rose...'

'You need to be patient and kind, like when they were toddlers.'

'You're very wise. I'll be kind, I promise.'

She sat opposite me, and the chair made a horrible cracking noise. 'Oh no, what have I done?'

'Let me have a look.'

She got up gingerly. 'Am I really fat, Kay? You'd tell me, wouldn't you?'

'You're a gorgeous waif. Look, one of the legs needs re-aligning, that's all.'

'Yeah, I'll take your word for it. I always forget you're basically a bloke when it comes to DIY.'

I fetched my Swiss army knife – it had an excellent screwdriver – and fixed the broken chair. Then I invited Rose to sit on it, and we were both pleased that there was no cracking this time.

'You don't need a husband at all,' Rose said. 'You can cook *and* fix things. You are basically a hermaphrodite.'

'Gee, thanks.'

'Well, look. Stella's here now, and you're off to Oz in a couple of days. I ought to get back to civilization.'

'Thanks for helping me book the flight, Rose.'

'You'd have done it without me. Eventually. Are you sure you don't want to call Bear, tell her you're coming?'

'I can't,' I said. 'It was our deal. We always said we would only phone if it was a World-Class Emergency. Originally that was because it cost so much to call Australia. Our parents would have killed us. But even when it got cheaper, we never phoned, not in all these years. Letters are our thing.'

'Isn't it an emergency now?'

'I hope not. Anyway, I've emailed her. If she wants to reply, she will.'

'You said she hardly ever looks at her email.'

'Well, maybe she will this time.' I didn't tell Rose my silly superstition: that if I went to Australia, Bear would be fine, but if I phoned, she wouldn't. I had to put in the effort in order for her to be fine. My rational brain pointed out that this was kind of irrational, and my irrational brain said, 'Yeah, so?'

The trains between Bangor and Crewe were a mess, so I lent Rose my car, which she promised to leave for me at Heathrow. She was already on my insurance from years back, the time when I stayed with her after Tim left, taking their shared car with him, the bastard. I knew I could get a lift back south with Stella, which would give me a chance to talk to her.

After Rose left in a cloud of exhaust and gravel, I felt strangely bereft. I was so lucky she'd been there to see me through these first few post-leaving days. She'd pushed me up mountains, made me book flights, helped me sort through my feelings, and sat me down with a pen and paper to make a list that amounted to a plan for the next few months, and... years.

I crept upstairs to see Stella but the door of the spare room was closed and I didn't want to be intrusive – Rose's 'be kind' command ringing in my ears. I pottered quietly about, tidying, cooking and cleaning. I made us a late lunch, but Stella didn't appear till gone 4 p.m., looking bleary-eyed.

'I fell asleep! I didn't mean to.' She sat down and devoured the lunch, though the sandwich was curling at the corners.

'So, er, what news from the front?' I asked, as if using a World War One soldier's voice would somehow make it seem a more casual question. 'How are you? How's the shop?'

'Fancy leaving Dad, when you have so much in common,' Stella said, her face blank. 'How's the shop? How's the shop?'

'Sorry. Old habits, you know.'

'The shop, at least, is fine. Thanks for convincing Anthony to come back. Until he does, Gran's in charge.'

'Seriously? Twenty-five years we've had that shop and Alice has never once stepped behind the counter. I'd love to see how she handles awkward customers.'

'She terrifies them. Talking of customers, guess what I sold!' Stella smiled at me for the first time since she'd arrived. 'Only the gold Cross fountain pen!'

'You *didn't!*' I almost dropped the glass of water I was holding. How many years had that pen been in the safe? How many times had I given it a polish, ready for the implausible event that a customer might buy it? 'That's amazing! What did Dad say?'

'Oh. He was like, "well done".'

'Good heavens, Sparkle, I'd have thought he'd be on Cloud Nine. Remember how he always says, "There's no better present than a smart fountain pen."'

'You know, Mum, he's not really himself right now.' Stella shook her head.

'Well, darling, please don't feel that you have to look after him. Don't let yourself be guilt-tripped into living back at home.'

'Don't you want to know how Dad is?'

'Yes, of course,' I said, because I knew it would be awful to say 'not really'. I stood up and turned on the kettle.

'He's in such a state, Mum. He's been crying loads.'

'But he never cries.' *Hurry up, kettle.*

'Well, you see,' Stella said, 'he's never been left by his wife of thirty years before.'

'Twenty-nine years.' I put my hand on her arm. 'Love, I don't expect you to understand.'

'That's a relief, Mum, because I don't.' Stella looked as if she might cry. 'I thought you two loved each other! You looked fine! Where has this come from?'

I got down two clean mugs. It turned out there was as much hot-drink-making after a separation as a bereavement. After Mum's death last year, I'd pretty much cried tears of tea.

'We grew apart, I guess. It does happen, love.'

'Daddy doesn't think you've grown apart!' Stella said. 'It's so crazy to split up now, when I'm finally out of your hair, and you have time to spend with each other.'

I fought hard against a sarky reply, but it was no good. 'It's the spending time with each other that's killing me.'

'Mum!'

'Sorry, love. Jokes are inappropriate.' I poured boiling water onto teabags and milk, relieved Rose wasn't here to tell me off. 'I genuinely didn't want to hurt him.'

Despite her long nap, Stella still looked tired. 'But you have, Mum. And I can't honestly understand why, unless you've met someone else.'

I hadn't felt, lately, that I occupied any moral high ground whatso-ever, but I definitely did over this. 'Gracious!' I said, putting our mugs down on the table. 'Why does everyone think there must be someone? It's not very feminist of you to assume I'm incapable of living my life without a man to lean on.'

'So there really isn't anyone?'

'There really isn't.'

I started tidying away Stella's lunch things. I needed to keep moving because I wanted to say something about her and Theo that she wasn't going to like, so delivering it casually was the key.

'Sparkle, have I ever told you how your father and I got together?'

'Weird topic, Mum, under the circumstances.'

'I know, but it's relevant.' I filled the washing bowl with warm soapy water. 'Your dad and I met when we were very young. I'd not been at university long, I was nineteen, maybe twenty. He was older, a postgraduate, doing business studies. He seemed ancient but he was only twenty-six.'

'You've told me this before. I still think it was a bit creepy that he picked you up when you were a first year. We were warned about that at uni.'

'It wasn't like that. The art department used to hold these mixers, cheese-and-wine evenings, seems awfully quaint now. It was the height of sophistication to me, coming from the back of beyond in the Wirral.'

'What if you didn't like cheese or wine?'

'You were out of luck. It was, here's a lump of cheddar, here's a glass of wine from a box, now go mingle.'

'Sounds wild.'

'Actually, they were pretty effective mixers, because there was always a lot more wine than cheese. I went to one with Rose, and your dad was there.'

'Great story, Mum.'

'I haven't finished.' I plunged a plate into the bowl. 'Anyway, we started going out, and things went along fine for a few months. But then I met David, who was friends with a girl in my halls.' It felt so strange to say David's name out loud to one of my children. Like breaking a taboo.

'Oh yes? David. I haven't heard of him before.'

'He was the same age as me and super-handsome.'

'Have you got any photos?'

'I do, actually. Back ho... back at the house. You know I studied art and photography. In fact, I was offered an apprenticeship in a photography studio when I graduated.'

'Wow, really? I didn't know that. Did you do it?'

'Er, no. I didn't graduate, remember. Anyway. I got on really well with David, I liked him a lot. Then one night we had a few drinks in the Students' Union...'

'Oh my God!' Stella put her mug down so fast she spilled tea on the table. 'You're not going to tell me that David is my father?'

I shivered, but I don't think she noticed. 'No,' I said, with more emphasis than I intended. 'Richard is absolutely your father. Here's a cloth.'

'Thanks. Phew.'

'Anyway, David confessed he'd liked me for ages but hadn't wanted to say anything because I had a boyfriend.' I thought back to that evening, one of the most amazing of my life, the memory of it glittering still, undimmed by time. 'So the very next day I finished with Richard—'

'Hang on a minute, you and Dad split up? I'm confused.'

It was a while since I'd given this account out loud, and I had to think for a moment. What came next?

'And I had a blissful few weeks with David—'

'Gah, TMI,' Stella said.

'And then I fainted on my way to a lecture, and discovered at the GPs that I was pregnant. With Richard's baby.'

'Ah, enter Baby Edward stage left.' Stella rolled her eyes at the thought of her brother. 'Hang on, though – how do you know that the baby was Dad's?'

'Oh, it was the timing. It was too far on to be David's. And anyway, we...' I hesitated, wondering if this was overdoing it, 'David and I had only just started, you know... we were taking it slow.'

'Mum!' Stella put her hands over her ears. 'Lalalala!'

'Sorry.'

'Didn't you think to pretend to David that it was his?'

'Certainly not, Stella!' I rubbed at a non-existent stain on the table so I didn't have to look at her.

'It's incredibly common, though, isn't it?' Stella sipped her tea. 'What's that statistic about a huge proportion of people who think the wrong man is their father?'

I moved on hastily. 'Richard was thrilled to have me back. He knew I'd want to keep the baby, being Catholic, you remember what my mum was like.'

'Nonetheless, I can't wait to tell Eduardo that he was nearly an abortion.'

'Stella, that's horrible, and he wasn't. I never even considered it. Your dad asked me to marry him, and although it was starting to be more acceptable back then to be an unmarried couple with a baby, it wasn't that common. So, we got married, and my parents were delighted. Richard's mother of course, that was a different story.'

'Gran likes you now, though. Well, she did, before you...'

'Yes, I imagine I'm not her favourite person right now.'

'So why are you telling me this?' Stella clapped her hands to her mouth. 'Oh God, he's the one, isn't he?'

'The one?'

'The other man! You're going to tell me that David was your one great love, so you're going looking for him to make up for all the lost years.'

'Certainly not, Stella. You're looking for a neat, black-and-white answer in a situation in which there isn't one. Anyway, that's not the point, that's not why I'm telling you this.' I sat down, and put my hand on her arm. 'I'm worried about you and Theo.'

'How are we on to Theo? Why are you worried?' Stella looked confused. 'I have to say, Mum, this doesn't feel like the most urgent item on our agenda.'

'It's been on my mind, is all. I've been thinking a lot about the folly of settling down too early. You're so young, Sparkle. I know you two have been talking about getting engaged, but from my vantage point, twenty-three is unbelievably young, no matter how it feels on the inside. Life is long. You need to spread your wings, try out lots of things, try out other people.'

'Honestly, Mum! Are we talking about me, or you? I'm going to go back to my house tomorrow, and find out if me and Theo have what it takes to last the distance, and I'm going to carry on with the catering business, because I like it, and I'm good at it. I don't think you should tell me what to do! I'm not the one hiding in an old cottage in the middle of nowhere because I left my home without a plan.'

Stella always did know how to do a walkout speech. She went out, and I heard her stomp upstairs. I thought of Rose telling me to be kind, and realised I hadn't been kind at all. I went upstairs after her, but hesitated outside her closed door, and decided to at least be patient, which was the other part of Rose's instructions. Instead, I went into my room, and sat on the grey chair.

I checked my phone, to see if Bear had answered my email. But there was nothing. I switched to contacts, and my finger hesitated over her number. Then I put the phone on the table. If it was a World-Class Emergency, I had to go there.

What had made me leave? Everyone wanted to know. Was there someone else, had something happened, what was the trigger? As I'd tried to explain to Rose, there were lots of things, an accumulation over many years. But if there *was* one specific moment, it was the afternoon a few weeks ago, on one of those days when you start looking for something and end up going down a wormhole of memories.

I'd pulled out from under my bed the shoe boxes containing Bear's most recent letters, to see if she'd said something outright that I hadn't noticed, or dropped in clues that I'd missed. I can't explain how odd it felt that she'd not written. We never missed a month. Came close a few times, of course, but as the calendar neared the fifteenth of my month, an alarm would go off in my head, and I'd sit down to write. I assumed it was the same for her. But now three of her months had been and gone.

Hours passed, as I read letter after letter, laughing at things she'd said in response to mine, tearing up at some of the sad bits. There was nothing obvious to explain her silence.

From day one of secondary school, Bear (real name Ursula, which she hated), Rose and I were an inseparable threesome. The best of best friends. For five years we did everything together. I could easily recall the pain I felt the awful day Bear told us her family was moving to Australia. We were fifteen, nearly sixteen. We'd been planning to all go to the same college for our A-levels. I don't know who cried more of the three of us. Bear and I made a pledge that we'd write every other month. The first month, she'd write to me, the next month, I'd write to her, and so on. This meant that every year I received six blue airmail envelopes filled with Bear's scrawling, slanty handwriting, her funny, wry voice, telling me about the horrors – at first – of her new life, and how Sydney wasn't a patch on Hoylake, which we laughed a lot about later. Then, of course, how she'd settled in, made friends, got herself a boyfriend, loved her college course.

And I wrote back long rambling updates on my life: what Rose and I had been up to, how much we missed her, what we thought she'd say if she was with us, the crazy times we had at college, then later, university, marriage, babies, work, kids… If I ever wanted to write my memoir, those letters would be a priceless resource, assuming she'd kept them, of course. Six letters a year from me to her, six letters back from her to me. Some were barely half a page, when life was busy, scrawled in haste; others four, five or more pages long full of the detail we both craved. They always ended the same way, with our special sign-off, the origin of which was lost in the long years of our correspondence: 'Till next time. Miss you. Always.'

I'd seen Bear in person over the years, of course. Rose and I went there during our gap year before university: six amazing, sunlit weeks travelling with Bear round Australia. The final night, drunk in a bar in Sydney, we promised we'd do it again when we all finished uni. But by then I had baby Edward, and Rose went alone. After that, children, work and life got in the way, and I'd not been to Australia since. Bear came back to the UK every few years; the last time was maybe three years ago. But those visits were always fleeting and unsatisfactory. She had so many people to see, and often tried to pack the whole of Europe into the trip. But on the page, our love for each other was easy to express; and always the letters came. There must be more than two hundred now, stored in boxes under my bed. We'd obviously both got email at some point, but Bear wasn't very interested in it, and anyway, neither of us had wanted to stop the old-fashioned letters.

When I went to retrieve the next box, I pulled out instead one I hadn't looked in for years. I'd cleared Mum's flat after she died, and saw that this box had my name on the lid in her clear capital letters. I hadn't yet got round to opening it, and I smiled when I realised what was in there: my youth. Ancient mementoes I could scarcely remember keeping. Photo-booth pictures of me and Bear, programmes for art exhibitions, old birthday cards from friends and boyfriends, including a special one from my mum that made me well up, tickets for gigs I'd been to in the 1980s, including Soft Cell's last concert, well, their first last concert, ah, that dated me. And some of my old photos taken back when I fancied I'd make a career out of photography, most in black and white, developed by myself at university, including a heart-stopping one of David Endevane, impossibly young and beautiful, all cheekbones and fair hair, like his namesake David Sylvian, the lead singer of Japan. As always, when I thought about David, I wondered what it would have been like if things had been different. Bear was the only person in the world, other than Richard, David and I who knew what had really happened.

At the bottom of the box was something I had forgotten so entirely, it was as though it belonged to someone else. It was a folded piece of yellowing paper, and in my childish writing, with hearts dotting the i's, I had written at the top: 'Things to do by the time I am thirty.' This was underlined twice in red biro. The date: 5 June 1982.

That was the year Rose, Bear and I finished our O levels, and Rose and I went to college. It was the year we turned sixteen. And it was the year Bear emigrated.

Thirty must have seemed unimaginably old when I was fifteen. I was impressed, retrospectively, at the girl who could look into the future and see so far ahead. Teenage Kay must have assumed she'd better get everything done by thirty; for afterwards, there'd be nothing but senility and the grave.

I read the list through, that day that started out with looking for clues about Bear, and one thing struck me right between the eyes: how few of the items on the list I'd actually done. Not by thirty, and not by fifty either. It wasn't a complete whitewash. I'd achieved the last one, which was 'have a baby'. In fact, I'd achieved it considerably earlier than young Kay might have envisaged, or wanted. And 'visit Bear in Australia' was also a tick, if I ignored the 'every other year' at the end of the sentence.

But so many things remained undone.

Sitting in the grey chair, I looked at the new list in my diary that Rose had helped me write: 'Things to do by the time I am sixty.' Climb Snowdon, tick. Visit Bear in Australia, nearly a tick. It was going well. Plus visit Venice and Lisbon, and try living alone for a while, something I'd never yet done. I'd gone from living with my parents to busy shared houses at university, then straight into my first home with Richard, joined a few months later by Baby Edward.

When I went back downstairs, Stella was in the kitchen chopping vegetables. Pans bubbled enticingly on the stove. I loved it when she cooked.

'Smells delicious,' I said.

'It's only veggie curry.'

'How lovely.' I wanted to hug her, but didn't yet dare. 'Stella, I was annoying about Theo. I'm really sorry.'

'That's OK.' She looked at me wearily. 'Mum, it still doesn't make sense. Do you not miss anything about home?'

My heart ached at how sad she looked. *Be kind.* 'Of course, I miss lots of things!' I sat at the table. 'I miss my kitchen, and my duvet, and having all my belongings around me. I stupidly left my favourite necklace behind, and my black polo-neck jumper, and my camera. I miss my yoga class, and I'd paid for it until July. I miss my friends, and the honeysuckle in the back garden, because this is the time of year it smells the best. I miss walking down our street to the corner shop, and I even miss Quiller Queen.'

There was a loaded silence, and I quickly went on, 'And of course, there's plenty I miss about Dad. I miss our Saturday evenings, glasses of wine in our hands, catching up on our weeks. I miss talking to him about what you and Edward are up to. I miss...' Wow, this was quite difficult. What else did I miss about him?

Stella tipped the vegetables into a pan. 'Did you feel this way when Edward and I were children?'

'What do you mean?'

The veggies sizzled wildly, and she tossed them about expertly with a wooden spoon. With her back to me, she said, 'Were you wanting to leave the whole time?'

'Oh, sweetheart, of course not!' I couldn't stand not holding her. I went over and put my arms round her shoulders, and she leaned back against me. 'Of course not,' I said again. 'I've had loads of happy years – happy times – with you. Having you two children was the greatest thing that ever happened to me. It's only been lately...' Careful, Kay, no more lies, '... it's only been a relatively short while, really, that I've been unhappy.'

Now, at last, Stella turned round, and took my hand in hers. It was so warm and soft that tears sprang into my eyes. It was simultaneously Stella's hand now, and little Stella's hand then, holding mine trustingly as we crossed a road.

'Why didn't you say anything before?' she said.

'I didn't really admit it, even to myself. I just felt as if, well, as if I was living half a life. Not because of you and Edward, not ever, but because your father and I were stuck in a rut. A dull rut.'

'Ruts are usually dull, Mum,' Stella said, letting go of my hand so she could turn the heat down under the vegetables. 'You don't hear people talking about exciting ruts.'

I laughed. 'You always cheer me up, Sparkle. I'm sorry. I never want to burden you with my unhappiness, but I have burdened you anyway, by leaving. Perhaps I shouldn't have left, after all.'

'No, Mum.' Stella looked serious. I loved her sombre grown-up expression, overlaid, like the warmth of her hand, with the child she once was, playing office dress-up in one of my old suit jackets, the sleeves several inches longer than her arms. 'If you really were unhappy, it was right to leave. Women should be able to leave, and I know they couldn't always in the past, like in Gran's generation.'

'Thank you, sweetie. I don't deserve you to be so understanding, but I'm really grateful for it.'

We ate her food together, and I told her about my plan for Australia. She offered, as I'd hoped, to drive me to Heathrow the next day, on her way back to Essex. I hoped the long journey would allow us to talk more with honesty and understanding.

Later, I went up to start packing. It was not quite light, but also not yet dark. I sat in the chair under the slanted window and gazed up into the teal sky. I thought of Bear, and Richard, and David. A flock of birds swirled into view, and I let my worries drift up into the sky with them.

Letter written on 27 June 2017

Dearest Bear,

Thanks for your lovely card. I still can't stop bloody crying. I don't think I did right by Mum at the end, though she honestly had no idea what was going on. I hated that she died in hospital. Not that she loved her flat, but at least she had all her things there. But I was there by her side when she went. I think she squeezed my hand one last time, though it was very faint, and then a moment later, the nurse said, 'She's gone, my love.'

There was so much to do for the funeral. It's lousy being an only child. At least when I go, E & S can argue about who does what. Weirdest of all was getting the death certificate, very formal and alienating. I didn't ask Richard to come with me, one of the shops is in between managers so he had to cover. Rose came, she was an absolute brick, and afterwards we went to a pub and had three gins each.

Not the chirpiest of letters, sorry, love.

Till next time.

Miss you.

Always, Kay

Chapter 9

Stella

The bags were in the boot, the electric sockets were switched off, the fridge was empty, but Mum was still working through her closing-up-the-cottage routine. I tapped my nails against the steering wheel. Mum appeared fleetingly at the door, and I sat up, but then she vanished again, and I sank back into my seat. It still felt odd to be able to see her whenever I wanted, after those weird few days of her absence.

I opened the glove compartment, hoping to find a tin of travel sweets. Dad always bought them when I was little. *Yes!* There was a tin. I pulled it out, and with it came a crumpled white envelope: Dad's letter that I'd forgotten to hand over yesterday. I put it on the passenger seat, intrigued as to what it said, and what Mum's reaction would be. I opened the sweet tin, and bitterly closed it again – it contained only coins and random screws.

The front door slammed, and Mum finally came out. She put the key in the safe box on the wall, came over to the car, then hesitated.

'I can't remember if I closed the window in the bathroom,' she said.

'I did it,' I said.

'Did you close it properly? It's not simply pushing the bottom window down, you have to flick the metal catch across.'

'I did that.'

'I'll quickly check. Rain might get in. Or a burglar.'

'You sound insane, Mum. The window's fine. Come on, let's go.'

She eased herself into the car, moving the letter so she could sit.

'That's for you,' I said. 'It's from Dad.'

'What?'

'He asked me to give it to you.'

I backed the car out of the driveway and onto the road. Mum turned the envelope over in her hands. 'Do you know what it says?'

'No, of course not. Why don't you open it?'

'I'll give it a minute.' Mum took a deep breath. 'No need to drive fast, sweetheart. My flight's not till tomorrow.'

I slowed down slightly. 'I find it very frustrating in movies,' I said, 'when they get a letter or present or something and take ages to open it.'

'I'm building up to it,' Mum said.

'He doesn't have a clue what's going on, you know. He doesn't understand why you left.'

I felt Mum's eyes on me as I slowed down at a roundabout. I knew she was wondering why I was being less accommodating than yesterday. What was it Gran had called her? *Evasive*, that was it. I'd been awake half the night thinking about our conversation. What she'd said about being unhappy made sense of her behaviour; at least, it made sense last night. But this morning there were still a lot of unanswered questions.

She breathed out heavily. 'I wish I could explain myself better.'

'Look, Mum, it's not that I think you should have stayed if you were unhappy.'

'What is it then?'

'Well, you're not being fair on Dad. Just leaving and not replying to any of his emails or voicemails, it's a big silence and he's reading all sorts of things into it.'

'I'm sure you're right.'

Her phone pinged, and she laughed. 'Talking of which...'

'Is it Dad?'

'No, it's Alice. Gran. She's another one I haven't replied to.' She read the message. 'She wants us to meet for "a little chat". Oh, marvellous.'

'That might be a good idea.'

'It's a terrible idea.'

'But, Mum, we're all having difficulty understanding why you've done this thing, this massive thing. I suppose I get it a bit more now, but I don't think Dad has any idea you were unhappy. He'd have you back like a shot.'

'Are you sure about that?' Mum picked up the envelope and opened it. 'Let's see.' She pulled out a piece of blue writing paper and unfolded it carefully. 'Basildon Bond paper.' She took a breath. 'OK. Here we go.'

She read it through in silence, while I restrained myself, with difficulty, from demanding to know what was in it. I focused my attention on the road ahead, the craggy mountains looming on one side, the shiny black piles of slate from the quarries glinting in the sunlight on the other. I focused on the tears floating round in my eyes, wanting to be released, and on the hard lump in my chest. I wasn't sure why I was so upset. Yesterday I thought I'd got some answers, but today the things Mum had said felt flimsy. The ground seemed to have shifted under my feet yet again, and nothing felt straightforward. Everything was confused, unclear. All I could think about was poor Dad, and also poor me, because now he was my responsibility.

But also, of course, poor Mum, if she really had been unhappy. Had she though? Or was that just a clever way of shutting down the conversation? No son or daughter could say to their parent, 'You should go back,' if the parent said, 'But it was making me unhappy.' Being unhappy was a deal-breaker. But nothing Mum had said sounded all that bad. Dad was kind, wasn't he? And generous. What was there to be unhappy about?

Mum let out a teary laugh, and put down the letter. I glanced at her, and saw that she was crying.

'It's very sweet.' Mum blew her nose, and started reading. '"Dear Kay, I hope you are well. I've been doing a lot of thinking since you left, and realise I haven't always been as attentive as I could or should have. If you ever decide you'd like to try again, I will be here. I'll do better this time. We could go to counselling, perhaps."' Mum broke off here to say, 'As if he ever would!' before she resumed reading. '"I remember you said you were going to Australia. I hope you find Bear well and happy. And maybe more travels after that – Venice, Russia, I can't recall where else you said. Hope you see some interesting sights, and maybe some interesting new stationery too." It wouldn't be a message from your father without the mention of stationery, would it?'

'It's his life's work,' I said, feeling that Mum no longer had a right to diss Dad about the shop.

'It is, indeed. "Let me know if you need more money. I have put some extra into our account if you wish to access it. With much love," and he's underlined "love" three times, "Your husband, Richard."'

'That's really nice,' I said.

'It's very forgiving, isn't it?' Mum said. 'Though it's a shame it took me leaving for him to realise that he wasn't very attentive.'

'Sometimes you have to spell things out, Mum.'

'Sparkle, where would I have started? I was just unhappy, most of the time.'

She still couldn't put her finger on it, I noticed. 'He's being very decent about money, too.'

'Yes, he is. I know. I'm lucky. He could be making it all extremely difficult.' She blew out air, as if she was making a decision, then said, 'I'll text your grandmother and see if she wants to meet tonight, before I go to Australia.'

'OK, that's good. I know you two haven't always got on, but…'

'I'm sure things will be hunky dory between us now, though.'

'Not funny, Mum.'

'Sorry.' She sent Gran a reply, and put her phone away.

'Will you write back to Dad?'

'Yes, I'll send him a proper letter from Sydney.'

'Well, so long as you don't think you can come back and start everything up again, OK?' This sounded harsher than I meant. Or maybe it didn't.

'Stella! That's a bit… I won't, of course.'

'Is that right what Dad said in the letter, that you're planning to travel after Australia?'

'Maybe. Come with me, Sparkle! It'll be amazing.'

'No thanks, Mum. I already had my gap year.'

'So did I, but I feel the need for another one.'

Something snapped in my brain, and I screeched to a halt by the side of the road.

'That's what this is!' I slammed my hand on the steering wheel.

'Are you sure we can stop here, Stella? The road's rather narrow.'

'For God's sake, Mum, I've just realised. This *is* your gap year, your grown-up gap year! You think you can go travelling and sleep with unsuitable people—'

'Stella!'

'And have lots of new experiences and take drugs and lose your luggage in Cairo. You're like a great big old student. For God's sake!'

Mum looked at me calmly. 'I've never fancied Cairo. Noisy. So, tell me, sweetheart, what's this about?'

I shook my head, trying to hold back more bloody tears. 'I expect you'll have a very fun year, turn everyone's lives upside down, then think you can come home afterwards.'

'With a backpack full of dirty laundry and a mild urinary infection?' I could hear the smile in Mum's voice, as if she wasn't being awful enough.

'I don't know why you think it's funny, it's really not.' I eased the car back onto the road and blinked furiously. It was lucky there were only a few other cars, as I couldn't see super-well right now.

We drove in silence for a few miles, then Mum said, 'Do you remember Leon?'

'Leon? My old boyfriend? What the f-, what the hell's he got to do with this?' Oh God! For one heart-stopping moment, I thought… oh God! If Mum was going to tell me that she'd left Dad for Leon, that spotty idiot who was young enough to be her son, I would just drive us straight into that tree, and save us ever having to have the rest of this conversation.

'Ah, you were very intense, texting each other non-stop, first love.'

'Mum! For God's sake!' This journey was clearly going to use up my monthly quota of 'for God's sake's'. 'Are you having an affair with Leon?'

'Leon?!' Mum started laughing, quietly at first, then hysterically. 'Leon!' she kept saying. 'Leon!'

'OK, calm down.' I waited till she'd got a grip. 'It's no stupider than anything else. I can't see any other reason why you'd mention Leon right now, it's so utterly random.'

'First Anthony, now Leon. I really don't seem to have a type when it comes to imaginary lovers, do I?'

She still seemed very amused, which made me so irritated I wanted to scream. 'Go on then, what about Leon?'

Mum stretched out her legs. 'Well, all I was going to say is that it was super-intense, remember, and then it was all over after about six months. You got bored of the poor old chap, remember?'

'I was only sixteen, it was kind of normal.'

'Well, my question, Stella, is: do you think two people – a couple – should have to stay together if one of them doesn't want to anymore?'

'No, of course not, but—'

'Because poor Leon was shattered when you chucked him, wasn't he?'

'I wouldn't say shattered. He was a bit upset.'

'He mooned around outside our house for weeks.'

'Then he started going out with Iola Gillespie,' I said, trying to steer the conversation back to Sanity Land, 'and forgot all about me.'

'Quite,' Mum said. 'The point is, if there's a couple, and one person wants to stay together but the other doesn't, we should give the final say to the person who wants out, shouldn't we? Morally, I mean? And indeed, practically?'

'Yes, but—'

'Otherwise you'd still have to be with Leon, right? And yet it was quite correct of you to want to let him go. He was a lousy match for you.'

'For God's sake, Mum! Are you seriously comparing my six-month meeting-up-twice-a-week teenage relationship with your twenty-nine-year marriage?'

'I'm simply pointing out a general principle that should surely apply to everyone. I shouldn't have to stay with your dad any longer, just because he doesn't want me to go.'

'*Any longer?*'

The silence that followed lasted until we reached the motorway.

Eventually, Mum said, 'I'm sorry, Sparkle.'

'Then don't do it, Mum. You'll upset everyone, go off for a while, then it'll be, "Oh I've had my fun, reckon I'll come home." Well guess what,' and my voice shook slightly as I said this, 'we might not be there waiting for you.'

'I wish I could show you how firmly I have closed the door behind me,' Mum said. She was being more patient than I'd have expected, presumably because she knew she was in the wrong. 'I have pushed down the sash, forced the rusty fastener into place to lock it, and turned a key for good measure, and before you say anything, I know I'm talking about a window not a door. But the principle applies.'

'Well for all your talk of principles,' and I took a breath, 'I think you're being fucking selfish.'

'Stella!' Mum shouted. Finally, it seemed, I'd found a way to make her angry.

But all at once, I was angrier. 'You *are* being selfish! It's so unfair to Dad. He's a kind man. By your own account, he was amazing when you got pregnant, even though you'd previously dumped him, and he's been amazing for most of the last thirty, sorry *twenty-nine* years, and now you've dumped him again. But instead of thinking about him, you've been all moony about some other bloke you barely knew for five minutes! What was so great about whatshisname, David, anyway? He wouldn't even consider taking on another man's child.'

'It wasn't like that, he—'

'What did you think would happen when you left? That Dad would say, "Oh, by the way, Stella, your mum's dumped me but no need to worry, I'm fine."'

'No, of course not, I—'

'Who did you think would be landed with the responsibility of Dad having a nervous breakdown? Who did you think would be expected to drop everything and rush to help?'

'Hasn't Edward—'

'He hasn't been near us, didn't you know?'

'But his messages made it sound like—'

'He hasn't shown his face. It's just been me. Me and Gran, who shouldn't have to look after her son at her age. You dumped him on us and went off without a thought.'

'Stella! That's enough! I'm sorry I've made you so angry, made everyone so upset. I don't love your dad anymore, and I was unhappy. If that means I'm selfish to leave, then so be it. Maybe I should have been a bit more selfish these last twenty-nine years, and I wouldn't feel the need now. But let me ask you this: was I selfish when I slept on your floor every night for a month when you had nightmares?'

'What, when I was, like, eight?'

'Was it *selfish* letting you go on that holiday with your friends when you were eighteen, without a murmur, even though you'd promised to go away with me?'

'Wow, you've been saving that up.'

'Welcoming you back when you couldn't find work after university, helping with your job applications, supporting you financially even now so you can pay your rent.'

'Stop shouting, Mum.'

'I never stopped helping you, boosting you up, encouraging you, urging you to have a more interesting life than I've had. Selfish! Are you joking?'

'No one made you live an uninteresting life,' I said, trying to keep my voice quiet. 'It was your choice.'

'God damn it, no it wasn't!' Mum yelled. 'I got pregnant by accident, and had to marry your father, and because of that, I lost *the love of my life*.'

Oh. My. God.

I prayed I hadn't run anyone over because I hadn't been focusing on my driving at all. Neither of us spoke for a long time. I tried to silently get my breathing back to normal. Finally, I forced myself to glance over at Mum. Her face was turned away, and she was staring out of the side window.

More miles went by, then very quietly, she said, 'I'm sorry.'

'You should be.'

'I shouldn't have said that. I feel awful.'

'So listen, Mum,' I said, as quietly as her, 'when you come home, even if Dad takes you back, I won't.'

'Oh, Sparkle!' Mum twisted in her seat. 'I know you're furious with me, and that's OK, but—'

'Do you mind,' I said, gritting my teeth, which for some reason helped soothe the pain in my chest, 'if we don't talk anymore?'

Mum sat back in her seat. 'Why don't you drop me at a station somewhere? I'll make my own way.'

'We're on a fucking motorway. I'll take you to Heathrow, like I said. Then that's me done.'

We drove on in a heavy mute fug. It should have felt good to have let it out, said how I felt. But all I wanted was to be on my own and cry. We didn't speak again until I came off the junction for Heathrow, and Mum directed me to her hotel. I pulled up outside it and left the engine running. I could feel Mum looking at me but I stared straight ahead at the car park, the people coming and going with wheelie suitcases and normal lives. I desperately wanted her to go.

'Thanks for the lift. I wish with all my heart that I hadn't upset you.' She leaned across the seat and kissed me on the cheek. 'Tell your father thanks for the letter.'

I wished I could say something nice, something to make it better, but I felt too far gone. Instead, I said, 'Hope Bear's OK.' I should have said this before; Mum must be expecting the worst, and I knew how important her friendship with Bear was.

'Thank you.' She put her hand on the door handle, then said, 'I know people sometimes push you around. Don't take any crap from anyone, Stella. *Anyone*.'

I let out a bark of laughter. 'Even you?'

'Especially me.' She smiled. 'I love you so much.'

I couldn't reply. I knew I'd cry if I said that I loved her and I didn't want to cry till she'd gone. She looked at me intensely for a moment, then said, 'Bye,' and quickly got out of the car. I watched her walk fast into the hotel – she didn't look back – then I turned the car round and headed for my house. The lump in my throat would not shift.

Chapter 10

Kay

There was no mistaking my mother-in-law – she stood out wherever she was. In this dull corporate hotel lounge, there were a few groups of businessmen, and some boozed-up women about my age who looked to be heading off for a riotous girls' weekend. And there, wearing the sort of anthropologically intrepid expression patented by the Queen during 1960s' tours of exotic countries, was Alice Bright.

Sitting upright in an armchair by the window, she ticked all the classic Alice Bright boxes. Navy skirt-suit in the Chanel style, tick. Perfectly neat ash-blonde hair, frostily unmoving, tick (and don't ever suggest for one moment that it might be covering up some grey, by the way). Immaculate understated make-up, tick. Navy court shoes to match the suit, with sensible-but-chic low blocky heel. Light-tan tights. Confident facial expression, giving clear expectation of winning whatever battle was coming her way. Tick, tick and tick.

'Kay!' Alice said, getting up with unbelievable agility for someone of seventy-eight. 'Isn't this place simply awful? Such an inglorious setting for your grand adventure! Why not go to a decent hotel? The Connaught is always very good.'

I kissed her powdery cheek. 'It's somewhere to lay my head tonight, Alice, that's all, before I fly to Australia.'

'Ah yes, the antipodes. Home of convicts and scoundrels since time immemorial.'

I grinned. 'Alice, anyone listening would think that rather racist.'

'I am most certainly not a racist, Kay. I voted Remain, as you know. Our little island is thoroughly enriched by people of all backgrounds.' She took both my hands in hers, and looked me up and down. 'Oh, you look just dreadful. Being bold is *such* a strain.'

I could see my reflection behind her in one of those huge mirrors all these places have, to make the room seem more spacious, I suppose. My straight brown hair, which only ever looked decent an hour after being washed, was pulled into a lank ponytail, and I was wearing comfortable travelling clothes, and no make-up. Next to Jackie Kennedy here, I was a bag lady.

'I might not look my best, Alice, but I assure you, inside I'm doing fine.' At least, I was until that horrific fight with Stella. I pushed it out of my mind; I could think about it another time. It was too recent, too raw to make sense of.

'Oh, my lovely girl.' Alice let go of me in order to place her hands on her chest in a gesture of pity.

A waiter came over and asked if we would like drinks. 'That's so kind,' Alice said in a noblesse oblige murmur, as if he was offering them for free. We ordered dry white wine, and sat down, two old adversaries facing each other. Over the years we had found a way to co-exist, but it had taken a very long time to get over our shaky start. I think she still believed, on one level, the same thing she had thirty years ago, the day Richard took me to his home and told her that we were getting married: that I had got pregnant deliberately to trap him. I'd never told her the truth, though Lord knows I longed to sometimes. Anyway, we'd eventually managed to develop a more cordial entente, and to be fair to Alice, she had always been an excellent grandmother, especially to Stella.

The irony was that for the first five or ten years of my marriage, Alice would have been delighted to hear I'd left Richard. A chance for her precious boy to marry the right sort of girl at last – what luck! But now I could see that, under her protective coating of powder and class, she was genuinely worried.

'So, my dear, thank you for meeting me. I know we haven't always seen eye to eye, but I'm simply here to, well, make sure that you're absolutely dead-set on this *scheme* of yours.'

'Do you mean my scheme to go to Australia? Or my scheme to leave Richard?'

'Obviously the latter, Kay.'

'I don't know if I'd classify it as a scheme, but OK. Yes, I am *absolutely dead-set* on it.'

'Would you mind, as a special favour to me, explaining why, exactly? Because I have to confess, I'm quite baffled. It has the whiff of mild insanity about it. Oh, thank you.' This last comment was directed at the waiter, who delivered our drinks with no panache whatsoever, a fact not lost on Alice, who muttered something about how they did things in the Connaught.

I thought about those lists that went around periodically on social media, outlining the outré behaviours that got women locked up in mental institutions in the 1800s, such as reading novels. It looked like my own equivalent was going to be 'leaving husband after long uneventful marriage while failing to express regret'.

Alice sipped her drink and made a face. 'Is this Asda's own grape, do you think?' she said, and put down her glass. 'Well, do go on.'

I launched into my now-familiar summary. 'Neither Richard nor I have been having an affair, hitting each other, or any of the other traditional marriage-ending things. I've not lost my mind, and if it's a midlife crisis, though it's a little late for that, then it still feels like the absolutely right thing to do. Oh, and it's not the menopause, either – I seem to be in peri-menopause, in case that matters.'

'My dear girl! Defensive much?'

I loved how Alice could make even slang sound like the Queen's English. She carried on. 'I suppose everyone's been trying to get answers out of you. Very well. I'll not try. I'm simply here to ask if you'll consider coming back after your jaunt to the southern hem, so you and Richard can talk properly, and he can attempt to understand what's going on. Perhaps get one of those mediator people in? They're quite the thing now, aren't they? Doesn't Richard deserve that, at the very least?'

She was very persuasive, her expression brimming with sympathy, but I'd had three decades of learning how to avoid getting suckered in. The trick was to not look her in the eye.

'I've already said everything I want to say to Richard,' I said.

'Well, what *did* you say? He professes himself utterly bewildered. Which is why we must suppose that he produced little Anthony, like a rabbit out of a hat as it were, as the likely culprit.'

I managed not to laugh at the thought of Anthony coming out of a hat, Richard holding him by the ears. 'I'm sure he knows now that Anthony had absolutely nothing to do with it.'

'Indeed, though he was initially rather fixated on the idea. I did suggest he was barking up quite the wrong tree with ghastly Anthony. I can call him that now I know he's not your paramour, though heavens, he will soon be my, what's the word, *colleague*. Sends shivers. Anyway, Richard, I said, when Kay's had steak at home, why would she go out for a cheap hamburger?'

I did laugh then, I couldn't help it, it had been building up.

'It's wonderful you can find humour in the situation,' Alice said. 'This is because of your mother dying, I suppose.'

'Me laughing?'

'You shaking everything up in this somewhat destructive fashion.'

'Why should it have anything to do with my mum?'

'My dear, I remember so well when my father died. It was more than twenty years ago now. Twenty-two. Stella was a babe-in-arms. You remember him, of course?'

I nodded, intrigued. Alice rarely talked about her parents.

'My mother, as you know, passed on when I was a child. Well, when my father died, and I was properly an orphan, I rather lost my head for a while. It's terribly destabilising to be all at once the older generation, don't you think?'

'I'm only fifty-one.'

'Yes, but now there's no one standing between you and the grave.'

'Great!'

'It sets one off-kilter. I had a funny little turn myself when Daddy passed.'

'What did you do?' I tried to imagine what Alice's midlife rebellion would have looked like.

'Between us girls…' Alice looked round the room and whispered, 'I took a lover.'

'You didn't!'

This wasn't totally shocking, as Alice's husband, Richard's father, had died long before, when Richard was a teenager, so she would have been very single at the time. I tried to remember what Alice was like twenty-two years ago, when she was in her mid-fifties. She was always very glamorous, of course, groomed, every hair in place.

'A younger man,' she said, her voice even lower. 'Married.'

'Goodness!'

Alice smiled dreamily, perhaps remembering long, lazy afternoons of love. Then, as if coming out of a trance, her expression snapped into its more habitual patrician mask. 'I came to my senses very quickly,' she said, and sipped more wine, followed by another wince. 'I'm only telling you this to explain that I do understand. I know how it feels to realise all at once that life is finite, that there is not unlimited time to do everything we would like to do, and that we had better get on with it.'

'That's it, Alice!' I could have hugged her, though she didn't do hugging. It was like she'd gone into my head and explained me to myself. 'That's exactly it! There isn't an endless supply of time!'

If I'd thought that sharing this revelation would bring her on side, I was sadly mistaken.

'Yes, my dear,' she said, tapping my knee with a bony finger. 'That's why we must use our precious time carefully. We must use it to look after our loved ones, and nurture our relationships, and serve our communities. Not squander it on hare-brained schemes to travel aimlessly, or smash up solid foundations. Use your time wisely – not to hurt the people who love you, but to be with them! Love them! Cherish them!'

I glanced at my watch. All at once, I'd had enough. 'Is this one of those things they do with drug addicts, an intervention?'

'Yes,' Alice said, sitting up even straighter. 'I do want to intervene. You've not thought any of this through. You're not in an unhappy marriage!'

'You're right, Alice,' I said, and stood up. 'I'm not, anymore.'

She stood too. 'Don't you think you can—'

'I don't, Alice. Goodbye. Thanks for everything.' I turned and walked through the bar, feeling her eyes boring into my back. I asked the receptionist to put the drinks on my bill, went up to my room, got into bed, and slept like a baby.

Chapter 11

Stella

It took a long time to get out of the environs of Heathrow, and by the time I reached Romford it was almost seven. I was still feeling flat as a crêpe about the horrible things Mum and I had said, and I was keen to think about something else for a bit. I let myself in to the house. I hadn't told Theo I was coming back today; my plan was to get unpacked, then go to his flat and surprise him. I was halfway up the stairs when I heard Gabby's unmistakable laugh coming from the living room. I don't know how, but I knew something sexual was going on. The fear I'd been pushing to the back of my mind all week, about Gabby and Theo, washed coldly over me. I crept back down, and went over to the door, which wasn't quite closed. I could hear Gabby's voice murmuring, then a man, so quiet I couldn't tell who it was. Then there was a different noise: the sound of two people in a clinch.

Holding my breath, I pushed the door a little way, just enough to slip through it, and stepped noiselessly into the room. It was dark in there, the curtains closed, and after the brightness of the hall it took me a moment to adjust. I could make out shapes on the sofa and it was clear they hadn't heard me come in. As I accommodated to the gloom, I could see that Gabby was sitting astride a man, kissing him.

My eyes blurred over and, as so often lately, I forced the tears away. At no time in my life had I more needed to be able to see. The man's face was obscured by the back of Gabby's head. Could it be Theo? I looked at the man's long bare legs along the sofa and realised with a burst of joy that they were unfamiliar. Thank God! I silently let out my breath; only now did I realise how long I'd been holding it for.

I turned, intending to slip out, go to Theo's as planned, and give him the kiss of his life. Then, to my astonishment, the door was pushed wide open, almost hitting me, letting in a shaft of light from the hall, and a man walked in, straight past me, not seeing me. He was completely naked, and because it was so unexpected, it took me a second or two to process that this *was* Theo.

My breath caught in my throat and I thought I might pass out.

Theo walked over to the sofa and said, 'You've started without me!'

I couldn't have moved away if my life depended on it. I was paralysed with horror. With the light from the hall I could now see that the couple were Gabby and Piet.

'We'll catch you up,' Gabby said, and she pulled him down to the sofa and started kissing him on the mouth, while Piet – oh Jesus – was doing something to Theo with his hand and even worse – actually, was it worse? – Theo was doing it back to Piet and also stroking Gabby's breasts.

I wasn't sure if I was really seeing this or if I was asleep and having the worst nightmare of my life. Somehow I got out into the hall and stood, blinking in the bright light. What a day, what a fucking appalling day. I could only think of getting the hell out of there, sliding into the safety of the car, going back to Dad's, where things were weird, sure, but not this weird. Then a voice came into my head, and it wasn't Bettina's, for once, but Mum's: 'Don't take any crap from anyone, Stella. *Anyone.*'

I looked longingly at the front door, then turned resolutely away
and went into the kitchen. Once again, I'd have to amend my mental
list of the top ten things I wished I'd never seen. I filled the kettle,
turned on the gas and took down four mugs, not caring if I made a
noise. I let the tears fall now without trying to stop them. Poor tears,
they were working overtime lately.

I realised I didn't blame Gabby, or Piet. If Theo wanted to see other
people, or try a threesome, he should have told me. I might not have
wanted to join him – let's face it, I'd definitely not have wanted to – but
we could have discussed it, like adults.

I thought back to the three little dots that had never materialised
into a message last week. Perhaps he'd wanted to tell me the truth, but
had lost his nerve. Perhaps we'd got out of the habit of talking. In the
months after the end of university, when we didn't see much of each
other, only the occasional weekend, he was always so busy with his
new job, his heavy workload. And then he'd introduced me to his old
friend Gabby, who needed a partner in her rapidly expanding catering
business. So I'd moved here, delighted to be near him, and we'd picked
up where we left off. Or so I'd thought. Perhaps what I thought was
the truth about me and Theo was actually just the story I'd told myself
about our relationship. Like Mum and Dad's two completely different
stories of their relationship. I realised I didn't know if my version of
our story matched Theo's version.

Why had I stopped crying? I thought for a moment. Bettina had
often encouraged me to name my feelings. *If you can name the feeling,
Stella, you can work through the feeling*. Well, I was sad. Theo and I had
been together a long time. We'd even talked about getting engaged.
But the thumping in my chest didn't feel like sadness.

I looked in the mirror over the sink. I'd never considered myself particularly pretty – Edward was the looker in our family– but I looked rather good myself right now. My eyes were sparkling from the tears, and my cheeks were flushed. I pulled my straight brown hair, inherited from Mum, off my face and twisted it into a bun. Perfect tendrils fell magically into place by my ears. I looked hot.

The kettle started to boil but I didn't take it off the gas. The shriek got louder and louder, and I pictured the three of them in the room next door, whispering in panic. 'Shit, someone's put the kettle on!' 'A burglar?' 'Go and see.' I guessed that Piet would be the one chosen to check, and sure enough, moments later he came into the room, wearing only a pair of startling orange underpants, blinking against the light and the kettle's screaming crescendo.

'Hello, Piet,' I said. I picked up the kettle at last, and started pouring water into the cups.

'Stella!' he said, so loudly that anyone who happened to be listening would be warned, and able to take evasive action. 'When did you arrive? I am very pleased to see you.'

'I should think you're actually rather surprised to see me,' I said. 'Tea?'

'Uh, yes please.' His eyes darted to the door. 'So, uh, have you been here long?'

'I have been here long enough,' I said, looking at the cups, rather than at him, 'to see enough.'

There was a silence. It was a new thing, seeing Piet at a loss. It made me want to laugh.

Name your feeling, Stella. Are you angry?

You know what, Bettina, I think I am *angry.*

'Let's sit down.' I handed Piet a cup.

'I ought to, uh, I ought to put on something…' Piet said, edging towards the door.

'Sit DOWN, Piet,' I said. And he did, abruptly.

'I am sorry, Stella,' Piet said. 'Do you wish to talk about it?'

'Let's do that,' I said, 'when the others arrive.' I put all the cups on the table, and sat down myself.

Name your feeling now, Stella.

I feel powerful, Bettina.

When did you last feel like this, Stella?

I can't remember ever feeling like this, Bettina.

I smiled broadly at Piet, and he smiled back, friendly but puzzled.

I made a bet with myself that the next one in would be Gabby, and so it proved. She was dressed, her hair tidy. 'Stella! How lovely! How's your dad?' She ran to my side and kissed my cheek, Judas-style.

'I made you tea,' I said.

'Oh, thank you! Yes, I heard the kettle so I came downstairs.'

I took my time. 'You came downstairs… from the living room?'

Gabby sat opposite Piet, and I saw him shake his head slightly at her. Gabby frowned in confusion at him. This was actively enjoyable.

'Piet is trying to tell you that I know, Gabby,' I said.

'Know… what?' Gabby said. Her acting was appalling, but she was saved by the front door opening and closing with a bang.

'Ah,' I said, 'that will be Theo pretending to come in, even though he doesn't have his own key. "Hi honey, I'm home!"'

'Oh God,' Gabby said, staring at the table. 'Do we have to do this?'

'Yes,' said Piet. 'It is correct for Stella to do this. We deserve it.'

'Thank you, Piet.'

'You are most welcome, Stella.'

Theo came in, wearing his jacket, his bag over his shoulder. 'Hi guys! Oh wow, Stella, how ace! I thought you might be coming back today, and I dropped in on the off chance.'

I looked at him, appraising him with an objective eye. There were always little things one didn't like about one's boyfriends. You tended to overlook them, prioritise other things as more important. Leon, for instance, had patches of awful acne on each cheek, and treated any mild suggestion that he speak to a pharmacist as an infringement of his human rights. Now, with Theo standing in front of me, fake-beaming, I realised that with his thin face and shifty eyes, he looked exactly like a weasel.

Theo seemed self-conscious that I was looking at him without saying anything. 'Er, so, how are things with your parents?' he said, slipping off his jacket. 'I'm sorry I couldn't make it down, wow, we've been so busy here.'

'So I see,' I said, watching Gabby and Piet trying and failing to catch Theo's eye. 'I don't think what I've been doing has been as interesting as what the three of you have been getting up to.'

'Er, well, er,' he said, looking slightly less relaxed.

'Though you know what they say,' I continued, sipping my tea, '"Three's a crowd".'

'Yes…' he said, glancing at the others, but still seemingly not picking up that all was not well. An idiot, then, as well as a weasel.

'Must be pretty crowded,' I said, 'on that sofa.'

Theo's eyes widened like a cartoon character's. 'What do you mean?'

'Give it up, fuckwit,' Gabby said. 'She knows.'

'Shit, shit, shit,' Theo said. 'Stell, it wasn't my idea—'

'You bastard,' Gabby said.

'It was just a stupid drunken thing, look can we talk about this on our own?'

I laughed. 'You're suddenly shy of large groups, Theo?'

'Am I still needed here?' Gabby stood up. 'Because if not, I'm off upstairs. I really don't want to watch this hideous post-mortem.'

'No, that's fine,' I said. 'Please feel free to leave.'

Gabby rolled her eyes. '*Fuck* me.'

'No thanks,' I said. 'I'm happy being the only person who doesn't get to do that.'

Gabby slammed the door behind her. I felt great. I expected that at some point soon, I would feel less great, when I thought about how comprehensively my life had been turned upside down, but right now, I felt that I could take on the world.

Awesome, Bettina. I feel awesome.

'Drink your tea,' I told Theo, who was gaping at me.

'What?' He looked in confusion at the cup in front of him, picked it up and took a big gulp, then spat it out all over the table. 'What the fuck?' He jumped up, and ran to the sink, poured a glass of water and drank it theatrically in one go. 'Have you…? Have you…?' He staggered back to the table and sat down heavily. 'Piet, I've been poisoned.'

Piet and I started laughing.

'It's not poison, you idiot,' I said. 'I just put in some spices, to give it a bit of a kick. Cumin, coriander, paprika.'

Piet picked up his cup and sniffed it. 'Mine seems fine,' he said.

'I didn't do it to yours, Piet.'

'That is very generous of you, Stella.'

'Well, until you screwed my boyfriend, you were always very kind to me, Piet.'

'If we are to be honest, Stella,' Piet said, 'I have not actually screwed your boyfriend. We did not get to that juncture before we heard the kettle boil.'

'You expect me to believe that was the first time?'

Piet glanced at Theo. 'I will let Theo explain,' he said, 'but yes, on my honour, that was the first time all three of us had got together to explore sexually in that way. I do not think I will be trying a threesome for a while after this. I will give you some privacy.' He stood up. 'Oh, Stella, I meant to tell you, I saw an interesting poster in the library today.'

'Is this really the time?' Theo said through gritted teeth.

'It is on my mind, so I would like to tell her now. It was about a support group, Stella, for adult children of divorce, such as you and me. It's on Wednesday evening. I am planning to attend and will accompany you, if you wish it.'

'Sounds interesting, Piet, thank you.'

'If you are still here, of course. I will be, though I fear in the long term it may be uncomfortable for me and Gabby to continue living under the same roof. She is a woman of large moods.'

He went out, and Theo and I looked at each other.

'And then there were two,' I said.

'Babe, I'm sorry.'

'Don't "babe" me. Sorry you cheated, sorry you lied, or sorry I caught you?'

'All of it.'

'I suppose Piet's cryptic comment meant that *you* have been sleeping with Gabby.'

Theo shook his head, no, but said, 'Yes.'

'She really is something…' I started to say, then realised that Gabby had made no promises to me. 'But unlike some people sitting here, she never pretended to be a good friend, or told me she would never hurt me.'

'She's sleeping with Piet, too,' Theo said.

'I guessed.'

He stared at the table. 'I'm sorry,' he said again. 'I promise I won't sleep with her, or anyone else, again, if you'll give me another chance.'

'It's a damn shame,' I said. 'Because I loved you, and thought you felt the same.'

'I did!' He looked up, and there were tears in his eyes. 'I do!'

I stood up and put on my coat. 'I needed you this last week, Theo. Really needed you. It's been the most difficult week of my life, but you ghosted out on me. You lied about what you were doing, you've been lying for I don't know how long.'

'Not long!'

'I don't need to know. See you.'

He jumped up and stood in front of the door. 'Where are you going?'

'Back to my dad's for tonight. I need to think about what I'm going to do about living and working with Gabby.'

'Please, Stella, don't go. I messed up so bad.'

'Blocking the door isn't going to make things better.'

'Let's talk some more. Give me another chance.'

'Can you get out of the way, Theo? I don't want to have to wrestle you.'

'Please, Stella!' His face was bright red. 'Please sit down and let me explain.'

I tried to get past him but he stood firm. We grappled for a few weird seconds, and my mum's words came into my head.

I know people sometimes push you around.

'Will. You. Fucking. MOVE!' I yelled, making us both jump.

Theo abruptly stepped aside.

I rushed past him, wrenched the door open, and ran out of the house. I drove in a random direction for ten minutes, then pulled over and rang Gran, who, unlike Dad, owned a mobile phone.

'Hello, Stella dear, are you all right? I've just seen your mother at a rather shabby hotel in Greater London.' No one could make 'Greater London' sound as unappealing as my grandmother. I couldn't wait to see her and get one of her affectionate pats.

'I'm fine, Gran. I'll see you back at Dad's later for a debrief.'

'Looking forward, dear gel. Kiss kiss!'

'Kiss kiss, Gran.' I hung up, and put my foot to the floor. Sometimes – maybe Mum knew this too – running away felt so very, very good.

Chapter 12

Kay

I waited till my coffee was in front of me, then pressed the green button on my phone, summoning this number I had never before called. My heart was thumping like a kangaroo's tail. Get me with the Aussie references. It rang four times, then she picked up.

'Good God! Kay!' Her voice sounded weird.

'Hey, Bear!' I aimed for a casual tone, but my voice was higher than usual.

'My God, Kay, what's wrong? Is it a World-Class Emergency?'

In spite of my nerves, I smiled at hearing her say our childhood expression. 'No…'

'Are you OK? You're not ill, are you? The kids? Richard?'

'We're all fine. Listen, Bear. I was just a little worried because you haven't written for a while.'

There was a pause. Then she said, 'I am so, so sorry. Time got away with me. You know how it is! Busy, busy. I got your letters, don't worry, I'll be back writing next month. Sorry love, I didn't mean to make you anxious.'

Oh dear. How anxious would she think I was when I told her where I was calling from? She chattered on, not giving me a chance to speak.

'So how are you, Kay? It's all good here, bit fed up with the weather, sun never stops bloody shining, haha, but I shouldn't be saying that to a Brit, right?'

Because I hadn't spoken to her on the phone for more than thirty-five years, I didn't know if she was always like this, or was just flustered to hear from me.

'So, I've got some news, Bear.'

'I knew it. Must be something pretty massive for you to phone me, my love. You better tell me now. I don't think I can wait for your next letter.'

'Well, you don't need to wait because…' Now it was time to say it, my hand clutching the phone shook with nerves. I felt foolish. Bear sounded fine. She'd simply been too busy to write. All my imaginings about what was going on with her seemed ridiculous. There was nothing to warrant this absurd journey; it looked overblown and melodramatic.

And yet…

She always wrote.

I took a breath, and said, 'You don't need to wait, because I'm here!'

'You're where, love?'

'Here! In Sydney!' In case she thought I meant Sydney in Hertfordshire or something, I added, 'Sydney, Australia!' in the daft Dame Edna Everage accent we used back when she first found out she was moving here.

There was a long silence. *Don't rush in*, I told myself. *Don't pre-empt what she might say. Don't try and guess what she is thinking.* But the silence went on so long – probably no more than ten seconds, i.e. an eternity – that I wondered if she'd fainted.

Finally, when I could stand it no longer, I said, 'Bear? Are you still there?'

Her voice came through, less upbeat than before. 'Yes, love, I'm here. And so, apparently, are you. Fuck! Where are you? Have you got a hotel? If you give me an hour I'll come to you. Kay, this is so wild! Did you write and say you were coming? Did I miss it? Are you here for work?'

'Bear, I'm in the…' I glanced at the menu on my table. 'The Jacked Up Coffee Shop.'

She let out a long loud breath, a long, whispered, 'Fu-u-u-u-u-u-u-u-u.'

'Round the corner from—'

'I know where Jacked Up is, Kay.'

'I'm not here for work, Bear. I'm here to see you.'

'Yeah, I'm getting that now. OK. That's cool. Very cool. Let me get my head into gear. Fuck. OK. I'm not dressed. Give me thirty minutes and I'll meet you there. I can't believe it, I can't believe you're here.'

'I can come to your house if it's easier,' I said.

'No! Stay there. That's fine. I'll see you in half an hour.' Bear hung up, and I closed my eyes for a moment. Everything seemed to be taking slightly longer than it should do. Bear's response, me processing Bear's response, the long lazy curve of water that arced into the air and onto the table, caused by me misjudging how close to my hand the water glass was…

'No worries!' The waitress arrived almost before I'd spilled it, mopped up and got me a fresh glass in an instant.

'Sorry, so sorry. Think I'm a little jet-lagged.'

'Oh yeah,' she said, already moving away and serving about six other people simultaneously, 'that'll do it to you.'

*

I'd never travelled anywhere this far before, never even had a flight with a break in the middle. The whole thing seemed so unreal. I'd thought I might sleep on the second flight, but I was far too wired, so I had two glasses of wine instead, at what might have been night-time but could as easily have been morning. With having had so little sleep on the planes, the sense of being outside my norms, of things being new and strange, was heightened by my conversation with the nice-looking woman I sat next to on the flight from Singapore, who chatted matter-of-factly about her work as an exotic dancer.

I'd also had plenty of time to reflect on the last few days. Way too much time. I thought about what Stella had told me, about Edward's continuing absence. I couldn't believe he'd not been home to see Richard yet. Something felt very off with him. I don't suppose he could have… but no, how could he? Richard had made a life-long promise and I couldn't believe he would go back on his word. But of course, I too had made a lifelong promise – till death us do part – and I'd just broken that. So maybe all bets were off when it came to promises.

I shook my head. There was too much to focus on at once. I would leave things with Edward for now, but the awful row with Stella still reverberated in my head. One traumatised child at a time. I decided that when I got back from Australia I'd see if I could meet her, make an apology she'd be willing to accept.

My flight got in at a little before seven in the morning. I went straight to my hotel, showered, changed my clothes, and called a cab. I was jagged with nerves and exhaustion and excitement. I didn't know what time Bear went to work, but assumed eight-ish would be early enough to catch her. I couldn't wait to see her face when I knocked on her door.

But when the cab dropped me outside her house, my chardon-nay-exotic-dancer feeling evaporated. I waited till the cabbie had disappeared, then I crossed to the other side of the road and stood looking at Bear's house. Number 192. For so long just an address that I wrote on an envelope every other month, in real life it was a long, two-storey house with a tiled roof, its front covered in cream-coloured wooden boards. The windows were concealed behind striped cotton awnings, so it wasn't possible to tell if anyone was in, but there was a large black jeep in the driveway.

Bear and Murray had divorced a few years ago. They had a son, Charlie, now a teenager. I half-expected to see him flying out of the front door, on his way to school, but the house was quiet, no sign of any activity. Perhaps he had already gone, or was staying at his dad's.

The Australian sun was already beating down on my head, despite the early hour. I could smell a faint whiff from my armpits.

Let's go! I told myself. All I had to do was cross the road and knock on the door. But my legs didn't move. I'd travelled ten thousand miles to be here, for one purpose only. *So what is the matter with me?* I asked myself firmly.

My jittery mind replied, *Bear won't thank you for arriving unannounced.* I might even give her a heart attack. Far better to call her first, perhaps from the nice-looking coffee place round the corner that I'd noticed from the cab.

I saw Bear before she saw me, the minute she pushed open the café door. The last time I'd seen her was three, four years ago. Maybe longer. It was on one of her fleeting European tours, with a tiny window for each country and an even tinier window for her friends. Nonetheless, Rose and I managed to meet her, and we had a wonderful evening in London. It must have been nearer five years ago, actually, I realised.

Bear was newly divorced and feeling the strain of being a single parent. She'd left Charlie with a UK-based cousin, and for a few hours, the old gang, the three amigos, were back together.

Bear's face was strained. Perhaps it was me, turning up out of the blue, that had caused the strain. She looked older, but then who of us didn't? Her copper-coloured hair was cut short and streaked with grey, and her face was more lined than I remembered. I stood up and she came over, breaking – to my intense relief – into what looked like a genuine smile.

'Kay!' She threw her arms round me and held me tightly. 'I can't believe you're here. You absolute nutter!'

I hugged her back, and blinked away a couple of stray tears. I was becoming so weepy in middle-age, I who, as a young woman, had prided myself on never crying. We broke apart, and she sat down, waving a hand at the waitress – 'My usual.'

'I guess this is your neighbourhood café,' I said.

'Yes, and it's so weird to see you in it! You are completely out of context.'

'I feel a bit out of context in general. Day before yesterday, I was in England.'

'So.' Bear leaned back in her chair and appraised me. 'What the hell is going on?' Despite all these years in Australia she still had something of her Liverpool accent, but there was an up-twang, an Antipodean lilt to it that hadn't been there in Hoylake.

'I wanted to see you,' I said.

'Did anyone tell you to come?'

An odd question. 'No. Why? Who would have told me to come?'

'Murray, perhaps?'

'Good Lord, I'm not in touch with him!'

'Someone else then?' In response to my puzzled expression, she went on, 'No, maybe... well, nothing. I don't know what I'm saying. I'm so confused to see you! And you look exactly the same as when I last saw you! What's your secret?'

'I don't know, I suppose not updating my look since my twenties is working for me. I love your hair, it looks really cute.' It didn't, really. She'd always had such pretty shoulder-length hair, the whole time I'd known her.

Bear lifted a hand to her head. 'I'm letting the grey come through.'

'I'm not ready for grey yet,' I said, 'but it definitely suits you.'

The waitress brought Bear a coffee, and they grinned at each other. 'Can you believe it, Marla?' Bear said. 'My oldest friend from England has turned up here, no warning, nothing!'

'Wow!' Marla smiled broadly at me. 'That's pretty cool.'

'It *is* cool,' Bear said, turning back to me as Marla returned to the counter. 'It's cool, not to mention brave, to fly across the world. It's not your usual style. So come on, then. What's brought you here?'

'You haven't written for six months,' I said. 'I missed three letters in a row.'

Bear nodded. 'I'm sorry. It just, well, this sounds bad, I'm not going to sugar-coat it. I guess it stopped being a priority.'

'I understand,' I lied, hoping I didn't show how much that hurt. Writing to Bear had always been an absolute priority to me. I'd written sitting up in a maternity unit bed after having Stella; behind the counter of Quiller Queen between customers; after Mum died; on holiday; on weekends; in so many precious free moments.

She reached out and took my hand. 'I'm so sorry my thoughtlessness cost you an expensive plane ticket, and no doubt a whole load of grief back home. How long are you here for?'

'I fly back Tuesday. But look, don't worry if you're busy, I'm not expecting you to spend time with me, I'm going to see all the sights, maybe an opera, and...'

'Don't be daft, you dag! This is an unexpected but wonderful treat. Of course I want to spend time with you. It'll be great. I'd invite you to stay, but things are a little tricky at home at the moment... but I definitely want to see you loads while you're here.'

'Are you sure?' I filed away the 'tricky at home' info for later interrogation, over a couple of drinks.

'Absolutely!' Bear gave me her biggest smile, her eyes crinkling. 'I can't think of anything nicer, now I'm over the shock! So look, how on earth have you swung this? How is Richard sparing you? You can't usually manage a day trip to Bournemouth without having to bring in a logistics team.'

Now it came to it, I didn't know how to say it. 'Oh, it's all fine.'

'Don't come the raw prawn with me!' Bear said, raising her voice. 'You've got high drama written all over you. You never do anything bonkers. Not since you were at uni!'

Fine. *Tell her, for heaven's sake.* 'I've left him.'

'Say again?'

'I've left Richard. I had enough of the marriage, and I left.'

I sat back and sipped my coffee, aware of Bear's eyes on me. I looked up defiantly.

'Well, good for you, love.'

'Really?'

'Yes.' She took my hand again. 'Really. This is a great move for you.'

'It is? Almost everyone else has told me what a terrible idea it is.'

'Screw them. You've been pedalling the same bicycle for thirty years.'

'Twenty-nine.' I grinned. 'Does that mean I need to buy a new bicycle?'

'You can choose a more fancy form of transport if you like. Honestly, Kay. I know Richard's been a good, solid husband. But life's fucking short, you know. I always wondered if he'd clipped your wings. You got stuck in a groove with kids, work. Maybe it's time to ditch good and solid for something else.'

'I don't want to meet anyone new.'

'No, that's not what I'm saying. Christ, I know that only too well! Last thing on my mind when Murray left. My overwhelming thought was, this split might be really painful, and it's doubtless having a horrible impact on Charlie, but at least I never need have sex again.'

I laughed. 'Shit, that's bad. I still quite like sex with Richard.'

'*Liked*, my love, it's past tense, if you've left him.'

'That's right. What I mean is, I don't have any desire to be part of a couple again.'

'That might change, though. It's all still so new. I've been uncoupled for nearly six years, and I'm afraid to report that it has plenty of disadvantages.'

'Yes, I'm a newbie at this. Maybe you can give me some tips.'

Bear sipped her coffee. 'The older I get, Kay, the more I realise that I know jack shit about what this crazy merry-go-round is meant to be about.'

'So, tell me about you, Bear.' I leaned forward. 'What's going on with you?'

'Oh, not much. Charlie is a handful. But school keeps him out of my hair. My job's fine.'

Bear was a PE teacher – she'd always been very energetic and sporty. 'Menopause not dragging you down yet?'

'Least of my worries!' She laughed. 'So how's the lag, talking of tiredness?'

'I'm pretty wiped out now. I'm starting to see auras round everything. I was running on adrenaline till I saw you.'

'Well, look.' She put some money on the table, waving away my attempt to pay. 'Why don't you go back to your hotel for a sleep? I've got to get to work, but this evening I'll take you to dinner at my favourite place, the Purple Kangaroo. 7 p.m. Don't let the stupid name put you off, it's the best Vietnamese in the city.'

'That sounds amazing.' I tried to stifle a yawn, but it was too large to be subdued. 'Ah, sorry.'

Bear grinned. 'It's creeping over you, I know the signs. Marla! Can we order this young lady a cab?'

Marla nodded, already dialling a number. 'Where to, Ursula?'

'The Park Royal,' I told her. Then, to Bear: 'Ursula?'

She'd hated that name as a teenager, had dead-eyed anyone who'd used it, so that even our teachers had got used to referring to her as Bear. The meaning of Ursula was 'little bear', a fact she'd latched onto when very young, even before Rose and I knew her.

'Yeah, I know. I've come back to it recently. Don't worry,' she said, 'I still answer to Bear, too. But when Dad died a few years ago, I discovered he'd chosen the name. I never knew that, and I did a bit of genealogy digging, well, Charlie did it for me, these kids and their tech-wizardry, eh? I discovered Dad had a sister who died when she was tiny, before she was one – cot death – called Ursula.'

'Ah, that's so sad.'

'I know, right? If he'd only have told me, I might have worn the name with pride.'

'Your dad was a sweet man,' I said.

'He was, and your mum was a top lady. I'm so sorry I couldn't make it to the funeral.'

'Ah, Bear, Ursula I mean, I didn't expect you to be there. It's funny, isn't it, how things work, because it's sort of to do with Mum dying that I'm here.'

'How so?'

'I cleared out her flat…'

'That's a grim job, isn't it?'

'Awful. But I found some of my old stuff. Including something interesting from when we were at school, that last year you were there, remember?'

'Like it was yesterday.'

'It was a list of all the things I wanted to do by the time I was thirty. And I've hardly done any of them, even though I am a tad past thirty. So, one thing led to another, and essentially, that list brought me here. I've updated it, and I'm going to do the things on it now. Better late than never.'

'Wow,' Bear said, smiling. 'There's something you're not remembering.'

'What?'

'Bring the list tonight, and I'll tell you.'

A horn beeped outside, and Bear stood up. 'Your taxi's here.'

I stood up too, aware now of how exhausted I was, the heaviness sweeping over me like stones. 'It was great to see you, Ursula.'

'You too, love. You crazy woman! Now I've got over the shock, I'm really happy you're here. I'll see you tonight.'

She walked me to the door, and saw me into the cab. I waved until she was out of sight, then closed my eyes. I must have slept for the twenty-minute ride, because it seemed no time at all that we were outside my hotel. I managed to pay the cabbie, get into my room, take my shoes off, and set my alarm for 6 p.m., but that was all. I fell onto the bed, as if someone had turned off a switch.

I slept right through the day, only surfacing when the alarm went off. I still felt weird, but after a shower and a tooth-brushing, better than before. I put on a clean dress, rang for a cab, and at the last minute remembered to put the 'things to do' list in my bag.

The Purple Kangaroo turned out to be embarrassingly near my hotel; I could have walked there in fifteen minutes. I was early, but Bear was already there, sitting at a table in the window. We kissed, and I got the giggles, as if we were still fifteen.

'I can't believe I'm really here, and it's really you!'

'I can't believe you're here either!' Bear shook her head at me. 'You look more rested.'

'I was solidly out of it for hours. I won't be able to sleep tonight. Mind you, I've been sleeping brilliantly since I left home, best sleeps I've had for years.'

'That's a good sign, isn't it?'

'I think so.' I started looking through the menu. 'I've never had Vietnamese before.'

'Shall I order some nice things, and we can share them?'

'Oh hell, yes.' I shut the menu with relief, and Bear rattled off an order to the waitress.

'Excellent choices,' the young woman said, 'you're gonna love it!'

After she'd gone, I started to say, 'Everyone here is so—'

But Bear interrupted me. 'Friendly? Yeah, I know. It bloody kills me.'

'Missing the old British service ethic, are you?' I mimed a salt-of-the-earth Liverpudlian waitress slamming a plate down on the table. '"That's yer lot!"'

'I do kind of miss it, oddly. So. Show me your list.'

I passed over the scrappy, much-folded piece of paper. Bear put on reading glasses, and examined it. 'Haha, become a famous photographer. Your ambition was impressive. Yes, yes, I remember this so well.'

'What do you mean? Do you remember me writing this?'

'Course I do.' She looked at me over the top of her glasses. 'We both wrote a list at the same time.' She rummaged in her bag and brought out her own folded piece of paper. 'Have you forgotten?'

'Completely! Jesus! When does early-onset Alzheimer's start?'

'We wrote these a few weeks before my family moved away. You and I were being all teenage and melancholy in your bedroom. You sat on your bed and I was on your blue beanbag.'

'Wow, Bear, you have the most amazing memory. I haven't thought of that beanbag in forever. It was so long ago.'

'Thirty-five years ago. No, thirty-six.'

'Where was Rose?'

'I'm afraid my memory doesn't extend that far. She wasn't there that day, that's all I know. We were sad about me going away. I think this was the same day we made the pledge to write every other month.'

'Oh! Well, I do remember that.'

'Then we each made a list of things we wanted to do by the time we were thirty. See?' She pointed to the lists. 'Your first one is to visit me every other year, and my first one is to visit *you* every other year!'

'Jesus, Bear, you did so much better with that one than me.'

The waitress brought over steaming bowls of food, and we stopped talking while she set them down, which unfortunately gave her the space to deliver an upbeat monologue about each one.

'Thanks,' Bear said firmly, in the middle of a eulogy about the pork pancakes, and the waitress took the hint.

'I'll leave you ladies to it!'

'You do that,' Bear said. Then, to me: 'So, start with some rice, and then try a little of each one. You bringing any food shizzle to the table: veggie, gluten-intolerant, no-carb? Guess I should have asked before I ordered.'

'No, I eat everything.' The food smelled amazing, and I started to ladle some onto my plate.

'Good for you.'

'Are there any other things on the lists that we had in common?'

'Yeah, we both wanted a baby. You obviously beat me to it by about thirteen years.'

'I was so stupidly young. Younger than Stella is now. Talking of kids... God, this is good.'

'It's amazing, right? Yes, what about kids?'

'You said things were awkward at home. Is that to do with Charlie?'

'Oh... yeah, he's at that difficult age. Not great around new people.'

'Edward was the same.'

As I ate another massive forkful of something delicious, I noticed that Bear was, in contrast, taking infrequent tiny mouthfuls. Her plate contained about a quarter of the food on mine. She'd often worried about her weight over the years – completely unnecessarily, she was always thin – and in her late teens had gone through periods of what I supposed we would now call bulimia. I realised with a jolt that must have been in the three or four years after she emigrated here. The move must have been a hell of an upheaval for her. A typical selfish teenager, I had only really thought about the impact of her departure on me.

'Also,' Bear went on, 'we both wanted to go to Venice. You wanted to eat ice cream by the Grand Canal, and I wanted a gondola ride.'

'Ha, yours is miles more touristy than mine.'

'Let's see… we both wanted to be famous in some way, me in athletics and you in photography. Ah well. How many of these did you do?'

'None, apart from have a baby. That's why I've updated it.' I opened my diary and showed her my new list. 'Visiting you is the first item. And look, Venice is still on here.'

'I can't believe you've never made it to Venice, you're hardly a minute away from it.'

'I always thought it was somewhere I'd go with Richard. It's not the sort of place I'd want to go alone. How come you never went, Bear, in all your many European travels?'

'I guess Murray wasn't keen on the idea. "No trucks? Just boats? Fuck that shit." You know,' she said, pointing at my diary, 'you haven't got anything on this new list about what you're going to do, work-wise I mean, now you're not in the shop anymore.'

'That's because I don't know yet,' I said. 'I'm a little bit worried about it. Fifty-one's kind of late to be starting a new career. I guess I'll have to wait and see where I end up living, then try and get a shop job.'

'You sound thrilled by the prospect.'

'Ah, I'm a bit over retail. But it's all I know.' I ripped a clean page out of my diary, and handed it to her, with a pen. 'You should do an updated list, too.'

'It doesn't have to be long, does it?' Bear said. 'I'm not sure I can think of many things.'

'Long or short as you like.' I ate while she made some notes, watching her covertly. She did look older than Rose and me. The granny haircut didn't help. And perhaps the Australian sun had been tough on her skin.

'There!' she said, putting down the pen. 'Four items. Go to Venice; drink tea on West Kirby beach; drink wine on the beach near my house here, which I have talked about doing for ten years; and make a photo album of my life for Charlie.'

'Those are great,' I said. 'Completely do-able. I'll come with you when you go back to Hoylake. I haven't actually been to Kirby beach for ages. You know…' And the ideas started coming so quickly, it was as if I had been thinking unconsciously of nothing else for days. 'I might go from here to Venice.'

'Wow, lucky you. No, not lucky.' Bear took another tiny mouthful of food, then laid her fork down in a decisive manner, as though she'd finished. 'You're making your own luck. You've unshackled yourself, and you're doing what you want for the first time in forever.'

'So come with me.'

'What?'

'Why don't you come to Venice, Bear? We can both go from there to West Kirby, and then you've done half your list in one go.'

Bear raised her eyebrows at me. 'Wow, look at you, Miss "I've just discovered air travel". Nice thought, but I can't.'

'Why not? Course you can! Is it work? Can't you take time off?'

'Exactly. "Sorry students and colleagues, I'm off to Europe now, catch you later."'

'You've worked there forever, I'm sure they'd give you a few days off. We don't have to go for very long. And won't Murray have Charlie?'

'Yes, he could have him. He's staying there now, in fact. But anyway, the thought of travelling is a bit hard going at the moment. All the logistics, think I'm getting stuck in my ways.'

If Charlie was with Murray, why couldn't I have stayed at her house? I decided to park that for now. 'I can do the logistics, bookings, everything.'

'Sorry, Kay, I can't.'

Now I'd had the idea, I felt disappointed she was shutting it down without even thinking about it. I could already picture the two of us strolling with ice creams by the Grand Canal, stopping for cappuccinos at an outside café, reclining on a gondola... now I'd imagined Bear there by my side, I couldn't unsee it. Surely I could bring her round to it. I let a few moments pass, ate some more of the delicious food and thought about what would convince me to go, if I were in Bear's shoes. In fact, what *had* convinced me to get off my butt, just ten days ago?

'You know, Ursula,' I said casually. 'Who knows how long we have while we're still healthy enough to travel? Not trying to be morbid, but we've got the opportunity now, and we don't know how long that door will be open for.'

I realised I was slurring slightly. The wine plus jet lag combo had gone to my head. I seemed to be the only one tackling the bottle; Bear's first glass looked untouched, while I was ready for a third. I decided not to pour it yet, in the spirit of moderation.

'None of us know how long we've got, Kay.'

'Exactly!' I banged my fork for emphasis. 'That's why I think we should go for it. I waited all these years for Richard to take me to Venice, but now I want to go with you, Bear.'

'Is this one of those late in life lesbian things I've been reading about in *That's Life!* magazine?'

'Bear, I love you, but not like that.'

'Talking of love, what about this one?' Bear held up our old lists. 'We both put "Fall in love with a beautiful man". How'd that work out for us, huh?'

'I did fall in love with a beautiful man,' I said, the heat rushing to my face. 'David Endevane. My first love. Maybe my only true love.'

'You sentimental old dag. He was very handsome, but from what you wrote to me, I don't remember him being all that nice to you.'

We looked at each other, the secret flickering between us.

'Have you ever…?' Bear said.

'No. I wanted to talk to you about that. About…' I hesitated. 'Whether it was a mistake, keeping it to myself.'

She nodded. 'Well, we have plenty of time to discuss it.'

'And discuss going to Venice? Carpe diem and all that.'

She laughed. 'I'll think about it, OK? I like your crazy side. I like you showing up here all mad and full of life.' She pushed her full plate away. 'I'm stuffed. Better get going. School night. But we could meet tomorrow afternoon, say four, and do some touristy things.'

'That'd be brilliant. Shall I collect you?'

'Nah, I'll come to you. Let's do the Manly Ferry tomorrow, that's a great little trip.'

She insisted on paying for our dinner – 'You've trekked all this way to see me!' – though I'd eaten three times as much. She got a cab outside, and I walked to the hotel, pleased that I knew where I was going this time.

I lay on my bed and texted the kids, even though Stella was angry with me and Edward had gone silent. *I'll never sleep, not after that massive nap earlier*, was the last thing I remember thinking before morning. Leaving my marriage certainly seemed to have improved my sleep. I wasn't quite sure what the significance of that was.

Letter written on 29 September 2002

Dearest Bear,

That is one adorable baby. Congratulations, darling. I love the name Charlie. He is the most beautiful thing I've ever seen – you are so clever! What does Murray think of his gorgeous little son? I've put the photo you sent on the fridge, and Stella, who is currently baby-mad, blows a kiss at it each time she goes past.

Hope labour wasn't too grim. We can compare war stories now. Tell me as much as you want to. I remember when I had Edward I didn't know anyone who'd had a baby and there were lots of things I found quite shocking.

It's very busy here. Now that Edward's old enough to collect Stella from school on his way home, I'm in the shop full-time. Richard has his hands full now he has two other shops. Sometimes I wish he was an accountant or civil servant, someone who comes home at six every evening and has weekends off. I'd never say this to Rose, but sometimes I too feel like a single parent. I know it's not the same, she's on it 24/7 with her kids and they are a lot younger than mine. Plus Tim is still behaving like an absolute shit over their house sale. And Richard is around now and then, of course. I guess sometimes I feel kind of lonely, Bear.

But you don't want to hear me whingeing when you've got gorgeous Charlie asleep (I hope!) in your arms.

Hope you get a decent time off with him. I don't have any advice really, other than get all the sleep you can, no matter what time of the day. Prioritise sleep over a clean house, getting washed, hell, prioritise it over everything except keeping the baby alive. Give him a squidgy hug from me. Now mine are older, I miss the baby stage. That lovely smell. Edward smells of Lynx deodorant.

Till next time.

Miss you.

Always, Kay

Chapter 13

Kay

I spent a lovely few days wandering round Sydney, feeling so dislocated from my ordinary life that it was like being another person. The Friday ferry trip was gorgeous; arriving into Manly at dusk and watching the lights sprinkle across the harbour was something I'd never forget. I was looking forward to spending the weekend with Bear, but unfortunately she was involved in organising an inter-school sports competition thing, which took up much of her time. I got in a routine of a leisurely breakfast on my own in one of the many cafés near my hotel, then some exploring while Bear was working, taking everything in: the Museum of Contemporary Art, a backstage tour of the opera house, and an organised walk round The Rocks district. What a beautiful city, what an amazing country.

Around four o'clock each day, Bear would text and we'd meet up. We went all over, and saw the famous sights, which were famous for a reason, but my favourite thing was to see the unsung ordinary places Bear knew about. Something that hadn't changed since we were young was her love of thrift shops, or 'op shops' as she said they were called here. On Saturday afternoon she took me to an amazing warehouse-style one where I supplemented my meagre running-away wardrobe with some beautiful new things. I got jeans, two dresses and some tops for little more than pennies.

I took them to the counter, gloating over them. 'Best shop ever!'

'It really is,' Bear said. 'I come here a lot.'

A man was in front of us, buying a vinyl single. I glanced over his shoulder: 'Ace of Spades' by Motörhead. It seemed an unlikely choice for the fellow, who looked like an accountant.

'That's seventy-five cents,' the woman behind the counter told him.

'I'll give you fifty for it,' the man said.

'I'm afraid seventy-five is the price,' the woman said.

'It's not worth it,' the man said.

I was feeling oddly skittish after a day in the warm Australian sunshine, and an afternoon of trying on pretty clothes. I tapped him on the shoulder, and he whirled round.

'Yes?'

'Do you think Lemmy would have quibbled about twenty-five cents?' I said. 'May he rest in peace.' I sensed that Bear, who'd been standing next to me, had moved away in embarrassment.

'Who?' said the man, looking puzzled.

'Lemmy! The lead singer of Motörhead, you philistine.'

The man grinned. Then he glanced past me, and his smile dropped. 'Ursula!'

I turned round. Bear was standing in the shadows by the dressing-room cubicle. 'Oh, hello, Frank.'

'God, Ursula, I heard from Murray about—'

Bear shook her head. Just once, a tiny movement, but it clearly meant 'shut right up', and he stopped instantly. After a pause, he turned back to me.

'You're right, lady,' he said. 'It's cheap to quibble about 25 cents. In fact,' and he handed some money to the saleswoman, 'here's a dollar.' He picked up his record. 'Bye, Ursula, good to see you,' he said, and went out.

The saleswoman began folding my new clothes.

'Who was that?' I said.

'Oh, an annoying friend of Murray's. Always gossiping about something, like an old woman.' Bear slapped down her credit card. 'Let me buy these for you.'

'No, Bear.'

'My treat. I want to. Such a thrill, to see you here, and decked out in proper good Aussie gear. Put your money away, it's no good here.'

'Well, that's really kind of you.'

'Wear that green dress tonight, we'll go dancing.'

'Really?'

'Nah, but I know a nice little Blues club.'

The club, called The Basement, was amazing, and the next afternoon we visited the stunning botanic gardens. On Monday, my last day, I discovered a huge stationery shop in Darling Harbour, and found an Ohto multi-function pen with two different colour ballpoints plus a propelling pencil. You hardly ever saw Ohto pens in Britain. I could imagine Richard's face if he could see it. I took a photo of it, but of course he didn't have a phone to send it to. If I sent a picture to Stella to show him she might delete it.

When you come back, even if Dad takes you back, I won't.

The pen was sixty dollars but I bought it anyway. When would I see something like that again? I had a sandwich lunch in a café, and wrapped the pen in brown paper, and wrote a little card to go with it. The woman in the café directed me to the nearest post office and I felt strangely elated when, with help from a cashier, I managed to send it. It was the first time in my life I'd sent anything more complicated than a postcard from a foreign country. I pictured Richard's face lighting up as he opened the parcel.

As I walked back towards town, I passed a huge secondary school, and realised it was the one where Bear worked. It was nearly three, so I thought it might be nice to collect her for once. I buzzed on the intercom, and explained myself to the friendly sounding receptionist, remembering to call Bear by her proper name. There was a pause, and the receptionist said, 'Please give me a moment.'

I waited for a couple of minutes, wondering if she'd forgotten about me, then she buzzed back. 'I'm so sorry, Ursula isn't here right now.'

'Oh!' I couldn't think where she might be. 'Is she in a meeting?'

'No,' the receptionist answered, 'she's not currently on school premises.'

I thanked her, feeling puzzled, and went back to the hotel. Perhaps she was at an off-site meeting, or had gone home early. But the text I received a little while later gave no hint of anything unusual: *Phew, just finished. Got a few things to do. Purple Kangaroo at 7 p.m.?*

I lay on my bed, staring at the telly, though I hadn't turned it on. I wondered what was going on with her, what she wasn't telling me, and what it was about the vibe she gave off that made it impossible to ask. I had two hours to kill before we met. Was this my future? Solitary meals, solitary travel, solitary hotel rooms. Richard hadn't exactly been a constant companion, but at least I'd usually had him to talk to at dinner time.

'I like my own company,' I told myself out loud. And then replied, also out loud, 'Yes, but not all the sodding time.' Great. I was starting to talk to myself.

'There are worse things than being lonely,' I remembered Mum saying to me, when she was ill and living in her flat in a rather unfriendly sheltered-housing block, 'but I can't think of them right now.'

Get a grip, I told myself, silently this time. *Man up, Kay! Tomorrow you'll be heading back to England.* I'd leave Venice for another time.

I worked out it was 8 a.m. in the UK, but Imogen was an early bird, so I decided to risk phoning her. Look at me, calling all the way from Australia, and it wasn't even a World-Class Emergency!

'Hello, Imo dear,' I said. 'I don't suppose lovely Bryn Glas is free...'

'Kay, my dear! You're bright-eyed and bushy-tailed! Weren't you just staying there?'

'I was, and it was wonderful as always! I'm abroad, coming back tomorrow. I wondered if I might take the cottage again, for a bit longer this time?'

'I'm so sorry, chérie,' Imo said. She sounded upset. 'My sons are insisting I get a permanent tenant in. They're putting it with a letting agency, can you believe? It's a "compromise" as I refuse to sell. Their decorators are going in next week, apparently it needs "blitzing" before they put it with an agency. You never minded the wallpaper, did you? I hate that you can't go there. It always felt like it was meant to be your place, really.'

'How much?' I blurted.

'Pardon, dear?'

'How much rent do they want?'

'Oh goodness, something ridiculous. I'm very cross about it, but they say I'm in need of regular income! Apparently I'm starting to run out! Isn't that silly!'

'The thing is, I've, er, I'm looking for my own place.'

'Are you, chérie?' There was a pause, but Imogen was too well-bred to ask why. 'Hang on, my sweet, I wrote the silly rent down somewhere.' There was a rustle of papers. 'Here we are. Yes, you won't believe it, the agent says they can ask for eight hundred pounds a month.'

I swallowed, and said, 'If you're able to let me have first dibs, Imo, I'll make sure I can pay that.' I'd worry about how another time.

'I'll try, my dear, but I don't seem to have much say in things at the moment.' Her voice, usually so strong, sounded frail and uncertain.

I said some nice things, I don't know what, and hung up, feeling that a rug had been pulled out from under me. I dreaded the thought of Bryn Glas slipping away, and was still thinking about it when I slid into a booth at the Purple Kangaroo next to Bear.

'Tough day?' I asked her. She was looking rather tired.

'No worse than usual.'

I didn't want to spoil our last evening by asking why she wasn't at the school earlier. If she didn't want to tell me, I didn't want to push it. She rattled off our order to the waitress, who knew better, by now, than to try to be our new best friend.

Bear said, 'Our first evening here, you said you wanted to talk about He Who Can't be Named, or is that Voldemort? You know who I mean.'

'He Whose Name I Shall Never Utter Again,' I said. My heart did the weird flip-flop it always did when I thought of David abruptly, without building up to it first. 'I might prefer this conversation to wait till I have a glass in my hand.' I looked around, and the waitress was already coming over with our bottle of wine. When she'd poured me a glass, I took a sip, and said, 'I'd always thought there was absolutely no need for Edward to know.'

'You were pretty adamant about that, if I recall.'

'There were Richard's feelings to consider, after all. And we haven't spoken about him ever since, we always swore we wouldn't. But then when I was leaving, Rich suddenly decided that I must be going off with him.'

'I can't believe he mentioned David, after all these years.'

'It was so strange. And he started to say something about Edward, I don't know what. I've been wondering if I was wrong, not to talk about it.'

'Well, David made it pretty clear he wasn't interested in being part of Edward's life.'

I took a larger sip. 'Yes. But it was a long time ago. We were kids then. I've been wondering if I should think about giving them a chance to get to know each other.'

Bear looked at me strangely. I couldn't read her expression. 'Hmm.'

'Hmm, what?'

'Just as long as it's Edward you're hoping to connect with David, and not yourself.'

'What do you mean?'

'You're fresh off the separation boat, lady. Fair game to fall for the "my life would have been so different if I'd stayed with my first love" fairy tale.'

'It probably would have been.' I took a large gulp of wine. Painful feelings swirled round my gut whenever I thought about what amount of the truth I owed to Edward. And I had to say, as the only person I could talk to about it, Bear wasn't exactly being super-helpful.

'I'm so sad it's my last day here,' I said, changing the subject. 'I won't half miss you, Ursula.'

'And I you. It's been great to catch up.'

Our food arrived, and we started eating, one of us with more enthusiasm than the other. We were silent for a while, busy with our own thoughts. Then Bear put her hand on mine, and startled, I looked up.

'Listen, Kay, I've been thinking a lot about what you said.'

'What *did* I say?'

'"Do you think Lemmy would have quibbled about twenty-five cents?"'

I laughed. 'What do you mean?'

'Venice. If you're still in, I'm in.'

'Really? You mean it?' I pressed my hand to my chest, trying to stay calm. 'You're serious?'

There was a pause, and I thought she was going to start laughing and say that of course it was a joke. But she said, 'I'm dead serious.'

Chapter 14

Stella

I slept so late that by the time I got downstairs, Gran was preparing lunch. She raised an eyebrow at me, while continuing her astonishingly speedy chopping. 'Good morning! Or afternoon, should I say.'

'Sorry, Gran. I was completely exhausted, I don't know why.'

'I'll pop on a bit of toast for you, shall I?' Without waiting for a reply, she put two slices of bread in the toaster, then picked up her knife and returned to massacring the vegetables. 'So are you going to enlighten me, dear heart?'

'About what?'

'Why you came back here last night, rather than to your Essex pied-a-terre? Not that it isn't lovely to see you, of course.'

'Ah, well, I wanted to see how the shop was. And how you and Dad are doing. '

'We're doing fine, dear, so there's no need for you to be here any longer. We both want you to get on with your own life, and so, I'm sure, does that wayward mother of yours.' She put down her knife. 'Do you know, I think I've missed my vocation in life. It's almost too much fun working in the shop!'

'But is this a long-term thing, Gran?'

'Stella, at my age, nothing is a long-term thing. But for now, I'm very happy to be Queen of Quiller Queen, and it means your father can stop worrying. You know how he feels about those shops. They're like the Windmill to him.'

'What windmill?' I felt as if I was being dragged along with the conversation, barely clinging to the coattails of meaning.

'The Windmill Theatre,' Gran said. 'We Never Close.' She tipped the contents of her chopping board into a pan, and smiled at the satisfying sizzle that instantly rose up. 'But never mind that. I want to know why you're here and not with Theo. Love's young dream, what a thing it is, to be sure, to be sure.' She lapsed into a shockingly bad Irish accent.

'OK.' I took a breath. 'We've split up.'

If I was hoping for a little sympathy, I was disappointed. Gran nodded, and said, 'I'm not surprised.'

'Pardon?'

'Never liked him. Shifty eyes.'

This was so exactly how I now felt about Theo's eyes that I wondered why I hadn't seen it before. 'Gosh, Gran, why didn't you say anything?'

'Well, *you* liked him. I didn't want to be rude.'

I laughed. 'Since when do you mind being rude?'

Gran coaxed the vegetables around with a wooden spoon, then lowered the heat under the pan. 'Not to people I love, dearest.' She took my hand in hers. 'Are you all right?'

'Yes,' I said, surprised by the rare physical contact. 'I really am.'

She let me go, and began buttering my toast. 'You'll meet someone lovely, someone worthy of you, when the time is right.'

'I'm planning to be single for a while.'

'Wonderful idea. Did me no harm at all.'

Perhaps I wouldn't want to be single for quite as long as Gran: forty years and counting. I took my toast upstairs and went to find Dad. To my surprise, he was in his study, working on a spreadsheet on the screen as if everything was normal.

'Ah, you're back!' He whirled his chair round. 'Why are you back?'

I told him about my split from Theo, and he hugged me tight. 'How are you, Sparkle?'

'Good. Strong. Resilient.'

'I must take a leaf out of your book. I need to remember my Viking heritage.'

'Our splits are a bit different, Daddy. I gave Mum your letter, by the way.'

'Thank you. What did she say?'

'She cried.'

'Did she?'

'She said she'll write to you from Australia.' I wished I could confide in Dad about how angry I'd been with Mum, and maybe exorcise some of the terrible things I'd said to her. But I didn't want to make Dad any more sad than he was.

'Seems so odd she's taking this momentous journey and I have no involvement in it. She didn't even ask me to get her some currency. Ah well.' He let me go, and said, 'What are you going to do about your home, and your business?'

'I'm not sure. Am I really not needed here?'

He looked at me with a kind expression. 'Don't take this the wrong way, Stella, but you're not. You've been amazing but you need to get on with your own life. Gran's an absolute powerhouse in the shop, and I think I'm ready to get back into the saddle.'

'Are you sure?'

'Positive. I need to be doing something. I'll tell you what. Yesterday your gran convinced me to close the shop at four, because she was going somewhere, West London, I think she said, and Callie had a doctor's appointment. Gran absolutely forbade me from taking over. That couple of hours when we had a 'closed' sign on the door of Quiller Queen, was a real wake-up call.'

'Oh Dad, I'm sorry I wasn't here to step in.'

'That's not what I meant.' He turned back to the computer. 'The shop was closed, and no one actually noticed. Perhaps your mother had a point. Perhaps I was a bit obsessed.'

'Bloody hell, Dad!' This was something that the whole family had been waiting for years, in vain, to hear him say. 'That's massive.'

'I'm going to be more sensible from now on, more balanced,' Dad said, slightly undermining his words by clicking on columns as he spoke. 'Then if your mother does come back, she will find me greatly improved.'

'That's wonderful,' I said, trying not to cry.

The ominous silence from Gabby since yesterday's Threesome-gate made me wonder if there was a business to go back to, and whether she and Theo were still… well, the only way to find out was to go back. If Dad was willing to start facing up to things, then I certainly should be. The following afternoon I got the train to Romford and let myself into the house. I breathed in a curry aroma wafting down the hall and, averting my eyes from the scene of horror, aka the living room, opened the kitchen door. Gabby was stirring something on the stove.

She whirled round and clutched her hand to her chest. 'Jesus, you scared me.'

'Sorry,' I said. 'How's it going?'

'Fine.' Gabby seemed nervous. 'Er, how are you?'

'Good, thanks.' *I feel reasonably confident, Bettina.* 'So where are we at? Haven't we got a party to cater this weekend?'

'Really?' Gabby's eyebrows could surely not go any higher. 'You want to carry on?'

'Gabby, if you don't want to work with me anymore, just tell me. There are easier ways of arranging it than shagging my boyfriend, you know.'

'Funny.' Gabby turned off the heat under the pan and sat down. 'Look, I'm sorry.'

'Sorry you slept with Theo, or sorry I found out?' I said, echoing my words to Theo that fateful night.

'Both, I guess. Ah, God, Stella. I wish I could put the clock back. Theo was here, you weren't, we were both a bit pissed. One thing just led to another.'

People were always saying that, as if they had no control over a situation. One thing led to another. But *how* did it?

'Well,' I said, realising that I had no interest in the gory details, 'let's get cracking.'

'OK. I'm relieved, actually.' Gabby ran her hand through her hair. 'Theo's cooking isn't up to much.'

It was a bit hard to hear Gabby talk about him so casually. But I wasn't going to show her that. 'His Thai green curry tastes like sick. Now let's move on. You and I have a business relationship, and I'll do my best to make it a success. We don't have to be friends, but I do expect you not to betray me in the future.' I imagined Mum applauding me as I spoke.

'Betrayal?' Gabby snorted. 'Hella fancy word for a few shags.'

'Let's just work together and keep it professional. If you want to keep seeing Theo, please be discreet.'

Piet came into the kitchen, and Gabby said, 'Piet, can you dish up? I'll be back in a sec.' She went to the door, and said over her shoulder. 'It wasn't a serious thing, you know. Theo still wants to be with you.'

'Nah, you're all right,' I called after her, 'I'm not into sloppy seconds.' I thought for a moment. 'Thirds, really, isn't it? Sloppy thirds!'

'Hello, Stella!' Piet took some bowls over to the stove. 'What is this sloppy thirds, a new kind of dish?'

'Something like that. Hey, Piet.'

'I am going to that meeting later, Stella, for adult children of divorce. Will you come?'

'Oh, I don't know, Piet. I'm not sure I'm in the—'

'OK. It's at six o'clock. I will be grateful for your company.' He held up a bowl. 'Would you like some of Gabby's curry?'

I realised I was starving. 'Yes, please.'

He and I were halfway through our food when Gabby came back in.

'This is delicious, Gabby,' I said. She might be a bit crap as a human being, but she was a good cook. 'What is it?'

'It's chicken – "Kukul mas kariya". The marinade's made with cashew nuts and coconut.' She took a bowl herself and sat down. 'I was thinking we could serve it at the thirtieth birthday party on Saturday. They want three curries: meat, fish and veggie.'

'This would certainly work for the meat one,' I said.

'I must say,' Piet said, piloting a huge forkful of curry and rice towards his mouth, 'you are being extremely professional, Stella. Isn't she, Gabby? Putting aside personal issues to focus on your work – I admire you greatly for it.'

'Mmm,' Gabby said.

'Thanks, Piet,' I said, genuinely touched, and amused, as always, by Piet's willingness to address the elephant in the room. Not just address it, but bring it right over to the table and invite it to pull up a chair and have a bowl of curry. Gabby looked gratifyingly uncomfortable, which was a bonus.

'I'm sure we can put all this behind us,' I said, scooping up another mouthful of curry. I felt oddly content. I liked the unusual feeling of someone else having messed up, and also the curry really was good.

There was a knock at the front door, and Gabby jumped up to get it. Moments later she came back in, a sheepish-looking Theo behind her.

'Hello, Stella,' he said.

'What the hell?' I said, looking from him to Gabby.

'You didn't answer any of my messages,' Theo said.

'No,' I said, adding in my head, *You shagging someone else kind of made me lose interest*. I realised that when Gabby slipped out of the room earlier she must have messaged him to say I was back. I frowned at her, wondering how it was that he seemed to have such a hold over her.

'What?' She shrugged. 'I know he's been wanting to speak to you.'

Piet said cheerily, 'Hello Theo, my old bum-boy!'

'For Christ's sake, Piet,' Theo said, going very red.

'What?' Piet said, looking puzzled. 'Is this not a real expression?'

'What do you think it means?' I said, starting to enjoy myself.

'Can I sit down?' Theo said.

'Sure, sit down on your bum, boy,' Gabby said, smirking.

'Piss off, Gabby,' Theo said.

'Is it not a male friend with whom you sometimes have anal intercourse?' Piet said, matter-of-factly.

'OK, you are using it correctly in that case,' I said, trying not to laugh.

'We haven't had anal, er, that thing you said,' Theo said. 'I'm not gay, Stella! Nothing happened between me and Piet, I swear! I don't like men! I was only even willing to try it because...' he dried up, presumably realising that his upcoming defence wasn't going to win him any credit.

'Because Gabby, who you *were* having sex with, suggested it,' I finished. 'Yeah, that's all right then.' I couldn't look at him now without seeing his weaselly face, his untrustworthy eyes. I should be heartbroken, but all I could do was wonder why I had wasted so much time and energy on him.

'Bloody hell,' Gabby muttered. She got up and started loading the dishwasher.

'Uh, Stella, can we talk?' Theo said.

'I'm sorry,' I said, thinking fast, 'I'm about to go out to a meeting with Piet.'

'Yes,' said Piet, reliably quick on the uptake, 'it starts soon, so we had better be on our way.'

'What time will you be back?'

'Late,' I said.

'I'll wait for you,' Theo said.

There was a pause, in which we all looked at Gabby, who had her back to us, but feeling our eyes on her, turned round, and said, 'Bloody hell,' again.

'On second thoughts, I'll come back later,' Theo said. 'Ten o'clock?'

'Let's leave it till another day,' I said.

'I really need to speak to you,' Theo said, 'so I'll come back later.'

'If he gets here before me,' I said to Gabby, 'try not to shag him.'

Theo turned and went out; we heard the front door close.

'Oh yes, she's so fucking professional, Piet.' Gabby slammed the dishwasher shut and all the crockery inside it rattled. 'Look, Stella, this isn't going to work if you're going to mention it at every single opportunity.'

'I know,' I said, 'but you went behind my back again just now, telling Theo I was here, literally seconds after I'd asked you not to betray me again.'

'There's that word again. You are really over-using it.'

'That's because you are really betraying me a lot.'

There was a pause. Then Gabby said, 'OK. Sorry I texted him.'

I noticed she didn't apologise for sleeping with him, but I was the one who wanted to move on, so I nodded, and gritted my teeth.

'I'm sorry, too, for going on about it.' It seemed a bit rum that I was the one apologising, but I owed it to the business to give it a go, and that meant making it work with Gabby. 'Really,' I added, 'you did me a favour.'

'Pardon?'

'Well, if Theo's not the faithful type, it's as well to find out now, isn't it, before we got engaged.'

'Er, yes, I suppose so.'

The uncertainty on Gabby's normally over-confident face made me smile. 'So, thanks, Gabby. I appreciate it.'

Piet grinned at me. 'Let's get to this meeting, Stella.'

'Oh, Piet. I only said I was going to get rid of Theo. I need to catch up with Gabby and the business.'

'I think you should come,' Piet said. 'It will be more authentic when you see Theo later, and also I wish very much to have someone with me.'

'Go,' Gabby said, 'we can talk tomorrow. I've had enough talking for now. I'm going to make two fish curries and you can taste-test them in the morning.'

I didn't fancy this weird support group. But though Theo had lied to me, I had never lied to him and I didn't want to start now, even if we were finished. Piet was right, it would be more authentic. And it was good karma to tell the truth. Not that good karma seemed to be particularly going my way right now, but still.

Chapter 15

Stella

Piet and I strolled companionably into town. I thought of him calling Theo his 'bum boy' and burst out laughing. He smiled down at me.

'It's nice to see you laugh,' he said, and added, with his usual impressive, but slightly muddled, command of English idiom, 'You have been through the mill and backwards again.'

'Thanks, Piet. I do seem to have had my share of challenging life events lately.'

'Yes, and for my part in this latest one, I sincerely apologise.'

'I don't blame you, Piet, and I don't even blame Gabby. Neither of you owed me anything.'

Piet stopped walking and put his hand on my shoulder. 'That is terrible, Stella, of course we owed you something. We owed you our friendship, and we let you down.'

'That's very sweet.'

'I will make it up to you, one way or another.'

'That's OK, there's no need.'

We arrived at the venue, an unremarkable town-centre pub, on the same road as the library. Piet bought us beers, and we carried them upstairs. I wondered why I'd come. I wasn't ready to bare my soul to a bunch of strangers. Would it be all, 'Hello, my name's Stella, it's been nine days since my parents split'?

I followed Piet through the door at the top of the stairs, into a scruffy room with a flamboyant orange-and-pink carpet that bore the battle scars of all the beer and cigarettes that had been ground into it. There was a circle of chairs in the centre of the room, which seemed more alarming than basic chairs ought to be. There were eight or nine people there, a mix of ages, most looking awkward or strung out. Apart from Piet, of course, who was always relaxed, and exactly the same wherever he went or whatever he did.

I couldn't help noticing that there was one good-looking boy standing in a corner clutching a beer glass and looking uncomfortable. There was something familiar about him.

A smiling woman who was clearly the organiser came over to us. 'Welcome! I'm Martine. I'll be running the session today.'

I wasn't sure how I felt about Martine, who was dressed in what looked like the exact same 1980s' puffball skirt Mum was wearing in ridiculous photos from her university days, and – hopefully – ironic blue eyeshadow from the same era. But Piet beamed genially at Martine, and held out his hand, and I decided that I should try to be more Piet. I told my shoulders to relax, and chugged down half my pint in an attempt to speed up the process.

At Martine's encouragement, we all took a seat in the circle and smiled awkwardly at each other, apart from Piet, who smiled un-awkwardly at everyone. I nodded shyly at the hottie opposite me, and he smiled back broadly, which was excellent. Then, to my surprise, he made the 'phone me' gesture with his hand, and pointed at me. I looked over my shoulder, to see if he was gesturing to someone else, but there was no one there. Puzzled, I pointed at myself, and he nodded, and carried on calling me on his pretend phone. Sure, I'd like to phone him, he was gorgeous! But one, I didn't have his number, and two, I had no idea who he was, and three, maybe I'd already gone off him as it was such a weird thing to do.

'I'd like to welcome you all to this, the first meeting of Romford ACODs,' Martine said, and Phone Boy put his hand down and made a 'let's talk later' face, which I greeted with a 'certainly, you handsome chap' face.

'Let's find out who's in the room,' Martine said. 'I'll start. I'm Martine, you know me, and my parents split five years ago. Let's go round this way.'

Though it was an excellent chance to find out Phone Boy's name, I hated introducing myself in groups like this. But no one else seemed to mind. The first woman, Carol, launched into a long rambling explanation of her parents' horrible divorce.

'That's great,' Martine said, as soon as she could get a word in. 'These are going to be quick intros for now, if that's OK?' She moved on to a middle-aged man sitting next to Phone Boy. The man introduced himself succinctly enough – 'I'm Michael' – and then gave a startling one-line summary: 'My parents were fuck-buddies who should never have had children.'

I was still wrestling with what that might mean when I realised too late that Martine had moved on to Phone Boy before I was ready. It sounded as if he said, 'I'm a new man,' but that wasn't the sort of thing people said, was it? Yet it must have been his name, as Martine simply smiled and said, 'Welcome.' There was no time to puzzle it over as it was coming round to my turn. An intense-looking woman with her hair in bunches mumbled that she was called 'Dreda', which also didn't seem like a real name, and that her parents had separated two years ago and both of them had remarried within six months. Piet whistled through his teeth at that.

Martine smiled at me. I mumbled, 'I'm Stella. My parents have only just split up. About a week ago. I guess I'm still processing it.'

'We are all still processing our parents' splits, Stella, but that is horribly recent, and I'm so sorry for your experience,' Martine said. Everyone nodded and made sympathetic faces.

'I am Piet, and my father had the affair with my aunt and they made my mother move out of the house,' Piet said. 'It was six years previously.'

'Wow, that's harsh,' Martine said. 'Is your mother OK now?'

'No, she is dead, I am afraid,' Piet said.

I whipped round so hard to look at him that I heard my neck crack. 'She's dead?'

Piet nodded. 'Well, it was not unexpected,' he said calmly. 'She was riddled with more than one disease.'

My God, Piet was a strange chap and no mistake. I sat back, and realised that Martine had already spoken to the last couple of people, and I'd failed to register their names. She shuffled some papers on her lap, cleared her throat, and said, 'ACODs stands for Adult Children of Divorce, and we are a much-overlooked group. Mostly, researchers who study the impact of divorce consider only young children, and of course they do suffer greatly. But so do those of us who were adults at the time. What are some of the things people have said to you when you told them that your parents were splitting up?'

Everyone but me chipped in immediately, talking over each other in their eagerness to share.

'It's not as bad as if you were a kid.'

'Good of them to wait till you were an adult so it has less impact.'

'How nice for them, starting again before it's too late.'

Martine nodded vigorously after each comment. 'Yes, exactly!' she said.

'I have one,' Piet said, leaning forward towards Martine. 'People said that at least I knew it wasn't my fault, because I was no longer living at home.'

'People said that to you?' I said, looking at Piet. He nodded solemnly.

'A friend of mine asked if I'd be having a bedroom in both parents' houses,' Phone Boy said, 'and started laughing, like it was a joke.'

'Yes,' Martine said, 'people do sometimes seem to find it quite funny. Why do we think that is?'

'It's a bit comical, I suppose,' an older man on Piet's other side said. 'Like instead of settling down to a pipe and slippers, the man is deluded that he's going to start again with a young girlfriend and a red sports car.'

'It's not only men who leave,' Martine said, 'but yes, thank you Adrian, that's part of it, isn't it? Our expectations of what an older marriage looks like.'

'And also,' said Carol, who was about Mum's age, 'everyone knows that divorce is awful for young kids, but if it happens to your parents when you're an adult, no one knows what to say. So they make a joke about it.'

'That is so true,' Martine said, nodding vigorously.

'You're expected to be able to cope, because you're not a child anymore,' Adrian said, 'but actually you're always your parents' child, aren't you?'

Others in the group muttered their agreement, and began sharing more horrific details of their experiences, but none of it seemed very relevant to me. Certainly none of them had stepped in to the family business and consequently discovered their boyfriend was unfaithful.

I sat back in my chair, and discreetly examined Phone Boy aka New Man. Dark hair, cut short but not too short, nice brown eyes. T-shirt and good jeans, the right blue and the right tightness around the, er, pelvic area. I drifted off into a pleasant little reverie about how Phone Boy would never be unfaithful, and how handsome he would look sitting up in my bed without his shirt on, smiling at me, making that 'call me' gesture…

I dragged my eyes upwards, back to his nice face, to discover, oh God, that he was looking straight at me, a faint smile on his lips. Had he witnessed my long slow laser-sweep down his body? I twanged my eyes away. Where *had* I seen him before?

'… but you know, it can be just as devastating for your parents to split when you're an adult as when you are a child.' Martine's voice broke into my thoughts. I looked round, and realised that everyone was nodding. Carol was crying quietly, tears rolling down her face.

'For some people,' Martine went on, 'the awareness that their parent might have waited for them to grow up and leave home before they themselves felt able to leave can be almost impossible to get over.'

I felt as if Martine had thrown a bucket of cold water over me. It had not occurred to me, until this moment, that Mum might have left earlier had I not come back home after university.

Piet nudged me, and handed me a pile of papers.

'Take one and pass it on,' Martine said.

I looked at the handout. It was reminiscent of a GCSE worksheet, with little squared-off sections and naff clipart decorations. Everyone else was already filling theirs in, and I didn't even have a pen. I turned hopefully to Piet, but he had his head down and was working diligently on the first question. Then someone was pressing a pen into my hand. I looked up into the kind brown eyes of Phone Boy.

'Thank you,' I whispered, for the room was silent as an exam room now, with everyone scratching away at their worksheets. I breathed in a wave of his scent – lemony and clean – and he grinned and sat back in his seat. The pen was a blue uniball, medium nib. Once a stationer's daughter, always a stationer's daughter. A good choice of pen: classic, dependable, nice flow.

I stared at the sheet. The opening question was: 'How did you first hear that your parents were separating?' I'd deliberately not thought too much about that awful phone call. But now, the question stark in black and white, it all came flooding back. I felt again the anxiety as I pushed coins into the phone box, the suspension of breath before Dad picked up, going over all the worst things that might have happened, the sheer frozen shock to the stomach on hearing him cry that his life was over, ranting and shouting, out of control, chaotic, about all he had done for Mum, all he had done for his family, and for what, what was it all for, it was all so pointless, there was no sense in going on with anything. And finally, my own regrettable words, telling him that Mum had clearly lost her mind, that I would tell her to come back, insist on it, I remembered promising. I hadn't managed this, had I? Instead I had bitched at Mum, told her off, accused her of taking a gap year, called her selfish, alienated her. My eyes blurred with tears and I could scarcely see my own writing.

When Piet started wailing it seemed at first a manifestation of my own inner state. Seconds later I realised that he was doubled-up as though in the most awful pain, his head against his knees, his whole body jackknifed in his chair, a horrible noise coming from his mouth. Like an air-raid siren, I thought dimly, remembering that sound from war films I'd watched with Dad. Everyone was staring at Piet, their own problems temporarily forgotten.

'Wah-wah-wah-wah-wah!' Piet cried, his face hidden in his hands. He began rocking backwards and forwards.

I put my hand on Piet's shoulder to comfort him, but it didn't seem to help. Martine came over and put her arms round him, not an easy task as he was rocking like a crazy person, but after a minute or so he started to calm down. Martine held him until he pulled away and sat up. His face was streaked with tears.

'It is so – so – painful,' he said.

'I know, Piet. I know,' Martine said. She had tears in her own eyes. 'We all understand. I do, and so do all your friends here.'

I wasn't sure that I did understand, really, but when he looked at me, I nodded vigorously.

'Thank you,' Piet whispered. 'I feel much better, and ready to continue.'

'Are you sure?' Martine got to her feet.

'I am quite sure, Martine, thank you so much!' He gave one of his beaming smiles, and if you hadn't seen him a few minutes earlier, you would never have known that he was in the slightest bit of turmoil.

Everyone turned their attention back to their worksheets, but I felt thoroughly shaken. If Piet, who took everything in his stride, had been so floored by his parents' separation, was I too going to have some kind of breakdown months or years down the line?

I went back to the form. 'How did you first hear that your parents were separating?' I wrote: 'Dad rang me but my phone had no battery left,' and noticed, almost as if watching it happen to someone else, that tears were dripping onto the paper.

Piet whispered, 'Are *you* OK?'

'Yes,' I said, giggling as I was clearly a teary mess and not OK.

I let the tears fall as I continued writing in shaky letters. I wrote about the panic, trying to find a phone box... then I realised all at once where I knew Phone Boy from, and my tears dried up like a tap being turned off. He was the nice librarian, the one who had directed me to the payphone on that awful day. *That* was why he'd made the phone gesture – he was trying to remind me of our connection. Silly to have done a mobile-phone gesture; I'd have got it much more quickly if he'd acted out a payphone. He'd be a lousy charades partner. I blew my nose and moved on to the next question, which was: 'Do you wish your parents were still together?' I hesitated. A few days ago I'd have ticked 'yes' so hard I'd have ripped the page, but now... I thought of Mum's face as she tried to think of things she missed about Dad, of her saying she'd been unhappy. After a moment, I ticked 'not sure'.

The next question seemed to have been written specifically for me: 'Strange things often happen to us as adults in the wake of a parental divorce. Did anything strange or unexpected happen to you?' I was still compiling what turned out to be a rather long list when Martine suggested that anyone who hadn't finished – looking round, I could see that category only included me – might like to complete the form at home.

Martine taught us some meditation exercises for when we felt overwhelmed, and then announced the date of the next meeting, in a month's time. Everyone thanked her and stood up. I started across the room towards Phone Library New Man Boy – if nothing else, I needed to find a more manageable name for him – but I was blocked by Carol, in full head-tilt mode. I smiled at her vaguely, hoping to be able to keep walking, but she reached out and clasped my hands.

'Are you all right?' she said, glancing between me and Piet. 'It's all still so raw for you. I saw you crying. You and your husband were really connecting with your feelings there, weren't you?'

'Oh, he's not my, uh…'

'It doesn't get any easier,' Carol said. 'My parents split in 1995, and I've never been the same. I was devastated.'

'Oh dear…' I could see that Lib-Pho-Boy-New-Man was putting on his leather jacket, which was so cute, very librarian-tries-to-be-edgy. I attempted to extricate myself, but Carol held on firmly.

'*Devastated,*' she confirmed, meaningfully, as though devastation was something we shared.

'I don't think I'm quite… well, you have to manage one day at a time, don't you?' I said, praying that a mundane platitude would get me out of being Carol's new best friend.

Damn it, LPB was heading for the door. I turned my head to him, my hands still held fast, and he caught my eye just as Carol said, in an unnecessarily loud voice, 'Still, you're lucky to have such a handsome and supportive hubby,' nodding at Piet, who was wrapping his long red scarf round his neck with a flamboyance even Liberace would have considered over the top. LPB made a brief smile of regret, and left the room.

CAROL! I wanted to shout. *You have alienated the hottest man in Essex, and after the ego-bashing I've had from Theo, I really need to know I can attract the hottest man in Essex. I'm not asking for him to be my new boyfriend, or anything. I only want a bit of a flirt, is that too much to ask?*

I pulled my hands away, and they slid out of Carol's damp ones with a slippery squelch. I said, 'Piet is not my husband.'

'Boyfriend then, sorry!' Carol trilled. 'I'm so old-fashioned!'

'He's not my boyfriend!'

But it was too late, LPB had gone, and Piet was looming over me saying, 'Ah, alas, Stella, if only I were,' and Carol was simpering and stroking the end of his scarf, and now Adrian was coming over to join in the fun, and I wanted to scream.

I tugged at Piet's sleeve. 'Come on,' I said, 'I want to go to bed.'

'Is this the invitation I have been waiting for?' Piet said gallantly. Carol laughed.

'No, Piet. My sights are set elsewhere,' I said. I linked my arm through his, and we clattered down the rickety stairs and out into the street. Perhaps there was a God, because LPB was standing outside, leaning against the pub wall, looking at his phone. He glanced up as we came out, and I saw him clock my arm in Piet's. He put his phone in his pocket and began to walk away. I extricated myself from Piet and called, 'Excuse me!'

The boy turned, and Piet stepped towards him. *Not now, Piet*, I thought. *I really need you to be somewhere else, any-bloody-where else, please just go away!*

But as the handsome boy looked quizzically at us, Piet said, 'Please, mate, my friend wants to talk to you.'

Piet sounded so funny saying 'mate' that I couldn't help laughing. The boy started laughing too.

'She does, does she?' he said.

'Yes, I do,' I said. We stood and stared at each other. His eyes were exactly the same colour as a tiger's eye pendant I owned, dark brown flecked with gold.

'I am surplus to requirements, I believe,' Piet said.

Carol tapped him on the shoulder. 'I'll keep you company,' she said.

'That is very kind,' Piet said, and he allowed himself to be led away. Good old Piet, taking one for the team like that! I thought of him earlier, saying, 'I will make it up to you, one way or another.'

'He's not your husband then,' the boy said.

'He's my housemate. I don't have a husband.' I decided I might as well clear it all up now. 'Or a boyfriend. I'm completely single.'

'This is useful information,' the boy said, grinning. 'I know you're Stella. I'm Newland.'

'Ah yes, I heard it in the group.' *New Man.* 'Unusual name.'

'Literary parents. They named me for Newland Archer from...'

'*The Age of Innocence.*' I had never in my life been more grateful for my school's English curriculum.

'Ahhhh!' Newland looked delighted. 'You're the first person who ever knew that.'

'I did it for A Level.' *Shut the fuck up, Stella!*

'It's a good book. A bit of a liability, though, for a name. Most of my friends call me Lan, which is shorter, at least. Do you remember me from the library?'

'Yes, you were really kind and let me use the payphone.'

It was obvious to both of us, I think, that we were talking in code. 'Do you remember me?' clearly meant 'do you like me?', and 'you were really kind' meant 'you were hot as hell'. It occurred to me with a flash of inspiration that if I stayed out late with Newland – if I, for instance, went back to his place – I could avoid the scheduled confrontation back at the house with Theo.

'Where are you going now?' I asked.

'Nowhere. What about you?'

'Same.'

'Then, Stella' – and he held out his hand – 'shall we go nowhere together?'

Chapter 16

Kay

'Stunning.'

'More than stunning. Exceptional.'

'Superlative.'

'Astonishing.'

'Exquisite.'

'Beyond compare.'

I sipped my cappuccino, closed my eyes briefly, then was rocked all over again by the view when I opened them. 'Bloody gorgeous!'

Bear laughed. 'So poetical.'

It was our third day in Venice, but it was the first time we had done the thing I'd dreamed of – sitting together in a café by the edge of the Grand Canal.

'I still can't believe we're really here,' I said.

'Me neither,' Bear said. 'Turns out all you need to achieve a lifelong dream is a bossy friend and a shitload of money.'

'Who knew?'

We went back to our new favourite pastime, which was gazing at the Grand Canal and failing to find the right adjective to sum up its appeal.

'It's like a film set,' I said.

'Except better, cos we're in it,' Bear said.

'It's like a painting.'

'Except better, cos we're in it.'

'Do you really feel that we add something extra to the timeless beauty of the scene, Ursula?'

'Yes, I do. We are, ourselves, timeless beauties.'

The water glittered in the low bright sun, and metres from where we were sitting there were gondolas tied up at the shore, bobbing gently up and down. Across from us, on the little island in the canal that housed the tower of San Giorgio Maggiore, someone was getting married. We were too far away to see their faces, but the bride posed for photos alone by the edge of the water, her long train spread out on the ground behind her. I missed my camera; my fingers itched to take her picture as well.

'You see all the films set in Venice,' Bear said.

'Like *Don't Look Now.*'

'That was a good one. But you don't really believe it's a real place, not till you're here.'

'And not even then.' I finished my coffee and sat back in my seat.

Bear put her hand on mine, startling me. 'Thanks,' she said. 'Thank you for making me come here.'

'I didn't make you, did I?'

'Well, you didn't *coerce* me. You just made me want to come. This is such a beautiful way to spend time. With you. Here.'

I hadn't yet dared ask Bear what made her change her mind. I didn't want to wreck the mood, which was friendly as always, but which I felt depended on me treading carefully. There was an agreement between us – unspoken but as loud and clear as if it had been yelled through a megaphone – to keep things light.

*

I was the one who'd booked this last-minute, off-the-clock-exorbitant trip. Bear had enough on her plate with organising a week's study leave from school at short notice. Rose would be proud when she heard how I'd managed all the complicated logistics. It had already cost an arm and a leg – hell, several arms and legs – for me to change my return flight with no notice. And as soon as Bear had said she wanted to come, she showed me the website of an unbelievably beautiful, unbelievably expensive palazzo. I said that a basic Airbnb apartment would be more my speed, but Bear insisted and offered to pay for the whole thing. I couldn't agree to that, of course, but reasoned that it was only five nights, and when would we ever do such a trip again? I also told myself to think of the fortune I'd saved on all the other holidays I hadn't had over the last twenty-nine years.

Our apartment was inside a three-storey golden-walled palace on the edge of the Castello district, and it was stunning. We had two floors to ourselves, including a large bedroom and bathroom each, and an enormous sitting room and kitchen. My bathroom alone was bigger than my bedroom at home. I mean, in the house I shared with Richard. The *room* I used to share with Richard. *God.*

I was discovering that long-haul travel made me manically wide awake, but Bear slept straight through almost the whole flight. However, she was still tired when at last we landed in Italy. Once the housekeeper had shown us round the palazzo, and we'd picked our dropped jaws off the floor, Bear went to lie down. Despite the beauty of the apartment, I was eager to get outside. The taxi-boat from the airport had shown me glimpses of a city even more thrilling than I'd imagined.

That first afternoon in Venice, by myself, strolling at will through the bright late sun, my shadows lengthening ahead of me as I walked, was one of the most glorious days of my life. I was alone, abroad, completely free. No one knew exactly where I was. Including me; I got lost straight away, but I didn't care. I flitted in and out of strange alleyways, stopping to inspect a shop window, or pause at the top of one of the sets of steps that bridged the little canals to stare at the view. I pretended I lived here, that I was a Venetian lady. *I always go to this café*, I thought to myself, *for my espresso. And to this market, for my fish and flowers.* Wandering around alone in Sydney, I'd thought my single life was going to be lonely, but I didn't feel that today, not at all.

I had to ask several people for directions on my way back. Though they mostly turned out to be tourists, they were all very friendly and helpful. I went into the golden palazzo to find Bear sitting on the window seat in the living room, looking out at the canal. She asked what I'd seen, where I'd been. She was pale and rather washed out, despite the epic amount of sleep she'd had. She blamed the jet lag, and seemed disinclined to go out. I'd been looking forward to dinner by the Grand Canal but I offered to make something in the apartment.

The kitchen was fully stocked, because it was an apartment for extremely rich people who presumably couldn't be arsed to get their own shopping in. Mind you, they'd have probably brought a chef with them; Bear just had me. I made a simple pasta – when in Italy – with a creamy sauce I'd learned from Alice, and a salad of delicious tomatoes that actually tasted of something. There was a separate fridge full of wine, so I cracked open a bottle and Bear and I sat at the huge kitchen table under a Venetian-glass chandelier, toasting each other and peeping out of the window every so often to check that the view was still there.

'I'll clear up,' Bear said after a while. She had barely eaten or drunk anything.

'You should rest,' I said. 'You'll want to feel strong for sightseeing tomorrow.' I went to take her bowl, but her hand curled protectively round it.

'Darling, I know you've not got much of an appetite, it's fine. You don't need to hide it from me.'

She gave me a tight little smile. 'OK. Thank you. Not sure where it's gone. Goddamn menopause. I'm sure I'll feel better tomorrow.' She stood. 'Do you mind if I go up?'

'Of course not!' I remembered that in Sydney she'd said the menopause was the least of her problems.

I stayed in the kitchen, sipping my wine, till the light faded. It was the last day of May, and the days were long. When I couldn't keep my eyes open any longer, I went to bed. I hoped Bear would be more of a travel companion in the morning.

But she wasn't. I breakfasted alone, wondering if the smell of coffee would bring her out. But she didn't appear. I had a bath in the huge bathroom, and got dressed slowly to give her time to surface, but eventually I gave up and went back out on my own. I felt a little down-hearted at first, but soon Venice worked its magic and I snapped back into my fantasy that I lived here and saw these sights every day. I drifted along with no clue of my direction until I saw the Rialto Bridge. It was crammed with people, so I didn't try to cross it. Instead, I walked down a nearby alley, and discovered at the end of it a tiny stationery shop, the window filled with glass fountain pens and tiny bottles of ink in every colour. Such beautiful things, so different from the stationery back home. Richard would have been in heaven. I went in and spent a very enjoyable fifteen minutes sorting through a display of soft suede-covered notebooks. Even the littlest ones were ten euros, but they were exquisite. I chose a sage-green one, tiny enough to fit in my pocket, and also a few sheets of thick cream writing paper with marbled edges.

I had a sandwich for lunch, and visited the Accademia art gallery. I got a text from Bear at about four, apologising for sleeping the whole day away. I hastened back to the apartment, thinking she'd be ready to go out now, but she was lying on a sofa, reading a book about Venice. I bit back a comment about why she was reading about it when the real thing was right outside the front door. Instead, I said, 'You look better.'

'I don't know why the jet lag's been so bad this time. Sorry I'm being a rubbish friend.'

'Not at all,' I said, hoping I sounded convincing.

She still wasn't up for going out in the evening, but I told myself that if we had to be stuck indoors, at least we were in a palace. I went out again and bought sardines from the market I'd seen yesterday, and grilled them with bread and more tomatoes. Bear ate more than the previous evening, and afterwards there was a little more colour in her cheeks.

'So, Kay,' she said softly, as she sipped her wine. 'Have you decided what to do about Edward?'

'Yes.' It had all been simmering away in the back of my head these last few days, and now I had reached a clear decision. 'I'm going to reach out to David—'

'Reach out, is it? How modern.'

'And offer him the chance to meet Edward.'

'What if he says no?'

'I'm going to tell Edward the truth anyway.'

'It's the right thing to do,' Bear said. 'Edward should be given the chance to decide what he wants to do.'

'I'm scared, though, Bear,' I said. 'What if Edward hates me for lying all this time? What if he's really angry?' I tried to smile, as if I didn't really mean it. But whenever I thought about telling him, I could only picture a furious reaction. Him towering over me, his face contorted with rage, yelling, pointing a finger at me, telling me to go, that I would never see him or the twins ever again.

'I'm sure he will understand,' Bear said, completely failing to engage with my angst. She stretched out her arms and yawned. 'Gosh, I'm sorry, I think I need a sleep.'

I couldn't help but glance at my watch; it wasn't even nine o'clock. 'Another one?' I said, regretting the words as soon as they were out of my mouth.

She looked at me for a moment, then said goodnight and went to her room.

I sent a few Venice photos from my phone to Stella and Edward, neither of whom acknowledged them, and to Rose, who did. I told her how knackered Bear was.

Is she ill?

Rose's stark text put into words the possibility that had been floating in my head for some time.

Maybe, but if she is, she is very keen not to tell me about it.

You should ask. She has come with you, after all. She might be waiting for you to ask.

I resolved to do so the following day, which was initially a replay of the first two days here: breakfast on my own and solo sightseeing. In the afternoon I returned to the palazzo, but this time Bear was waiting for me, keen to go out for coffee, and she looked so much better that questions about her health seemed intrusive and rude.

And that was where we were now, sipping coffee by the canal, testing out superlatives to describe the view, as the light started to fade.

'Delectable.'

'Sumptuous.'

'Delicious.'

'On a more prosaic note,' I said, 'shall I buy more fish to cook tonight?' Last night's sardines had seemed to go down well, better than the pasta, which perhaps she found a bit heavy.

'I think we should go out.'

'Oh great! There's a book of recommended places back at the palazzo.'

'I'd like to go to the Club del Doge,' Bear said, without hesitation.

'The what now?'

'It's the restaurant of the Gritti Palace.'

'Have you been looking at guidebooks this *arvo*, Miss Ursula?'

'It's somewhere I've always wanted to go. It has this terrace over-looking the canal.'

'Surely that's true of pretty much every restaurant here.'

'It's special. Look.' Bear got out her phone and showed me a picture of a stunning restaurant. 'When Murray and I planned our honeymoon to Venice, we were going to stay at the Gritti.'

'Oh! I didn't remember you came here for your honeymoon.'

'We didn't.' Bear's face darkened. 'Once he worked out how much it would cost he persuaded me we should save the money for a deposit on our first house instead.'

'I guess that was practical.'

'Yeah, exactly what a gal wants from her new husband: extreme parsimoniousness. Is that even a word? Tightness. Stinginess. I should have run for the hills right then. It was a warning sign.'

'So remind me where you did go?'

'Perth.' Bear snorted. 'His mother had a holiday home there. Look, I made the best of it, but somewhere, who knows where, there's another Ursula who went to Venice on her honeymoon and lived happily ever after.'

I knew exactly what she meant. Somewhere there was another Kay, who lived in Venice and made a living from her world-renowned photography. 'Ah, that's sad.'

'Yeah, so now I've tugged your heartstrings, let's go to the Gritti.'

'Honestly, I'd love to, it looks beautiful, and I don't want to be a Murray, but I'm slightly worried about my cash flow. I spent five times my entire Venice budget on my flight and our apartment.'

'Ah, don't even think about it, Kay, it's my treat tonight.'

'Ursula, you can't.'

'I can. I want to. In fact, I insist. It would be an absolute pleasure. First, you've been super-patient with me being under the weather, and haven't complained once about having to go sightseeing on your own. Second, you've made me dinner two nights running. Third – look, Kay – if it wasn't for you, I wouldn't be here now. And if I wasn't here now, I might never have got to see Venice at all.'

Her face was glowing with pleasure at being here. That was what this whole thing was about, wasn't it? Doing things we had always

wanted to do. I pushed down into a dark place what her last sentence
might mean, and said, 'Let's go for it, Bear.'

'Yay! I can't wait!'

'Shall I ring them?' I took my phone out.

'No need.'

'Really? It doesn't look the sort of place where you can just rock up.'

'Oh,' Bear said, 'now I need to tell you that I took the liberty of
booking it yesterday.'

'You cheeky monkey!' I laughed. 'What if I had refused to go?'

'I knew you wouldn't. But also, I knew I could cancel the booking
if you turned out to be as much fun as Murray.'

I felt that I had passed some sort of test, which was slightly uncomfortable. But, what the hell. After all those years with Miserly Murray,
perhaps she'd got into the habit of making plans under the radar.

I smiled at her. 'Shall we pretend it's your honeymoon?'

'Are you offering to drag up?'

'Maybe not. I'd make a lousy man. Let's just be two old friends,
having a wonderful time.'

'Yes, that's what I want.'

I saw that there were tears in her eyes. I put my arm round her.

'Are you OK, love?'

'Fine. Bit emosh. Can't believe we're here, and I've finally made it
outside.' She squeezed my hand, and turned her head back to the view.
'I mean, fucking look at it. Glorious.'

'Outstanding.'

'Spectacular.'

'Sensational.'

*

Both done up to the nines, we were shown to our table at the Club del Doge. We hadn't saved up any adjectives for this particular setting, but it would have been pointless anyway, as it was beyond words. We sat out on the terrace, right over the canal. The combined effect of the subtle lights of the restaurant, and the dark inky water, the quiet lapping of the canal below our feet, the gentle swooshing of the occasional gondola gliding past, meant that we were silent for several minutes, drinking it in. It was still warm enough not to need the cardigans that we'd brought with us, middle-aged lady-style. There were other diners out on the terrace, but the tables were far apart, and anyway they were all quiet too; any conversation was undertaken in low tones, so as not to disturb the tranquillity.

'Wow, Bear,' I whispered, forgetting in my astonishment to call her by her proper name. But she didn't seem to notice.

'I'm here,' she whispered back, talking to herself as much as me. 'I'm really here.'

The waiter, treading so softly as to be pretty much silent, and thus a little startling, appeared at my side with bread, water and menus. Despite the candles glittering on every table, it was pretty dark, and I didn't have my reading glasses, but I could see that the prices were something else.

'Ursula, are you sure…'

She held up a hand. 'Not another word. Let's really go for it. Three courses, champagne, the works.'

The waiter re-materialised at the word 'champagne', quietly spoken though it was. Ursula spoke to him in Italian – she was always good at languages, I remembered – and he smiled and disappeared.

'What did you order?' I said.

'I knew they had a Billecart-Salmon champagne, so I asked for that.'

'Is it expensive?' I asked, pointlessly. I'd already seen that one of the starters was thirty-five euros, so we weren't in the ballpark of my usual nine-pound Sainsbury's prosecco.

'Devastatingly so,' she said, and raised her empty glass to me. There was something so reckless, so brittle, about the way she smiled as she said this that I was forced to address the thing I wished with all my heart I could ignore.

'Ursula, this is difficult… can I ask you…?'

'Not yet, darling. Don't ask me anything yet.' She turned to me, her eyes lit by candlelight, a tiny flickering flame dancing in the middle of each pupil. The dreadful answer to my question was on her face, visible as a birthmark. 'Let's have the most wonderful meal together. What shall we eat?'

I forced myself to look at the menu, but the printed words, already tiny, swam in front of my eyes. My heart was beating hard. I chose almost blindly, more or less the first things I could see, and closed the menu the better to focus on Bear. But she didn't want to be focused on. The champagne arrived and she glanced at the label and grinned.

'I had this once before,' she said, 'and it's the nicest thing I ever tasted.'

'I hope it lives up to your memory,' I said, doing my best to match her tone. A breeze ruffled my hair, making me cold, and I pulled my cardigan over my shoulders.

The waiter popped the cork with the perfect amount of drama. After he'd poured, Bear and I clinked our fizzing glasses together.

'To us,' Bear said, 'and our long-lasting friendship.'

'To us,' I repeated, and sipped my champagne. It tasted astonishing, like melted ice cream, but it could have been lemonade for all I cared.

'Like it?' Bear said.

'Delicious.' I managed to make my face match the sentiment. 'When did you have it before?'

'Ah, it was years ago, when Murray took me home to meet his parents after we were engaged. His dad was in the wine trade then, and clearly thought Murray had done well with me as he cracked this little beauty open. I drank too much and got giggly with his mum. I miss them. That's something you never think of with divorce, that you're gonna miss the in-laws. They were always terribly sweet to me.'

'Did they keep in touch after you got divorced?'

'They tried. But it's hard, they live near Perth, it's a huge distance. And they're pretty elderly now. Murray takes Charlie to see them twice a year.'

'I wouldn't mind a chance to miss my mother-in-law. Do you know she's moved in with Richard and taken over my shop?'

'Wow, she's a bit of a gal, isn't she? So, darling. Talking of divorce, how are you feeling about Richard now?'

This wasn't what I wanted to talk about, it seemed all at once completely irrelevant, but it was her call. I mustered my thoughts as best I could. *How did I feel?*

'Well, I suppose I'm a little warmer towards him than I was. I don't know if that's just because we've had some time apart. I was so angry with him when I left, and completely certain that we'd reached the end of the road.'

'And now?'

'Oh, I'm still sure it's the end of the road. But I can think of him without feeling the usual rush of pissed-off emotions. When I bought him that pen in Sydney, I know it sounds stupid, but choosing it and sending it to him, imagining his face when he opened the parcel, made me feel closer to him than I have done for a long time.'

Bear took a long swig of her champagne, and a waiter silently appeared and topped up her glass. She waited till he'd gone, then said, 'I'm sorry to hear that.'

'Sorry to hear I felt closer to him? Well, I know what you mean, but don't worry, I'm not flitting about here, I—'

'No, Kay. I'm sorry you think it's still the end of the road.'

'Oh.' I sat back in my chair. 'What do you mean, exactly?'

'Being on your own is shitty.'

'Well, it can be...'

'It's *shitty*, Kay. Oh, it's fine at the start. Lovely freedom, exciting independence. Then it gets progressively less fine as life happens, crap happens, and then there comes a time when it's not fucking fine at all.'

'Bear...' I reached for her hand but she moved it out of the way and wrapped it round her glass.

'I'm fine,' she said. Her ironic repeat of 'fine' here didn't seem deliberate.

'You're not. Talk to me.'

The waiter set down two exquisite-looking plates of food, as far as I could see, anyway, in the now almost-complete darkness.

'Yum!' Bear said, and started eating immediately.

'Darling, please talk to me.'

'No, thank you,' Bear said. 'I want to eat my food, I want to drink my champagne, I want to gaze at the view, and I'll tell you what I don't want, very much, way more than I want all of those things put together, I don't want your fucking pity, OK?'

Silent tears began streaming down my face. Thank God it was dark. I shovelled in some of my food. I couldn't have told you what it tasted like. It tasted like fucking pity, I suppose.

'So,' Bear said brightly, after a long pause, 'all I'm trying to say is, that with my long experience of divorce and separation, and my current perspective on life, I'm suggesting that you think very carefully before you throw into the mud what is fundamentally a positive and solid relationship.'

I swallowed the food, whatever it was, that was clogging up my mouth, and spoke steadily and carefully, in an attempt to cover up my quavering, tearful voice.

'This is very different from your response when I first told you I'd left Richard. Your initial reaction was amazing.'

'Yeah, I know. There are some good things about ending a long-term relationship, don't get me wrong. And you'd come all that way to see me; I wanted to be supportive.'

'And now?'

'And now I want to be honest.'

'I have always greatly admired your honesty, Bear.'

She laughed. 'How ironic, when I've been so dishonest with you lately. But OK, here's some honesty now. You might not admire this, though. Do you remember when you wrote to me, all those years ago, about being pregnant with Edward?'

'The defining moment of my life – of course I remember! God, I was in such a terrible state. Do you still have my letters from back then?'

'I do – would you like them?'

'Oh, no. Only when you've finished with them.' I bit my lip after I said this. You bloody idiot, Kay. But she didn't react.

'Well, even at the time, I wondered why you handled things the way you did. Why you didn't get an abortion. I know that's a weird impossible hindsight thing to think of now, you'd obviously never be without Edward. But at the time, why didn't you?'

I hadn't thought about this part for so long, I couldn't quite think how to answer. 'I'm not sure. Worried about my mum's reaction, I guess… abortion was a massive thing, we didn't talk about it…'

'Except we did. Rose and I both had abortions, before you got pregnant.'

'Gosh, I didn't realise all the cool girls were doing it.'

'There's some weird subconscious shit going on here if you don't remember that. I'd been in Oz for three years when I had mine. I wrote to you about it.'

'I do remember.' I dredged into the rusty filing cabinet in my brain. 'Weren't you on the pill, and it didn't work?'

'Yes, I had a stomach bug.'

'You were unlucky.'

'So was Rose. Hers was around the same time, first year at university.'

'That's right.' I was the one who'd held Rose's hand afterwards, not that she needed comforting. She knew she'd done the right thing. A one-night stand, a split condom. I hadn't thought about that for years.

'We didn't have the morning-after pill then,' I said. 'What a godsend that would have been.'

'Or if not an abortion, why you didn't have the baby on your own?' Bear said.

'Gosh, it would have been so difficult…'

'Difficult, but not impossible. Lots of girls did it, even in the dark days of the late 1980s.' Bear rested her chin on her hands, and looked at me. 'Do you want to know what I think?'

I didn't, really, but I nodded.

'I'm calling you out on David being your one great love.'

'He *was*, Bear.'

'You let him go pretty easily. Ran back to Richard. Gave yourself a nice origin story about how you and Richard had to get married, and how David was the one who got away. I think you actually believe your own tale, now.'

'Abortion was a big deal, Bear, whatever you remember. So was being a single parent. My family were Catholics.'

'So were mine. So were Rose's. Look, Kay, you're a big girl now. I'm only asking whether you might be using the whole David-and-I-were-parted-by-fate story to explain why things have gone wrong with you and Richard.'

'No, I…'

'Because actually they took a long time to go wrong, didn't they? Twenty-nine years, as you keep reminding me. And who knows what things would have been like with David? He wasn't always that nice to you, remember? He might have turned out to be a bore, or an abuser. You weren't with him long enough to see anything more than his golden light. By leaving him before you really got to know him, you could always think of Richard as second-best.'

'Wow, that's pretty harsh, Bear.' I forced a smile, trying not to show how much her words hurt.

'Honest, Kay. I'm being honest. Yes, life is short. So is it a good idea to throw away a good relationship? One built on more solid foundations than a pretty boy who let you down a third of a century ago? My honest opinion is, make sure – *really* sure – that it's the right thing before you close the door behind you and Richard for good.'

She sounded like Alice. I swallowed down what I wanted to say, and managed, 'Thank you, I will consider what you say very carefully.'

'Bullshit answer,' Bear said immediately, 'but all right. Let's leave that there. Tell me more about Rose's new man.'

When Bear and I had first met in Sydney I'd told her about Graham. I wasn't sure how interested Bear was, as she and Rose weren't all that close anymore, communicating mainly by Christmas cards. But now Bear seemed to be implying that Rose was worthy of attention because she had at last appreciated the value of being coupled-up. Which was unfair to Rose in every way; she hadn't wanted to get divorced in the first place, but she had worked bloody hard to make a single life for herself, and had taken her time finding someone who she cared about.

How well did I know Bear, really? Not the Bear I knew as a teenager, or the one of the letters, but real Bear, Ursula, the grown woman in front of me. No wonder she had stopped writing; when finally there was something big to talk about, she'd stoppered up her mouth.

I managed to make a few comments about Rose and Graham, and Bear seemed interested. Then she said, 'Do you remember when you and Rose came to Oz, before university, and you took a photo of the three of us? All together, with your timer?'

I used to love taking pictures that way. Young people and their selfies would never know the hit-and-miss joy of the camera timer. 'I don't know what happened to that photo. I've a vague feeling that Rose might have it.'

'If she finds it,' Bear said, and she swept a finger under her eyes, 'I wouldn't mind a copy. For Charlie.'

'Sure,' I said, dabbing a finger under my own eyes.

The waiter collected our plates, giving me a chance to get a grip. I discreetly wiped my face with my napkin and watched Bear knocking back her second or third glass of champagne. I wondered how it might affect her, this woman who had barely eaten or drunk anything for days.

'Are you OK?' I whispered, when the waiter had gone. 'Is the alcohol OK for you?'

It was now too dark to see her expression properly. It struck me that perhaps the shrouding night was one of the reasons she'd wanted to come here.

'I distinctly remember that when I put in my order,' Bear said, 'fucking pity was not on it.'

'I'm not—'

'Ah great!' Bear turned her attention to the approaching waiter, a different one I think, though in the gloom they all looked the same. He served us our main courses, and we began to eat.

'This chicken is gorgeous,' Bear said. 'Do you want to try it?'

'No, thanks. Mine's lovely too.' I was pretty sure I'd ordered fish, and it tasted like fish, so that was OK. I felt hollowed out, the sort of hollow that no amount of food or drink or beautiful views could fill.

'What are you going to do about Stella and Edward?' Bear said.

'I don't know. We've always been close. It feels awful to not be speaking. I suppose I just have to wait till they come round.'

'It's all change, isn't it, for all of you?' Bear said. 'I'm surprised about Steady Eddie going silent on you, though. I always picture him plodding along his respectable pathway. Born with a briefcase under his arm, that one.'

I wasn't sure I liked my family being held up to Bear's scrutiny. The waiter topped up our glasses again, and turned the bottle upside down in the bucket, waiter-speak for, 'You need to order another one.'

I decided to tackle the Snowdon-sized mountain between us one more time. 'This is not a pity question,' I said.

Bear laughed humourlessly. 'I'll be the judge of that.'

'You must have had to put up with a lot of people saying the wrong thing,' I said, 'if you're finding so much fault in everything I say.'

'Is that your question?'

'No, my question is, is there anything I can do?'

Bear put her cutlery down. 'That is a sweet thing to ask.'

'I mean it.'

'I know. Thank you. There *is* something. Can I tell you tomorrow?' Her voice was different, less guarded.

Whether or not she hated it, there seemed to be no point pretending how I felt. 'Of course,' I said, and pushed my plate away. 'It's lovely here, the most beautiful restaurant I've ever seen, in the most beautiful place I've ever visited, but I feel just sad sitting here with you.'

'I'm sorry, darling,' Bear said. 'I think I'm currently Sadness personified. Turns out it's contagious.'

We sat separately for a moment, then as if it had been arranged, we reached for each other's hands. We both stared straight ahead, gazing into the blackness of the water.

'It's shitty, isn't it?' Bear said. I could hear her crying, and she could probably hear me crying.

'Yes, it really is,' I managed to say.

A waiter flitted near, then discreetly disappeared. It was ten minutes, maybe more, before we were together enough to tell him just coffee and the bill. We talked of inconsequential things over coffee – her house, my grandchildren, Charlie's exam results.

When we stood up to go, Bear said, 'Oh dear.'

'What is it, darling?'

She kept moving, through the door into the brightly lit restaurant, and when she turned back to look at me I could see, blinking in the unfamiliar light, the immense strain on her face.

'I think I'm too tired to walk back. How silly!' She sank down on a chair at an empty table. A couple of waiters hovered nearby, looking anxious.

With my pitiful Italian, I managed to ask where the nearest vaporetto stop was. It was less than five minutes away, but Bear didn't look able even for that.

A young waitress with big concerned eyes told us there was a gondola station right next to the restaurant.

'Sure,' Bear said when I told her, 'I can manage that.'

I tried to take her arm but she shook me off. 'I have low energy, is all. I'm not an invalid.'

We got out of the restaurant and, thank God, the gondolas were right outside, some so close they were tied to the restaurant's fence.

I'd decided not to bother with a gondola ride when we arrived, after I learned it cost more than one hundred euros. Now it seemed cheap at twice the price to get Bear safely back to our apartment. The gondolier took her hand and helped her in, and she sank down onto the cushions, looking utterly wrung out. I allowed myself to be helped in too, and the gondolier pushed the boat away from the edge with the efficient movement of someone who has done it a thousand times. We made our way along the main canal, which was completely silent, other than the gentle swoosh of the black water next to us.

'You can see the stars,' Bear whispered. She was lying right back on the cushions. I sidled down and joined her in gazing at the night sky from a horizontal position. 'Isn't it beautiful?'

'It really is,' I said. A peaceful feeling descended on me, as if I were in the grey chair under the skylight at Bryn Glas, watching clouds and birds.

'The whole world is so beautiful,' Bear said. 'I wish I had realised that before.'

We turned deftly into a narrow side canal, where it was even darker, and so silent I could hear Bear's gentle breathing next to me.

'We're having a proper Venice experience, aren't we?' I said. 'Staying in a palazzo, eating at a restaurant on the Grand Canal, going in a gondola…'

'This always seemed such a cliché,' she said, 'but actually, at night, it's wonderful. It's so peaceful, almost meditative.'

She was right. I'd seen plenty of tourists sitting in gondolas during the day, holding up their phones to video scenes they were passing, the canal a crowded highway, their gondoliers weaving them round other boats like dodgems. At night, it was very different.

We turned into another side canal and we could hear, in the far distance, a woman's voice, singing opera. It was very faint, but got louder as we glided along. I turned to ask our gondolier, standing behind us, if he knew where it was coming from. But he was looking at his phone, one hand idly guiding the pole in the water, immune to the charms of the Venetian night.

'I know this music,' Bear whispered. 'It's Verdi.'

Neither of us said anymore, not wanting to break the spell. *If I died now*, I thought, *this would be a perfect moment to go*. Out of the corner of my eye I looked at Bear and wondered if she was thinking the same.

As we seemed to be getting nearer to the singing's source, perhaps an opera house, or maybe someone rehearsing, we turned into a different side canal and it began to fade away. I let out my breath, and Bear rested her head on my shoulder.

'That was one of the most perfect minutes of my life,' she said.

Soon – much too soon – we arrived alongside our palazzo. The gondolier helped us up the steps onto dry land, and Bear paid, dismissing my attempts to contribute with the emergency fifty-euro note tucked in my phone case. She looked more energetic than in the restaurant, and climbed the steps to our apartment in, if not a sprightly manner, at least not like an elderly person.

'Do you feel less knackered?' I asked her as we made our way into our gorgeous kitchen.

'A bit. I ate too much, or maybe had too much champagne. I have to take it easier. Can't overdo it.'

We stood in the centre of the room, looking at each other.

'Ursula…' I said.

'Darling, I'm feeling better but I'm still super-tired. I'm going to bed. Thank you for a wonderful evening, and for a brilliant trip to Venice.'

'We've still got two more days!' I said.

She put her arms round me and pulled me into a tight hug. It was the first time she had held me so close since we met in Sydney, and I could feel how thin she was, how many layers she must be wearing to keep looking well.

'Night, darling,' she said, and went out.

I sat in the kitchen for a while, thinking, then I put out the lights and went to bed. Bear had the bedroom on the main floor, and mine was on the floor above, up an exquisite but impractical winding staircase. By the time I got up there, I felt utterly low-energy myself. My last thought, as I got into bed, was that I must make sure that Bear didn't overdo it the next day. We would go to St Mark's Square, as planned, but then I'd encourage her to come back and rest. My eyes were so heavy, I couldn't let myself think about anything difficult now. I put it all out of my head and focused on the dark, sliding, starry sky that had been our canopy in the gondola. In moments, I was asleep.

Letter written on 23 May 1996

Dearest Bear,

I'm writing to you, a prisoner on day release, from a gorgeous little cottage in the North Welsh mountains. I am blissfully, ecstatically alone. No one is following me to the toilet, no one's singing 'Old Mac-Bloody-Donald' at five in the morning, there are no nappies to change, and no meals to make, other than my own.

You know how Alice's always hated me? So I can't account for this, but she came round the other day when I was up to my elbows in screaming children, and she helped out. She was surprisingly effective at getting Stella to eat her lunch. When Richard got home she had a right old go at him, telling him I was exhausted and how had he not noticed? Of course, he hadn't, being pretty exhausted himself with the shops (he has two now, did I tell you?), and also he's not the world's most observant husband. She said she had never seen such massive eye-bags and that I looked about 102 years old. <u>Cheers, Alice.</u> She told me she'd look after the children for five days while I went off to this cottage which belongs to her friend. She wrote down the address, gave me a code for the key box and pretty much pushed me out of the door.

When I got here, I made the bed, fell into it, and slept for twelve hours straight. I've been a parent for seven years, and I am <u>knackered</u>, Bear.

I love it here. I'd miss my kids eventually, but I wouldn't mind staying here a while longer. Maybe a year or two. I have to go back tomorrow, alas and alack, but I do feel properly rested for the first time since Edward was born.

I loved hearing about your marathon success. You are an Olympian in my eyes. Especially when getting up the stairs is sometimes as much exercise as I can manage without a sit-down.

Till next time.

Miss you.

Always, Kay

Chapter 17

Kay

The sun was streaming through the windows when I woke, and I knew straight away that something was different. It's weird, isn't it, how you know instinctively if you're alone or if there's someone else in the house. Or luxury palazzo, in this case. It felt empty. Stalling, to prolong the inevitable moment when I'd have to get up and face whatever had happened, I looked at my watch. Gone ten. When had I ever slept so late?

I did a little of the one-nostril-at-a-time yoga breathing, which seemed to be the thing I turned to at moments of crisis. Then I padded downstairs in bare feet, averting my eyes from Bear's bedroom door. When I opened the door to the kitchen, I prayed that she would be sitting at the table sipping coffee. But the room was empty. On the table were several sheets of lined A4, ripped from a pad, plus some of the fancy cream-and-marbled paper I'd bought yesterday. My name was written on the top page in Bear's familiar handwriting. From the length of it, this was not so much a note as a manifesto.

I took another couple of one-sided breaths, then sat down and unfolded the lined paper.

'Dearest Kay, this is my last letter to you,' it began, and I started crying.

3 June 2018

Dearest Kay,

This is my last letter to you. I could see last night that you knew. Forgive me for running out on you. Firstly, I just don't want to talk about it. Not with you, not with anyone. Murray says I'm in denial, though who gives a toss what he says? He's stressed about having to step up and be Charlie's only parent. But maybe I am in denial. I had to laugh last night when you said you'd always admired my honesty. I've found that when it comes to this fucking disease, honesty doesn't work for me.

Secondly, I can't explain how exhausted I am, right down to my bones. Chemo took it out of me completely last year, and even now, though I'm taking nothing more invasive than painkillers and steroids, I'm always very low on energy. I find stairs particularly knackering, I nearly lost it when we first got here and saw that spiral staircase, so thanks for taking the upstairs room. At home, everything I need's been moved downstairs. My bedroom's in the living room, and the only one who goes upstairs now is Charlie. For all I know, he's got a crack den up there.

You might be wondering how I managed to get out this morning. First, I have bad days and good days. Or increasingly, bad days and bearable days. Today is bearable. Second, I woke really early, before four. I don't get my best sleeps at night anymore. I am, as you saw, very into daytime naps. And third, these steroids are amazing, like a big short blast of cocaine. I don't take them very often because of the shitty side effects, but they are good for when I need a boost.

I thought I could manage this trip without them, that the adrenaline would see me through, but I need to be at home now, where everything is set up for me. I have a ton of help there, from people who know I don't want to talk about it. And I can sleep whenever I want, without having to explain why. That's not a dig at you. It's hard to explain to anyone; I've really struggled with how much to tell Charlie. He knows I'm ill, but not how ill.

Kay, I'm sorry I stopped writing to you. I stopped because I didn't have anything to say. I didn't want to talk about my illness, didn't want to be treated differently by you, or anyone. The pity, the head-on-the-side – those things make me feel physically sick. I didn't want to talk about my illness, but there wasn't anything else going on. I haven't worked in a year, sorry I lied to you about that, but I imagine you guessed. When I said I couldn't see you at the weekend because of a school sports competition, I was actually asleep for most of the time. I haven't done anything much in the last year except sleep, have my blood markers monitored and go to the gym for sitting-down exercises. My life has narrowed, apart from this crazy trip to Italy with you, so thank you for that.

I couldn't believe it when you turned up in Oz. I was furious with Murray, because I thought he must have told you. When I found out he hadn't, that you'd shown up because you were worried I hadn't written (and, let's be honest – I know how you love my honesty! – because you'd left Richard and were looking for a mission), I thought you'd guess straight away. And I didn't want that. So I put on a good show, I think. After I saw you that first night, when I could barely eat, I felt so ill, there were a few days when I couldn't get out of bed till after lunch. I thought it was the end. But then I felt better, and I thought, this will be the last time I can ever do something crazy.

I'm not going to be able to visit Hoylake with you. I only have one flight left in me, so I'm using it to go home. I'm full of energy now, false medicated energy, but energy nonetheless. I'm sorry I'm wasting it on getting to the airport. But I need to be home. That's not to say I regret coming here, it was the most brilliant thing that has happened in this last lousy shitty year. Eating that amazing meal in that amazing restaurant was an experience I thought I wouldn't be able to have, but now I can cross it off my list. That's massive, and you should be proud of yourself for being there at the right time.

The A4 paper ran out here, and Bear had gone onto the creamy marbled notepaper. I paused too, to make coffee, and collect myself. I did more breathing while I waited for the machine to brew. In, two, three, four. Out, two, three, four. I sat back at the table and took a sip of coffee. *OK. Here we go.* I picked up the next page.

You asked if there was anything you could do for me. Yes. Four things. Another list. Brace yourself, it's very bossy.

First, something to add to your list: please do something with your photography. I'm pretty sure you're not going to be a famous photographer now, as you thought you might when you were fifteen. But I'd like to think you were doing something with your long-repressed creative side. You're talented and I remember how much you used to love taking pictures.

Two, make absolutely sure you're doing the right thing with Richard. I know you think you are, but please check. I've obviously been thinking a lot about 'what it's all about, Alfie', ha ha, and I want you to make really sure that ending your marriage is the right thing, you're not just doing it because you're bored. Sorry for being blunt. Divorce is brutal. I don't think I ever recovered from Murray leaving me. I'd have given anything not to have gone through this last year alone.

Three, tell Edward the truth about his dad. He deserves to know for sure, and maybe David deserves to be given a second chance to meet his son. Even though he didn't behave well at the time. Look at me, being all about the forgiveness. Ugh.

Finally. I'd like a little part of me to be forever in Hoylake. In the water at West Kirby beach. I'll get Murray to send some ashes to you – there's no need to come out to Oz for the funeral, it'll be family only, anyway. Will you do that? Maybe with Rose?

Phew, I didn't think this would take so long to write. More than two hours! My hand hurts. It's nearly six in the morning now, and the sun is coming up over the canal. It's so gorgeous here.

Miss you.

Always, Bear

Reading our usual sign-off, minus the 'till next time', pushed me over the edge. For ten minutes, maybe more, I couldn't do anything but cry; jagged, breathless, out-of-control weeping I hadn't done since my mum died, and before that, never. If someone had come in with a gun and ordered me to stop weeping on pain of death I couldn't have. I was absolutely depleted when it had passed. Wrung out.

I wiped my face and went into Bear's room. It was as empty as if she had never been here, the shutters open and the bed neatly made.

Amazing to think she'd managed to get out and find a water taxi, get herself to the airport. *Bad days and bearable days.* I thought perhaps I should go to the airport, see if she was still there. But no; I'd be doing that for me, not her. She had a limited amount of time left and she was using it as she wanted. Who was I to get in the way of that?

This was becoming a habit: being upset and alone in foreign countries. I stood at Bear's window and looked, as she might have done this morning before she left, at the Grand Canal, shimmering in the sun. Burning it into her memory, knowing she would never see it again. I thought of all the years the canal had been there, the heartache and happiness it had seen. This is a fleeting moment, I told myself. What was that George Harrison album I had in my teens? *All Things Must Pass.*

In other words, *Man up, Kay!*

I showered, dressed, and went out, to the café Bear and I had sat in yesterday. I ordered a cappuccino, got out my pen and the last sheet of creamy notepaper. My letter to Bear was as short as hers was long.

3 June 2018

Dearest Bear,

Thank you for your letter. I promise I will do everything on your list. Go well, my darling.

Till next time.

Miss you. Really.

Always, Kay

I put it in an envelope, and turned my attention to the view. For five minutes, I told myself, I am going to sit here, and think about nothing but the scenery, the sun on my shoulders, and the smell of my coffee. I am alive, and I am here. I observed the dots of people on the tiny San Giorgio Maggiore island opposite, and followed the passage of several small boats and water taxis, and in this way, managed not to think about anything sad for a short, blissful time.

My coffee finished, I took out my Venice guidebook. Denial and distraction, those were my plans for today. I went everywhere, walking till I could walk no longer, then caught a vaporetto, then walked some more. There wasn't a Tintoretto I didn't see. I visited the Lido, and the island of Burano, and walked round the original Jewish ghetto, stopping there for a lunch of chopped liver on rye bread. I went round the Guggenheim, and four churches, lighting a candle in each one. I threaded my way through some glamorous shopping areas, and in a designer boutique I bought Stella a beautiful bag in butter-soft brown leather. I browsed the market under the Rialto Bridge, and chose some blue, fur-lined gloves for Rose.

All day, I thought about Richard. It was easier than thinking about Bear, though occasionally snippets from last night or from the letter would surface against my will. In particular, how terrible Bear said she felt when Murray left her. That really hit home. I'd thought Richard wouldn't feel it so badly, as we were, really, already living quite separate lives. But Bear knocked that certainty out of me, and now all I could focus on was the pain he must be feeling, the pain I had inflicted on him. I felt so raw, I seemed to have lost a layer of skin, so that whenever I thought about how Richard might be feeling, I flinched with the pain myself.

I thought of Alice, calling me destructive; Bear insisting I make absolutely sure; Edward giving me the silent treatment; Stella upset and angry, telling me I was selfish. Perhaps I *had* really fucked up. I could no longer access so clearly the feelings I'd had when I walked out. I'd been so sure. Now, a few short weeks later, it didn't seem quite so cut and dried. Why *couldn't* I be married and still do the things I wanted, like everyone had said? Was I right to turn so many people's lives upside down, to hurt Rich so badly, for some mirage of freedom?

Life was short. Bear was proof of that. Did I want to spend whatever time I had left in a state of upheaval, living alone, not quite part of something? Had I made a massive mistake? Bear's words ricocheted in my head. My reasons for leaving seemed far away right now. Richard had been a good husband, hadn't he? Didn't I owe it to him, to myself – heck, to everyone – to make sure I had done the right thing?

I noticed a woman looking at me oddly, and realised I wasn't sure how long I'd been standing here, in a smart clothing store, holding a pair of trousers I didn't remember picking up. They were soft velvet, a reddish-bronze colour, and I was gripping them with the tight clutch of a crazy person. Possibly more to the point, and more the reason for the funny look, tears were rolling down my face. I put the trousers down hastily and hurried out of the shop. I walked back to the palazzo, sat on my bed, and looked at my phone for a long time before I tapped in Richard's number.

It wasn't just his number, of course; it was listed on my phone, under 'Home', but there was no way I was going to look that up. The symbolism would finish me off. It was our landline, because Richard had never owned a mobile phone. He'd been pretty resistant to me getting one, too, for unspecified reasons, and in the end I'd given money to Edward and asked him to buy one for me, so I could justify it to Richard as a gift. Thinking about this, the subterfuge, the worry of what he'd say, the arguments that followed, gave me a moment's pause. But somehow I had already pressed the call button, made the connection, and the phone was ringing at his end, at our house. *His* house.

I prayed Alice wouldn't pick up. Then I heard him say, 'Hello?'

My stomach knotted at the sound of his voice, as familiar to me as my own, yet also now exotic and unknowable. Did he sound anxious? Upset? Harassed?

As well as mobile phones, he was also resistant to any fancy landline add-ons such as call recognition, so until I spoke, he wouldn't know it was me. I could hang up, and give this all more thought. But then I said, 'Hi, Richard.'

'Jesus! Kay!'

'Sorry, it's, er, sorry if this is…'

'It's great to hear from you!'

'It is?' I hadn't expected that.

'Yes! Where are you? You sound far away. I hope this isn't costing you a fortune.'

I laughed. It was so adorably Richard that his first concern should be my phone bill.

'It's fine. A drop in the ocean compared to how much everything else costs here. I'm in Venice.'

'Wow, Venice! Is it amazing?'

'Absolutely breathtaking. How's everything there, Richard?'

'Good. The shops are running smoothly. Anthony's back, thankfully, and he's the manager at Quiller Queen now, with Mum his assistant. They're a tour de force, those two.'

'That's great.' A familiar dull ache of boredom started to wash over me, and I shook my head to try and dislodge it. Was this an awful mistake? Phoning him, wondering if I should be thinking of trying again – Bear was wrong, surely.

'Mum's enjoying staying here, and feeding me. It's good for her to look after someone, you know what she's like.'

I did, indeed. How she would love taking command of my kitchen, putting all the herbs into alphabetical order, clearing away the appliances she had so often told me were a waste of space. 'A clear counter, Kay, is the first step to becoming a decent cook.' Alice had been in constant despair that I had never taken even that first step.

'Sorry about all that Anthony business, Kay,' Richard said abruptly.

'Oh gosh, that's…'

'Think I lost my mind! I'm awfully embarrassed now. Thank goodness he was able to forgive me.'

'Yes, that's really good…'

'Are *you* all right, Kay? Enjoying your travels? Feeling happier?'

'I'm not sure, Richard. That's why I'm phoning, you see…' I took a breath. I'd started this, so I ought to finish. Mistake or not, I was knee-deep in now. I'd tell him that his original idea for me to take a few weeks' break and then for us try again, was a good one. Perhaps he would consider couples' counselling. But before I could say anything, he started speaking again, and I remembered that he never was very good at listening.

'I hope you *are* happy, Kay, because I wanted to tell you that I am so, so sorry I made it so difficult for you to leave.'

'Well, that's all…'

'It was a shock, you see.'

'Of course it was. I…'

'But you were completely right.'

'I was? But I...'

'We had ground to a halt. Our marriage, I mean. I didn't even see it. You were so wise, Kay. I would never have seen it, either, if you hadn't said anything.'

'Oh! That's great that you feel better about things...'

'More than better. I'm a new man, thanks to you. You were right! Rip the sticking plaster off in one go. Ouch, super painful, but then you start to realise, hey, it's not so bad. I'm healing every day.'

What was this? *Healing?* This wasn't the man I had known.

'You sound in a good place, Richard,' I said. 'That's amazing. As for me...'

'I'm in a terrific place. Kay, I hope you won't mind if I tell you that I've met someone. It's very early days, of course, we've only been out a couple of times, but it makes me remember our courting days, you and me before the babies, that lovely feeling of wanting to be with someone every second of the day. Oh listen to me, I'm babbling.'

It became more difficult, all at once, to hear what he was saying. Something about what a gift I'd given him... his freedom... who would have thought that at nearly sixty he'd find... so compatible... did I want to collect my things from the house... I must be needing them... ready to clear that space and move on... she'd persuaded him to get a mobile phone... he'd have to give me the number... she'd been under his nose all this time, would never have realised if... she was so good for him... she was making him take a week off to go to Paris.

The mention of Paris snapped me out of it.

'I'm so sorry, Richard, I seem to have lost the connection, I can't hear you. I'm going to hang up now and try you later.' I pressed 'end' and turned off the phone.

*

I sat for a while, facing the window. The palazzo had glamorous long white lacy curtains, the sort that feature in adverts for expensive perfumes. A light breeze made them quiver slightly, casting dappled shadows onto the floor. I felt as unsubstantial, as ephemeral, as those shadows. I pressed my thumbs into my forehead to make sure I was still here. Just about.

He'd said, *If you ever decide you'd like to try again, I will be here.* But that promise wasn't worth the Basildon Bond paper that it was written on.

Time passed, and the shadows deepened, until they weren't dappled any longer, and then there weren't any more shadows. I got up, and went out into the dark, walked to the Gritti, and asked for a table for one. I'm not sure exactly what I would have done had they been full, perhaps thrown some kind of fit, but thankfully they had a space for me, a few tables along from where Bear and I had sat last night. I ordered food, and the same champagne we'd had, and stared out onto the waters of the Grand Canal and I felt… I don't know what I felt. I didn't even know if I was feeling *something* rather than nothing.

I couldn't feel, but I could think. I could think about how close I had come to going back. If Richard had said, *How lovely to hear from you, I miss you, shall we try again?* I would have said yes. I didn't know how to work out what I really wanted. When I'd left, I thought I'd really wanted to go. *Wanted* was too feeble a term for it; I'd *needed* to go, to jump into the unknown, to be my own person. But today I'd thought that maybe I'd had enough freedom. I suppose Bear had made me feel that; her words, and also her sadness at being alone at the end of her life. Being rootless in a foreign country probably wasn't helping. I'd expected the door back into my old life would still be open, but surprise! It wasn't. I'd thought Richard would stand still, wait for me, but he hadn't even stood still for a month. Surely that was impossibly soon to have met someone and shrugged off the heft of a long marriage. I turned my phone back on, ignored his missed calls, and wrote the message I should have sent days ago.

Sparkle, I'm sorry for being an idiot. I love you.

Stella was usually a good communicator, responding promptly to texts and phone messages. Of course, things weren't usual between us, and she hadn't replied to my last few travelogue texts, so I didn't expect anything. I sipped the champagne, which was even more delicious than last night, like drinking soft, creamy velvet.

My phone buzzing made me jump.

I'm sorry too, Mum, and I love you.

It was the best message I'd ever been sent. My mood soared upwards. All at once, I couldn't wait to get back to England, and put things right with Stella. I turned off the phone, and finished my starter. The delicious flavours of shallots, garlic, wine and salt filled my mouth. All at once, it seemed that I could taste absolutely everything.

So now what?

You go through life, you make choices, they lead to other choices, and before you know it, you're in a place you wouldn't have started from. It was time to make new decisions, and change the story.

My main course arrived, and I focused my attention on that, and it was exquisite. When I'd eaten enough, I poured my third glass of champagne, and made a silent toast to Bear. She was probably still in the air, somewhere over India, perhaps, heading towards her stopover in Singapore. Napping, no doubt.

To Bear, I said in my head, *may the rest of your life be pity-free.* I took another sip. *To Mum. I miss you.* I let a tear fall, as it always would whenever I thought about Mum. And then, finally, *To Richard. Thank you for setting me free.*

I left half the bottle of champagne, perhaps because it was the most un-Richard gesture I could think of making. Let the staff enjoy it. I paid the enormous bill without whimpering, and left a large tip too.

No gondola tonight. I walked back through the dark strange city, feeling at home here, and at home in my skin for the first time in a long time. Tomorrow, I needed to make plans for what I was going to do with the rest of my life.

Chapter 18

Stella

It was rather a nice party, all fairy lights and flickering tealights in glass jars. Though Claire, the birthday girl, didn't have many guests – probably no more than twenty-five – it seemed buzzy and crowded in her small, neat flat. I wished I was one of the guests, but alas, Gabby and I, in matching aprons and matching black moods, were at the far end of the living room, behind two trestle tables loaded with huge pots of curry. If you saw us from a distance you might think we looked like a cohesive team, but come a little closer and you'd see how stiff and formal we were with each other.

'You do the veggie and the rice, I'll do the others,' Gabby said for the third time. We were struggling to come up with new things to say to each other. I think I was finding the whole thing slightly less awkward than Gabby. As Newland said the other night, it was easier to recover if you were the injured party rather than the injurer. You could tell he'd done a year of Law before switching to English Lit.

What it wouldn't have occurred to him to say – he was far too modest – was that it was also easier to get over Threesome-gate now I'd met such a gorgeous chap. Not that anything had happened between us, of course. It was way too soon after Theo for another relationship, or even a one-night stand. After the ACODs meeting, I went back to Newland's place and told him the whole story. We stayed up till four in the morning talking about our lives. When I told him I'd wanted to stay out so as to avoid having to see Theo, he kindly offered me his bed, and he slept on the sofa.

In the morning I woke to a lot of furious texts from Theo. Feeling bolshie, I replied that I'd spent the night with someone else. Well, it was technically true. Theo had the sheer brass nerve to call me a slag in his reply, and I blocked his number. It was difficult not to compare him unfavourably to Newland, who was so lovely and kind, and those eyes…

'Did you hear that?' Gabby said, bursting into my daydream. 'They've announced that the food is ready.'

'Right. Action stations,' I said, standing up straight. Someone turned down the music and partygoers started to make their way towards us. Twenty-five people seemed a lot when they all arrived at once, but I focused on serving them quickly and tidily, remembering to smile and chat, and giving clear ingredient information when asked.

We'd served about three-quarters of the guests when I became aware that Gabby was having an altercation with a woman who'd already collected her food.

'This tastes nothing like green shrimp curry,' the woman was saying. 'It doesn't have any coconut milk in it, for a start.'

'You know about Sri Lankan food, do you?' Gabby said, in a foolishly confrontational tone, because I was fairly sure the woman was Sri Lankan.

'I lived there for the first twenty years of my life,' the woman said. 'You know, you shouldn't describe your food as Sri Lankan if you've just read about it in cookery books. It's cultural appropriation.'

'Actually,' Gabby said, raising her voice, 'I have an aunt by marriage who's Sri Lankan, who taught me everything she knows.'

'Really?' the woman said, looking like she didn't believe a word.

'Yes, really.' Gabby folded her arms.

The woman glanced over at me, and I looked away, embarrassed, because I knew that Gabby's entire knowledge of Sri Lankan cuisine came from a week's holiday there a couple of years ago.

'Everything all right, Hinni?' Claire, the host, came over, looking worried.

'Yes thanks,' the woman said politely.

Claire glanced worriedly at Gabby, who was still looking rather aggressive.

'Your friend was asking about the food,' Gabby said.

'Oh, do you like it?' Claire turned to Hinni. 'I thought of you when I booked Yummi Scrummi. Taste of home!'

'That was very thoughtful of you, Claire,' Hinni said. No one wanted to upset the host.

Claire smiled, and wandered off. Hinni shook her head, and Gabby smirked at her until she too walked away.

We finished serving, and started to clear up. I'd just about unclenched my buttocks from their tight knot of excruciating mortification, the words 'cultural appropriation' ringing in my ears, when Gabby hissed at me, 'You could have backed me up there.'

'You told me yourself you forgot to add the coconut milk.'

'You are part of this business, Stella. You can't fade into the background when things get difficult.'

'Don't you think she was right, though?' I said. 'We don't know how to make the food properly authentic.'

'Hardly anyone knows what it should taste like. That was just unlucky. And I'm a bloody good cook.'

'That's not what I'm talking about. Your imaginary aunt can't take the place of genuine knowledge.'

'Oh, fuck off.'

'No,' I said, and I undid my apron, '*you* fuck off.' I hadn't planned to say this at all, but God, it felt good.

'What?'

'I'm done. I'm through.' I balled up the apron and threw it on the floor. 'I don't know how I thought I could carry on working with you when I can't trust you. I can't trust you to take care with the recipes. I can't trust you not to lie to customers about your phoney credentials. I can't even trust you not to screw my boyfriend.'

'Fine!' Gabby picked up my apron and flung it over the top of the table, where it landed at the feet of a group of guests, who looked at us in confusion. 'Good fucking riddance. I was an idiot to let Theo talk me into taking you on. Said you'd been all pathetic about getting a job and leaving your mummy. Should have trusted my gut, knew as soon as I met you that you were a waste of space.'

I walked away without looking back, pushing past groups of people talking and dancing.

'I'll pack up here by myself then, shall I!' Gabby yelled after me.

Outside the house I stood in the darkness for a moment, trying to catch my breath. I didn't know exactly where I was; Gabby had driven us in her van. I got to the end of the road and saw a bus stop. I sat at it and called Newland. I'd only known him for three days, but he was already the person I most wanted to talk to.

He picked up straight away. 'Hey, are you OK?'

'I've had a row with Gabby and I've left the business,' I said, as calmly as I could. 'I'm going to go back to the house, pack, and go to my dad's till I work out what to do.'

'Wow, all I've done today is decide between ham or cheese sandwiches.'

A woman sitting further along the seat clucked her tongue sympathetically. I cradled the phone tighter and whispered, 'I'm sorry. You've only just met me, I don't want to pull you into my drama.'

'Don't be sorry,' Newland said. 'This is a good decision for you.'

'It is?'

'Obviously I don't know Gabby, but from what you said, she really undermines you. I couldn't understand why you went back to work with her after she'd been so horrible.'

'Oh, Lan. I don't know either, anymore. I didn't want her to feel she'd beaten me, or something. And it was Theo's fault, to be honest, not hers.'

'It was both their faults. Where are you? I'll come and get you.'

'Don't worry, I'm at a bus stop somewhere.'

'They're only every forty minutes this time of night, love,' the clucking woman said, 'and we've not long missed one.'

I turned to her. 'Where are we, exactly?'

'Hutton Road, Shenfield.'

I repeated this to Lan and he said, 'Near Brentwood? I know it.'

'Tell him we're opposite the library,' the woman said.

I did so, and he laughed. 'I know exactly where that is, I was at a Young Essex Librarians meeting there the other week. I'll be there in twenty minutes. Look out for a pink car.'

'Why's your car pink?'

'Tell you later.'

'Lan, I...' in an emotional state, I nearly said, 'I love you'! And we hadn't even kissed yet! I said goodbye hastily and hung up.

'He seems like a lovely fella,' the clucking lady said.

'He is,' I said.

By the time Lan turned up in his crazy little Noddy car, me and clucking Linda were mates. I'd promised her Lan would drop her at her house in Harold Wood. He took this in his stride, and the three of us chatted animatedly all the way there, about Linda's job as a hospital orderly, about my abrupt resignation from Gabby's business, and about how young you had to be to qualify for membership in the Young Essex Librarian's group (under forty, incredibly). We also uncovered the truth of the pink car: it had belonged to his cousin, and when she went travelling she'd offered it to him at too good a price to worry about the colour.

'I thought I might spray it,' he said, 'but I've become quite fond of it.'

'I like a fella who's confident in his masculinity,' Linda said approvingly.

Lan took her right to her door and she shook his hand as she got out. 'You're an old-school gent, you are,' she said. Then in a stage whisper to me, she said, 'Definitely a keeper,' and winked.

With Linda gone from the back seat, I felt a bit less relaxed, though not in a bad way. There was a definite charge between us. The truth is, that when that funny little pink Nissan pulled up at the bus stop and I saw him looking out for me, I realised that I did love him, even though it was obviously far too early to know that, let alone say it.

'That was so good of you, Lan, to rescue all the waifs and strays of Shenfield. You're a complete star.'

'So are you, Stella. Your name means "star". I looked it up today in an idle moment.'

'You did? That's so sweet.' I thought of Gabby, and shuddered. 'Are you sure I'm not a waste of space?'

'You what?'

'Nothing. I'm being silly. Anyway, I'm really grateful.'

'For what? It's no hardship to be nice to you. You're a star and, apparently, I'm a keeper.'

At the house there was no sign of Gabby's van, and I prayed we could get out of there before she returned. I let us in, and paused outside the living room. That night I'd come back here and stood silently in this same spot – the moment before everything changed – I felt as if I no longer belonged here. I should have trusted that instinct. It amazed me now that just a few days ago I'd thought I could carry on as if nothing had happened.

We went into the kitchen to get some of my utensils. I was startled to see Piet sitting at the table.

'Hi, Piet. I thought you were working tonight.' He had a lot of odd jobs, including bar work.

'Hello, Stella and Newland. They didn't need me after all, I am afraid.'

'Oh, I'm sorry.'

'It was my own fault, I was late. But I must admit, I am starting to worry a little about money.' He got up and filled the kettle. 'What about you? Has the party ended?'

'I came back early. Actually, I've left the business.'

'That is a sensible decision.'

'It is?'

'Gabby is not a team player.'

Newland laughed. 'You can say that again.'

'What will you do now?' Piet asked. 'Tea?'

'Go on then. Quick one. I'm moving out now. My rent's paid till the end of the month. I'll stay at Dad's for a while, I guess. Then, I don't know.' I knew I had to go, but the thought of going back yet again to my family home, with no job and no money, filled me with anxiety. It couldn't be like before. It mustn't be.

Piet clattered about with cups and milk. 'I do not feel so comfortable living here with Gabby myself. She is too unpredictable. She was very rude to Carol the other morning.'

'Carol? From the ACODs meeting?' I blinked in surprise.

'She and I had a night of highly enjoyable casual sex. Gabby was then extremely unpleasant to Carol, who is certainly *not* old enough to be my mother.'

'No... OK,' I said, resolutely avoiding Lan's eye, though I could see that he was grinning hugely. I was sure Carol was at least twenty-five years older than Piet. You had to admire his appetite for random sexual encounters. He was so unashamed, so *European* about sex. It was kind of refreshing.

'If you get any ideas about work or living arrangements please keep me on the loop.'

'*In* the loop. I will, Piet.'

'Because I suspect,' and he smiled at Lan, 'you will be wanting to live back in this area, and I too should like to stay here. I must mention that I enjoy sharing a house with you.'

Lan and I took our tea upstairs. I found that I was smiling. What was it about Piet? He always made me feel better. I promised myself that I would come back to this town; I really liked it, and I had a potential housemate here. Going back to Dad's this time would just be a stopgap, I was determined about that. I could feel that Gabby's words about me being a waste of space were sliding off my shoulders, not embedding into my brain as they would have done last year, when I felt so unconfident.

How do you feel?

Surprisingly fine, thanks Bettina.

With Lan helping me pack my stuff into bin bags it was all very quick – I didn't have much stuff – but even so, we hadn't quite finished when I heard Gabby come in. There was a lot of door-slamming and swearing, and after ten minutes I heard Piet run upstairs and go into his room, presumably to get away from Gabby in full flow.

As we crept downstairs with my things, there was a knock on the front door. I opened it, and Theo was standing there.

'Oh,' he said.

'Oh, indeed,' I said. 'I guess you're here to comfort poor Gabby?'

'Er… sorry. I didn't know you were here.' He glanced at Newland. It was probably shallow of me to notice that he was gratifyingly taller and more handsome than Theo, but what the hell. I was owed this moment.

'Newland, this is Theo.'

'Hello, Theo,' Newland said, his face inscrutable. 'I've heard all about you.'

'Oh,' Theo said. He started to hold out his hand, then changed his mind. The kitchen door banged open behind us.

'Get the fuck in here, Theo,' Gabby's voice came wafting menacingly down the hall.

'Well, er, I'd better…'

'Good luck, Theo.' I stood aside to let him in, and he scuttled off down the hall. Quietly, I added, 'You're going to need it.'

*

I'd have liked to stay forever in the comfortable passenger seat of Lan's pink car, chatting about the weirdness of the day and listening to the steadying normality of his. But in little more than an hour, we pulled up outside my dad's.

'I'll help you in with your bags,' he said.

'Thank you. It's so late, I'm sure no one will be up. In fact, it's so late, you ought to stay over.'

'I can easily drive home.'

'Lan, it's one in the morning. Anyway, I want you to stay. You can meet my dad, and my grandma.'

I realised this was the sort of thing one said to a proper boyfriend, and I blushed; luckily it was dark so he couldn't see. And also luckily, he said, 'That would be great.'

I unlocked the door quietly, but to my astonishment my dad appeared in the hall, and threw his arms round me. 'Stella! What a lovely surprise!'

Dad's appearance was a lovely surprise too – he'd had a shave, washed his hair, and was smartly dressed. 'Sorry it's so late, Dad. Why are you up?'

'I've, er, been out,' Dad said, looking shifty.

'You have?! Where?'

'Oh, nowhere much, really.' He let me go, and looked behind me to Newland standing a respectful distance away. 'Do you need me to pay the driver?'

'No, Dad, this is Newfriend. I mean, Newland, my, er, new friend.'

'Pleased to meet you, Mr Bright.' He and Dad shook hands politely.

'Yes, indeed, yes.' Dad glanced at me quizzically. 'Did you drive Stella here? Very kind. I was about to have a nightcap. Care to join me, you two? Newland? Is that from Edith Wharton, by any chance?' He put his arm round Newland's shoulder and led him towards the kitchen, leaving me to follow on behind, grinning to myself.

Chapter 19

Kay

My last full day in Venice got off to a shaky start, with a phone call to Imogen. She told me her sons had received an offer on the cottage from a wealthy parent wanting it for his student daughter and her friend; he was willing to pay £900 a month.

'My sons are thinking about it, chérie, because although they don't really want undergraduates in, the money is, it seems, too good to turn down.' Imogen's voice was quavery. 'They know the price of everything, my sons, and the value of nothing.'

'I understand, Imo,' I said.

'If you think you can match it, dear, I'm sure I could get them to offer it to you instead.'

I knew I couldn't match it, far less outbid it. In truth, I couldn't even afford the original rent she'd mentioned. My savings would disappear in no time. With many regrets, I waved Bryn Glas goodbye.

I was saying goodbye a lot, lately: Bear, Richard, Bryn Glas. So with today's disappointment out of the way, I wandered round Venice with, as usual, no particular aim in mind, taking photos on my phone. Most were utter clichés, but I wanted to see if I could get my eye back in. Once again, I really missed my proper camera. Why the hell had I left it behind, as if it were no more important than an old jumper?

In the afternoon I found myself – no idea how – back at the stationery shop where I'd bought my sage-green suede notebook. I went in and chose a bigger, more expensive one for Richard, in a delicate silver-grey, and another pile of the creamy notepaper. I took my purchases to the café outside, ordered a cappuccino, and uncapped my favourite Waterman fountain pen.

Dear Richard,

I hope you like this notebook. The stationery shop here is full of them, and I wish I could bring hundreds home. They're too fancy for most of the shops, but they might do well in His Nibs.

I'm so pleased you're happy. It's wonderful that we can both move on, and be glad for each other. I want to thank you for respecting me enough to take me at my word. I didn't realise how serious I was about us, about our separation, until I heard it from you.

I will really miss you. Twenty-nine years is a triumph, not a failure. There's a lot of great things to take from it, not least our wonderful children. What's that thing, don't cry because it's over, smile because it happened. Naff maybe, but it's how I feel.

I stopped writing because I became aware of someone standing at my elbow. I turned to say, 'No, grazie,' to the waiter, assuming he was about to offer me more coffee, but it wasn't a waiter. It was a tall man with dark hair, about my age, perhaps a little younger, wearing a light-grey suit and a blue scarf. He said something in Italian, and I looked up at him, puzzled.

'English?' he said.

'Yes.'

He smiled. 'You dropped this.' He handed me the lid of my fountain pen.

'Oh! Thank you.' I hadn't noticed, it must have rolled off the table. I turned back to my letter, but he didn't move away. I looked up at him again, a 'what?' expression on my face.

'It is a rare thing, nowadays, to see someone writing with an ink pen,' he said. 'You look like a woman from a Henry James novel.'

'Er, thanks,' I said. Was it a compliment, even? I couldn't remember if Henry James was the one who had frumpy buttoned-up women, or was that Thomas Hardy?

'I am also sitting alone,' the man went on, 'and wondered if you cared to sit together.'

A pick-up! My first for a while. Decades, probably.

'No, thank you,' I said, smiling to show no hard feelings. I gestured at my letter. 'I'm busy.'

'I will say goodbye, then. I just wanted to tell you that I was dining at the Gritti last night with my father, and I noticed you, sitting alone, perfectly self-contained. You sometimes smiled to yourself, and I was very intrigued. My father told me to speak to you, but I'm afraid I was too shy. Anyway. I wish you a lovely stay in Venice.' He began to walk away.

Self-contained? Intrigued? Shy?

'Actually,' I said, 'please do sit for a moment.'

'Thank you,' he said, and did so.

Well, it wouldn't be Venice without a little romantic frisson, right? I needed something to tell Rose when I got back that wasn't about our friend's terminal illness or my almost-not-quite attempt to return to Richard.

'I'm Kay,' I said.

'K, as in the alphabetic letter?'

'K-a-y, short for Kathleen.'

'Kathleen is a lovely name. I am Luca.'

'Your English is excellent, Luca,' I said.

The waiter brought over his coffee, and he thanked him. 'I studied in Oxford.'

'Er, what college did you go to?' My flirty chatter was extremely rusty.

'Keble.'

He raised his cup to his lips, and I stole a glance. Mid-to-late forties? The suit was expensive. White shirt, no tie, one button open at the neck, cashmere scarf. Little too much Sacha Distel about the tan and the swept-back hair, but undoubtedly good-looking.

'May I ask, to whom are you writing?'

I glanced down at the letter. It was hopefully at the wrong angle for him to read it. 'My husband,' I said.

'Ah, I see. A lucky man.'

'My ex-husband. We are separated,' I said. It felt fine to say it out loud. Good, in fact.

'Then maybe I am the lucky man.'

I laughed. 'Your lines are very cheesy, Luca. Have you not polished them since you were at Oxford?'

He smiled. Hell, it was a nice smile. 'No, you are quite right. I am stuck in the nineties, I am afraid. But I do feel lucky, sitting here, talking to a beautiful lady who writes letters with a fountain pen and orders champagne just for herself.'

'I don't usually,' I said. 'The champagne, I mean. I do of course always use a fountain pen.'

'Of course.'

We smiled at each other. 'How much longer do you have in Venice?' he said.

'I'm going home tomorrow.' Of course, I didn't really have a home, but it was too complicated to explain.

'To your husband?'

'No, but back to England. Work out what I'm going to do next.'

'Do you have plans, then, for this, your last night?'

I looked into his eyes, which were crinkled at the side. I was very fond of eye crinkles. 'Yes,' I said, surprising both of us, 'I am going to have dinner with you.'

He looked at me, amused. 'That is very good to hear.' He called the waiter over, and paid for both our coffees, ignoring my offer of cash. We agreed to meet outside the Gritti at 8 p.m., but he said he would take me somewhere else, 'somewhere Venetians go'. I honestly thought he might kiss my hand when he stood up to leave, but clearly even for him it was a cliché too far, and he simply said, 'Arrivederci, Kathleen. See you tonight.'

When he'd gone, I texted Rose, my fingers skidding awkwardly across the letters.

Henry James heroine – good or bad?

She must have already been looking at her phone because the reply came back straight away:

Venice obvs having fine literary effect on you. Generally good. Spirited, bookish, complex, independent. Why? Are you writing an essay?

Haha no. Talking of literary matters, how are things with Graham?

I was careful to always make sure I asked about him.

Good thanks. Wonderful. Stayed in bed till 10 this morning, I was late for work!

TMI, as Stella would say.

But good for Rose. Sex with someone new – it must be weird. But maybe sex with someone new, someone handsome, someone with a lovely smile, might be pretty nice. *Someone hot*, another of Stella's expressions. Someone with no strings attached, in a foreign country one was about to leave… well. I wish I hadn't left my fan in the apartment as it seemed rather warm, all of a sudden.

I finished my letter to Richard, rather more breezily than I would have if I hadn't been interrupted. Then I walked back to the palazzo, stopping off at the little Castello post office to send the letter and silver-grey notebook to Richard, and my last letter to Bear.

Back at the apartment, I had a bath and did all the woman-going-on-a-date things I hadn't done for years. Well, I'd done them, but not all at once, with a date mindset. I washed my hair, shaved my legs and pits, and had a little trim of the old lady-garden, not that I was planning to sleep with him, obviously not, he was clearly a café-lothario, but just in case…

In case what? I heard Rose say. *In case there was a freak accident that involved your pants coming off in public?*

OK, Rose, I said to myself, *in case I do decide to sleep with him.*

There's nothing wrong with casual sex, Rose replied. *As long as you have a...*

Oh God, of course I didn't have a condom. Why would I? I'd been married for a hundred years. Richard and I used the cap, and funnily enough, that wasn't one of the things I'd packed in my rucksack. Anyway, a cap wouldn't be good with a strange man, you had to have a condom to protect yourself against all his likely diseases. Ugh, maybe I wouldn't sleep with him after all. In my mind he was morphing into a tacky medallion-man type with a hairy chest. Was I really going on a date with a man I didn't know, just because he said I looked like a woman out of Henry James?

Apparently I was, as I put on my not-sensible bra, and my hitherto-unused fancy lipstick. I suspected it was too red for me but what the hell. My nicest dress was the one from the Sydney op shop, which I'd already worn the last two evenings to the Gritti. I sniffed it but it didn't seem too bad, so I sprayed some perfume on it, and put it on.

All the way to the Gritti I told myself he probably wouldn't even show up. But I knew he would. I was early, but he was already there, and we smiled hugely at each other and kissed on both cheeks.

'You look lovely,' he said. 'I didn't think you'd come.'

He took me to a restaurant I wouldn't ever have found on my own. It was up one alley and down another and sideways and heaven knows where it was. And even if I had found it, I wouldn't have gone in, as it looked completely undistinguished from the outside. But it was crowded with lively, noisy Italians of all ages, and it had a terrific buzz. How different it was from the awed hush at the Gritti, the whispering couples. Here, everyone was laughing and shouting, and most of the people sounded as if they were flirting wildly with each other, though given my lack of Italian they could as easily have been discussing high finance.

Luca and I squeezed in to a little table at the back, and talked non-stop. He told me about his life; unusually for someone living in Venice, he had grown up here. He and his friends used to earn money in the school holidays by helping lost tourists find their way. He'd lived in the UK and many other places in Europe, been married twice, and had a grown-up daughter in Canada. He worked for a non-profit organisation that had something to do with energy and the environment, but he was on a six-month sabbatical to look after his father who was ill. During that time he needed to find residential care for him, of which there wasn't much in Venice. He wanted to move them both to Milan, but his father was resisting.

I told him about my kids, and I relaxed so much, I even told him about my grandkids. He couldn't believe I was a grandmother, did a genuine double-take. 'I was a child bride,' I told him, but I could see he was trying to work out my age, too polite to ask outright. I realised I didn't care if it put him off. I was very much in a 'this is who I am, take it or leave it' kind of mood. I told him about my dashed photography plans too – Lord knows how we got onto that.

'So you were going to work in a studio?'

'Yes, a great place right in the centre of London. They did weddings but also some celebrity and fashion work. Terrific opportunity.'

'Then you got pregnant?'

I nodded. 'Told you I was young. Up the duff, crashed out of my degree, never finished it, couldn't take up the apprenticeship. Got married instead.'

'I can guess "up the duff", though it is a new phrase to me,' he said. 'Life is a strange and complicated journey that does not follow a straight path.'

'How profound, Luca!'

'So what did you do instead? What are your special skills?'

'Gosh, I'm not sure I have any. I've worked in a shop for twenty-five years. I guess I'm good at being cheerful with customers. Is that a skill?'

'Certainly not all in the service industries have it.'

'True. Oh, and I'm pretty good at DIY.' Luca looked puzzled, so I continued, 'I was the one who did all the repairs around the house. Put up shelves, did plumbing and electrical things, you know.'

'Not your husband?'

'Well, he wasn't at home much. And I'm more handy. You should see me with a screwdriver.'

'I would like to see that,' Luca said, in so sexy a voice that I hid my flustered face in my glass, and drank a big slurp of wine.

'And where is your accent from, Kathleen? I have been trying to work it out.'

'I'm from Hoylake, near Liverpool.'

'Ah, it is a Beatles accent!'

'Well, it's a bit grander than theirs. In fact, the most famous celebrity from Hoylake was John Lennon's first wife, Cynthia. She was his bit of posh. My mum knew her cousin quite well.'

'I am in the presence of greatness.'

'Yes, I'm only three degrees of separation from John Lennon.'

'I have always loved the Beatles,' Luca said.

'Everyone loves them.'

When Rose and I were at university in London, we dined out on being from Liverpool. Rose even developed a convincing little routine about being the secret love child of Paul and his first serious girlfriend, Dot. Thinking about that made me smile, and Luca raised his glass to me.

'To Cynthia Lennon, and Kathleen – beautiful women from Hoylake.' He pronounced it 'Oh-lick', which was weirdly sexy.

As we ate delicious home-made pasta we discussed our marriages. I told him a little about Richard and me, and how tiring it was to ricochet from feeling that things were fine when I first left, to feeling lost and afraid.

'Divorce is like a death,' Luca said, pouring more wine. 'You have to grieve it in a similar way.'

He'd been through it twice, so I supposed he knew what he was talking about.

We had the most exquisite chocolate tart I'd ever eaten, and more wine, and coffee. He put his hand over the bill so I couldn't see it.

'I would like to pay,' I said.

'I'm embarrassed for you to see how little it is,' he said, 'and I asked you to dinner, so I must pay.'

'Actually, if you remember, I asked you.'

He handed the waiter his card and said, 'I don't remember.'

'Look here, Luca,' I said, my words slurring slightly. 'I'm not going to have sex with you just because you paid for my dinner.'

'I should think not,' he said, 'after such a cheap dinner.'

We both laughed, and I thought, *Actually, maybe I will sleep with you…* but the thought of it terrified as much as excited me.

He let me leave the tip, and we weaved out into the cool dark night. He put his arm round my shoulders, which felt very natural, and we strolled in some direction or other. With Venice, who knew where we were going? It wasn't as if it mattered.

'What would you like to do?' he asked.

'I guess, a walk along the Grand Canal towards my apartment, and then I should go to bed. I have an early flight.'

'Where are you staying?'

'Castello. In the Palazzo Luce Dorata.'

'Ah, that's a beautiful building. "Golden light".'

'Is that what it means?' I had assumed it was someone's name. 'Well, everything in Venice is beautiful,' I said.

He stopped walking and turned to face me. 'You're quite right,' he said, and before I could register it, his soft lips were on mine. Immediately I worried that I wouldn't be able to remember how to do this. I hadn't kissed anyone except Richard for three decades, and it wasn't as if he and I had spent a lot of time lately locked in a snog. Did you move your lips, and how open should your mouth be, or…

These thoughts evaporated in a millisecond because I stopped thinking and kissed him back. It turned out that I had muscle memories that meant that my rusty lips knew what to do without needing me to get involved.

The kiss went on for a long time and after we broke apart, we stood looking at each other. My breathing felt a bit odd.

He smiled. 'Yes, *everything* in Venice is beautiful.'

'You old corn-master,' I said.

'What is a corn-master?'

'A polite term I just made up for a bullshitter.'

'I'm not bullshitting, Kathleen. You are lovely.'

'Well, thanks.' The way he pronounced Kathleen – a name I'd never liked – with a hard 't' in the middle instead of 'th', did something interesting to my insides. For the record, I was not beautiful. I was usually a five or six at best. But I had put in a good effort with my hair and make-up tonight, so call it a seven. And it was dark, and we were drunk. So maybe an eight. And he thought he was on a promise, so let's call it a nine.

We continued walking along the canal, and he pointed out various interesting buildings, and told me stories about the bridges we walked across. I wondered if he would kiss me again, but he didn't.

'Do you like being back here?' I asked.

'It's a wonderful place to live, and also a terrible place. Sometimes both at the same time.'

'Why terrible?'

'Ah, it's a playground for tourists, you know. It is not for the people who live here. We are pushed aside, our needs are always secondary.'

As a tourist myself, I felt I should apologise, but it seemed a bit trite. I said, 'Is that why you want to move to Milan?'

'For my father's sake, we need to move. But I am sad about it. It is terrible here, but of all the places I have lived, I love it here the best.'

We reached the palazzo, and my heart, which had been thuddy all evening, ratcheted up a level. I could feel it reverberating all the way up to my throat.

'Christ, I'm scared,' I blurted.

Luca took his arm from my shoulder and looked at me, his face gentle. 'Why, Kay?'

'Because I want to ask you in but I'm terrified.'

'Am I as frightening as all that?'

'Hell, yes. Well, not you personally, you're very nice, it's just…'

It's just, the last time I slept with someone who wasn't Richard, it was David Endevane in 1988. It's just, I am a middle-aged woman with sagging boobs and a flabby stomach, and my neck isn't as firm as it once was and even my feet have callouses on them, there isn't any part of my body that could reasonably be called pretty, actually my forearms aren't too bad but I guess their interest won't hold you for long. It's just, I don't know how to do sex that isn't familiar married sex. It's just, we need a condom but I don't have one and I would die rather than ask if you have one, even though I always told Stella that she must insist that her boyfriend use one. It's just, I'm not sure how old you think I am. It's just, what if you're a cad, or a thief, or into some stupid kink that will make me laugh?

'I'm not long separated,' I said, instead. 'It feels like it might all be a bit soon.'

'That's completely fine, Kathleen,' he said. 'I had a lovely evening with you. I would hate for things to be spoiled by you being uncomfortable.' He kissed me on the cheek, and stepped back. 'I tuoi occhi sono come il mare.'

'That sounds lovely, but for all I know, you might be telling me I have pasta sauce on my face.'

'I enjoy speaking English very much, but sometimes it is too English. Italian is the language of romance. I told you that your eyes were like the sea.'

'Murky and polluted?'

He laughed. 'Have a safe flight tomorrow. It was wonderful to meet you.' He turned and began to walk away, as he had done in the café. If this was a clever psychological technique, it was highly effective.

'Luca,' I called, 'hang on a minute.'

He stopped, and waited. 'Yes, Kay?'

'Please do come in,' I said.

Well, why the fuck not. Life is short.

Isn't it, Bear?

Chapter 20

Stella

I got up late, and staggered down to the kitchen to discover Gran was whipping up a world-class Sunday brunch.

'Ooh that smells lovely, Gran. I'm starving.'

She gave me one of her looks. 'And what time did you arrive here last night, young woman?'

'Late. Dad was still up. Has Newland appeared yet?'

'Can I assume that Newland is the slumbering form on the sofa, who almost gave me a coronary when I went in to tidy up?'

'Oops!'

'I must say, he has nice manners. My small scream roused him, and he said, "Hello, you must be Stella's grandmother," introduced himself, then went back to sleep.'

I laughed. 'He is extremely polite.'

'Is he your new beau?'

'We've only just met. I really like him, but I'm not going to rush into anything so soon after Theo.'

'Very wise. Well, do let him know that there are pancakes and bacon awaiting him.'

I went into the living room and stood quietly for a moment, looking down at the sleeping Newland. He looked utterly gorgeous, all mussed brown hair and long dark lashes, one hand under his cheek. I said his name, and his eyes flickered open. He gave me a beaming smile. 'Hello, Star.'

I fought back an urge to tell him how handsome he was, and mumbled, 'Hello, Keeper,' instead.

He wriggled into a sitting position, still covered by the duvet, but I caught a glimpse of shoulder and realised – be still my heart – that he wasn't wearing a top. What else wasn't he wearing? All at once it seemed silly to keep him at a chaste arms' length, silly and self-defeating. I leaned down to kiss him, lost my nerve halfway, and bizarrely blew a puff of air onto his face instead.

'What was that?' he said.

'You looked hot,' I said, blushing like a peony. 'Not *hot*-hot, I meant warm. Though you looked *hot*-hot as well.' *Oh God! Shut up, Stella!*

He grinned. 'Well, I'm much cooler now, thanks.'

'Um, Gran's doing us a big breakfast.' I went over to the door.

He said, 'I'll be there in a minute.'

I turned back briefly and caught a glimpse of him throwing off the duvet. I don't think he saw that I saw, but now I knew exactly what he wasn't wearing, and had to take a moment once I was outside the door, to stand quietly and wait for the heat to leave my face.

A few minutes later he appeared in the kitchen fully dressed, and won Gran over instantly with his keen appetite for her cooking.

'These are the best pancakes I've ever had,' he said, eating a fourth one.

'Shall I tell you the secret ingredient?' she said. 'You'll have to promise never to reveal it.'

'I swear on my life,' Newland said.

'How come you've never told me, Gran?' I said.

'You never asked, dear heart.'

'Nor did he!'

Gran ignored me. To Newland, she whispered loudly, 'Mayonnaise.'

'I'd never have guessed,' he said.

'Makes them fluffy,' Gran said with satisfaction.

Seeing as she was in a confiding mood, I said, 'Where was Dad last night? He was out very late.'

Gran frowned, and indicated with the minutest shift of her eyebrows that cooking secrets were one thing, but it wasn't appropriate to discuss family matters in front of Newland when she didn't know him from Adam, nice as he seemed. My grandmother's semaphore was impressive enough to get her a job at MI5.

Mind you, Newland was no slouch at decoding signals either. 'I can go into the living room while you talk,' he said.

'No!' I said, surprising myself with my own vehemence. *I know people sometimes push you around.* 'I want to be able to decide when and what I talk about, and in front of whom.'

'Liking your use of "whom" there,' Newland said.

'She had a decent education, you know,' Gran said, who never minded me speaking up for myself. 'Even if it was in a state comprehensive.'

'So come on, Gran, spill.'

My grandmother picked delicately at her own small plate of pancakes. 'I believe he was out with a lady, and that is all I know.'

'No way!' I said. 'Isn't it incredibly, insanely, way too soon for that?'

Gran put down her fork. 'You'll know how much I hate saying this, Stella,' she said, 'because you're aware of my feelings about amateur psychology. And indeed, professional psychology. But I think it's good for your father to do something positive, take a bit of control, in a world which seems somewhat out of control.'

'Wow, Gran, you sound very modern when you talk like that.'

'Oh dear, do I? How ghastly.'

'When my father left, four years ago,' Newland said, 'my mother emptied every cupboard and drawer in the house, cleaned absolutely everything. It took her weeks to do the whole house like that. She went off sick from work and spent her time cleaning. Like you say, it's something about what you can control. It's good to let them get on with it, I think. Who knows how they're feeling?'

Gran and I looked at Newland.

'You're a thoughtful young fellow, aren't you?' Gran said.

'He's a librarian,' I said.

'A libertarian, did you say?'

I laughed.

Newland pushed his empty plate away. 'That was outstanding,' he said, 'and us libertarians know our carbohydrates.'

'Gran used to cook for the royal family,' I said, continuing my new series of delivering awkward despatches about people's jobs.

'You must have some amazing stories,' Newland said.

'I signed a non-disclosure agreement,' Gran replied, haughtily.

'Gran, talking of cooking,' I said, 'I've quit the Sri Lankan business.'

'I'm glad to hear it.'

'You are?'

'I couldn't understand why you and your friend with the irritating name, Tabby, was it?'

'Gabby.'

'Why you and Gabby were offering Sri Lankan food. You didn't have any connection to it, after all. It lacked authenticity.'

I stared at her. 'Wow, that's exactly what I've been thinking.'

'Having tasted your food,' she continued, 'I was forced to conclude that you both made up for your lack of knowledge with a surfeit of coriander leaves.'

'I've left my house as well,' I said, thinking I might as well tell her everything in one go. 'Can I stay here for a bit?'

'Of course,' Gran said. 'I'll need someone to drive me to the supermarket this afternoon, in that case.'

'I will,' Newland said.

'There's a good chap.'

Once Newland had gone off with Gran, I went up to my room, intending to do some clearing out. I didn't want Newland to see how thoroughly my childhood was preserved here; it wasn't even as if I was particularly sentimental. I started putting aside old clothes and toys for the charity shop, and it was going well till I pulled out a box full of photos from my cupboard. I'll have a quick look, I told myself, and an hour later I was still sitting on the floor going through them. I couldn't believe how many there were of Nita and me. Before university she'd been my closest friend, and I couldn't remember now why we'd drifted apart. She came to see me a few times when I was in my first year, but she seemed uncomfortable and out of place, and I didn't always have time to catch up with her when I came back to see Mum and Dad.

I heard the front door slam, and went downstairs to find Newland and Gran back from the shops, chatting like old friends.

In the evening Gran cooked us shepherd's pie, and Dad and Newland chatted about working with the 'great British public', as Newland called them, or 'the great unwashed' as Dad preferred. How well Newland slotted in to my life; in one day he was more comfortable with my family than Theo had managed in years.

After dinner, I suggested to him that we go out for a drink. 'I can show you the pub where I had my first legal drink, and the one where I had my first underage drink, and the one where I threw up in someone's handbag.'

'That's one hell of a guided tour,' Newland said. 'Bring it on.'

'Stella, how revolting!' Gran said. 'Go on, you two. Have fun.'

I thought about taking Newland's arm as we walked down the road, but bottled it.

'They seem nice,' he said.

'Mmm. They're both on quite weird form at the moment. You did very well.'

'They must have been used to seeing you with Theo, so even though I'm not officially your boyfriend it must be odd to see you with another guy.'

I shivered deliciously at the word 'boyfriend'.

'Actually, Theo didn't visit me here that often,' I said. 'When I moved back after university, he only came once or twice.' As I steered Newland into the Three Horseshoes it occurred to me that perhaps Theo was so distant back then because he was already seeing other people. Maybe even Gabby. It was easy to name my feeling at that: hurt pride. Nothing more fatal.

'Wow, a proper old-school boozer,' Newland said admiringly. 'Horse brasses and everything. I'm guessing this is your first-underage-drink venue.'

'Good catch.'

The pub was exactly the same as when sixteen-year-old me and Nita had taken advantage of the lax bar staff, who barely glanced at our fake IDs. Same red carpet, same plates and unfunny framed cartoons filling the walls, and what looked exactly like the same old blokes sitting at the bar. I ordered two halves of the local beer and we clinked glasses.

'It's so weird you being here,' I said. 'My teenage world and my current world are colliding.'

Newland grinned and took a sip of his drink. 'This is pretty nice beer. I'll have to take you round my own memory lane in St Albans some time.'

'Do you go back much?'

'Well, Mum's still there. Not as often as I should. It's all a bit painful.'

'She still not over the divorce?'

'They're not even divorced yet.'

'How come?'

'When Dad left, Mum was so angry she refused to agree to a divorce. He has to wait till they've been separated for five years and it's only been four.'

'Blimey. That's quite a grudge.'

'To be fair, it was a pretty messy break-up. He saved up twenty-five years of irritation and gave it to her all in one go. Oh, and then he went off with her friend.'

'Jesus. I'm starting to think I got off lightly with my parents' split.'

'It's like that woman running the group said. Martine. As adults, we're expected to quickly get over our parents separating, be grown-up and supportive. But that means we don't really always address how we feel about it, as their children.'

'Do you think I haven't addressed how I feel?'

'I don't think you can have done yet, Stella. No one could have, it's still so recent. I think you're pushing your feelings away, to protect yourself. I get it totally, I did the same for months.'

'I did have a horrible row with my mum. And a cry at the group.'

'Those are good starts.'

'Ready for the next pub?'

'Sure,' he said, and chugged down the last of his beer.

We went out into the evening, and to my delight, he took my hand. I said, 'I told Gabby that she did me a favour by sleeping with Theo.'

'How so?'

'It showed what he was really like, and it meant I got out of a bad relationship.' I squeezed his hand. In my head, I added, *And I met you.*

'You don't have to rush into anything with me,' Newland said, as if he had heard the unspoken words. 'I'm really happy to wait.'

I didn't reply, but steered him down an alleyway.

'I'm liking these little byways you're taking me on,' Newland said. 'Wow, there's a pub hidden down here!'

'This is where I had my first legal drink,' I said, and pushed open the door to the King's Head.

'This is more like it,' Newland said, looking round the modern pub, with its wooden tables and floor. 'Let's stay here. I don't need to see the pub where you threw up into someone's handbag.'

As I'd expected, Nita was behind the bar, serving a group of young men. God, she worked hard, and always had; her aunt's café during the day, her parents' chip shop in the early evening, and the King's Head at night.

'Hey, Stella! Good to see you.'

'Newland, this is Nita, my oldest friend.'

Newland shook Nita's hand, and she winked at me. 'A gentleman, huh? Nice change of pace for you.'

'Shurrup,' I said, as if we were still at school. 'I'm showing him our old hangouts.'

'Lucky you, a grand tour of all the dumps,' Nita said. 'Mind you, some of us still hang out here.'

Newland handed me a twenty for the drinks, said, 'Excuse me,' and disappeared to the loo. Nita gave his departing back an appraising look. 'Niiiiice. Very nice. What happened to that one from university?'

'I'm not seeing Theo anymore. Newland and I are just friends,' I said. 'And I've moved out of my house-share.'

'God, your life continues to be about a million per cent more interesting than mine.'

'If I buy you a drink, Ni, would you be able to sit with us? I want to ask you something.'

'Yeah, sure. Give me five minutes. I'll serve these people and come over.'

I sat at a table and minutes later Newland joined me. 'Beer then wine, you'll be fine,' I said, handing him his glass. 'Nita's joining us in a minute.'

'Are you plotting something?'

'Yes. I've realised what I want to do, but it will only work if Nita is in. I need someone like her as a business partner: hard-working and trustworthy. And I've got to think carefully about the food – it has to be something I have a connection to.'

'None of that foreign muck, eh?' Newland said, in a 'Brits abroad' accent.

I gave him a shove. 'I want to do something I can justify. To myself and others.'

'Fish and chips?'

'Nita's probably had enough fish and chips to last her whole life.'

'Pies? But pie stalls are ten-a-penny.'

'That sounds like a nursery rhyme,' I said. 'Didn't Simple Simon try and buy a pie for ten pennies?'

'I believe it was only one penny, but he didn't even have that, poor sod.' Newland drank some wine, then said, 'What about the sort of food your gran makes? Classic British dishes? They're not exactly fashionable, but everyone likes them.'

I sat up. 'Shepherd's pie!'

'Yes, that sort of thing. Hotpot, whatever that is.'

'Newland, you're a genius.'

'I am, I suppose. It's quite the burden.'

Nita came over, clutching a glass. 'Thanks for the wine, guys.' She sat down. 'Stell, have your parents really split? I heard it from my dad, but you know, he is such a gossip and he doesn't always get it right.'

I nodded. 'I'm afraid they have.'

'God, I'm sorry. So weird. I always thought they were a very together couple.' Nita shook her head. 'Must have hit you hard. How have you been coping?'

'This nice handsome librarian's been helping,' I said. I must be more drunk than I thought.

'Not all librarians are nice,' he said. 'I used to work with this woman who made all the children cry during Rhyme Time.'

'I like the sound of her,' Nita said. She turned to me, and in a loud whisper, she said, 'He seems great. Worth a shag, surely.'

Newland started laughing.

'Nita!' I said. 'I'm still getting over Theo turning out to be a rat.'

'So, shagging's not on the table then?' Nita said.

All three of us looked at the table.

'Yeah, don't shag on this table,' Nita said. 'I'm the one who'll have to clean it.'

'Can we stop talking about shagging for a moment,' I said, 'so I can run my idea past you?'

'I'm all ears,' Nita said. 'I'm praying it has something to do with me getting out of this godforsaken town.'

'Yeah. I'd like to take you to a different godforsaken town.'

'The answer's yes, in that case. Now tell me what the question is.'

It was almost midnight by the time Newland and I got back to Dad's. I was rather drunk, and extremely happy. We sat at the kitchen table and ate toast.

'That was a really productive evening,' Newland said.

'I know, I can't believe how far we got. I need to talk to Gran tomorrow. It was because of her I went into catering in the first place. I did hospitality at university but I didn't get such a good degree. My other granny got very ill just before my finals, well, I can't use her as an excuse, but my mind was elsewhere.' I must have been more than rather drunk if I was about to tell him this next bit. 'And I messed up. Only got a third. As bad as not having a degree at all.'

I stared at my plate. It was the first time I'd told anyone, other than my family and prospective employers, that I'd got a third. I got that creeping, prickly feeling running up and down my back, which I always got whenever I thought about my finals, how all my job applications were rejected automatically, because of that useless little three.

But Newland didn't turn a hair. 'Degrees are overrated,' he said. 'You're smart, talented and interesting. I can't wait to see what you do next.'

I looked up at him, into his sparkling eyes, and for a moment, I saw myself as he was seeing me. I liked, very much, what I saw.

Chapter 21

Kay

'You're an utter barbarian, you know that?' Rose took the cup firmly out of my hand.

'You have mentioned it once or twice.'

'*I'll* make it. In a pot. Go and sit down.' Rose pushed me towards a chair. 'You are officially excused from tea-making duties from now till the end of time.'

I sat down and grinned as Rose tipped out my bag-and-milk-in-the-cup-all-together teas, and boiled a fresh kettle.

'Honestly,' she muttered, 'I go upstairs for five minutes, and when I get back you're putting on a horror show.'

'I'm just doing it badly so you end up doing it,' I said.

'Yeah. Tim used to do that with every domestic chore.'

'I bet Graham doesn't.'

'Too right.' Rose winked at me. 'So, what are you going to do while I'm out today?'

'First, contact Imogen and put in my offer for renting the cottage. Thanks to Graham.'

'He's brilliant, isn't he?'

'I'd never have thought of Airbnb, and his barn idea is genius. I can only hope that Imogen's family thinks so too. I also need to sort out a bank account. It's beyond embarrassing that I still only have a joint account with Richard. Oh, and there's the small matter of trying to reconnect with my children.' There was one other thing I needed to do, but it wasn't something I could tell her about.

'That'll be a solid day's work.' Rose put the teapot on the table and sat down. 'I emailed Bear this morning.'

'Ah, I'm glad.'

'Do you think she's still looking at her email?'

'I don't know. She never used it much at the best of times.' I remembered Bear's expression, gazing up at the stars in the gondola. It made me think of my mum's face, the last time I saw her conscious in that awful hospital. *I'm ready.* 'I don't think she can have very much longer.'

'Jesus,' Rose said. She pressed her lips tightly together. The news of Bear's illness had hit Rose hard, even though they weren't particularly close anymore. I too was still reeling from it, and from all the other uncertainty in my life. Thank God Rose had been there to take me in when I got back from Venice, and to help me process my strange wanderings. As on Running Away Day, there was no question of who to ring when I arrived back in Heathrow. But this time, she picked up.

That first evening in Winchester, I poured it all out about Bear, and Rose and I cried together. When we'd got past that, I cried some more, this time about what I was going to do with my life. Rose – and Graham, too, a wonderful man – listened patiently, and helped me piece together something that looked like a plan, something that might just be a way of making my life resemble more closely the ever-expanding list in my diary. While Rose boosted me up, Graham was practical, writing down timescales and making estimates of how much I'd need to live on each month, and how long my savings could last.

'You excited?' Rose said.

'About the tea we're waiting an absurd amount of time for?'

'About the possibilities for your new life. Though this tea will be amazing.' She lifted the lid and gave it a stir. 'Patience is a virtue.'

'Excited, yes, and also terrified and anxious.'

'All the good emotions. I hope Richard will be able to move on soon, as well.' Rose stood up to get the milk out of the fridge.

'He's already got a girlfriend.' It was only now I realised I'd forgotten to tell her this, because I'd forgotten about it myself. I wondered what the significance of that was.

'You're kidding!' Rose whirled round so hard I feared she'd get whiplash. 'How do you know? When did you find out? Who? When? How? I have so many questions.'

'I rang him from Venice and he told me.'

'You rang him from Venice? Why?' Rose sat down and fixed me with a suspicious eye.

'I, er, well. I sort of briefly changed my mind and wanted to see if he'd take me back.'

Rose gave me a 'WTF' look.

'After everything I said. I know. Lost my nerve. Dark night of the soul. It was straight after Bear bailed out and went back home.'

'I guess you were feeling pretty vulnerable,' Rose said. She poured the tea.

'Yes, I think so. I suppose I felt adrift, and he seemed safe. It was an existential crisis. I still feel adrift, and there will probably be other crises, but I'm OK for now.'

'So what did he say when you offered to try again?'

'Thank the Lord it didn't get that far. He talked over me, so I didn't get to say my piece, and he said his instead.'

Rose laughed. 'He was always one of those men who says, "who wants to go first, OK I will".'

'I'm now extremely grateful to him that he shut the door behind me so decisively.'

'So who is she?'

'I don't know, but whoever she is, she's already got him to buy a mobile phone and take her to Paris.'

'Wow, that's *so* annoying!'

'I know.' I laughed, surprising myself. 'But maybe he had got in a rut too, with me, and needed someone new to spring him out of it.'

'You're being very mature,' Rose said.

'I won't be mature when I find out she's a twenty-five-year-old dolly bird. But honestly, I'm relieved. It clarifies things. That option is no longer open, and I don't want it to be.'

'Men sure move on quickly, don't they? Tim certainly did,' Rose said, sipping her tea. 'Mmm, this is what tea should taste like.'

'I don't know about all men. I think Richard certainly isn't designed to be on his own.'

'And what about you?'

'I don't know if I'm any good at being alone because I haven't been single since 1980.' I picked up my cup. 'Tastes exactly the same as the way I make it.'

'Jeez, who the hell did you go out with in 1980? Weren't we like, thirteen?'

'Do you remember that boy Steven in the year above us?'

'Vaguely.' Rose put her hand to her head. 'I'm getting ice-skating…'

'Well remembered! We went to the ice rink. Everyone thought he was the best boyfriend ever, because he took me somewhere more fancy than the Wimpy.'

'What happened to him?' Rose said.

'No idea. But after that I had one boyfriend after another.'

'Serial monogamy, they call it now.'

'Back then they called it something a lot ruder.'

'So come on, Kay, tell me more about your travels. The non-sad-Bear parts, I mean. You must have had some fun as well.'

'As a matter of fact…'

'Kay Bright! Is that a dirty smile? What, what, what?'

'As a matter of fact, in Venice I had sex with someone.'

Rose, who had just taken a sip of tea, looked as if she was going to have to spit it out. She stared at me for several seconds, her mouth stoppered with liquid, till she was able to swallow it down. 'Good God, Kay, for a minute there I thought you said you'd had sex with someone!'

I put on an insouciant expression.

'I can't believe you haven't told me this already! Waffling on about Richard's girlfriend, who cares about that?' She slapped her hand on the table. 'Speak, damn you!'

'It was really nice,' I said.

'REALLY NICE? I am going to tip the rest of this pot of tea over your head, young Kay. I need details and I need them *now*. First off, is calling the person you slept with "someone" a deliberate ambiguity? Should I assume "someone" was a woman?'

'I'm afraid not. Apologies for my boring adherence to gender norms.'

Rose waved her hand graciously.

'He picked me up in a café by the Grand Canal.'

'Romantic setting. He was handsome, I presume.'

I swiped through the photos on my phone and showed her one I'd taken of Luca the morning after our date. He was standing outside the palazzo, wearing the same clothes from the night before. His hair was a little mussed, and he was smiling that smile.

'Ooh, he's sexy. Well done! Was it weird?'

I didn't need to ask Rose what sort of weird she was referring to.

'Yes. Completely weird. I kept expecting him to do things the way Richard did them.'

'And was it nice, or not nice, that he didn't do them?'

'Really nice.'

'You should see your face, Kay. Cat that got the creamy Italian stallion doesn't even begin to express it.'

I thought of Luca, in the half-dark, raised up on his elbows, looking into my eyes. It had been a long time since Richard had looked at me like that. Familiarity was only part of it. Somewhere along the line, Richard and I had stopped seeing each other as desirable. I wondered if Richard's new woman made him feel that way, the way Luca had made me feel.

'Will you see him again?'

I shook my head. 'It was a classic one-night stand.'

'Didn't he take your number?'

'Yes, but only out of politeness.'

'Bet it wasn't.'

'Honestly, Rose, I'm not holding out for him. I'm not eighteen anymore, waiting for the phone to ring. It was a lovely night, exactly what I needed.'

I didn't tell Rose how utterly life-affirming that night had been. How uncomplicated, how physically fulfilling. Bear had been resolutely turned towards the place she was soon to be heading and, standing alongside her, I had been staring in that direction too. Then Luca helped turn me back towards the light. For that I would always be grateful. Well, for that, and for the outstanding orgasms, too. Plural intended.

'You're smirking again,' Rose said.

'I know.'

Rose looked at her watch. 'Damn! I'm already late.' She swigged down her tea, and said, 'I'll see you this evening. And I *will* get some more details out of you, don't think I won't.'

'Imo, dear, have your sons accepted a tenant yet?'

'They're making a final decision tomorrow,' she said. 'Oh, I do hope you're able to take it. Tell me you are.'

'I think so. I think I have an offer that they won't be able to refuse.'

After I'd told her my (actually Graham's) ideas, Imogen whooped delightedly. She promised to call her sons right away and ring me back.

While I waited, I opened up Rose's laptop and took a breath. I knew David Endevane had a Facebook account, and an open-access one at that, because a few years ago I'd come across it by chance in an idle hour of googling. OK, *fine*, I had gone looking for him. I just wanted to see what he was up to. Nothing much, it had seemed – some random posts about films and music, and a few photos.

I looked at the page now, and it was as uninteresting as I remembered. He obviously didn't use it much as he only had thirty-seven friends, and his posts were very sporadic. In fact, the last one was from more than a year ago, and was of people in a restaurant looking at the camera with fixed smiles, David in the middle, holding up a glass bottle of Coke. Though the picture was pretty lousy, I could see that he didn't look at all like the David of my memory. He was older of course, but also much heavier, his face puffy, his eyes lined and baggy, his hairline receded. There were some other photos of him with what I presumed must be his wife and kids, and with older people who might have been his parents. I scrolled through some more, stopping at a picture of him holding a child of around seven with the caption, 'Having fun at Corfe Castle'.

I couldn't quite deal with the thought of the children in the pictures, and what their connection was to me. I turned my attention instead to his wife. He clearly had a type; we were both slim and flat-chested, with straight, brown shoulder-length hair. She was really pretty though, with a beautiful beaming smile. She was the upgraded version of me, and probably about ten years younger – the sort of new model Richard had got for himself, most likely.

Quickly, before I lost my nerve, I sent David a brief message, saying who I was, reminding him of our long-ago friendship, and asking if he'd be willing to speak to me. If he didn't check Facebook very often, it could be a while before I heard from him. I then opened another tab and googled his name, not expecting much. There were a couple of results featuring people with the same name, both in America. One was a news item in a finance magazine announcing that David Endevane had been promoted to head of Missouri Multi-assets, and one from a music website discussing how David Endevane's band had found fresh sounds in their 1960s' inspirations. There were a few images, none of which were of my David.

And then – *Christ* – an article from a Dorset newspaper last year. My heart flipped over.

David Endevane, aged 50. Beloved Husband of Verity, much loved Dad of Ben, Owen and Abbie and a treasured Brother and Uncle. Sadly missed by his family and friends. Service Bournemouth Crematorium on Thursday 12 October at 11 a.m. Family flowers only please. Donations made payable to 'Addaction' may be sent c/o Peter Layton Funeral Services.

Fuck.

Oh, Edward. I was too late.

I was too stunned to cry. I'd told Bear I wasn't going to behave as if there was unlimited time any longer, and here was the life lesson in not having done that come back to bite me. I'd had years to tell Edward the truth – decades – and I'd blown it. If I'd told him at any point during the last twenty-eight years, right up to last autumn, he would have had the chance…

Hang on a minute, though. A tiny hope gripped me. Perhaps this was another David. I turned back to the laptop and scanned the obituary details. Sure, it was an unusual surname, and this man was the right age, but actually, this could really still be someone else. You know what? I was *sure* it was someone else. I just didn't have that feeling that he had died. When Bear had left the palazzo I knew I was alone, but I didn't have that same feeling about David having left the world. But I had to act quickly, before it really was too late. I texted Edward, suggesting I come up and see him and Georgia at the weekend. It was going to be the worst conversation of my life, but it would be even worse if David died and the choice for Edward to meet him was taken away.

The phone rang: Imogen. I closed my eyes. I wasn't sure how much more tension I could handle.

'Kay, dear! Good news! My sons love your ideas, and would like to offer you the tenancy.'

'Oh, that is so wonderful!' I could hardly believe that Bryn Glas would be mine.

'They're even willing to accept a small rent reduction in return for your hard work. How does £700 a month sound?'

'Marvellous, Imo.' It sounded awful. But I knew I would be able to manage it, one way or another.

After we hung up, I was about to text Rose and tell her the exciting news, when the computer beeped: a Facebook message. Oh, God. I did a quick bit of yoga breathing, then clicked it open.

Hi Kay, I'm Ben, David's eldest child. I'm monitoring his FB page for my mum. I'm sorry to tell you that Dad died last year. Mum is happy to make contact with any of Dad's old friends. If you'd like to, please send me your contact details. Best, Ben.

Well, I guess I could stop deluding myself that it was the obituary of some other David Endevane. *You bloody idiot, Kay.* Thinking I could *feel* that he was still in the world. What an arrogant idiot I was. What an utter, useless mess I had made of everything. I closed the computer, and rested my head on the table.

Everything in my life that had gone wrong was because I'd let David push me away. When I told him I was pregnant, and he didn't want to know, why wasn't I more persistent? Why didn't I wait it out? Why wasn't I brave enough to have had the baby on my own? David would doubtless have come round eventually, if not to me, then to his son. If I'd done that, I wouldn't have rushed into marrying Richard, wouldn't have had to feel grateful for so long that he'd rescued me. I wouldn't have been living behind glass all these years, never doing quite what I wanted, not achieving anything. And Edward would have known his biological father, or at least known who he was, had the choice to approach him or not. What a stupid mess I'd made of it all. I couldn't even remember why I'd done what I did, couldn't connect to the girl who made those fateful decisions all those years ago.

I felt hollowed out, too bleak to cry. David, Bear, my mum. Everything was utter crap. Even the thought of Bryn Glas couldn't work its usual magic.

My phone pinged: Edward, saying I would be very welcome to come up this weekend. Oh, *terrific*. I thought about what I was going to have to tell him, and wondered exactly how I was going to be able to find the words.

Letter written on 16 August 1988

Dearest Bear,

Thank you, darling, for your lovely kind letter, but I am in a
much better place now. Buy a hat, I'm getting married! No, not
to HWNISNUA, but to Richard. How the hell did this happen,
thinks Bear, all confused!

I'm hardly sure myself. It was a few weeks ago, not long
after HWNISNUA dumped me, and I bumped into Richard
in the Students' Union. It was the first time I'd seen him since
we split, and he looked so handsome. Fickle old Kay, eh? He
asked how I was, so nicely, that I plucked up the courage to
tell him my news. We spent the evening together, and long
story short, he proposed. He said he'd missed me terribly,
that he loved me, and that, being a few years older than me,
he felt ready to be a father. We made a solemn pact that we
wouldn't tell anyone the truth, ever, and that we would never
speak of it again.

I didn't tell him you already knew. But I'm going to keep
my promise to him, and not tell anyone else. Not even Rose.
Not Mum. Not the baby. And certainly not Richard's terrifying
mother, who I'm pretty sure despises me for 'trapping' Richard.
Imagine if she knew the truth!

I'm not going to finish my degree. At first I thought I could take a year out, have the baby, then come back. But I went to see Dad's friend, the one who liked my work and offered me an apprenticeship in his Soho studio. I told him about the baby, and asked if he could wait a year and he said the timing wouldn't work, and that was that. It all feels a bit pointless now. It's going to be marriage and a baby instead, and perhaps it was silly to think I could make it a career, there's so many brilliant photographers out there. Richard has big plans after his MBA for a shop he wants to open, and when the baby is older I can work there.

Richard isn't as handsome as HWNISNUA, but he is something better than that: he's kind. And he loves me. He's generous, and hard-working, and I think he'll be a great dad. And I do love him, Bear. I really do. I think what I felt with HWNISNUA was infatuation. It's the real thing with Richard. I didn't see it when we were dating before, but I do now.

It's going to be a quick and tiny wedding next week, register office. By the time you read this, it will already have happened, I will be Mrs Bright, so don't really buy a hat, unless you want one anyway. Mum's disappointed it won't be in church but she knows we want to move quickly. Hope I don't look too preg in the photos! I'm already showing a little. I know you won't be here for it but I'll be thinking of you. Thanks for all your brilliant support these last crazy few months. Love ya, Honey Bear.

Till next time.

Miss you.

Always, Kay

Chapter 22

Kay

My arms ached, but the boys still had boundless energy, hurtling from one piece of playground equipment to the other. I'd already done a very long grandmotherly stint at swing-pushing, way longer than I used to manage when Edward and Stella were little. It had seemed so boring, then. Push, wait, push, wait. You couldn't switch off while doing it, in case you absent-mindedly shoved them too high, or got hit in the chest on the return trajectory. I must have been a rather impatient young mother.

It was different this time round. There was pleasure in finding the exact right spot for my feet in between the two swings, so I didn't have to keep moving forwards and back; a simple bend at the waist was enough. There was pleasure in the repetitive rhythm, too, and in arranging it so that as I pushed one, the other one was coming back. Once I got into the groove, I felt like some kind of Swing Queen. Above all, there was huge pleasure in the twins' delighted screams, crying, 'More!' and 'Who's highest, Nana?' I let myself properly experience each second with them, in case this was it, in case this was the last time I was allowed to see them.

When at last they'd had enough, I took them for a brief turn round the greenhouse, though they were still too little for it, really. Then we went to the botanic gardens' outdoor café where Edward was working on some papers. How grown-up he looked, sitting there beavering away in his shirt and jacket, a coffee in front of him. It was so easy to see underneath his façade of a father of nearly thirty to the little boy he'd been: sitting at the kitchen table in his school uniform, studiously doing his homework, frowning in concentration, pushing the hair out of his eyes.

I bought the boys each an ice-cream square sandwiched by chewy wafers. 'Double nuggets!' Finlay cried in disbelief, suggesting they weren't usually allowed such a treat. I then sat them down on the grass to watch an inept juggler, and took my coffee over to Edward.

'Nice stamina, Mum,' Edward said, putting down his pen. 'That was great, thank you, it gave me a chance to finish reading a couple of reports.'

'Shame you have to do work on a Sunday.'

'Oh, it'll save me time tomorrow at the meeting.' He glanced over at the boys. 'Double nuggets. What kind of crazy fool are you?'

'Messy, aren't they? Hope Georgia doesn't mind.' I glanced at the papers he was looking at, but they could have been written in Chinese for all the sense they made to me. I often felt like an out-of-touch granny when I was with Edward. At least I wasn't quite at the shawl stage yet.

I still hadn't worked out what to say to Edward. He and Georgia had been particularly sweet since I arrived last night, fussing over me, asking how I was. Edward didn't quite say, 'Now you've gone insane and left

Dad, how's it going?' but the gentle, kid-glove treatment I was getting
suggested it was what he was thinking.

'So how were your travels, Mum?' he said now, though I knew he
wasn't super-interested. Probably he thought of them as one of the
symptoms of my madness.

'You want to see some photos?' I took my phone out.

'Sure. You sent me a couple from Venice, but I'd like to see more.'
He flicked through them, making polite comments. 'Some of these
are pretty good. This one, the little canals, gorgeous. You should send
these somewhere. The *Herald* run this photo competition every week.'

'The newspaper? Ah no, they're just on my phone.' I put on my
sunglasses. The Glasgow sunshine was stronger than I'd come to expect
from my previous, usually rainy, visits here.

'I'll AirDrop a couple to myself,' he said, fiddling about with our
phones. 'Maybe I'll send some in for you.' He then sat back, and said,
with the air of someone who's finally plucked up the courage to say
what's on their mind, 'Go on, then, Mum.'

'Go on, what?' My heart stuttered – did he somehow know what
I wanted to tell him?

'Haven't you come up here to have a go at me?'

I hadn't expected this conversational turn. Surely it should be the
other way round. 'What have you done,' I said, 'that I should be telling
you off about?' I was happy to stall the inevitable moment when he
realised that he was the one who should be telling me off.

'Because I haven't been to see Dad,' he muttered. 'Since you, er,
left. Or Stella.'

Ah! 'I know, darling, and I'm sure they'd love to see you.'

'Well, go on, then,' he said, avoiding my eye. 'Tell me what a prick
I am. Abandoning them in their hour of need, blah blah.'

'Certainly not. That's not why I'm here, Edward.'

'It's not?'

'No. I wanted to see you. And actually, I'm here to say that *I'm* sorry, sweetheart.' It felt good to say it. Great, in fact. I should say it more.

'What for?'

'For leaving Dad. For making a big mess for everyone to clear up. And...' I took a breath. 'For not always being honest with you.'

'Oh.' He stared at the table. 'Well, I guess I... I don't know... Georgia thinks I should tell... I want to. God, how to start?'

He was clearly bursting to say something, so keen in fact that he didn't seem to notice my 'not always been honest' confession. Fine. Let's keep stalling forever, sitting in these pretty gardens, my grandchildren nearby, the sun on my back, coffee in my hand. Because once I told him, who knew what he'd say? If he didn't want to see me ever again, I knew how to get to the train station from here. I had all my essentials on me, and Georgia would probably be willing to send on the rest of my things that were back at their house. I had to tell him, it had to be today, and I had to face whatever consequences there were, however bad. But I was happy to postpone the moment for as long as possible.

'Go ahead,' I said. 'Say what you need to say.'

He shook his head. For a moment, I thought he wasn't going to say anything. Then he said in a rush, 'Aren't you pissed off with Dad?'

'With Dad?' Fleetingly, I wondered if Edward had got the wrong end of the stick, if he thought it was Rich who'd left me. 'Why?'

'About how quickly he replaced you?'

Ah, again! 'You've heard about his new woman, have you?'

'Stella texted me. He's going to *Paris*, the bastard.'

Yes, indeed. A week with Rich in Paris, or anywhere, really – how we had all dreamed of that for so many years.

'Well, look,' I said, my voice low, in case of eavesdroppers, 'it does seem very quick to me – unflatteringly quick! – but I guess it's what your dad needs to get him through our split. If so, I'm all for it. I hope the person he's found is nice, someone who will take care of him. And look, it's someone who can persuade him out of his rut, who can get him to go on holiday! I never could. I genuinely hope it works out for him.'

'Wow.' Edward looked at me intensely. 'You *really* did want to fucking leave him, didn't you?'

'It was the right thing for me. I'm hoping it will turn out to be right for all of us.' I smiled, though I didn't feel like it, and started to gather my courage. *Be brave*, I thought. *Remember, you've climbed Snowdon. You are tough, a mighty woman. Oh, hell.* 'Edward, I'm here because I really wanted to see you and the twins, and Georgia too, of course. But it's also because there's something I have to tell you.'

'About Dad?'

'Not really, it's about you.' I stirred my coffee unnecessarily, to buy time. 'It's something I wish I'd told you years ago. The reasons why I didn't are complicated, your father and I thought, well, it was a long time ago, but we thought…' *God!* This was even harder than I'd imagined.

'Spit it out, Mum,' Edward said. He looked almost amused.

'Spit it out. Good idea.' My heart pounding, feeling sick, I said all in a rush, 'Dad isn't your real father. Your real father was a man called David who I met at university. We hadn't been together long when I got pregnant and he didn't want it – you. To cut a long story short, your father offered to raise you as his own and we agreed we would keep it secret and that seemed terribly important at the time but it doesn't anymore, and—'

'Mum.' Edward was holding up his hand. 'I—'

'Please, there's a tiny bit more. The worst bit. Let me get it out then you can speak for as long as you want.' I braced both hands on the table, for moral support, or something. 'I recently decided to tell you and I tracked David down but he... he...' I didn't know how to say it. Now it came to it, I didn't have the words. 'He... oh, God...'

'He died last year,' Edward said.

I stared at him. 'Pardon?'

'Mum. I know about David.'

The sunlight in the gardens seemed whiter all at once, brighter. I thought I might faint. I gripped harder onto the edge of the table, closing my eyes to stop the dizziness. He knew. He already knew! But how? Only four of us knew: me, David, Richard and Bear. Three, of course, now that David...

I opened my eyes. 'Did Dad tell you?'

'Yes, he did.'

'I can't believe that!' How could Richard have broken our pact, and then not told me he'd broken it? That bastard. *Why* had he? Edward was looking at me, waiting for me to go on.

'I'm so sorry I didn't tell you years ago,' I said. I took a deep breath. 'I'd pushed it so thoroughly under the carpet that I pretty much forgot about it. But I wish I'd given you the chance to see him.'

The twins came running over, covered in ice cream. 'Nana! Daddy! We're bored!'

'Come on then,' Edward said, taking a packet of wet wipes out of his inside pocket and expertly mopping their faces, 'let's go home.' He turned to me, and said, 'To be continued.'

Somehow I got to my feet and walked back to the car with them, a sticky little hand in each of mine.

By the time we got back to their place, a lovely airy high-ceilinged house in Shawlands, I felt completely weird. Having to sing fifteen verses of 'Old MacDonald' in the car to distract Jamie from feeling sick probably hadn't helped. Who knew that Old MacDonald had iPads and laser guns on his farm, eh? It certainly was a more modern enterprise than the one I sang about when their dad was little.

Georgia was out at her mum's, so I didn't have to put on a front for her. Edward sat the kids in front of CBeebies, and he and I went into the kitchen. I stood there, rather lost in the large room.

'I'll get their tea together,' he said.

'Can I help?'

'It's only fish fingers. Why don't you make us some tea? You look a bit shell-shocked.'

My strange, unknowable child. He'd always been so much more enigmatic than Stella. She might not be great at naming her feelings, but she always showed them. You knew straight away if she was happy or upset. Edward was self-contained, had been since he was little. You had to prise under the surface to glimpse what he was thinking.

I filled the kettle, and sat down. 'Go on, then, love,' I said, trying not to sound like I was begging, even if I was. 'Tell me.'

Edward put fish fingers under the grill, and started chopping carrots into neat little sticks. 'Do you remember when the twins were tiny, a couple of years ago, and they got bronchitis?'

I nodded. I'd flown up to Glasgow to help out; Edward and Georgia were both exhausted. I'd have stayed longer, but Richard had phoned several times, making pointed comments about the shop. Remembering that now made me ashamed I'd let him talk me into returning home before I wanted; ashamed that I'd bought into the obvious nonsense of treating work as more important than my family.

Edward went on, 'Georgia was completely freaked, and after they recovered, she got it in her head that we should do genetic tests, see if there were medical issues that might affect them as they got older. I thought it was a daft idea, but there was no talking her out of it, and, actually, once I got my results, it was pretty interesting. It showed my Irish heritage from you; in fact, amazingly, it nailed it down to Donegal. I remember you saying your great-grandmother came from Donegal.'

'Yes, she did...' I wasn't sure where this was going. 'Was there anything about hereditary illnesses?'

'We showed the report to the boys' paediatrician but he didn't think there was anything to worry about. Anyway, the relevant thing,' and Edward raised his eyebrows, 'was that Dad's famous Scandinavian heritage was missing.'

'Oh.' I turned away, under the guise of making tea. With trembling hands, I poured water into mugs.

'You know how he's always gone on about being descended from Vikings?'

'I certainly do.' God, how often, and how thoroughly, Richard had told me about it.

'I even did a school project on it, do you remember? Drew myself as a Viking boy? So,' Edward said, buttering some bread, 'I thought Dad must have made a mistake, or been misinformed. So I asked him, how come my test didn't show up any Scandinavian DNA.'

I dug my nails into my legs. *Oh God, poor Richard.* 'And after fudging for a bit, about how those tests weren't necessarily accurate, he told me he wasn't my biological father.'

'Jesus. Edward, I am so, so sorry.' I splashed too much milk into the mugs and sat down. A few minutes ago I'd been furious with Richard; now I felt heartbroken for him. All those years we'd not

talked about it, all those years he'd considered himself as much a
true father to Edward as he was to Stella. What a horrible blow it
must have been, to have had to finally reveal the painful truth we
had worked so hard to suppress.

'Bit of a facer, as you can imagine,' Edward said, running his hand
over his eyes.

'Sweetheart. I handled it all so badly. I'm so sorry.' A thought occurred
to me. 'Is that why we've not seen anything of you for such a long time?'

He nodded. 'Been processing it.' He sipped his tea, winced, and
fished out the teabag I'd failed to remove. 'I was really bloody angry
for a long time.'

'God, I'm sure you were. I'm so sorry.'

'It felt as if you and Dad had played a trick on me. Like I was the
butt of a joke that everyone knew except me.'

'Oh, darling! It wasn't like that at all.'

'I know, and I don't think like that anymore. But I'm telling you
how I felt then.'

I nodded, determined to stop interrupting. I must let him speak.

'Georgia said I should talk to you about it, but I wasn't ready.
Actually, I'm not sure I'm ready now.' Even as a little kid, he'd rarely
cried, but his eyes were watery. 'I didn't even know if I was part of my
family anymore.'

'Oh, Edward.' I inadvertently let out a sob, and covered my mouth.
'Of course you are!'

'No, it's fine, I know that. Logically.' He attended to the grill, turned
fish fingers over. How prosaic life was, the way it just went on, with fish
fingers and tea, when one's whole world had been turned upside down. Not
looking at me, he said, 'Thank goodness for Georgia. And my therapist.'

'You have a therapist?'

'Why not? Stella had one. All the kids from complicated families are doing it these days.'

'Ah God, I didn't want to give you a complicated family.'

'They all are, though, aren't they? That's what my therapist says. Boom times for her. But no, I'll be honest, it was hard. It's weird, you know, to discover that you're not who you thought you were.'

I shook my head. There must have been a better way for me to manage all this.

'So what did Dad… Richard…'

'It's all right, Mum. He's still my dad.' Edward smiled. 'He told me what had happened, and that you'd both agreed to keep it a secret. He told me he was,' Edward paused, and continued in a lower voice, 'always very proud that I was his son.' He was definitely crying a bit, and he definitely didn't want me to acknowledge that.

'Jesus, Edward. I can't believe Richard didn't tell me any of this.'

'I asked him not to, Mum.' He slid the fish fingers onto plates. 'I didn't want to rake things up for you, and Dad didn't either, especially as Granny Hurst was so ill. I did wonder, when you left him, whether he had told you after all, and it had caused a huge row.'

'No, he never said a word.' Poor Richard, carrying all that on his own. 'So did you try and contact, er, David?' How bizarre it felt, saying David's name out loud, to Edward, of all people.

'I met him.'

'You met him?!' My heart started banging as fast as if I'd been running.

'I've met his wife.'

'You've met his wife?!'

'This is like that infuriating game Finlay plays,' Edward said, 'where he repeats everything you say.' He picked up the plates. 'I'll let them eat in front of the telly, for a treat.'

He went out, and before I had time to even think, my phone buzzed, making me jump; mind you, anything would make me jump right now. It was a text from Rose, checking in. She knew I'd come up here, but assumed the visit was purely to spend time with Edward. At some point I would have to tell her the whole thing. God, there was so much more to tell than even I had known. I hoped Rose wouldn't be too angry that I hadn't confided in her before now. For the time being, I decided that, like Edward, I just needed to express my feelings.

The revelations keep on coming, Rose

What's happening, K?

All my chickens are coming home to roost

Has your phone been hijacked by a cliché-bot?

I'll tell you when I see you. We are going to need a LOT of wine

Edward came back in and I put my phone away.

'Would you like something to eat?' he said. 'There's some nice beef casserole Georgia made, left over from the other night.'

'Sod the casserole!' Maybe I was still an impatient mother. 'Tell me about meeting him, please!'

'OK.' Edward sat down next to me. 'Once Dad told me David's name, it was easy to track him down.'

I nodded. I'd found this out myself.

'Endevane is incredibly rare. It's a corruption of an obscure Welsh name, did you know?' Edward went on.

'Yes,' I said, faintly. My heart still seemed to think we were doing a marathon.

'Is that why you love going to that cottage in Wales?'

'I don't think there's any connection.' But as I said it, I wondered if there was some weird subconscious shit going on, as Bear might have said.

'I expect I've got quite a lot of Welsh DNA myself, thanks to David,' Edward said, 'and the boys too. The DNA test confirmed we've got a lot of Celtic in us, at any rate.' Luckily he didn't expect a reply. It was going to take me a while to, as Edward put it, "process" that.

'Anyway,' he continued, 'I tracked him down on Facebook, told him who I was, and he said he'd like to meet me.' He took a nonchalant sip of tea.

'How? When? Where?' I held out my arms wide, in a visual representation of *tell me everything*.

'It was a few months before he died, I guess. He lived in Dorset, and I was coming down south for work, so we met in Chelsea for a drink.'

My son, and the father of my son, met in London. I would have been no more than a few miles away from them at the time. I'm surprised I didn't get some kind of alert, like a plague of locusts, or the water in the taps running red.

'It was just the one time,' Edward said. 'I could see he would have been a very nice-looking bloke when he was young.'

'Yes, he was.'

'He looked a bit like me.'

'You are a nice-looking bloke, yourself.' I studied him, allowing myself to catalogue the resemblances I'd always seen but never spoken of, except in letters to Bear: the fair hair flopping over the forehead, the grey-blue eyes, similar in colour but not shape to Stella's, the cast of the jawline. 'Was his wife there?'

'No, she wasn't, but she knew about me. I don't know if he'd only told her after I contacted him, or if she'd always known.'

'Were they happy, do you think?'

'I'm not sure. He was a drinker. He told me that a few years ago his wife had had enough of him boozing, and left him.'

I hadn't expected David to turn out to be a drinker. But then, I didn't really know him at all. 'Were they separated, then?'

'No, he managed to give up drinking, and she came back, but then he was diagnosed with cancer.'

'What kind?' I wasn't sure why I needed to know that, and nor was Edward, because he looked at me oddly.

'Oesophageal, I think he said. He described himself as a former alcoholic. He was up front about it. He drank orange juice. He told me straight away that he was ill, and that he didn't know how much longer he had. He was really glad I'd got in touch.'

I couldn't believe Edward had, after all, despite my foolish inertia, got the chance to meet David before it was too late. It was such a relief, only relief was too small a word to describe it. I felt as if an actual physical burden had been lifted off me, that a heavy rucksack was no longer weighing me down. My heart started slowing at last.

'Did you like him?' I asked. It was an inadequate question to cover everything I wanted to know.

'I don't know. I guess so. It was only a couple of hours. He was nice enough. I didn't feel there was a particular connection. He stared at me a lot, I suppose he was trying to see his face in mine.'

Nice enough. All these years I'd held David in a special, magical place in my heart, the road not travelled, the one who got away. And yet other people could see him and think, *nice enough.* The thought made me smile.

'I didn't think of him as a replacement for Dad, or anything like that,' Edward said. 'Your dad's the one who brings you up.'

'I've always wondered, though, how things might have been different.' I looked intently at Edward, hoping he would realise the significance of what I was saying, the guilt I felt about not giving David more time to decide if he wanted to be with me, be the father to my child. 'How it would have been if David and I had stayed together, brought you up together.'

'It probably would have been different, Mum,' Edward said, 'but it might not have been any better. It could easily have been worse.'

'Your dad wasn't exactly round a great deal when you were a kid, though,' I said. 'He was so busy, working all the hours.'

'I was never in any doubt that he loved me,' Edward said. 'He was, and is, a good dad.'

Bear told me I'd made up an imaginary love story. That things with me and David weren't how I remembered them. 'He was very handsome,' she'd said, 'but I don't remember him being all that nice to you.' Maybe she and Edward were right, and things wouldn't have been better with David. Either way, it was high time to draw a line under it. I hadn't married David, I'd married Richard. It hadn't been perfect, not by any means, but for a long time, it had been good enough.

'David asked me to pass on a message to you, Mum.'

'To me?' Christ. *Like I said, Rose, the revelations keep on coming.*

'He said he wasn't very nice to you when you told him about me, and to tell you he was sorry.'

'Ah.' I closed my eyes for a moment, to let that one wash over me. 'He was terribly young. We both were.'

'Are you OK?'

I opened my eyes. 'Yes, darling.' *Just squashing down thirty years of repressed stuff here, but otherwise, I'm dandy.* 'Are you?'

'I'm very relieved I've told you.'

'Right back atcha.' I smiled at him. 'Did he want a relationship with you, do you think?'

'I don't think so, and I didn't want one with him. I kind of needed to see him, but once was fine. His wife Verity called me when he died, said she thought he'd have appreciated me coming to the funeral. So I went with Georgia. We didn't talk to anyone apart from Verity. I spotted his kids, but I wasn't sure if they knew about me or not. So I didn't approach them.'

'Bloody hell, Edward. You're such a… such a…'

'What?'

'Such an amazing grown-up.' I stroked his cheek, and then took his hand in mine. He held onto it tightly and we sat for a few moments in silence. I burned with a thousand questions, but I knew that if there was any more to tell, he would tell me in his own time. Perhaps it would take a while for him to open up any further. Perhaps I'd never know. Perhaps there wasn't any more to tell.

'Mum,' he said, breaking into my thoughts. 'Can I ask you something?'

'Yes, of course.'

He took a mouthful of tea, made a face as it was cold, and said, 'Do you not love Dad anymore?'

Edward – a mature man, and yet sometimes, still my little boy.

'I do love him, sweetie. I thought I didn't, before. But I've realised I do, it's just in a different way, a way I didn't immediately recognise as love.'

'Love is complicated, isn't it?' he said, and he came over and put his arms round me. It was our first hug in I don't know how long.

'It must have been hard for you, back then,' he said, 'when you were pregnant with me.'

'Oh, darling.' My eyes filled with tears. In his arms I allowed myself to remember, for the first time in forever, the paralysing cold dread I'd felt when I realised David didn't want to know. Imagining Mum's reaction – 'You must give the baby up for adoption.' Or Rose's – 'I'll book you an abortion.' Not knowing the right thing to do, making decisions that resonated down the years.

'Sorry I haven't been there for you and Dad these last few months,' he said.

'You've been dealing with a lot,' I said. 'We both understand.' I knew I could speak for Richard when I said this. 'And I'm sure Stella would too, if you ever want to tell her.'

'God, I suppose I should.' I felt him shake his head against my shoulder. 'I'll never hear the end of it. I'll go and see them soon.' He let me go and sat back in his seat. 'And can we come to Bryn Glas for a few days in the summer holidays?'

You would never know that moments earlier he had been in the grip of powerful emotions. I admired his ability to bounce right into the next thing.

'I was telling Georgia what a great place it was for a run-around when I was a kid, and she's mad keen for the twins to be somewhere outdoorsy with no internet.'

'How lovely!' I decided I'd let them find out when they arrived that Imogen's sons were installing super-fast Wi-Fi.

'When can you move in? Are the renovations finished?'

'Nearly. I've arranged to take it from Wednesday. Imogen's managed to convince her family to give me a rent reduction on the grounds that I am a sensible and mature woman. Ha! If only they knew. And because I'm going to restore the barn.'

'You'll stay with us a few more days, then, won't you?' Edward asked. 'No point rushing off if it's not ready yet, and the boys love having you around.'

'I love seeing them. And you.' I had to press my lips together to avoid any more teary outbursts. My son wanted me to stay. I hadn't blown everything.

I'd been accustomed, lately, to looking back on my life as a series of minor disasters and major errors. But actually, you could look at it in an entirely different way. My life was full of exceptional children and wonderful friends. New possibilities were right around the corner. When you compared my life to a lot of other people's, it turned out that I was really extremely lucky.

'Daddy!' Jamie called from the living room. 'Can we have pudding?'

'Cheeky sods,' Edward said, 'they had a massive ice cream with you.'

'I'll make them a fruit salad,' I said, getting up. I gave him one last kiss, my golden-haired boy, and then I started slicing apples and bananas, and let the prosaic slide back into my life. It was less exciting, for sure, but considerably more restful.

Letter written on 17 June 1988

Dearest Bear,

Oh God, B. I don't know how to even start this letter. I don't know if I'm coming or going. Shit, shit, I'm so all over the place. I wish you were here and I could sit next to you with a couple of rum and Cokes and tell you the whole thing. Or maybe just Coke for me… that's a big clue right there. I daren't tell Rose, she'd start fussing and I really don't want any fussing. As for my mum, she will kill me. I'm never telling her, full stop.

OK. Long story short. You know I've been seeing David and I'm in love, love, love? It's been absolute bliss. I've barely seen the inside of a lecture theatre these last few months, we've hardly been out of bed. So, deep breath Bear, that little chick's come home to roost. A few days ago I fainted on the way to a lecture, and my tutor sent me to the GP. He did a preggers test, and I expect you can guess the result.

It took me till yesterday to pluck up the nerve to tell David. Oh, Bear, it was awful. Awful doesn't even cover it. It was like he was a different person. I suppose I'd sort of hoped that he would kiss me, hold me, tell me it would be OK, ask me if I wanted to get married, even. But he kind of acted like it was all a major inconvenience that I needed to sort out. He was so matter-of-fact, I even wondered if this wasn't the first time a girl had given him this news. Basically, he assumed I'd get an abortion. He didn't ask how I was feeling, or anything. His first comment was, 'I can pay half if that helps.' I didn't even clock what he meant, I thought he meant half of the costs of the baby, or maybe even half of the cost of the wedding. Thank God the penny dropped before I said anything about a wedding!

I said, 'Do you think I'm getting an abortion?' and he went, 'Well yes of course, I'm only twenty-one,' and I said, 'But I'm Catholic,' and he said, 'You don't even go to church,' and I said, 'I am lapsed but we don't do that,' and he said, 'Oh dear, then we have a bit of a problem.' I know what it means now when people say their blood ran cold.

I've got 'have a baby' on my 'to do by 30' list, but I don't want one yet. I remember you writing to me about your abortion, a couple of years ago. That was definitely the right thing for you. But I don't know if it's right for me, Bear. Shit.

Anyway, I cried, and begged He Whose Name I Shall Never Utter Again (henceforth HWNISNUA) to at least stay with me and the baby even if we didn't get married, but he laughed. He said we were kids ourselves and if I wanted to have the baby that was fine, but I was on my own. And then he finished with me.

Please write back soon, Bear. I feel terribly alone. The little bump might start to show soon and I will have to tell people. I have stopped fainting but I feel so sick, and I know you will say I must tell Rose or Mum but I don't know what to say to them. Rose didn't even like HWNISNUA very much, but I know she will help, BUT she will try and get me to have an abortion or maybe think about adoption and I just don't know, Bear.

Is it stupid to think I could look after the baby on my own? With HWNISNUA, it will be a very beautiful golden-haired baby.

I need to think.

Till next time.

Miss you.

Always, Kay

Chapter 23

Kay

I slid into my car, where it had sat for almost a week in the staggeringly expensive car park at Heathrow. I was planning to drive to Wales through the night, Bryn Glas's siren call loud in my ear. I started the engine, then thought, but I'd love to have my little stool in Bryn Glas. It was nothing special, but it had belonged to Mum: a three-legged stool with an embroidered cover. It was in the bedroom I'd shared with Richard, and I could see a space for it so clearly, next to the grey chair in my new bedroom. This fleeting thought flowered instantly into a plan to go back to the house, the 'marital home' as they called it on Radio 4 dramas, and get some of my things. Richard had said I could, after all, in the Venice phone call.

I started driving towards London. I wondered if I should ring him, let him know I was coming. I called out to the in-car phone dictation thing, which I rarely used, because it often sent such weird messages. I got the impression that it didn't like my accent.

'Who do you want to call?' the robot voice said, and the call screen on the dashboard lit up.

Saying 'Home' stuck in my throat. 'No one,' I said.

'OK.'

I was pleasantly surprised that it didn't attempt to call Norman or Noreen or some other made-up person.

Right then. I would just turn up. Great idea. Well, possibly a very bad idea, but at least I would have the advantage of surprise. It would be about seven by the time I got there, so Rich might not yet be home. The thought of seeing him was odd. Not unpleasant. Just odd. Too odd to dwell on. Instead, I made an inventory in my head of the things I should bring. The stool, and my camera, of course. And some clothes – I was sick of the ones I had, and as the weather was getting warmer I would need more summer things. Even in North Wales. Plus the boxes of Bear's letters under the bed, and that other box, the one with photos and memorabilia from my past.

Before I knew it, I was in my old street. I still had my resident's parking permit on the windscreen, though my usual space was filled by another car. I pulled into a space behind it, and looked at the house. Seeing it again, after a month – good Lord, it was exactly one month to the day – I realised how much I hadn't missed it. I'd never felt as at home, despite all the years I lived in this house, as I did in Bryn Glas.

Heavy-legged, I got out of the car, and rang the doorbell; it felt wrong to use my key.

'Good heavens!' Alice said on opening the door.

'Hello, Alice. How are you?'

I knew I could rely on her icily correct manners to kick in automatically. 'Very well, thank you, and you?'

'Richard said I could collect some of my things,' I said, still standing on the doorstep, feeling about as welcome as one of those poor fellows who go door-to-door with holdalls full of surprisingly pricy tea towels and yellow dusters.

'He didn't mention anything,' Alice said, not moving to let me in. 'He's, er, out currently.'

'I didn't tell him I was coming, I was just passing.' This was ridiculous. I could easily take Alice in a fight if I had to, but I'd prefer to be let in peaceably.

'Very well.' At last she stood aside, and I stepped into the hall. The house smelled different. Furniture polish, perhaps? 'I suppose you'll be wanting tea.'

'No thanks,' I said, surprising both of us – when had I ever said no to tea? 'Please can I have a glass of water?' To be honest, I'd had enough of sitting at kitchen tables drinking tea and discussing heavy stuff. *Heavy.* This would be a pleasant change. Well, not pleasant, this was Alice we were talking about, but it would be a change.

She led me through, as if I didn't know where the kitchen was, and with a silent gesture, invited me to sit at the table. I chose a different place from my habitual one, and did a speedy inventory, noting the neatness of everything. Cups hanging on hooks, surfaces clear of any impediment to cooking, the few privileged appliances still allowed to be out of cupboards sparkling clean. Where there is discord, said Francis of Assisi and, more aptly for Alice, Margaret Thatcher, may we bring harmony.

'You've not long missed Stella,' Alice said. 'She was here briefly, between houses, but she's moved back to Essex with Nita.'

'Oh, how lovely she's moving in with Nita. They used to get on so well.'

'They are living with a Dutch fellow, I hear.' Alice transformed 'Dutch' into a swear word. She placed a glass of water in front of me with exaggerated care. 'How have you been?' she asked, formally.

'Fine, thanks,' I said. Thank heavens for small talk. How long would it take me to answer truthfully, rather than just 'fine'? I'd still be speaking when the sun went down, and possibly when it rose again the next morning. 'You?'

'Fine.'

I looked around wildly for something to talk about, and noticed that amidst all the pristine, something was odd and out of place: three serviettes, lined up along the counter near the sink, shaped like swans. You'd be looking at Alice a long time before you'd identify her as a woman who fashions origami napkins in her spare time. It was surely one of the million things she'd dismiss as déclassé. I stared pointedly at the napkins, and Alice's gaze followed mine, but then her eyes snapped away and I could see that if we were going to get to the bottom of the mystery, I would have to be the one to raise it.

I didn't quite have the nerve. Instead, I said, 'I hear you're enjoying working in the shop.'

'I am, rather,' she said. To my astonishment, she smiled. 'I was there today. It's heaps of fun!'

'It *is*?'

'You must miss it terribly! Anthony's such a tonic, isn't he? He has me in fits from morning till night.'

Good Lord, she had fallen for Anthony's charms. Who'd have thought it?

'He is very witty,' I said, politely. Would it amuse her if I said, *Now you can see why I had an affair with him*? Perhaps not. 'Do you enjoy serving customers?'

'Adore it,' she said. 'Anthony says I am very good at upselling. Do you know what that is?'

I suppressed a smile. No, Alice, I only worked in retail for a quarter of a fucking century, why don't you tell me all about it? 'Er, yes, I believe I do.'

'A customer will come in for a cheap rollerball, and I will send him out with a Sheaffer!' she said, proudly.

'Well, good for you,' I said.

'So, are you still dashing about, Kathleen? Hither and thither, as it were.'

'Yes, I've just been up to see Edward and Georgia.'

'Oh, we haven't seen them for ages. Is he terribly busy?'

'He told me they'll be visiting soon.' I could stand it no longer. 'Alice, I'm very impressed by your swans.'

Tight-lipped, she said, '*Thank* you, Kathleen. Actually, those were created by Mrs Macrae.'

I looked at her, puzzled. The name rang a bell, but I couldn't think who she meant. She seemed rather flustered, but there was no time to think about it further, because the front door slammed and I heard Richard call, 'Mum, we're back!'

We?

Alice and I locked eyes, and I wondered if she could see the extreme horror in mine.

Richard came into the room, his coat still on, noisily larger than life, chatting as he entered. 'They didn't have Rioja, can you believe, so we had to go even further, lovely evening for a walk, though... oh!' He saw me, sitting cowed on my chair, holding onto my water glass as if it was an ejector button. Why wasn't it an ejector button? There really was a massive lack of ejector buttons in my life. He looked exactly how I remembered him, and also utterly unfamiliar: everything was in its usual place, hair, eyes, shoulders etc, but it was as if they were attached to a stranger.

He recovered quickly. 'Kay! How lovely to see you! I didn't know you were coming. Is everything OK?' He bustled over and I stood up, and after a tiny hesitation, do we kiss or not, we hugged. Then he darted back to the door. 'You remember Aileen, of course?' He ushered into the centre of the room a woman who I'd been dimly aware of for the last minute, but hadn't been able to connect who she was in my brain.

Aileen Macrae. Mrs Macrae. Of course. The manager at Pencil Us In.

'Hello, Mrs Bright, er, Kay,' Aileen said. She gazed at me awkwardly, an anxious smile flickering on and off.

'I'll make tea!' Alice cried, wisely deciding that this was the right moment to opt out. She turned her back on the whole messy scene and started mucking about with cups and the kettle. I wished I could think of a similar task, but nothing came to mind. It would be kind of weird if I suggested I nip out and clean the loo or something. So here I was, facing my ex-husband and his new girlfriend in my former kitchen, and a furious letter to the editor composing itself in my mind about the chronic shortage of ejector buttons.

Meanwhile another part of my busy brain was dredging its memory banks for Aileen intel. The first thing it came up with was how long it took me to teach her to use the new till. She was not a fan of technology, something she and Richard had in common. She point-blank refused to do her daily round-up by email, always insisting on speaking on the phone. She and Richard would have spoken on the phone six days a week, for the last goodness knows how many years. She was the longest-serving manager, other than me. They probably knew each other inside out after all this time.

My brain reminded me that Aileen was Scottish, and a divorcee (or widow, I couldn't recall), and loved to bake. She was always bringing in home-made cakes and biscuits to work, and her assistants over the years would say, 'Aileen, you are a nightmare for my waistline.'

One thing I'd not previously noticed about her was that she was rather pretty. I'd never seen her in anything but her working clothes in the shop, but here she was in an elegant blue dress, her hair swept into a proper chignon. Lucky Richard. At last he was with a woman who knew how to do her hair; I'd never graduated beyond a messy bun. In the early days of our courtship I'd once asked if he wouldn't prefer someone tidier, but he always faithfully denied it.

'Sorry for turning up unannounced,' I said. 'I was on my way back from seeing Edward and thought I'd grab some of my things. If that's OK.'

'Well, it's lovely to see you!' Aileen said, full of sudden enthusiasm. Her smile went up a notch in authenticity and she came over and kissed my cheek. Had she wondered if I'd returned to claim my rightful place at my husband's side?

'Of course it's OK!' Richard beamed. Perhaps he, too, had been frozen rigid by the prospect of a loving reunion between us. 'How was Edward?'

'Really good. We had an excellent chat.' I looked meaningfully at Richard. 'About the past.'

Richard knew immediately what I meant, because the telepathy of a long marriage didn't switch off simply because the marriage had ended. He made a very slight shift of his mouth, which meant, 'Oh God, was it OK? I wish I had been able to tell you, but you understand why I didn't.' With my eyes, I telegraphed back, 'Yes, I understand, and thank you.'

He smiled, relieved.

Aileen, who'd been avidly following our facial ping pong, said, 'Would you be wanting to help Kay fetch her things, Richard? I'll get on with the supper.'

'No, it's fine,' I said, 'Alice can help me.'

'Yes, of course,' Alice said, looking startled. She abandoned her pretence of making tea, and straightened up into even more of a ramrod position than normal.

I longed to say something nice to Aileen, to show her I didn't feel displaced, but for some reason I blurted, 'I was admiring your lovely swans.'

'Oh! Thank you.'

'Yes,' Alice said, thin-lipped, 'they're awfully *clever*, aren't they?'

The amount of vitriol Alice managed to pour into 'clever' was a masterclass in contempt. I felt a sisterly pang for poor old Aileen, who'd be on the receiving end of Alice's infinite disdain now. But it was definitely someone else's turn; I'd done my time.

And perhaps Aileen was up to it. I thought I saw a mischievous twinkle in her eye. 'Och you daftie, Alice,' she said, her Highlands accent seeming broader by the minute. 'Like I said before, I can show you how to do the swans in a jiffy. They're not very difficult.'

'Marvellous,' Alice said, gritting her teeth so hard I thought I saw enamel dust.

I went out, Alice following, and climbed upstairs slowly, clinging on to the bannister for support. It felt so odd being back here, so wrong, an old coat I'd outgrown. At the top of the stairs I stood for a moment outside my former bedroom. Mine and Richard's former bedroom. God, this was requiring considerably more grit than I possessed. I looked at Alice, willing her to help me get through this, and she pushed a glass into my hand.

'Medicinal,' she whispered.

It was brandy, the best present anyone could have given me at that point. She must have poured it during the pretend tea-making. Probably for herself, so giving it to me was a true gesture of kindness.

'Thank you,' I said, and chucked half of it down my throat. *Man up, Kay!* Then I tentatively pushed open the door and went inside.

My chair still had all the clothes slung over it that had been there when I left, presumably now covered in dust. I was pretty sure the duvet cover was different to the one I had last seen on this bed. Alice, surely, would make him change the sheets. Or would that be Aileen's remit now? The room looked different, but I couldn't put my finger on why.

It was so airless in there that I sat on the bed, trying to catch my breath, doing the slow yoga breathing, wondering as I did if it actually helped calm me or was just a placebo.

'Are you all right?' Alice said. Her voice seemed to come from a long way off.

'Is it different in here, somehow?' I asked.

'I don't think so. I don't come in here except to change the sheets.' Bingo. 'Does it look different to you?'

'Yes. Perhaps it's because I'd forgotten what it looked like.'

'Or perhaps you no longer regard it as your room,' Alice said.

I turned and looked at her, surprised. 'You might be right.'

'Mmm. So. Shall we start with the wardrobe?' She walked over and opened it slowly, as though expecting a large snake to slither out. I stared at my clothes in amazement. Wow, I had so many. I'd been managing all this time with my backpack supplies, supplemented by my Sydney op-shop purchases. I flicked through the hangers, but most of the things felt as if they belonged to someone else. I took a couple of dresses, and a handful of shirts and jumpers, and Alice folded them efficiently and put them into an old weekend bag of mine. Then I went quickly through my bedside drawers, but other than a couple of bits of jewellery, there was nothing to detain me. I crouched down and pulled out the boxes of Bear's letters from under the bed. I planned to go through them and summarise some of the events in them for Charlie. I coughed at the dust that rose up, and piled them outside the door, along with the little stool and the box of memorabilia from Mum's flat.

'Would you be willing to sort the rest, Alice?'

'Certainly,' she said. I pictured her rolling up her sleeves with gusto, pulling on rubber gloves to avoid being contaminated by my bad taste, and sending Richard out with bin bags full of my belongings to the charity shops and the dump.

'Thank you. I really appreciate your help.'

'I'm not a fool, Kathleen,' she said, zipping up the holdall. 'I can see how utterly delighted Richard is by his new friendship, how happy it makes him. It's made me realise just how, well, how *depressed* he was before.'

I should have known Alice would find a way to get in a good solid barb. *I made him depressed, did I?* But thirty years of building up resistance to her eternal disapproval stood me in good stead. *He made me depressed too, you know*, I said in my head, then handed her back the brandy glass.

'I'd better not finish this, I've got to drive.'

'Well, I'll say goodbye,' Alice said. 'I'm going to rest in my room. Mrs Macrae appears to be making the evening meal, so I am a trifle de trop.' She reached out her hand. 'Goodbye, Kathleen. Good luck with your future endeavours.'

'Endeavours' in Alice's voice sounded extremely unsavoury, and rather exciting. I shook her hand, and she turned and went into Edward's old room, where she was currently staying, and closed the door. As I walked downstairs, I wondered how much longer Alice would be living here, and what was happening to her own flat, and whether Richard dating Aileen had put a crimp in Alice's secret plans to move in permanently. Then I realised, with a marvellous lightening of my mood, that none of that need concern me.

I took my things out to the car, and went back to say goodbye. I stood in the kitchen doorway for a moment, before Richard or Aileen noticed me. She was beating egg yolks in a bowl, and he was sitting at the table, a glass of red in his hand, saying something to her and chewing an apple vigorously at the same time, revealing the food in his mouth. It was a trait I had never much enjoyed. But I shook myself; there was nothing to be gained by finding fault. Everyone had irritating habits, including me. Just ask Rose about the teabags. I needed to remember that I had my freedom, and despite his shock when I left, Richard now seemed eager for us to be on good terms. I needed to give thanks for that miracle every day.

Aileen was laughing at something he'd said, and I saw that, really, she was perfect for him. She was the right age – a little older than me – and she was funny, and warm, and kind, and really into stationery. Also, she was bosomy. He'd appreciate that. I knew I'd always been a little too flat in that department for his liking.

'Er,' I said, to alert them to my presence, 'I'm off now.' They looked over at me, and I had a very strong sense that I was now the outsider.

'Ah, Kay!' Richard said. 'I meant to thank you for the amazing pen from Sydney.'

'I'm glad you like it. I thought it was pretty cool.'

'It's smashing.'

'I've sent you something from Venice, too.'

'I look forward to that.'

There was an awkward silence.

'It was lovely to see you, Kay,' Aileen said. 'I hope everything works out for you.' She put down the bowl and sat next to Richard.

'Thank you, that's very kind.' I knew that was my cue to leave, but it felt a bit abrupt to go without any attempt to let them know all was well between us. 'So, Aileen…' I started, but I couldn't think how to end my sentence. *So, Aileen, what do you think of my husband's sexual technique?* Perhaps not. *So, Aileen, how quickly are you planning to move in? Come on, Kay! Why not simply be honest but kind?*

'So, Aileen, I'm really pleased that you and Richard are happy together.'

'Oh, Kay.' She looked as if she might cry. 'That is the nicest thing to say.'

'I mean it,' I said, truthfully.

Richard smiled at me. 'Thank you, Kayla. That means a lot.' Him using my pet name also meant a lot.

'We're taking it slowly,' Aileen said, clearly eager to reassure me. 'I don't live here, you know.'

'We're not in a rush, are we?' Richard said, and put his hand on hers. This gesture, which had, for almost thirty years, been mine to experience alone, rocked me a little. But only a little. I could almost feel the comforting warm weight of his hand on my own. And then it lifted, and I felt not bereft, but lighter.

I waved vaguely at both of them, said, 'See ya!' and in my head, heard a childhood echo from long ago. *See ya! Wouldn't want to be ya!*

I drove for about twenty minutes, then remembered that in the whole Aileen-swans-Alice-brandy confusion, I'd forgotten my damn camera again. I thought about going back, but even stronger than the desire for the camera, was the desire to not ever go into that house again. I kept driving, my mind pleasantly blank, for a couple of hours.

I was past Birmingham, on the motorway heading towards Wolverhampton, when my phone rang. I glanced at the screen on my dash, in case it was Stella or Edward, but it was a long mobile number unknown to me. I didn't usually take those calls, having had my fill of being asked if I'd been involved in an accident that wasn't my fault, but something made me tell the car thing to answer it.

A man's voice said, 'Hello? Is that Kay?' He had an Australian accent.

Oh God.

Even though I knew this was coming, I still felt the cold hollowness of shock in my stomach. World-Class Emergency. My mouth dried up, and I barely managed to squeak, 'Hello.'

'This is Murray, Ursula's husband. Ex-husband. I'm afraid I've got bad news.'

Chapter 24

Stella

'Did you see that Gabby is here?' Piet said.

'God, is she?' I knew I shouldn't be surprised; every trendy food stall I'd ever seen in my time on the markets seemed to be here. This was our first festival, and though it felt too soon to be testing our food on such a large crowd, the classic rockers on stage would attract our perfect demographic of older couples and families.

'Is the sign straight?' Piet asked, stepping back from the stall.

Nita and I squinted at it. It was our banner's first outing, and it looked brilliant. Piet had persuaded Theo to design it for free, possibly using mild blackmail. The name of our business, 'Back to my Roots', was at the top in large letters, with 'Traditional, Veggie and Vegan Options' in smaller letters underneath, and cute artwork of carrots, potatoes and parsnips round the sides. At the bottom, it said, 'As enjoyed by royalty' – a piece of artistic license based on Gran serving similar meals to the lesser-known princes and princesses fifty-something years ago. We all thought this very funny.

'Bit higher on the right, Piet,' Nita said.

'Yes, boss,' he said, and went back to adjust it.

'Very handy,' Nita said to me in an undertone, 'having someone that tall around.'

Nita was clearly rather taken with Piet. A couple of weeks ago the three of us had moved in together, a mile or so from where Piet and I had lived with Gabby. Things had so far gone abnormally smoothly. Nita referred to our flat as 'House on Fire', because that's how well we all got on.

We'd been there about a week when I bumped into Theo at the supermarket. I thanked him for the banner and he mumbled something self-deprecating, confirming my done-under-blackmail-conditions hypothesis. He'd been keen to tell me he was no longer seeing Gabby.

'I wish it had all never happened,' he said. 'I really regret mucking you about, Stell.'

'Well, that's good of you to say,' I said, and we parted with no hard feelings. I could see that if I'd given him any encouragement at all, he would have asked to try again. Which was a nice ego boost. He didn't inspire any feelings in me any longer – not sad ones, and not angry either. When I looked at his face, all I could see was his weaselly expression the night of Threesome-gate.

Theo's duplicity, coming at the same time as Mum leaving, had really shaken my sense of who I could and couldn't trust. But I was ready now to fling myself back into the murky waters of relationships, ready to hand my heart to someone who might equally treasure or trash it. Not that I could picture Newland hurting me.

But that was the risk you took, when you let people into your life. How could you ever know what they were going to do? Friends might turn out to be liars, might sleep with your boyfriend; other friends you'd drifted apart from might turn out to be absolute jewels; parents who seemed solidly and unmovably around forever might suddenly up and go; parents who were married for thirty years might fall in love with someone else. Like Mum said, not every situation had a black-and-white answer. The future was unknowable, yet that was starting to feel exciting and tingly, rather than scary and out of control.

Nita was putting out our recyclable food boxes, while recounting a lurid story about an old boyfriend of hers who'd liked her to walk up and down his spine while wearing stilettos. It was clearly for Piet's benefit; he was sorting condiments and listening intently, expressions of respect and lust doing battle across his face.

'Right, brace yourselves, I'm firing up this oven,' Nita said.

With contributions from mine and Nita's dads, and Gran, we'd bought a second-hand catering oven, a trailer, and a tow bar to attach it to Nita's car. We intended to pay it all back if we made enough money. I was secretly daring to think that we might, because in 'Back to my Roots' trial runs at street and food markets we had done brilliantly, far beyond our expectations. But the potential audience at this festival was on a completely different scale, and we were all nervous. When the site opened to the public in a couple of hours, we'd be in unchartered territory.

'We are one stall amongst dozens of others,' Nita said, seemingly for her own benefit, as she bustled about getting the oven hooked up and ready. I watched her for a moment, impressed once again at how professional and capable she was. Then I started getting our pre-prepared ingredients together for the toads in the hole. Or was it toad in the holes? Even Gran hadn't been able to decide on the plural. I smiled, thinking about Gran enunciating 'toads in the holes'.

Preparing and planning this business, and testing out the recipes with Nita and Gran, had been the most enjoyable few weeks of my working life.

*

'We should put you on YouTube,' Nita said to Gran. 'You'd be a sensation.'

It was early June, and Gran was teaching us some classic recipes. Nita was as in awe of Gran's hyper-fast chopping technique as me, the way she reduced helpless onions into thousands of bits of shrapnel in seconds. We applauded each time she did it.

'Thank you, dear gels.' Gran smiled modestly. 'But in my own mind I am already all the sensation I need to be.'

'Too right, Mrs B,' Nita said, tipping the onions into a pan. 'I'll never be even half that fast.'

'It's just practice, Nita dear, and good wrist action.'

'To be fair,' Nita muttered, so only I could hear, 'my wrist action has often been complimented.'

'Now how's that batter coming along? Stella dear, put some elbow grease into it, for heaven's sake.'

'If something's worth doing, it's worth doing properly, isn't it, Mrs B?' Nita said, grinning.

'Indeed. You young people need *that* tattooed on your arms, not misspelled Hindi proverbs.'

'Neither of us have tattoos like that, Gran,' I said. 'I've got a butterfly on my ankle.'

'And I've got the moon and stars, but I'm not saying where,' Nita said.

'Sausages!' Dad said, bursting into the kitchen, bringing a blast of outside cool air with him. 'Golly, it's hot in here.'

'We've got all the rings going, and both ovens,' I said, relieving him of his carrier bag. 'Thanks, Dad. Gran is very particular about the toad ingredients.'

'That's why I was so long,' he said, taking off his coat. 'I had to go all the way to Waitrose to get organic.'

'We won't be using posh sausages every time,' Nita said.

'Quality tells, Nita!' Gran said.

'Profit margins tell, an' all,' Nita said, and winked at me.

'Oh yes, Alan Sugar,' Gran said, pouring oil into a frying pan. 'Come back to me when you can't work out how to spend your second million.'

After all her years in catering, Nita was a shrewd businesswoman as well as an excellent cook. Gran rated her highly, regularly telling me how much better a business partner she was than Gabby, and throwing in some disparaging remarks about coriander for good measure.

I always worried that I wasn't a very good cook, or great at business. But as Gran complimented the smoothness of my batter, and Nita kept raving about how terrific my ideas were, I wondered if Newland was right, and that since my crappy degree I'd been unnecessarily hard on myself. I did *love* cooking, and people usually liked what I made. Not Dad, to be fair, but most other people. Mum, for instance, always requested my special strawberry cake for her birthday, ever since I was fourteen.

'I'm heading out again,' Dad said. 'Got to check on, er, some things, and I'll be staying late.'

I noticed a secret smile pass between Dad and Gran, before he kissed me abstractedly on the top of my head, and hurried out.

'Is he off out with Aileen *again*, Gran?'

'Nita, I think this needs more salt,' she said.

'Gran, he's been out with her every evening this week.' Dad's sudden relationship with Aileen was very slightly freaking me out. Wasn't it a bit fast? More than a bit – wasn't it unbelievably fast?

'Well, Stella, if your mother can go gallivanting round the world, surely your father can go out for a drink without exciting the interest of the national media,' Gran said. 'Time for some tasting.'

'The bit I've been waiting for,' Nita said. 'I'm starving.'

I decided to put Dad's weird new love life out of my mind. The food smelled amazing. Gran was right, why shouldn't Dad have some fun? It hadn't been his idea to split up with Mum.

There was silence while we tried the vegetarian shepherd's pie.

'Delicious!' Nita said.

'Not bad at all,' Gran said, her highest form of praise.

It did taste great. But in order to be ready for festivals, we'd have to scale up so much. There were so many possible difficulties ahead, and so much to do if we were going to literally get this show on the road. I was afraid of dragging Nita down with me if it failed.

Trying to keep the anxiety out of my voice, I said, 'Do you think this is going to work, Gran?'

She looked me straight in the eye. I knew she wouldn't lie. 'You know,' she said, and I held my breath, 'I think it will. I think it will be hugely successful. Don't you, Nita?'

'Absolutely!' Nita banged her fork on the table. 'There are so many festivals and events with an older crowd. I'm not saying older people aren't adventurous of course.' And she smiled at Gran. 'But they won't all want chipotle chicken in harissa. Loads of them will love to see the nostalgic food they grew up with. I think it'll be a big hit.'

I heard Bettina's voice. *Take a leap of faith, Stella.*

'OK. Good.' I reached across and took Nita's hand in mine. 'So we're doing this?'

'Oh, we're doing this.'

*

And now, less than a month later, here we were, doing this. I looked out at the huge field, and the dozens of other stalls setting up, and I had to take a few slow breaths. *There is going to be a limit to what I can achieve today.*

Piet caught my eye. 'It will be fine, Stella,' he said. 'We are well-prepared, we have a great team and a superb product, and we have our secret weapon.'

'What's that, Piet?'

'Madame Nita can walk all over anyone who complains with her fierce shoes.'

'Oh you!' Nita flicked a tea towel at him, and he giggled. It was going to be a long day in a small enclosed space with these two undressing each other with their eyes any chance they got.

But once the gates opened and the punters flooded in, there was no time for any eye-undressing. The classic cooler-than-expected British summer weather meant that everyone wanted something warm to eat. The family crowd were very keen to introduce their kids to toad in the hole and bubble and squeak, while the twenty-somethings appreciated the vegan shepherd's pie. Several times during the day I compared our queue to the one at the taco place next to us, and noted with satisfaction and panic that ours was twice as long. Yet with the unflappable and charming Piet serving at the front, and Nita and I cooking together like we'd done it all our lives, everything went like clockwork. We worked non-stop throughout the entire lunchtime period and for an hour afterwards. But as Billy Bragg stepped up and started strumming his opening number, the lunchtime rush at last seemed to be over, and we were able to breathe out.

Once the final few customers dispersed, we did a speedy inventory, and realised our stocks wouldn't be nearly enough for the evening. Nita and Piet volunteered to go back to the flat to collect more supplies. I grinned as they rushed off together to the traders' car park. If they weren't a couple by the end of the night, I would eat Piet's daft beanie hat. I closed the front of the stall, put up a 'back soon' sign, and checked my phone, which I'd felt buzzing in my pocket a few times. There was a lovely text from Mum.

Sparkle, good luck at the festival today. I'm so proud of you. Hope it goes brilliantly, I know it will. You are so smart and clever. Can't wait to try your new food! Hope to see you soon. Love you.

I replied, thanking her and said 'love you too'. I put my phone away and began scrubbing down the prep surfaces. I still hadn't seen Mum, though she'd been back from Venice for a while, and was living permanently in Wales. She'd sent me some lovely messages, but neither of us seemed to have the courage to suggest meeting up. I'd had several awful nights waking up with a gasp, twisting out of a horribly realistic dream in which I yelled at her, 'You're fucking *selfish*!' Would she really want to hear from me after I'd said such awful things?

Nonetheless, I felt relieved and happy that we were at least talking via text, sending messages several times a week. I realised that I was whistling as I wrung out my cloth.

Notice when you're content, Stella, Bettina used to say. *It's important to notice those moments as much as the difficult ones.*

Out loud, I said, 'I'm more than content, Bettina. I'm absolutely exhilarated, actually.'

There was a knock at the back door of the stall. I opened it, expecting to see a member of the friendly festival staff, come to check in.

But Gabby stood there, wearing a Yummi Scrummi apron, holding two coffee cups.

'Am I interrupting?' she said. 'I heard you talking to someone.'

'I was talking to myself,' I said. Once I'd have been embarrassed to admit something like that to cool Gabby, but now it seemed pointless to pretend to be someone I wasn't. There were worse things than having conversations with someone in your head, and Gabby should know; she had done lots of them.

She held out a takeaway cup. 'Latte with skimmed milk, how you like it.'

I put the cup on the counter. 'Thanks.'

'Sorry,' Gabby said. 'I know it's a pretty shit peace offering.'

'Yeah,' I said. 'Cup of coffee in return for my boyfriend. Doesn't seem quite enough, does it?'

'Fuck, no. Sorry, Stell. Well, er, how's it going? Your stall was the busiest, I saw the queues.'

'Yes, we did well,' I said, dishing out my words in small portions.

'Was that Piet I saw out front, serving?'

'You know it was, Gabby. No one else looks like Piet. And you've seen him up very close, you know how he looks.'

'Bam! Pow!' Gabby swerved her head from side to side, as though avoiding imaginary punches. 'You're totally bossing it.'

'Look, I'm a bit busy, and you must be too, so…'

'Stella.' Gabby looked at her feet. 'I wanted to say sorry properly. I know I fucked up, and I don't even know how it happened.'

'How can you not know? How can you sleep with someone's boyfriend and not know how it happened?'

Gabby's shoulders sagged, and out of nowhere, she started to cry. 'I'm – *sob!* – such – *sob!* – a fucking – *sob!* – idiot – *sob!*'

At least there was something we could agree on.

It felt weird seeing her cry, because she'd always given the impression of being made of granite. I tentatively put my arms round her, and she immediately gripped me tightly back and continued sobbing.

I patted her shoulder and muttered, 'there, there,' in an attempt to speed this along. When her crying seemed a little less intense, I asked, 'Who's helping you on the Yummi Scrummi stall?'

'No one,' she mumbled.

'You're not running it on your own, are you?'

'Yes,' Gabby said, leaning heavily against me. 'Three drunk women shouted at me because I didn't do their order quickly enough.' Her words were interspersed with little sniffs.

'Gabby, it's far too hectic here for one person. That's insane.'

She moved out of my arms. 'I guess I am insane, right?' She wiped her face with her apron. 'Why did I mess things up between us?'

'I don't know. I'm not a therapist, Gabby.'

'Please tell me, Stella.'

'Look, I don't have any special insight into your brain. Perhaps you wanted to run the business alone. Maybe you were sick of living with me and didn't know how to say so. Maybe you secretly wanted to sleep with me, so slept with my boyfriend instead.'

'Wow, steady on there, Dr Freud. You're not *that* hot.'

'Perhaps,' and this came to me in a flash, by far the most likely explanation for Gabby's unfathomable behaviour, 'you're in love with Theo.'

'Sorry, *what*?' A red blush started to rise up her neck.

'You're in love with Theo. You've loved him for years. You jumped at the chance to have me move in because it meant you could get closer to him, then you couldn't work out how to play it.' This came out fully formed, as if it had been pre-prepared in my brain, the ingredients all in place, ready to be served up.

'That's absolute bollocks.' Gabby's face was completely tomato-hued now.

'Well, take it or leave it. There are a lot of possibilities, Gabby, but it's up to you to work it out. It was Theo who hurt me, but you were part of that, and that's not what friends do.' She didn't say anything, and I added, 'Why don't you tell Theo how you feel? Be completely honest, see what he says. I don't think he has any idea how much you like him.'

If this was a therapy session, Gabby would soon have to fork over fifty quid.

In the distance, I saw Newland making his way towards the food area, and my heart lifted. 'Sorry, I have to get on.'

I moved towards the sink, in the hope that Gabby would go, but she stood there looking sad.

'Stella, everything's gone to shit since you left.'

'Uh huh.'

'I know, I know, it's my own stupid fault. I was wondering though… would you consider trying again? With the Sri Lankan food? I know you won't want to move back into the house, though you can if you want, like a shot, these unfriendly people are living there, and…'

Newland was close enough for me to see his face now. He was scanning the stalls, looking for me. I waved, and Gabby turned to see who I was signalling to.

'Who's that?'

'Someone you're not allowed to sleep with,' I said, and a moment later I was in Newland's arms. It felt really natural; no one looking at us would guess that it was the first time we had really held each other

tight. When we broke apart, I was gratified to see on Newland's face
that he too got the significance of the embrace.

'Hey, this looks fantastic!' he said, sweeping his arm round the stall.

'It's going amazingly well,' I said.

Newland stepped back, and looked at Gabby. 'Hello,' he said.

'This is Gabby.'

'*The* Gabby? Man, I've heard a lot about you.'

'Oh cool, I'm famous,' Gabby said with a flirtatious smile.

'I've heard a lot of toxic stuff about you,' Newland clarified.

I stifled a smile.

'I'll be going then, I guess,' Gabby said, not moving.

She looked so pathetic that I took pity on her.

'Look, here's something that might help.' I took out my phone. 'I'm
texting you the number of my old therapist. She's in London so it's a
bit of a trek, but I really recommend her.' I sent her Bettina's contact
details, then put my phone back in my pocket so decisively that Gabby
had no option other than to go.

'Bye, then.' She turned to Newland. 'Good to meet you.'

'Mmm,' said the usually polite Newland, and he turned and started
washing his hands at the little sink.

Once Gabby had gone, I kissed Newland on the cheek.

'What was that for?'

'For not falling for Gabby's charms.'

'I didn't notice any,' he said.

'I like you, Mr Davies,' I said, as I helped him tie on his apron.

'I like you too, Ms Bright.'

'I've been thinking…' I said.

'I've been thinking the same,' he said.

'How do you know it's the same?'

'Because I see a twinkle in your eye.'

There was no need for me to put my reply into words. I threw my arms round his neck and kissed my answer instead.

The evening was even busier than lunch and I was extremely grateful to have Newland with us. He and Piet were a brilliant front-of-stall team, and Nita and I got even more efficient at the back, dancing round each other like *Strictly* professionals. Even with the extra supplies, we came close to selling out. Plenty of people came back more than once.

One family returned three times to try everything; and a frazzled-looking mum confided in Piet, with tears in her eyes, that her young daughter had eaten the bubble and squeak, the first time ever that she had liked cooked vegetables. 'It's a bloody miracle,' the girl's father said, and it seemed as if he was speaking for the entire day, our entire enterprise.

It wasn't all smooth sailing, of course. At one point the oven stopped working, having come apart from the gas supply and we had to temporarily shut up shop while we reconnected it. Then we ran out of wooden cutlery. Piet abandoned his post and dashed to the nearest supermarket to buy up what he claimed was their whole supply, while Nita ran round nearby stalls asking to borrow some to keep us going.

But undoubtedly, it was a triumph. I couldn't remember ever being so physically exhausted, yet so mentally energised. When we finally brought down the shutters at 10.30 p.m., we smiled at each other with the incredulous smiles of people who have got away with something. It turned out that there *wasn't* a limit to what we could achieve that day.

'That was fricking awesome,' Nita said. Even her bubbliness, which generally operated on a 24/7 basis, was slightly dimmed. She spoke more quietly than usual, and sat on the trailer steps looking as if she could go to sleep right there and then.

'Never thought we could do it,' I said. I sank down onto the steps next to her, and we gave each other a tired hug.

Piet had been counting the card and cash takings. He said, 'It is clear from this profit that British people really love root-vegetable-based dishes.'

'A big profit?' Nita said.

'Enormous,' Piet said, with a smile just for Nita.

Nita and I slapped our palms together feebly. 'Let's get packed up,' I said. 'It's another two hours before we'll be allowed off site and I want to be ready the minute we can move.'

Nita heaved herself into a standing position. She looked across at Lan, who was leaning against a counter smiling at us. 'You're awfully quiet, New Boy. Whatcha thinking?'

'Oh, just what a brilliant achievement this was, and how well we worked together, and how superbly you two planned and executed the whole thing.' He beamed at me. 'I couldn't be more impressed.'

I beamed back. 'We had a lot of help,' I said, 'from some terrific young men.'

'That's us,' Piet said proudly, shaking hands with Newland.

'It's a hell of a team,' Nita said. 'Shame you two have real jobs.'

'I don't,' Piet said. 'I can combine my studies and my bar and courier work with this splendid new business venture.'

'And I'd love to help on weekends,' Newland said.

'Yes,' Piet concluded, 'we would very much like to be part of Rooty-Tooty.'

'You know that's not its name, don't you, Piet?' Nita put her arms round Piet's neck.

'It should be, though, Madame Nita.' His arms went round her waist.

'Well!' I said, jumping up. 'Shall we have a little walk round the site, Newland?'

Nita and Piet were already locked into a massive snog as Newland and I hurried down the trailer steps, giggling. Outside, the festival was winding down. The main stage was empty, though a couple of smaller marquees were still blasting out music. The site was dark, and I looked up at the sky, speckled with stars. Arm-in-arm, we wandered round the few stalls that were still open, and got a couple of beers. Most of the younger festival-goers had been taken home, and there was a sense of several small, intense parties going on in various corners of the site.

'What about Piet and Nita, then?' Newland said.

'Ah, I saw that coming a while ago. I hope they're not going to be committing PDAs like that at home. I've already seen enough of Piet in the buff to last a lifetime.'

Newland laughed. 'You're a brave little soldier. Perhaps you'd better come back with me tonight. I have a feeling there might be some serious romping at your place.'

'And at yours too, I hope.'

'Is that a promise?'

I shivered with anticipation. 'Yes, it is.'

'That makes me very happy. And it's Sunday tomorrow. We can have a long lie-in, and I'll bring you breakfast in bed.'

'And then will you bring me a Newland in bed?'

'It would be my pleasure. Literally and metaphorically. Stella, I am honestly so proud of you. You had a vision and you made it happen.'

I stopped and turned to him. It was too dark to see his face properly. But that was a blessing, because he couldn't see mine either. 'If I said it happened because you believed in me, would you think we were on an American soap opera?'

'Yes. Are we?' He put his beer down on the ground and wrapped his arms round me. 'Is your mother really your sister?'

'Is that always what happens in American soap operas?'

'I believe so,' he said, his voice a little muffled as he buried his face in my hair. 'And talking of mothers, I bet yours will be really proud of you too.'

'She's sent me loads of nice texts.'

'I know you were really upset with her,' Newland said. 'But she has always been there for you, hasn't she?'

'I suppose…'

'When my parents split they were so self-obsessed. Perhaps they were like that before. But they never ask how I'm doing, never check in with me, never have anything much to say to me unless it's to slag each other off. Your parents, on the other hand, it's been such a short time since they separated, but they are both still right there with you. Especially your mum.'

'Damn!'

'Why damn?'

'You're right. I'm going to have to do some proper grovelling to Mum.'

'I'll help. I'll do back-up grovelling.'

'What does that look like?'

'I'm not sure. I'll hold all the bunches of flowers for you, or something.'

I tightened my arms round him. 'Newland?'

'Mmm?'

'I, er, I think I love you, you know.'

I felt him breathe out against my hair, a long warm sigh. 'I think I love you too.'

It felt as if we were quite alone, though there were hundreds of people milling about, weaving past us. One woman, a little the worse for wear, bumped into us and we broke apart. 'Oops! Sorry! Didn't see you! God, it's so dark!' She reeled away, and I reached for Newland's hand.

'We're standing in a thoroughfare. Let's go back and see if the others have stopped kissing yet.'

'I don't think we've quite stopped ourselves, yet, have we?' Newland said. He bent down and gently kissed me on the lips. I responded enthusiastically, and it was only when someone else almost walked into us that finally, hand-in-hand, we strolled back to the trailer to pack up and go home.

Chapter 25

Kay

'Ah, it's amazing to see this again.'

Rose nodded. 'Gorgeous, weren't we?'

The photo was a little crumpled round the edges, but – please excuse my lack of modesty – there was no denying the quality. It was a tight headshot in black and white of three pretty young women: Rose on the left, smiling and looking sideways at Bear next to her; me on Bear's right, looking simultaneously pleased and harassed. Setting up the camera timer and making sure everyone stayed in the right place was a bit stressful. With film, you couldn't keep trying again and again till you got it right. You had to get everything in place, then hold your breath and hope.

The photo was from the one visit to Australia that Rose and I took together, during our gap year, when we were still in our teens. When everything in life was there to be looked forward to, and it was too early for us to have made any mistakes. Before I met Richard, or David; before I got pregnant and crashed out of my degree. I looked again at our unlined, hopeful faces. So beautiful, so young.

Bear's laughing face, in the middle, made that photo. The eye was drawn to her. It was absolutely impossible to believe that this radiant, lit-up person was no longer alive.

I'd assumed that trip would be the first of many, as per my list, but less than two years later I was pregnant and the free lazy days of my youth came to an abrupt, juddering halt. It had been years since I'd seen this photo, but I remembered that cheeky version of Rose so well, before marriage and life knocked the stuffing out of her. Not permanently, as it turned out. Fifty-something Rose had started to find her old groove. I remembered that version of Bear, before illness cropped her hair and radiated lines of pain onto her face. And that version of the other girl, Kay Hurst, before her life turned into a series of compromises – whatever happened to her?

A tear dropped onto my hand, and I placed the photo carefully on the table so it wouldn't get wet.

'Ah, darling,' Rose said. She put her arms round me. Her eyes were damp too. We'd done plenty of crying about Bear's death, and you'd think there would be no more tears left, but we both kept welling up whenever we thought about it. Which was most of the time.

'You know,' I said, against Rose's shoulder, 'if she was alive, I'd be writing to her about now.'

'There's nothing to stop you writing letters to her,' Rose said. 'Nothing says you have to send them. Or you can start writing to me, now. Keep me up to date with your Welsh student adventures.'

I let Rose go, and wiped my face with the edge of a tea towel. 'How come you ended up with the photo?'

She sat next to me. 'You gave it to me, along with the negative. I think I'd offered to get copies done for all of us, but I must have forgotten.'

'I don't suppose you still have the negative?'

'No, but you don't need them anymore, David Bailey. Photography's moved on a bit since then.' Rose triumphantly produced two copies of the picture. 'You just scan it in and print as many as you want. The quality's pretty good.'

'Thank you,' I said. 'I'll send one to Murray, ask him to pass it on to Charlie.'

'Did he put a note in with the, er, the...'

'Ashes? Yes, very brief, thanking me for doing it. It was all unofficial, you know. I assume he couldn't be arsed with the paperwork and expense to do it properly, so I opened a jiffy bag that came via normal airmail and found—'

'Oh, Christ.'

'A small amount of Bear in a Ziploc bag.'

'Please don't show me.' Rose shook her head. 'I still can't believe she's... you know. Left the planet.'

'I know, chick. Me neither. I don't know if she got my last letter, from Venice. But that letter she left there for me was the last I heard from her. When she said goodbye, she really meant it.'

Rose let out a long sigh. 'Wish I'd come with you now.'

'You weren't to know. I'll tell you what else Murray sent me. Bear asked him to. It came in a massive parcel – all my letters to her. Arranged chronologically, with the most recent on top.'

'Oh, Kay.'

'When I'm feeling stronger, I'm going to read them through. My entire adult life on record.'

'That was thoughtful of her.' Rose shook her head. 'It feels unfinished, doesn't it? So weird that the last time I saw her turned out to be the last time I will ever see her. We always think there will be more time.' Her voice cracked on the last few words. 'Jeez, Kay, you realised all this, even before Bear, didn't you?'

'What do you mean?'

'All your carpe diem stuff, chucking your marriage in, you already realised that this could all end any second.' Rose indicated 'this' by gesturing round the room, but I knew she meant 'everything' and not just the kitchen.

'I feel it more keenly than ever now, though,' I said.

'*Heavy*,' Rose said.

'*Heavy*,' I replied.

'Oh blast, the tea!' Rose jumped up and grabbed the pot, hastily poured us mugs of stewed-looking dark tea.

I added a lot of milk, and smirked at her. 'Yeah, this is so much nicer than the stuff I make.'

'Sod off. You know I left it too long.' She looked again at the photo. 'You really were a terrific photographer.'

'Aw, shucks.' I took out my phone. 'Still am. Look at this.'

'The *Scottish Herald*. What am I looking at?'

'Edward sent them one of my Venice pictures and they chose it as their photo of the week.'

'Oh, wow! That's fantastic!' Rose took a closer look. 'It says your picture is magical.'

'Yes, "a magical, unusual image, that reveals something new to us about this much-photographed city". Oh mercy me, I seem to have memorised it.'

'Well, of course, I was there first with famous photographer Kay Bright. You did my wedding photos, remember?' Rose said.

I could still capture the pure flush of pride I'd felt when I showed Rose the wedding album I'd made for her. 'Yeah, they turned out pretty well, didn't they?'

'Considerably better than the marriage.' Rose made a face. 'And look at this photo of us three. It really captures something about the essence of each of us.'

'I was so intense about photography back then.'

'You took your camera and lenses and the whole shebang to Australia that gap-year trip. Do I remember a tripod coming with us too? You hardly had any room for clothes so you had to borrow stuff off me and Bear the whole time.'

'Ah, to be so single-minded. Before I encumbered myself with responsibilities.' I smiled. 'Bear lent me a blue T-shirt with a rainbow on it that trip, and I accidentally took it home with me.'

'Was it really an accident?'

'It suited me better than her.'

'Well.' Rose let out a long shuddering sigh. 'She don't need it now.'

We looked at each other. I still couldn't believe it, even though I'd known it was coming. Despite having gone through it not long ago with my mum, I couldn't take in that David and Bear were no longer in the world. People my own age. I was closer than ever to the edge myself.

'So,' Rose said, 'what now?'

The sunlight, which had earlier filled the cottage kitchen with a summer gold, was starting to fade. Rose's face was becoming less distinct, but I didn't want to turn on the new overhead spotlights.

'Well, tomorrow we go to Hoylake. Then when I get back I have to finish my application for the photography course. I'm going to have to buy a new camera, I can't face asking Richard to send me my old one. And I've made notes for the Airbnb listing. I just need to work out how to use the website.'

'I love your plans. It feels like you've made things happen so quickly. What a turnaround.'

'Couldn't have done it without you and Graham helping me.'

'It was a pleasure.' Rose leaned back in her chair. 'I love it here. Imogen's guys did a good job on the redecoration, don't you think?'

'It's maybe a bit too much soothing grey for me, I like a bit of colour. But I can liven it up with pictures and cushions, can't I?'

'I'll get you some pretty cushions for a house-warming gift,' Rose said. 'You'll let me come and stay here whenever you don't have lodgers, won't you?'

'You're always welcome. But won't Graham mind you popping up here all the time?'

'Hell, no. Do you know what I like most about Graham?'

'Is this going to be X-rated?' I leaned forward.

'The way he makes the most of any situation. I say, "Graham, I'm going to Kay's for a bit," and he goes, "Great, that'll be nice." Or, "Graham, I've got to go to the supermarket, do you want to come?" and he'll say, "Yes, it'll be good to hang out with you." And if I say, "Actually on second thoughts it'll be quicker on my own," he'll say, "Sure, why don't I get started on supper while you're gone." It's perfect, to be honest.'

'Somewhat different from Tim, huh?'

'Tim always made the least of any situation. And as Oprah Winfrey used to say, "Honey, I do not need that negative energy around me, nuh-uh."'

I rolled my eyes like Stella would. How I wished she was here. I still hadn't seen her since our fight in the car, and I missed her with a physical ache. I so wanted to ask her to meet, but was afraid to push her into it too soon, before she was properly ready to forgive me.

I went on quickly, before I got too maudlin, 'Listen, thanks for coming tomorrow. I know you don't like going back to Hoylake.'

'I can't let you handle Bear on your own.' Rose scrunched up her face. 'But it'll be so weird. I've not been back there, Kay, not for years.'

'I know.'

'After Mum moved away, there was nothing there for me anymore.'

'You've always been amazing, Rose, at moving forwards. At not looking back.'

'Have I? That's good. I think. Is it good?'

'Yes. It's admirable. We both escaped the Wirral and went to uni in London, but I never went much further. Till now. But look at you. You've lived in Cardiff, France, the States, then back here to Manchester, then… where?'

'Southwold.'

'Oh yes, do you remember your lovely house on the beach?'

'Glorious. But so isolated. You know what I remember most about living there? You coming up every weekend after Tim left. You got me through that hellish time, and I will never forget it.'

'I don't think I did anything much.'

'You only had one day off work a week, Sunday, and every Saturday night for about six months you'd faithfully drive up to Southwold. Not exactly a short journey, is it? You'd take the kids out, let me sleep, cook for me, make me laugh, wipe my tears, give me wine, clean the kitchen. Then in the early hours of Monday morning you'd drive back to London and go straight in to work.'

'You've more than paid me back, Rose, given my recent shenanigans. Didn't you come back to London after Southwold?'

'God, yes, it was a relief to get away from Tim's idea of an idyllic place to live. Back to London, and finally to Winchester.'

'I need to be more like that. More like you. Not get static, stuck in a place.'

'You've been doing pretty well lately, Kay. And Bryn Glas is a very nice place to be stuck.'

'Yes, well remind me not to stay here for twenty-nine years, won't you?'

'I hope we get twenty-nine more years,' Rose said, and shivered. 'So, you don't think you'll get lonely here? No handsome Italian stallions coming to keep you company?'

'Funnily enough, I heard from Luca last week.'

'You did?' Rose sat up straight. 'Tell me *everything*.'

'He texted to say he'd be in the UK for a conference in September, if I'd like to meet up.'

'And? AND?' Rose said.

'I said I wasn't sure where I'd be then, and I'd let him know.'

'What? But you will be here! You'll be starting your course then.'

'I know. I want to think about it.'

'You're being very cool, Miss Kay, I must say. Ice Queen.'

'I know you'll encourage me to go for it, Rose—'

'Too right I will!'

'And it might be wonderful to see him. But it also might tarnish the memories of that brilliant night.'

Rose nodded. 'I get it. If he turns out to be less gorgeous than you remember.'

'Or less fun, or kind, or good at listening. I need to think for a bit longer about what I want.' I glanced at the clock. 'Look, it's getting late, and we are on ash-duty tomorrow. We're going to need a good night's sleep if we're to be emotionally resilient.'

Rose yawned. 'Fine. I'll interrogate you further about your sex life tomorrow.' We stood up, and I put my arms round her.

'Listen, Rose, thank you for helping me make my plans into something real.'

'You're welcome.' She rested her head on my shoulder. 'You've made brilliant choices.'

'Apart from in my tea-making.'

'Hell yes. I can't believe that you'll soon be here alone in charge of a box of innocent teabags.'

'You go up, I'll turn out the lights.'

'Night, Kay.'

As I got ready for bed, Bear's face was in my head, her face when we sat in the restaurant. 'Not yet, darling. Don't ask me anything yet.'

I hoped she knew how much I appreciated her throwing everything in to come with me to Venice. I hoped it didn't hasten her end, though that was something I'd never know. But it had been her decision to come. I sat on the grey chair and let myself cry. For her, for me, for our friendship. For the way she'd stopped writing ahead of her death, perhaps to prepare me for the letters I would no longer receive, and for the loss of writing my own letters to her, putting my thoughts down on paper.

It was getting cold. I wrapped a blanket round my shoulders, picked up my writing pad from its home on the little embroidered stool, and under the sloping window's picture of inky-black sky, I uncapped my pen.

19 July 2018

Dearest Bear/Ursula (I will never get used to your real name),

So you upped and died. That was hasty of you. I hope you weren't in pain, and that there were people with you who loved you.

Rose has offered to be my correspondent now, so this will be my last letter to you. Well, of course it will, Bear, because you're dead. Why you had to go and be dead, I don't know. I have some of your ashes. They don't look like you.

I told you how much I love the cottage in Wales. Well, I'm living here now. Sure, it's remote and creaky, but it's got a fresh lick of paint and it feels more like home than anywhere else. I love being here alone. I've always been around a lot of people. What with the kids and the shops, I never had much solitude, and I've realised that I really need it. But then, of course, sometimes I really miss noise and people.

I've taken a long lease on the cottage, and I've agreed with Imogen that I'll put the spare room on Airbnb a few times a month. It'll mean I can cover the rent, and it'll be company now and then. Yes, Bear, I'll try not to let any serial killers stay. I've already put a lock on my bedroom door, in case. Plus, I'm going to restore the barn, and slowly make it into a couple of bedrooms and a bathroom. I have carte blanche as long as I make it better not worse, and so they'll be able to use that for more tenants in the future.

Thank you for your list. I've pretty much tackled all of it. Firstly, the photography – I <u>am</u> going to do something with it. Thank you so much for suggesting it. I'm kicking off with a part-time degree in photography. The university is only thirty-odd miles away. I haven't applied yet, but they've told me informally that I'm likely to get a place. This time I will finish it. Degrees are considerably more expensive than they were when I flunked out last time. I'm not sure it's the best use of Mum's money, but the course is very practical, and there are lots of work-placement opportunities in various studios and labs. Some are in Liverpool, so I'd be going right back to where we started if I got one there.

I'm hoping I'll be able to support myself with it at some stage. More to the point, I want to spend my time doing something I love. I feel excited, reinvigorated, in a way I've not felt for years.

The second item on your list was Richard. You were right to tell me to check. I thought, briefly, perhaps I did want to go back to him. It wasn't right, as it turned out. But it helped me reach the clarity I needed, and allowed me to properly move on in a way I hadn't been able to before. We are being strangely benign towards each other, now. I think we both feel that we have given each other our freedom.

Then, Edward. Finally, years too late, we talked about David. It brought us close together, closer than we've been for a long time. I found an old photo of David that I took, back when we were an item. I sent one copy to Edward, and another to David's widow, Verity. I contacted her via David's son on Facebook. She wrote such a lovely note, said she would put the photo in a frame on the wall, that she wanted to think of him like that, not how he looked when he was ill.

The one cloud still in the sky, apart from you, dear girl – maybe you're a star up there now? – is that things still aren't right with Stella. I haven't seen her for two months, and I feel so terrible about the harsh things I said. I don't know how to make it right. But I won't bore you with that, Bear, not now you're dead.

So, you've had your funeral, just close family, in Oz. Charlie is living full-time with Murray, and they're going to sell your house because his is bigger. Murray tells me that the proceeds from the house will go into Charlie's college fund, so that's good news, isn't it?

I guess I'm scrabbling around for good news.

Tomorrow, Rose and I will make a pilgrimage to Hoylake. You wanted to go there one last time, and you will, Bear, even if in weird gritty form. The final item on your list. We'll walk to West Kirby beach, where you wanted to drink tea, and we'll do that in your memory.

I was thinking about that time we went there, we were fourteen or so, because we reckoned the peace and quiet would help us revise. You were mucking about on the rocks and fell in the water. Rose was nearly sick, she laughed so much. Your geography notes got ruined and I had to get my dad to photocopy mine for you. Well, we're going to sit on that same rock, if we can find it, and put you back in the water. This time there are no exams to worry about. There's nothing, in fact, for you to worry about, anymore.

Love you.

Miss you.

Always, Kay

I put the pen down, got into bed, and stared up at the skylight. I thought I would never get to sleep, and then it was morning, and the light was streaming in. I could hear Rose clattering around downstairs, no doubt doing something homely with the teapot, and I got up. It was not a day for lying in bed. It was a day for saying goodbye.

Letter written on 12 October 1982

Dearest Bear,

Loved your letter, thank you, it was so loooooong, I have read it six times. Thank you for the photo of your new house, it looks lovely. I'm sorry your college isn't very good, I wish you could have stayed here and your parents have gone without you. You could have lived with me. Rose and I miss you <u>so so so</u> much. College is fun but it would have been so much better with you, that nice lady lecturer we saw on the open day with the plaits saw me and Rose and she remembered us and said, 'Where's your friend?', meaning you. We both started crying and she gave us tissues and some chewy mints.

Anyway, it doesn't matter how far away you are because we will visit each other regularly, as inscribed in our lists, and we will always be friends, forever and ever, in sickness and health, till death us do part, amen. I think we might accidentally be married now, hope that's OK with you.

Till next time.

Miss you.

Always, Kay

Chapter 26

Kay

'Is it here?'

'I don't think so, Rose. In my memory, they were right next to the sea.'

'I know, chick, but the tide's much further out than it was that day.'

'How is it that there are so many damn rocks?'

Rose and I walked further along the beach, trying to identify the rock that Bear had fallen off more than three decades ago. It was tricky, because there were lots of possible rocks. And also, because it was more than three decades ago.

Apart from a few solitary dog-walkers, the beach was almost deserted. You'd think there would be some early holidaymakers, but schools hadn't broken up yet; anyway, it had never been a particularly touristy beach. We were surrounded by water. On one side of us, the sea, far off in the distance, glinted appealingly. On the other side there was the marine lake, with its yachts bobbing about. I remembered my dad spending time there when I was young, but I realised I had no idea what he had been doing. Did he sail? Or just hang out with boating friends? There was no one I could ask, now.

'After this,' I said, 'no one can die for a while.'

'Too right,' Rose said. 'It's been a rough old year for you, first your mum, and now Bear.'

'And David.' I hadn't planned to tell Rose yet, but it came out, unbidden.

'Who?' Rose turned and looked at me.

'David Endevane.'

'That name rings a bell.'

'He was the boy I was seeing before I married Richard.'

'Oh yes! I remember. I saw him with you a couple of times in the Students' Union. He was gorgeous, wasn't he?'

'Yes.'

'Looked like a pop star. You were rather smitten, I recall. Why did you split up with him again?'

'I discovered I was pregnant.'

'Oh yes! I remember. Richard got you pregnant. You cheeky dog! Those were the days, when we juggled several men… ' Rose stopped and made a shocked face. 'Don't tell me he's died?'

'Yes, October, but I only heard recently.'

'Oh. I'm sorry, Kay. I didn't know you were still in touch with him.'

'I wasn't. I haven't seen him since I was twenty-one.' I started walking, and Rose scurried to catch me up.

'Hang on, miss! What's going on? What aren't you telling me?'

'Rose, there is a lot to tell you, but we should wait till we have very large drinks in our hands.'

'Ooh, you said this in one of your texts. This all sounds very intriguing.'

'I'm praying you won't be cross with me for not telling you a long time ago.'

'How old is this secret?'

'I've been keeping it since I was twenty-one.'

'That's a coincidence, it's the last time you saw David.'

'You're like Hercule Poirot, Rose.'

She twirled an imaginary moustache. 'Did you murder anyone?'
I shook my head.

'OK, well, I expect I won't be too cross, then.'

I kissed her cheek. 'What did I do to deserve a friend like you?'

'You're not a bad friend yourself, soft lad.' We grinned at each other.

'Come on, then,' I said. 'Let's get this done.'

'Hang on,' Rose said. She stopped walking, and looked across the beach, the way we'd come, back towards Hoylake.

'What for?' I said, but as I spoke, I heard the faint sound of someone calling Rose's name. I turned and saw that in the far distance, a woman was walking towards us. Rose started waving extravagantly with both arms.

'Who's that?' I said, and then I realised. 'Ohhh, Rose.'

'Thought it would be nice if she was here,' Rose said, not looking at me.

As Stella got nearer, walking tentatively across the hard sand, I knew how anxious she was from her body language. She looked a little thinner since I last saw her. Her hair was pinned up and made her look more adult. I tried to make my face welcoming, not wary.

'You found us!' Rose cried, pulling Stella into a massive hug. 'I'd forgotten how many great piles of rocks there are! Sorry about that.'

'It's fine,' Stella said. She untangled herself from Rose, and she and I looked uncertainly at each other.

'Hello, sweetheart,' I said.

'Hello, Mummy,' she said, and the baby-name made my eyes prickle.

'Come here,' I said, and she walked into my arms and held me as fiercely as when she was a teenager and had been vile to me all day; her intense night-time hugs were her way of saying sorry. The final crack in my heart started to heal over.

We let go, and stood, smiling foolishly at each other. 'It's unbelievably kind of you to drag Stella here,' I said to Rose.

'She didn't drag me,' Stella said quietly. 'I wanted to see you.'

'You did? You were so angry…'

'I'm sure everyone said things they didn't mean,' Rose said, briskly. 'What better way to reconnect than over the scattering of ashes?'

'It's not the jolliest team-building activity you could have thought of, Rose.'

'I'm afraid the obstacle course was all booked up,' Rose said. She put her arm through Stella's. 'This lovely girl has schlepped here to support you on a difficult day.'

'Thank you for coming, Sparkle.' I put my arm through Stella's free one, sandwiching her between me and Rose. 'I've been dreading today.' I planted a kiss on her lovely cheek.

'We'd hoped to launch her off the rocks where we used to sit,' Rose said to Stella, pointing. 'Probably those ones there, but the tide's too far out. We will have to have a little walk, is all.'

'I'd like a walk,' Stella said. 'I've been on a train for ages.'

'It's not quite as warm as I'd thought, bloody July in England, and I am fatally under-dressed,' Rose said. 'Let's get Bear into the sea, and us into a nice pub.'

Linked together, feeling contained and whole with my two favourite women, we set off. The water, sparkling faintly in the distance, looked miles away, across a vast expanse of hard cold sand.

'How's everything going with "Back to my Roots"?' I asked. 'Your father tells me it's going brilliantly.'

'It is a big success. I'm glad you and Dad are speaking to each other.'

'We're being terribly mature.' I laughed. 'Dad also told me that your new boyfriend is great.'

'Dad really likes Newland, so you'll have been getting a biased account.'

'Your grandmother likes him too, apparently, so he's either a saint, or minor royalty.'

'Jeepers, it's like a bush telegraph!' Stella said. 'You know everything. Well, it's early days, Mum. But he's really great.'

'I'd like to meet him some time.'

'Actually, I was thinking of bringing him to Wales for a few days, and we could help with your barn renovations.'

'That would be wonderful!' I frowned. 'But how do you know I was planning to do up the barn?'

Stella tilted her head at Rose, who I could see grinning out of the corner of my eye.

'Jeepers,' I said, 'it's like a bush telegraph!'

'Also, we wanted to ask if you'd take some photos for our website.'

'I'd be honoured to.'

'Plus, we've got a stall next month at a new festival in mid Wales, not far from you, so we hoped you might come along to that, see us in situ.'

Stella clearly wanted me back in her life, and then some. 'Shit,' I said, getting a tissue out of my pocket. 'I was planning to save my tears for Bear but I seem to be using some up now.'

'Aw, Mum. I'm sorry.'

'No, *I'm* sorry.'

'We're all sorry,' Rose butted in. 'Good. Now that's established, let's get this show on the road.'

When at last we reached the water's edge, we stopped and all instinctively looked out at the horizon, and to the dark land mass of Wales. So often I had gazed at it from here as a child, never dreaming that I would end up living there, far less that it would be part of my son's DNA. How right it felt, to be standing here now, the light glinting on the water as the waves moved gently in and out, lapping close to our shoes. I took a plastic bag from my backpack. Rose and Stella examined it.

'Ashes are weird,' Stella said, speaking for us all.

It was impossible to think that this had once been a person, far less a person I knew. How could all that life, all that energy, come down to this static, unremarkable dust?

'First,' Rose said, 'we need to drink tea with Bear.' She took a thermos out of her bag, and four plastic cups. She set them down on the sand and poured a small amount of milky tea into each one. We each took a cup, and Rose held the extra one for Bear. We clinked them together, said, 'To Bear,' and drank.

'Nice cuppa that, Rose,' I said. 'Not stewed at all.'

Rose raised an eyebrow at me. 'At least you recognise decent tea when it's in front of you.'

I opened the bag of ashes and looked at Rose.

'What do we do?' she whispered.

I shrugged. 'I haven't done this before, I've only seen it on the telly.'

'In films the ashes always get caught in the wind and they blow all over the person,' Stella said.

'Luckily it's not windy today,' Rose said.

I hesitated, then scooped out a small handful. 'Till next time, then, dear Ursula. Miss you, Bear.' I flung the ashes into the sea. They sat on the top of the water for a moment, then a wave came in and washed them away.

'Is it polluting?' Stella asked.

'You're so modern,' I said. 'I'd never have thought of that.'

'I don't think so,' Rose said, 'aren't humans biodegradable?' She took a handful of ashes and sent them into the water. 'Bye, then, Bear. It was good knowing you.' Her voice cracked on the last word, and I put my hand on Rose's shoulder.

'May I?' Stella said.

'Of course!' Rose said.

Stella stepped forward, and looked out to sea. 'Bear,' she said, 'I only met you a couple of times when you came to England, so I didn't really know you. But I felt like I knew you through Mum. And I want to tell you that you inspired me. You, and Rose, and my mum.'

Stella threw her handful of ashes into the sea, then turned to look at us, and I felt pride warming my whole body. Little more than a year ago she had seemed lost, uncertain. Now here she was, eyes shining, her voice strong and sure. Rose squeezed my hand.

Stella went on. 'Bear, you had to move to a foreign country when you were young, and you didn't want to, but you made a life for yourself there. It took Mum a bit longer to make the life she wanted for herself, but she's doing it now. We only have one go-round this planet, don't we, and it's up to us to make it what we want it to be. But friends, good friends, like Rose, and Nita, can help us make those things happen.'

'My God, Stella,' I said, tears pouring down my face. 'What are you doing to us?'

'I feel like we've all been trying to work out what we want to do,' Rose said, 'with our one go-round this planet.' She wiped her eyes.

We all three stood looking out at the horizon, and no one spoke for several minutes.

'I know this is a terribly sad day,' I said at last, 'but I do feel unusually peaceful.'

'I do too,' Rose said. 'I feel like we have done right by Bear. That's a good feeling.'

'I've been going to this funny support group, with Newland and Piet,' Stella said, and Rose and I both turned to look at her. 'The group's big into acknowledging when things are difficult. But also they encourage us to say when things are going well, otherwise we might miss it. Bettina used to say the same. Anyway, I want to say that, though you're right that it's a sad day, I'm happy that I'm here, with both of you.'

'How did you manage to create someone so wise?' Rose said to me.

'Sparkle, you know at twenty-three what it's taken me twice as long to learn.' Then I whispered, 'I'm so sorry. Those awful things I said.'

'Oh, Mum, I said far worse things.'

'I deserved it.'

'You didn't. You just wanted a fresh start.'

'A fresh start shouldn't have to hurt people, though.'

'It can't always help it.'

'Rose is right – how did you get to be so wise, Stella?'

'I put it down to my upbringing.'

'I'm so glad,' Rose said, putting her arms round us both, 'that you two have remembered that you love each other.'

'All thanks to you, Rose. Is that what we're supposed to say?' I said.

'You're welcome!'

I stepped forward. 'Let's finish saying goodbye.' I tipped the rest of the contents of the bag into the water, and we stood and watched the sea sweep in and out until there was no more sign of the ashes.

'Well,' Rose said, 'that's that.' She took out her phone. 'I think we should commemorate this moment with a selfie, if you're not too posh for that, Kay.'

'Ugh, a selfie,' I said. 'How millennial of you, Rose.'

'I've brought your old camera,' Stella said.

I looked at her. 'You have?'

Stella smiled at Rose. 'Yes, I, er, heard you were going to be doing a photography course, so I thought you might need it.' She took my camera out of her bag, and gave it to me. I could scarcely believe I was finally holding it again, the familiar weight of it in my hand.

'Oh, Stella.'

'Dad put a new film in it,' she said. 'I didn't know how.'

'Ohhhhh, Stella.'

Rose winked at Stella. 'Good work, kid.'

I took off the lens cap and looked at Stella through the camera. 'I remember all its little quirks.' I lowered it and said, 'Let's go back to the rocks where Bear fell into the sea.'

We walked back, and I set up the camera on a flat boulder, facing the water. Rose and Stella posed patiently as I fiddled with the timer, then dashed over to join them.

'Ten seconds!' I gasped, as I took my place next to Stella.

We smiled, a little fixedly, then started laughing properly with the age-old embarrassment of waiting for the shutter to click. When it finally did, Rose said, 'I think that will be a good one.'

Arms linked again, this time with me in the middle, we walked back across the sand towards the town, and a pub lunch, and our one brilliant go-round the planet.

A Letter from Beth

Thank you so much for reading *The Missing Letters of Mrs Bright*. If you'd like to be kept up to date on my new releases, click on the link below to sign up for a newsletter. I promise to only contact you when I have a new book out, and I'll never share your email with anyone else.

www.bookouture.com/beth-miller

I hope you enjoyed reading *The Missing Letters of Mrs Bright*, and I'd love to hear what you thought, so please leave a review. I read all the reviews, so tell me what you thought!

If you don't like leaving reviews but just want to say hello, you can get in touch on my Facebook page, through Twitter, or my website.

With thanks,
Beth Miller

drbethmiller

BethMillerAuthor

www.bethmiller.co.uk

Acknowledgements

Huge thanks to:
- My writing friends: Melissa Bailey, Jo Bloom, Sharon Duggal, Lulah Ellender, Abbie Headon and Becca Mascull, and the Prime Writers, for all the top chats.
- Liz Bahs and Jacq Molloy, for the non-stop encouragement, first-class editorial advice, absorbent shoulders to cry on, and generally being the world's greatest writing buddies. And Jacq again, for vital Aussie info.
- Juliette Mitchell, for being there at a crucial point of the second draft – the dark before the dawn – and for reading it in a weekend and coming up with a stunning blueprint for a way forward. Couldn't have done it without you.
- Saskia Gent, my first reader, who loved even the messy first draft, claiming it definitely *wasn't* too long at 115,000 words. I hope you still like it now it's a little briefer.
- Stu Robarts, Georgina Spraggan, Tim Vaughan, and the twitter account West Kirby Today, for excellent and detailed information about West Kirby Beach.
- My agent, Judith Murdoch, who helped me come up with the initial idea for the book.

– My editor, Maisie Lawrence, who helped turn a big mush of words
   into something coherent, giving me lots of laughs and encouragement
   along the way.

Finally, as always, to my family: my children, for being continually
proud and interested, or at least, doing a good impression of being
proud and interested. And most of all, thanks to John, who always
gives me the self-belief, time and space to get on with writing.